THE COL[...]

Valerie Blument[...] [...]
1950 and was edu[...]
land. She worked [...]
while writing for her own pleasure, but is now
writing full-time. She lives in Oxfordshire. *The
Colours of Her Days* is her second novel, following
'*To Anna' – about whom nothing is known* (Collins,
1988).

Available in Fontana by the same author

'To Anna' – about whom nothing is known

VALERIE BLUMENTHAL

The Colours of Her Days

FONTANA/Collins

First published by William Collins Sons & Co. Ltd 1989
First issued in Fontana Paperbacks 1990

Copyright © Valerie Blumenthal 1989

Printed and bound in Great Britain by
William Collins Sons & Co. Ltd, Glasgow

To Diana, a wonderful mother,
with my love

Contents

Acknowledgements

My especial thanks go to George J. D. Bruce, the portrait painter, for his invaluable advice on art; to Bruce Hanson, who spoon-fed me with details of John Ruskin and Brantwood; to Dee and Harding Laity of Norway House, St Ives, who were a fount of local knowledge; and to Stanley Cox of the St Ives museum, for giving me an insight into nineteenth-century St Ives.

Prologue

The Coachman's Inn had once been a farmhouse and was situated on rising ground above the eastern shore of the lake. An unmade, furrowed track led from the Coniston road, and climbed and wound gently for perhaps half a mile before petering out into a fold of the hills. Here was to be found Altwood Ground Farm, a mile and three-quarters from Coniston, surrounded by conifers and tangled hazelnuts and birches. On its own except for the shells of a couple of cottages and a disused churchyard, it was a low building jointed like an 'L' with a dilapidated barn, and constructed of the same lakeland slate and stone as nearly all the other buildings in this part of England, which was then in Lancashire. The house was almost derelict but behind the crumbling walls around the yard bushes burst with rhododendrons the colour of blood, and around the rotten front door honeysuckle ran amok.

To the 28-year-old newly-wedded farmhand who visited Altwood one day in late July 1850 it held limitless possibilities. With his arm about his 19-year-old bride he stared at the stillness of Coniston Water, which mirrored the fells now swathed in ochre. He viewed it all with longing.

'It'll be ours,' he said to the small dark-haired girl nestling against him. 'I tell you I've had it working for others. Working all hours for an extra two shillings a week. No thanks at th'end.'

'But how'll we afford it?' she asked dubiously, lacking his enthusiasm, lonely already, as in her mind she projected herself forward to a time when she had lived in this isolated spot for years, deprived of all gaiety.

'With my money and yours, my little bit of inheritance added to it, there would be just sufficient.'

9

'And the house – see its state!'

Their visions were entirely different: he saw himself as a landowner – a farmer instead of a farmhand or yet another shepherd; she saw herself as a drudge.

'We'd soon put the house to rights,' he answered confidently.

She looked disbelieving and saw her husband – that huge, spare-framed, red-haired man – as a stranger who was intending to whisk her away from all that was merry.

Her spirit asserted itself: 'I don't like it.' She raised her voice and gritted her teeth.

'Well I do.' He looked down at her small pale face and scowled, defying her to argue.

'A lot of the money's mine you was wanting to use,' she persevered, regardless.

She came from Ulverston and had a small dowry – had married beneath her, so her mother continually said.

'Flora, when you married you took vows. I'll not need to remind you . . .'

So Thomas Ruddock bought his twenty-nine-acre farm with its scrub and blighted oats, and all day and into the night he and his wife laboured, first on the house itself, striving together to put it in good repair, and then on the land – up and down the field in all weathers, side by side or calling to one another across the expanse. They were too tired to quarrel, she too weary to miss the town or her friends, and soon her aims, by necessity, became his, because they were all she had left to grasp.

She learned not to complain about their lack of furniture and instead reminded herself how fortunate they were to have their own well and a fast-flowing beck running through their land. There was a certain satisfaction to be derived from being thrifty and from seeing their sow fatten – filling buckets with peelings and anything she found in the hedgerows, watching the animal guzzle and snort. She had become attached to the creature, which privately she considered more intelligent than her husband's mongrel. However, cleaning out the sty was not a job to be savoured.

Young though she was, Flora's was an indomitable character – she had defied her parents by marrying Thomas – and she threw aside her girlhood to immerse herself in her role. She was scrupulous in her cleanliness and the swilling-out of the privy housed in a tumbledown outshed; rose before her husband in the morning in order to draw water from the well; and learned to cook economically, seasoning the pot with rosemary and frying the bread in flavoured lard instead of cooking meat . . .

But Thomas Ruddock was no businessman and he had not researched the running of a business as a profitable enterprise. To make twenty-nine acres of oats pay was virtually impossible, and no surrounding land was available to rent. After a couple of years of poor yield, disheartened, he decided to change to dairy farming, and duly ploughed and re-seeded his field and then filled it with cows. Every evening he would round them up with the trained dog he had bought, and drive them into the yard and into their sheds to be milked: one after the other, endless rubbery teats sliding through his fingers; and the performance to be repeated at five o'clock the following morning.

Two more years elapsed – by which time he had a daughter, Rosaleen – then his cows rewarded him for his good care by breaking out of their field and into the overgrown churchyard which was surrounded by yew hedges. Nearly all of them died from the poisonous effects of their gluttony.

Destitute, the proud, fiery-tempered man who had only ever wanted what had seemed reasonable, and whose ambitions had not been outlandish, defended his case before his little, equally hot-tempered wife, and much shouting went on. But the shouting offered only recriminations, and no plans for remedying the situation. When they were finally exhausted, a thought dawned upon Flora in the ensuing hiatus.

'Well what are we going to do 'bout it then?' she asked.

'What do you mean?'

'It's obvious what I mean. There ain't no money coming in, is there? And there's the three of us. What'll we do to live? You'll not be suggesting I beg in the streets?'

''Course not.'

They were sitting in the parlour before a fire, their little copper-haired child crawling around energetically, and suddenly the fight went from the man. He watched her rapid progress as she travelled around the room and was filled with sad tenderness.

'Oh Flora, what are we to do?'

And with his mellowing she was by his side in an instant, in love again with his humbleness.

'Leave it t'me.'

The same farmer who had not been prepared to rent out his adjoining land was more than prepared to accumulate more – but not before chiding Thomas:

'You should've put it to sheep or beef. It's nearly all grazing in these parts. You should've known better.'

'It were oats before I took it on.'

'And look at what happened. Why d'you think it were run-down when you took it? Oats don't work on these slopes.'

'But I was wanting to try sommat else.' Thomas was stubborn in his self-justication.

'You should've stuck with sheep,' the farmer insisted, 'then you wouldn't be coming running t'me now.'

But he bought twenty-five acres at a fair price, which left them with enough land to be self-sufficient, and the money to instigate the next stage of Flora's plan.

Within six months the old farmhouse was transformed into a comfortable inn with four letting bedrooms, and over the years business increased and their reputation grew.

❧ One ❧

FORMATIVE YEARS

Once I saw it all
As it really was.

Rosaleen was born into their lives amidst quarrels and hardship on May 1st 1854. She was a tiny baby and then a tiny child, with dainty features and wide slanting eyes whose irises were an extraordinary pale lilac defined by a thin black rim. But it was her hair that one first noticed: golden auburn, like her father's, it lacked the wiry texture of his and waved lustrously to the small of her back.

Rosaleen could not remember the Coachman's as a farm, or the destitute years, and by the time she was old enough to formulate her thoughts, matters were already on the turn for the better and the inn was becoming established. Flora insisted that Rosaleen go to school.

'But why?' Thomas asked. 'What does a lass want with learning things?'

'Times is changing,' Flora replied firmly, her hand on her hip in that aggressive pose she assumed when she prepared for battle. 'A lass must've things in her head,' she continued, nodding sagely as she spoke. 'Ros'leen's inclined to be wild. 'Sides, think what a help she'd be when she's older if she was good at writing and numbers.'

Flora persuaded him. And soon her husband believed it had been his idea. He'd proudly tell everyone he met, smiling his genial smile: ''Course my little'n goes to school. I told Flora one has to be modern thinking . . .'

He'd take his daughter himself – everyone in Coniston knew

them with their similar bright hair – and at the back of the cart, beside the prick-eared mongrel, the five-year-old child bounced up and down on the sacks of animal-feed whilst the old pony trotted out smartly.

Her mother fetched her from school, and alone with Rosaleen, Flora would often show the softer aspect of her nature. She was so young, and she had had her day and her joy, and perhaps recognized in her daughter something of herself.

'Ah, little Ros'leen,' she mused once, 'you'll be lucky. And it were me that decided you'd do best t'go to school. He's forgotten that.'

Rosaleen had inherited her mother's delicate bone structure and creamy complexion. Thomas's skin, in comparison, was rough-textured, and the freckles on his face so beaten by the years of outdoor life that they merged in an orange-tinged ruddiness. Above his full lips was then a thick moustache, a bristling ridge of gold, and Rosaleen would tug its hairs – coarse as a pig's.

Her brother Robbie was born when she was six. Six years old, and she was a creature of her countryside. Her hair was the bracken of the mountains, and she picked pieces and struck them in her curls like spiked feathers . . . She climbed and she ran and taught herself to swim with her father watching anxiously over her. Thomas doted on her.

'Take me on the gondola,' she'd plead. This was the steamship owned by the Furness railway, which crossed the stretch of lake from Waterhead and back.

'You spoil her,' Flora scolded him.

'Aw Flora, it don't do no harm. She helps when you ask her.'

'Well I say you spoil her, and one day you'll not get thanks for it.'

But there was work too, and as Rosaleen grew up many duties were assigned to her. Apart from drawing from the well, a task her mother had delegated to her, these duties included taking charge of the chickens – rearing them, feeding them, collecting the eggs, and wringing the necks of the older birds – and endless

picking of the fruit through the summer and into early autumn –
rhubarb and gooseberries and blackcurrants, barrow-loads of
Worcesters and great green cooking apples, yellow plums and
dark purple ones . . . Her pale fingers would be stained with
their various deep-toned juices, and when she brushed them
against her cheeks or rubbed her eyes, inky patches would be
left.

Inevitably, during those rich-picking summer months, she
developed stomach pains from cramming so much fruit into her
mouth, and sometimes to Flora's horror she got worms. She
would scratch her bottom like a terrier and jump up and down in
her discomfort – and then came the medicine, a strong and
vile-tasting substance which purged her insides so that the
creatures fled from her body in a puddle of uncontrollable
diarrhoea.

'You mustn't eat the fruit unwashed, Ros'leen,' Flora casti-
gated her.

'No, Mother.'

But each year she forgot, and continued to cram the luscious
raw fruits into her mouth, and it was a matter of luck whether or
not she caught worms.

Her other chores included sweeping the grate before breakfast, dressing Robbie and cleaning all the shoes and boots. When
all these things had been done she sat down to a bowl of poddish
– thick porridge made in a pan over an open fire, and stirred with
a stick called a thible. It was served in basins which were
afterwards filled with tea. In between duties and school hours
she was free. How fortunate she felt then; and she explored with
zestful eagerness. She was always disappearing, and Flora, who
had young Robbie to concern herself with now, besides all her
other domestic duties, had neither the time nor the energy to
worry or reprimand. During her hours of freedom Rosaleen was
unchecked. And in return for her liberty she was always willing
to help when asked.

She learned to drive the pony and cart, sat alongside her father
and watched every wrist movement, learned to use the same
words he did, and her strange gruff voice would ring out: 'Do a

halt lad . . . Go right. Trot out will you? Walk, whoa, whoa, walk laddie.'

Sometimes on a Friday she missed school, and then, by herself, drove the eight and a half miles to Ambleside market. One day she returned with two Herdwick lambs.

'What did you do that for, Ros'leen?' Flora cried.

'They looked sick, Mother. The ewe rejected them.' Rosaleen's eyes pleaded.

'But they're *male*!'

'Oh!'

'Well they're your responsibility, Ros'leen, and you'll have to feed them by the bottle by the looks of them. I gave you good money for cloth, not for buying livestock.'

Rosaleen thought for a moment, and a sweetness came into her expression. She began to babble, as she always did when she was in the wrong:

'We can loan the sheep out when they're older and take a female lamb in return for their services. You just see.'

She knew all about animals' mating habits and already understood about bartering and dealing in livestock. '. . . And we can make cloth, Mother. I'll learn to spin and weave. They'll teach me to weave at school, and Nana Annie'll teach me t'spin.'

Nana Annie was Thomas's mother who lived in Coniston. She gave Rosaleen her own wheel which she no longer used, and showed the girl how to work it. Thomas made her a loom – he was a fine craftsman when he could be bothered – and he made this gift for his daughter with much care and love, carving his name on one side and his initials on the other. But it was a year before Rosaleen's young rams were shorn and she could use it, and meanwhile she fed her babies and combed their wool as though they were high-class dogs, and in the end not much cloth could be made from two sheep. She was a resourceful girl and she experimented with dyes, soaking the yarn overnight in tin vessels filled with different colours. The wool dried out unevenly, but when she wove it, all the colours intertwined and became wild abstract patterns which thrilled her. She experimented further. Soon she had her own little business going – word spread fast, carried as it was initially by the local postmistress – and women came to her with their own yarn to be dyed and woven into cloth . . .

Those years of childhood were on balance happy years. Each Sunday they attended St Andrew's Church in Coniston, dressed in their best clothes to mark the occasion, and Thomas wore braces instead of tying string around the waist of his trousers. On Sundays they always had mutton and spicy dumplings, and Nana Annie and Flora's parents joined them.

Those years there was even a pleasure about one's duties: Rosaleen loved to collect the still-warm eggs which were to be found in such obscure places, to fill the buckets from the well and feel the freshness of soft water on her early-morning face; even polishing shoes had its rewards when one could almost see oneself in the old creviced leather. And to see the grate swept and newly made up with logs, ready to light, instilled in her a feeling of homeliness. She did not enjoy wringing the chickens' necks and wished that they would keep still to make it easier. But it was a job to be done, and as such it was best done as quickly as possible: her little hands would clasp and twist and crack deftly – and then it was over, and the immobile bird was presented to her mother to be plucked.

The inn flourished, and whilst the Ruddocks could certainly not be termed prosperous, they were no longer abysmally poor. Rosaleen's feet did not have to slip about in boots and shoes which were sizes too large and worn thin.

She grew up accustomed to the sound of men's laughter; came to trust those deep-bellied sounds of hearty pleasure and recognized her father's above the others. Men seemed reassuring figures, but more – they were to be envied because they were their own masters. In between errands she would sit on the window seat in the corner of the sitting-room with its assorted chairs, stools and tables, and from her position she watched, fascinated and unshocked, the behaviour of adult men: local tradesmen, men who toiled down the slate or copper mines that were Coniston's main industry, shepherds, travellers who had spotted the sign on the main road. Sometimes there were women and other children, but it was the men who interested Rosaleen.

She observed how they held their pewter tankards; how they stood and propped their elbows on the oak bar; how they sipped or slurped their beer or cider or wine or whatever it was they drank – in the winter spiced mulled wine that Flora made. She listened to their rumbling voices, noted the loosening of waist-coats and the corpulence of the heavy drinkers and heard more than a few rude tales. Men held no illusions, but surrounded by them she felt secure. Here in the dark-beamed flagstoned inn with its odours of ale and food mingling with beeswax and leather and brass and animals, with her father at the fore of all the other men, she was content.

And beyond the inn, always there but never the same, stretch-ing as far as the eye could see, was her countryside: her fells she climbed, her woodland she roamed, her lake in which she swam. Her sky. She embraced her sky, ever-changing like a frivolous girl, transforming the landscape beneath it from one minute to the next.

Rosaleen would spend as long as she could on her own, never lonely in her solitude. People loved her because of the way she looked, but she had no real friends. There was no time for friends. Her days were so full, with almost every waking moment accounted for, that she was possessive of her precious rare hours of leisure. However, she did not mind sharing them with Robbie. Robbie was always quiet and undemanding – hanging on to her hand, never questioning what she was doing and valiantly keeping pace with her endless energy. She sang nursery rhymes to him, played marbles or hopscotch with him; even when she was at her busiest she would always make time for Robbie. She was the only person who never pushed him away saying: 'Leave me be, can't you see I'm busy?'

When she was twelve Rosaleen left school, for even with the newly-appointed cook to assist in the kitchen there was just too much for Flora to do.

She cried in private when she left that summer. She had been happy there. She missed, too, the journeys with her father when

18

they both felt so close to one another whilst speaking so little – and then, the quick embrace goodbye for the day, before she disappeared into the little school building, into the classroom with its scrubbed tables and hard bench seats which numbed her bottom, its slates and broken pieces of chalk.

It was Robbie's turn now, and she drove him there, proud despite herself, the reins bunched in her right hand – a girl with a woman's life to look forward to; and her knowledge was left suspended, dangling like an unfinished sentence.

'Do a halt lad. Go right. Trot out now will you. Walk then, whoa, whoa, walk laddie . . .'

And the sadness at depositing her brother where she would wish to be herself, watching the clusters of children and listening to them clamour and singing songs. Remembering. Slower home – and maybe a visit to Nana Annie on the way, taking some salted mutton or herb pudding, or a side of bacon or a length of Cumberland sausage.

'Ros'leen, my tiny lass.'

'H'llo Nana.'

'You're so pale.' She always said this.

And Rosaleen answered every time: 'I was always this colour, Nana.'

'A kiss for your Nana then.'

Barely taller than the child, the old lady tilted her seamed cheek with its lumps and pits and hairs. There would be a momentary pause as Rosaleen hesitated, veering between affection for her grandmother and revulsion at the damage life had wrought to her face; and then she pursed her lips and kissed her briefly.

Nana Annie was not in fact as old as she appeared. She was, maybe, sixty-eight, but could have been at least ten years older. With the absence of any teeth her mouth fell away in a dark sucked-in *moue*. Her eyes were olives lost in the surrounding creases and pouches, and darted about restlessly. When they alighted they fixed upon their object a relentless and critical stare. Her chin jutted like the rocky face of Old Man, and from it her neck was a sinewy stalk no different to the chickens' Rosaleen wrung. Around her small head the thin tired threads of her hair showed the vestiges of red, but mostly it was the dull grey of an old dog's beard and was bound in two skinny plaits and fastened on top. If she had not been her grandmother, Rosaleen would have believed her to be a witch. Impossible to think she had ever been young, or that she had borne not only Thomas, but two other sons – both moved away now – and a daughter who had died in infancy.

Nana would take the mutton or bacon, lurch her body lopsidedly on bowed legs to the giant hook attached to a low beam, and suspend the joint, and they would both stare upward as it swung back and forth for several seconds.

Her cottage was one of those known as the Banks – a short terrace of dark narrow cottages in a tiny lane cut into the mountainside as it started to climb steeply. Its wideswept views encompassed the fells – muted, across the lake. But on a bad day there was nothing muted about the Banks. Gales raged around the cottages and the wind howled. In front of the row were the allotments shelving downwards, and between the vegetables were beaten tall posts. The washing lines were strung to these posts – zig-zagging and crossing one another with everyone's laundry waving like drab flags. A tailor lived next to Annie Ruddock, so his line was always more crowded and more flamboyant.

Nana Annie's home had a single room downstairs and a single room upstairs, and had once housed two adults, three rum-bustious boys and a dog or two; and from here also, old Bartholomew Ruddock, Thomas's father who had died long before Rosaleen was born, had conducted his cobbler's business.

'Finest cobbler outside o' Carlisle, my husband was,' Nana told everyone when he was dead. But it was well known she had not cared much for him when he was alive. He had been mean and penny-pinching, although his careful attention to their finances meant he had left two of his sons twenty-two pounds two shillings and sixpence in his will, and the house to her. The third son had quarrelled with him, and he received nothing but a broken shoemaker's needle wrapped in waxed paper. It was symbolic of the old man's feelings.

Nana's life, no different to others of her background, was one of extreme hardship, and she accepted her lot the same as all the other women. While the men drank for relief, they gossiped. Nana Annie loved gossip. She was also supremely superstitious, and beside her bible – which she could not read and had a tendency to hold upside-down – she kept an assortment of curios: 'lucky objects', she called them. She was obsessed by omens. 'It's an omen,' she cried when Thomas was ill once on his birthday, or when a cloud formed a particular shape; she often gazed at the clouds, assessing their portent.

But she was, despite these pessimistic idiosyncrasies, essentially an optimistic old lady, over-ready with her advice, and stubborn when it came to accepting it in return. And she loved Rosaleen. To Rosaleen, had she been rich, she would have given her wealth. Instead she could only pick a wild flower or tempt her with warm rough bread, or fill her head with gossip. And once – that special once – she had had something proper to give. She had given Rosaleen her spinning wheel and taught her to work it, placing Rosaleen's fingers beneath her own and turning the wheel, feeding in and pulling through. And in return Rosaleen had given her squares of glowing colours which she herself had made.

Two years passed and it was early June of 1868. Flora, heavily pregnant, dragged herself about during the exceptionally hot weather. Apart from her immense belly she was pitifully thin, her cheeks were hollow and her eyes dull and sunken. She proceeded with her chores as usual, out of habit and obligation, and did not protest, not because she was a martyr, but simply because there was no point.

'Mother, you look ever so tired,' Rosaleen said, when she finally noticed. 'Go lie down, do.'

'I couldn't do that, Ros'leen. There's the laundry to be seen to still.'

'I can see to it, Mother.'

'Bless your heart, you've already quite sufficient to do for a lass your age.'

She appreciated Rosaleen now the girl was older, understood her a little better, and recognized that inner fortitude she herself possessed.

'Mother, please rest. Please let me do it. You look proper poorly.'

Flora capitulated. A few days later she went into labour.

It was Sunday, and after church all the family were gathered together at the inn: Flora's parents from Ulverston, Nana Annie, Thomas, Flora, Rosaleen and Robbie. The occasion was special for there was a visiting circus in Coniston, and after lunch they planned to go. Rosaleen had helped Flora prepare the food in advance – cold veal pie and slices of tongue and ham, Cumberland sauce and various salads, followed by a bread pudding with cream. An extra girl had been hired to take Thomas's place behind the bar, and the family were free for the afternoon.

The mood was one of forced jollity; forced because Flora's parents – William Snell, the stout fast-talking butcher, owner of three shops, and his prim little wife Nellie – disliked Thomas quite as much as he disliked them. Nana Annie thought them stuck-up and muttered loudly under her breath, and they thought her one of the most dreadful old women they had ever encountered. The tension between the adults usually rebounded on the children and Thomas would become impatient with Robbie and was inclined to cuff his ear, whilst Flora would nag at Rosaleen.

However, this afternoon there was a tacit agreement to avoid disputes. The circus was a major event; there would be plenty to do and see and talk about, plenty of good ale and cider to drink, and festivities would go on well into the evening. Nobody wanted to mar such a jolly outing with a show of mood.

They sat in the snug at an oak table, its gate-legs extended.

'Will there be bears and funny men, and ladies with beards?' Robbie asked Rosaleen.

'I expect so, mankin,' his sister replied.

22

'And wrestling,' Thomas said. 'I like to watch a good wrestling match.'

'And juggling,' Nana Annie croaked. 'All them skittles twirling 'bout at once.'

'I expect there'll be the odd skirmish,' Flora's mother said nervously, fiddling with the brooch on her lace collar. 'There's always skirmishes at these do's.'

'You fuss too much,' her husband accused her, then masked his annoyance with a friendly: 'Tut, tut – women. Always fussing.'

Flora was unusually quiet; she had a low backache which would intermittently ease, only to recur with a stabbing pain. She thought: 'The bairn's not due for another couple of weeks. It can't be that.'

Tiredly she wiped the flat of her hand against her forehead. It was clammy and damp. 'I must be sickening for sommat,' she mused. 'And on such an afternoon. Well I'll not be spoiling everyone's fun.'

Rosaleen noticed the way her mother picked at her food. 'Mother, you've not eaten a thing.'

'Hush child, will you? I've been picking at bread aforehand. I fair stuffed myself.'

'I didn't see you.'

'And was I asking you to watch over me?'

'I only –'

'Enough. Come help me clear this lot away.'

They went into the kitchen – a large rectangular and steamy room dominated by a huge and crowded pine dresser against one wall. Against another was the big black Kitchiner range. It had cost £23.10s., and Flora was justly proud of it. Upon the hotplate stood various pots, grid-iron and kettle – all big enough to cater for any number of people. Overhead assorted implements made a fine show hanging from a low rail, and beneath the window was a butcher's block upon which rested a side of ham and a knife. The work table where they also ate was in the centre of the room and now Rosaleen and Flora stacked the used plates and bowls and cutlery upon it. The mongrel lay beneath it. So ancient that he could barely move, and retaining only his sense of smell, neither his blind eyes nor his deaf ears registered anyone entering the room. He wheezed in his heavy sleep and a stench emanated from the area in which he rested.

'Father should ought t'put the gun to its head. It ain't nice t'see a creature like that,' Flora observed in a pitying tone.

'I've never seen a man so tender-hearted over an animal as Father is over this dog,' Rosaleen said, bending to stroke its ears gently.

'Your father's a tender soul beneath all the ranting.'

For a moment Flora's expression was wistful. She was thirty-seven and all the clarity of youth had gone from her face. Now her cheeks were the colour of light washed stone and lines ran from either side of her nostrils to the corners of her lower lip.

She gave a little unconscious sigh and then a wince as the blade of pain caught her. Rosaleen was immediately at her side.

'What's wrong, Mother? Is it the bairn?'

'No, child. It ain't due for more'n two weeks yet.'

'Maybe you shouldn't go to the circus.'

'I'll not be spoiling everyone's fun.' Flora voiced firmly her earlier thought. She stood up defiantly and for a moment gazed with rare tenderness at her fourteen-year-old daughter.

She saw, of course, that the girl was beautiful – so perfect of feature, such a small vivid creature – but she saw more besides. She saw in the expression both intelligence and sensitivity, and Flora felt a violent sense of urgency. She touched Rosaleen's chin – a firm, pointed little thing – and then said something strange:

'Ros'leen, when you grow up you'll do what you want to.'

'What d'you mean, Mother?' Her eyes were puzzled.

'I mean that you don't have to be like me.'

'Aw Mother – I'm fine as I am.' But she shifted her feet, uneasy at her mother's insight.

They prepared to go to the circus and stood together outside the inn, the men organizing the means of transport.

Thomas, wearing his new check waistcoat and sweating already, had taken charge.

'I'll take Ros'leen and Nana with me in th'cart, and Flora and Robbie can go in the dog-cart.'

'It'll be more comfortable for you, dear,' said Flora's mother, deliberately loudly so that Thomas could hear.

The latter scowled and retaliated: 'She lacks no comforts with me, I'll have you know.'

They set off, down the winding track and on to the main Coniston road, which was busy with other vehicles and people on foot heading in the same direction. They had barely gone a couple of hundred yards, travelling in convoy, when Rosaleen heard her mother emit a shrill cry, and then another.

'Flora, Flora.' The grandmother's voice rose high.

'We're turning around,' the butcher called to Thomas who was following behind.

'What's happened? What's up with my Flora?' Thomas called back, brandishing the whip and jerking the reins in his anxiety.

'She's gone into labour, that's what,' the other shouted, across the hub and clatter of wheels, whilst passers-by looked askance.

They sped back to the farm.

'Robbie, you go find the doctor,' Thomas instructed his son when they arrived at the yard. And tenderly he lifted his white-faced wife and carried her from the dog-cart, followed by a troop of clamouring adults and Rosaleen.

'There's blood on her. Oh my Flora, there's blood on you,' Thomas said softly, horrified, as he carried her up the stairs and into their room.

'She's bleeding!' echoed Flora's mother.

'Oh cut off your tongue,' snapped Nana Annie.

'How dare you?' the other lady bristled – and then began to moan as Flora was laid on the bed: 'My lass . . . My daughter.'

Flora lay panting like a dog while they quarrelled, and it was left to Rosaleen, the only calm one amongst them, to cope. She hustled the men from the room, separated the shrieking grand-mothers, and mopped up the unstoppable red flow.

Appalled, she thought: 'I didn't know we had so much blood in us. I didn't think so much could come out of us.'

She laid cool wet flannels on her mother's forehead and held her hand when the heaving began again. The groans were rasping sounds that became weaker as Flora became rapidly debilitated.

Some time later Thomas knocked on the door. He smelt of whisky. 'What's happening with her?' he asked Rosaleen thickly, and peered round the door.

'Nothing, Father. Leave now. There's nothing you can do,' she whispered, smelling his breath and recoiling a little. 'Is there no sign of Robbie and the doctor yet?'

'No,' answered Thomas, his face darkening as he recalled his son's mission. 'Where is that lad? I'll take the strap to him, I will. Wandered off dreaming more'n like.'

'I expect he can't find the doctor, Father,' Rosaleen told him shrewdly, looking up into his freckled, worry-furrowed face. 'Everyone's at the circus.'

'Bloody circus!' Thomas shouted. 'Bloody stupid thing.'

'Hush Father. Now leave us, do.'

His blue eyes entreated her fearfully. 'Will she live, d'you think?' he asked her, in a tremulous voice.

Rosaleen lowered her lashes to hide her tears and whispered, 'Oh Father . . . I don't rightly know.' Her whisper caught in her throat and she gave a little sob. Then she recovered herself and insisted again: 'Leave us, do.'

He left, chastened, his head bowed. Rosaleen returned to her mother, who was quiet now, her eyes glazed, and changed the towels yet again; the other two women had resumed their bickering, when suddenly Flora gave an unearthly scream. She attempted to sit up and then slid down again. The blood seeped from her; and then the door burst open and Thomas charged in with the butcher in pursuit.

'Flora, Flora,' Thomas cried, putting his hands to his eyes in despair at the sight of his wife.

'Mother's gone, Father,' Rosaleen said in a flat voice. Her stomach trembled with nausea. 'Mother's gone,' she thought. 'Mother's gone.'

The grandmother recommenced her shrieking.

'You killed her. You killed her.' She hurled her abuse in a

torrent at Thomas: 'Sure as anything it were all the hard work you forced on her which killed her.'

'You stupid woman,' shrilled Nana. 'Your daughter did no more'n any working woman. A little work never killed nobody.'

The furious squabbling and shouting continued, and Rosaleen, unable to bear this undignified scene over her mother's deathbed, put her fists to her ears to blot out the sound.

At that point Robbie returned with the doctor, arriving in the midst of this chaos and horror and ghastly mess of blood which had finally stopped pumping out . . .

'You slaughtered her. You slaughtered her . . .'

And in front of them all Thomas struck his mother-in-law, before collapsing in a heap of grief.

❦ Two ❧

RESPONSIBILITIES

We sing away our childhood
Until our throats constrict.

She was buried in the little graveyard of St Andrew's Church, and the bell peeled from the castellated tower. Afterwards a few mourners went straight to the Blackbull Inn opposite and got drunk.

The old mongrel died that evening and Nana Annie muttered about omens. Thomas, broken-hearted anew, dug a grave for it in the orchard, his eyes streaming as he laid the bedraggled body of his pet in the trough.

'It were a sign from above,' Nana Annie told him in a knowing voice when he returned inside. Though what kind of sign, she could not have said.

Her son ignored her, but privately he felt there must be some sinister reason for the passing-away of his dog on the day of his wife's funeral.

Thomas could not operate without his Flora. Hers had been the stronger and more resolute of the two characters.

'I've the brain and he the brawn,' she used to quip. But she had had little sense of humour. Her husband had been the laugher in the family.

That changed. Then a strange viral infection left him totally deaf in one ear, with the hearing of the other impaired, and at the age of forty-six he was abruptly old, his vigour gone, his joy taken from him, and his decline began. He stopped shaving altogether, and his moustache became a beard – a burst of fire that just grew and grew, and was more often than not speckled with the foam of beer. He only bathed when Rosaleen nagged him, when she personally filled the tin tub in the kitchen and supervised his undressing, soaping his back with carbolic soap and scrubbing him and crooning to him in her gruff voice as though he was her child:

'You're all gleaming clean now. See how nice it feels, Father. You're all spruced-up and clean.'

He'd stand up meekly and let her rub his legs, and tenderly she would sponge all his parts, her face aglow with maternal pride. There was no modesty between them. She was used to nakedness, used to the sight of animals copulating, used to witnessing birth and death. She was matter-of-fact about it all; it was an integral part of life.

She coaxed her father to eat at meals, sitting next to him in the kitchen at the side of his better ear – the left one.

'I made this hotpot – see how good it tastes,' she'd wheedle. 'See – I made a Brown Betty pudding specially for you. I put plenty of nutmeg in, like mother used to.'

But she could not speak of Flora without tears coming into his eyes.

Thomas looked to Rosaleen now. He who had pampered her and encouraged her freedom now confiscated that freedom with his dependence. He depended on her as he had once depended on his wife. With Robbie he had no patience, and Robbie was incapable of speaking loudly, which meant that Thomas could never hear what he said until it had been repeated several times. During all this he became frustrated, his temper would erupt, and his son be reduced to a gibbering mess. With the cook and the new girl he'd hired to help, he was as bad, and they only stayed out of kindness and affection towards Rosaleen. It was different with customers – then Thomas only had to stand with a drink in his hand. For that alone he was considered worthy.

A couple of times a week the beer was delivered. Rosaleen loved to watch the men unload the cart – the big dray horse standing immobile, its face buried in a nosebag full of chaff, whilst her father helped hoist the barrels off, and then roll them through the side door and down to the cellar. Stripped to their shirtsleeves, with sweat staining their armpits, the men would work swiftly, set the barrels in their proper order – and then they were off, the horse startled by the crack of the whip, trotting a few steps before slowing into a regular plod . . .

A year passed, and Nana Annie, now partially blind, came to live with them. Thomas's room was divided by a partition wall, and with much protest as a demonstration of her independence, old Nana Annie moved in. Cantankerous with her disability, angered that it had forced her to leave her cottage, she tried to guard the last embers of her pride. But she was incontinent, and with sodden sheets and mattress which suffered morning inspection when Rosaleen helped her make her bed, Nana Annie felt her humiliation sorely.

At first she insisted on trying to help in the kitchen, or carrying plates of food to customers, but there were countless mishaps, and eventually she conceded her disability, and from then on spent most of her time in the lounge huddled where Rosaleen had used to sit; a hag-like figure with her toothless mouth forever in motion, chewing on itself. She sat there day and night, soaking up men's conversation, drinking too much cider and knitting mechanically – running her swollen fingers along the knobbly rows to ascertain the approximate length.

Rosaleen was fifteen and she felt old. There was no time even to mourn her mother. If momentarily she allowed herself to luxuriate in grief, then some mundanity would pluck her away from her private thoughts. She was mistress of the inn, mother to Robbie, nurse to Nana Annie, housemaid – quite apart from all her usual tasks, although it was now Robbie's duty to see to the well and to polish the shoes and boots and do the grate, besides helping their father with the large vegetable plot.

Once a week, whatever the weather, she drove the cart to Ambleside market. Occasionally she drove further – fifteen miles to Ulverston, and she jostled with the other folk, all those who like her had travelled from near or far, some on the special market-day train, to make or save a few pennies. She evaded the groping hands of men, the outstretched hands of beggars, picked up items, fingered lengths of cloth, stopped – fascinated – at the apothecary's stand, breathed in the smells of white farm-churned butter and ripe rancid goat's cheese, bargained and cajoled to get the best prices. Everyone knew her with her bright hair and the shawl she had made herself.

Several local lads came to the inn to drink in the evenings:

'Fill my glass for me, Ros'leen, and I'll fill you,' they would leer.

But she had no time for them; they were vulgar with their innuendoes. She would toss back her head and purse her lips against a sharp remark which would only have caused further provocation.

She wore her hair drawn back, but the severity of its style only emphasized the loveliness of her face; neither did the plainness of her faded skirt and simple white blouse disguise the developing curves of her body. Rosaleen's appearance excited reaction, while she herself remained impervious and a little mystified – longing for her old freedom and for something else that was yet obscure. She was not ready to be a woman.

Scant time to dream any more.

But very infrequently there was the odd, rare day when she would tuck up her skirt and petticoat and clamber up rocks with Robbie behind stretching out to reach her. They would balance on a narrow ledge – and there would be the falcon's nest, and they would lift the eggs. Occasionally they spotted an eagle, swooping down from its eyrie on a crag, its immense wingspan casting a shadow on the rocks . . .

Or they would catch small fish with home-made nets attached to sticks and release the wriggling creatures before they suffocated, watching them swim vigorously away, reprieved.

Once, in August, they 'borrowed' a little row-boat. Rosaleen stood up in it causing it to tilt. Stripped to her bleached cotton chemise and drawers she jumped in the lake and swam round and round in small circles, gasping and laughing, as Robbie clasped the oars with a terrified expression.

'It's icy,' she cried joyfully. 'Oh Robbie it's so icy. Oh you *must* come in. It's ever so icy, but it's *good*.'

He shook his head silently, his mouth clenched in fright – that his sister might drown, that the boat might drift or sink, that its owner might have seen them take it.

Rosaleen hauled herself into the boat and Robbie whitened as it rocked.

'Ros'leen –'

'Ah but that was *good*.'

Her lips were blue-tinged and parted in laughter, her teeth chattered a little and her flesh was alive with goose-pimples. She lay back and shook her head, her hair clinging in wet curls down her back.

'You can row now,' she told the boy. 'It's your turn.' And then, in a tone of sudden inspiration: 'Let's visit Brantwood. Row towards there, Robbie.'

'We *can't*.' He looked shocked.

'Why ever not? The lake doesn't belong to Brantwood. It's ours as much as anybody's.'

Slowly Brantwood came into view, and Rosaleen stood up in her skimpy wet underclothes to stare at the large yellow house. The boat rocked and Robbie gave her a beseeching look.

'Oh how I'd love to go inside. We could at least walk in the garden.'

She was oblivious to her brother's distress, transported by the romance of the house, so close to the ordinariness of her life.

'Ros'leen – we oughtn't.'

'No one would *know*. I'd so like to draw closer.'

'Please, Ros'leen.'

He was in tears now, and realizing her unkindness she was contrite.

'Aw Robbie – don't cry, my mankin.'

Robbie was her charge – like the two lambs she'd rescued from the market which were now rather ill-tempered rams. She felt like a mother to her brother, who, although six years younger, was already taller than her. His button-brown eyes shone in a face as heavily freckled as his father's, and his dark hair was wiry, tending to stand on end no matter how hard Rosaleen tried to tame it.

'You're a proper catastrophe,' she'd tease him. 'God had a proper fright just before he made you!'

He was an earnest obliging child, academic and serious, and his desire was to please everybody. Poor Robbie – always so afraid. Everything he did that took the slightest physical courage, he did because of Rosaleen, and always with trepidation in his heart. He would have preferred to sit writing poetry or inventing weird contraptions from odd bits he found lying around in the barn.

At nights he lay beside Rosaleen in bed, gazing wide-eyed at the shadows and the distortions they assumed in the light from the flickering candle flame. He could not sleep without the candle, even with his sister there. Sometimes she would come in late after working – so late it was nearer morning – and she knew he had been waiting for her, and only when she had said her prayers and crawled into bed would he fall asleep, coiled against her.

'Ros'leen, Ros'leen, I've a surprise for you,' he called to her when he returned from school one day. He dumped a large bundle at her feet.

'What is it, Robbie?' She bent to inspect the package and her forehead puckered inquiringly.

'They're for you. Teacher gave them me. She says we're a nice family.' His teacher, the vicar's wife, had also been hers.

'Feels sorry for us more'n like,' Rosaleen told Robbie in a wry tone.

He became impatient. 'Well look see what they are, Ros'leen.'

She opened the parcel. It contained about twenty assorted magazines – copies of *The Cornhill*, *MacMillan's*, *Family Herald*, *Christian World* . . . And several books. Speechlessly she turned the pages as though each one was precious.

'Oh . . . Oh!' she exclaimed at last. 'How kind. How truly, truly kind.' She flung her arms around her brother. 'Thank you for bringing them, my mankin.'

She had never had such a gift. It slipped her mind then how little time there was for reading; she belonged to everyone else and never to herself. But she would make time. And within her, something clicked into place.

When she was nearly sixteen her father was suddenly aware of the changes in her body, and without preamble told her that from now on the attic room – that small disused room with its cobweb-draped rafters and bats and mice – would be hers.

'But Father, I can't leave Robbie by himself.'

'Why not? Lad's nearly ten now, Ros'leen. He's too timid for his own good.'

'Well, it's not his fault, Father. That's the way he is.'

'You're turning him into a girl,' Thomas accused her belligerently.

'I'm not, Father. I'm giving him affection that's all.' She rubbed agitatedly at the tip of her nose.

'Well you're moving up to the attic, Ros'leen, and I'm not speaking no more on the subject.'

'But I *like* my room, Father. What've I done wrong?'

Then he looked remorseful, because he had not considered her feelings.

'Why must I move, Father?' she persisted.

She had washed and scrubbed him as though he was her child, seen him naked, as he had seen her, but now, confronted by Rosaleen's question, Thomas was embarrassed. He reddened to the roots of his hair, and stared at her hopelessly, wishing that his Flora were there with her quick tongue and ready answers.

Rosaleen awaited an explanation.

'It ain't natural for a grown lass – a grown woman – t'sleep with her brother.'

'Oh I hadn't thought . . . Hadn't realized . . .' She said no more but helped her father and brother prepare her new room – scrub the rafters and floorboards, seal off the mouseholes . . .

The vicar had found her a bed. It had belonged to the old widow Mrs Cromby who had recently died and had no family to whom to leave things; and for the first few nights Rosaleen felt the old woman's bones in that bed, smelt her and touched her loose dry skin – and imagined her own bed and Robbie's lonely

34

warmth; Robbie awake, staring at some awful phantom on the wall.

'How sad it all is, Robbie, isn't it?' she thought, herself gazing at the shadows cast on the sloping ceiling. 'Nana Annie half blind, Father three-quarters deaf, you with your terrors and me with my drudgery and an old woman's bones in my bed and nothing to dream of any more, and the sky so gloomy day after day that you cannot imagine that beyond the grey there is beauty.'

1872 was already half gone; Robbie had his twelfth birthday, and June – that month of fairs and circuses, touring players and sports – drew to a close. One minute the countryside was drenched, then it was dry, then it was drenched again. Sometimes all in the space of an hour. That small lakeland area abided by its own rules, had its own skies and clouds and sunsets; and its skies were always more vivid, its clouds more dramatic and its sunsets more outrageously flamboyant than anywhere else.

In July Rosaleen's rams won prizes at three major fairs. She herself showed them off; and the clusters of shepherds and farmers leaning on their sticks or against the flimsy fencing, beer tankards in hands, found their eyes more riveted by the diminutive girl issuing orders to the pair of rams as if they understood, than by the beasts themselves.

'We'll sell 'em, Ros'leen,' Thomas exclaimed delightedly after their third success. 'They'll fetch good money.' He set the latest cup amongst the paraphernalia behind the bar.

'But Father, we'd do better t'keep them and charge more for them at stud. That way the money would keep coming.' She gazed up at him, her little face wise.

Her father scratched his head uncertainly: 'Well . . . I don't rightly know that'd be so, lass. What do we want with them two beasts? And b'sides – there wouldn't be many prepared to spend more on stud fees. No, Ros'leen, I think it's best we auction them. They'll be too old in a year or so.'

Rosaleen looked sad. 'They'll end their days in someone's belly, Father. I like them. I nursed them as babes.'

'Aw lass, you're growed-up now. There plenty t'do without

seeing to the likes of them. And they've become proper bad-tempered of late. Why – only the other day one of 'em near as got my leg when he charged.'

Rosaleen's expression became cunning. 'Father, I've had an idea!'

Thomas, in good spirits, smiled indulgently at his daughter – 'his Darlin', he still thought of her privately.

'I'm not sure as I trust your ideas, Ros'leen.'

'That's not fair – is it, Nana?' She turned to Nana Annie, who jolted from her doze at the sound of her name.

'Eh . . . What's that?' she shrilled.

'Nothing, Nana, it's not important.'

'Ros'leen's had one of her ideas,' Thomas shouted in his mother's general direction.

'I heard, I heard. No need t'shout. It ain't me that's deaf. What idea have you had then, tiny lass?'

'I'll tell you, Nana. Sit down, Father, do.' Rosaleen tugged at his sleeve.

'Aw . . . All right then.'

He allowed himself to be led to a chair, and when they were sitting down Rosaleen spoke loudly into his left ear: 'Father, the inn gets ever so busy nowadays –'

'Aye, thank the Lord for it.'

'Thank the Lord,' echoed Nana Annie.

'Father, even with Robbie helping more now, there's so much for me to do. Sometimes I've scarce time to breathe.'

'It's like that in hostelry, Ros'leen, you know that.' Thomas's voice held a warning note. He withdrew his arm from under hers.

A feeling of annoyance rose in her that he should so discount her feelings but she repressed it and continued: 'Father, if you got a good price for the rams like you said, we could afford extra help here at the inn. Only yesterday I was hearing that Nancy from the Banks – her daughter was wanting some work –'

'Why do I need Nancy's girl when I've got my own?' Thomas asked, pretending to be puzzled, but in fact understanding full well.

'You heard the tiny lass,' Nana Annie chimed in. 'There's too much for her t'do. She gets tired.'

'You stay out of it, Mother.'

'That's a fine way t'talk to your mother that is.' But she mumbled it and Thomas did not hear her.

'There's myself and Robbie and cook and the girl – ain't that plenty of help enough?' Thomas's tone defied her to argue; and Rosaleen knew that it would do her no good to catalogue those innumerable duties which usually kept her busy from the second she awoke until last thing at night, or to tell her father that he did half what anybody else did.

However, she was not quite ready to abandon her tactics.

'Father, if I was not here you'd have to find somebody else.'

And at that he roared at her: 'But you are here. Of course you're here. Where else will you be? You're getting as bad as your brother, you are. Always moaning.'

Later he recovered himself; held her to him, apologized in a way: 'I lost my temper a bit before didn't I, eh lass? You didn't take it too bad then?'

'No, Father.'

'I mean – we're friends, like?'

''Course, Father.'

But the words haunted her: 'Where else will you be?' As though she would never be entitled to be anywhere else. It was expected she would be bound to him for ever. Her lot. He could be as rich as Croesus, and able to employ a dozen servants – but his expectations would be the same.

A few days later a traveller stopped at the inn. He arrived on horseback during the afternoon, as the sudden appearance of the sun was dispersing the rain clouds.

From the doorway Rosaleen saw her father unstrap the bags from the saddle, set them on the ground beside the traveller and lead the enormous horse to a spare stable. Almost tripping over a chicken that got under her feet, she hurried out to assist the man. He was in his late twenties or early thirties, of medium height and powerfully built. He stared at her as she stood smiling unselfconsciously, her hand extended towards the two pieces of luggage, then he smiled jauntily back at her.

'They are too heavy for you,' he said in a cultured voice.

Rosaleen laughed. 'I'll bet I'm almost as strong as you!'

He appraised her – a lively expression in his rather sorrowful brown eyes. 'You're so tiny.'

'But I'm strong!' she insisted – and lifted the tan leather bags, which were really not very heavy.

'We shall compromise. A bag each.' He took one from her and followed her inside.

'Is that a flute?' Rosaleen asked, pointing with her free hand to the wooden tube protruding from his coat pocket.

'Yes.'

'And you play it?'

'A little.'

'Oh how lovely – will you play it for me?'

'*Die Zauberflöte.*'

'What?'

'An opera by a genius called Mozart – *The Magic Flute*. I shall be Papageno and you shall be Papagena.'

She showed him to his room and he reappeared in the lounge about half an hour later, informally dressed in loose-fitting trousers and jacket.

Rosaleen spotted the flute as she poured him a beer. 'Please will you play it?' she asked him again, handing him the tankard.

'If you sit beside me.'

'Aw sir. I've other customers to tend to.'

'I see no other customers,' he said softly.

She glanced around. There were four others, all locals she knew well, talking amongst themselves. And Nana Annie in her usual place. Thomas was behind the bar, loudly berating Robbie over some triviality; and the stranger still looked questioningly at Rosaleen.

She wanted to join him, but was worried about antagonizing Thomas further. She hesitated, then said: 'Let me ask my father. He's ever so deaf, I must warn you. He's only shouting so at

Robbie because he can't hear himself. The locals are used to him.'

The man was touched at her defence of her father.

Rosaleen tapped Thomas's shoulder, interrupting his tirade, and he whirled round. Then his expression softened and his rough index finger stroked her cheek. 'What do you want of me, lass? You've that look about you.'

She laughed, and snuggled against him for a second, fleetingly recapturing that unique, safe feeling she'd had with him as a child. Robbie, taking advantage of the diversion, scuttled off outside, where he could be at peace with his vegetables.

'Father, the newcomer wishes to play his flute. Well it were my idea actually; I saw it sticking out of his pocket, but it would be a fine way to entertain everybody.'

'He doesn't need my permission to play his flute, Ros'leen. Come, lass, there's more to it than that, to see your face.'

She caught the stranger's eye and was embarrassed, having to say everything so loudly into Thomas's ear. 'He wants me to sit next to him, Father.' She bent her neck so that nobody should see the pink rush into her cheeks.

Thomas studied the fair-haired man who had come over to them, his hand held out in greeting, and shook it perfunctorily. 'Well there ain't no harm in that I suppose,' he said stiffly. Then, recalling his displeasure with his son, he looked about for Robbie. 'Where's that lad gone?' he roared. 'I'll have the hide off him.' And he left to look for him.

Rosaleen shrugged apologetically. 'He doesn't mean anything. He's been like it since my mother died. Will you play now? See – I'm sitting down all ready to hear you.' She crossed her legs and cupped her chin in her hands expectantly.

He sat down also and swivelled his chair so that it faced her, then, having buffed the mouthpiece of the instrument on his yellow waistcoat, he put it to his lips. Inhaling deeply and watching her all the while, he began to play.

One tune led into the next; some Rosaleen knew and others she did not, and she moved her body gently in time to the lovely sounds, noting the expression on the man's face as he blew, and the dexterity of his fingers. In her corner Nana Annie rocked and croaked to the music, and the four men stood, nursing their tankards, their faces glowing in appreciation. Thomas had returned without Robbie, and even though the sounds that filtered his way were slight, he began to smile and look happier.

Eventually the man put his flute away and everyone clapped. He thanked them modestly, licking his dry lips, and Thomas said, 'Another beer, sir – and on the house.'

'Thank you,' the other said. 'That would be most welcome.'

Thomas returned with a fresh beer and Rosaleen was about to get up when the traveller detained her.

'You're not going to leave me.'

'Sir, I must. It's not proper.' She never said 'ain't' like her father.

'And why not? Am I not a proper gentleman?' he teased.

'Yes most certainly . . .' Rosaleen felt flustered.

'Then what is not proper?'

'My father wouldn't like it.'

'I am certain he will not object. Now stay by me and be sociable or I shall go into a state of decline.'

Rosaleen sat on the edge of her seat, conscious of Nana Annie's blind gaze in her direction, and the fact that the clicking of her knitting needles had stopped; conscious of her father's gathering disapproval and the four affable miners nudging one another.

'Little Ros'leen Ruddock was soft-talked by a real gentleman,' she imagined them saying to their wives later. But soothed by the pleasantly modulated voice of the man beside her she relaxed gradually and sat back in her seat.

He was not handsome, but his face was kind, and his mouth – neatly framed by a pale moustache and trimmed beard – was sensitive. She liked, too, the way the dolefulness of his downward eyes was abolished when he smiled: then they gleamed like the devil's; and he smiled often.

He asked her about her life, and then he mentioned Brantwood, and Rosaleen was immediately alert.

'Brantwood is my favourite place,' she confided.

'Well it has been sold, you know. John Ruskin has bought it from that old Radical William Linton for fifteen hundred pounds without having set eyes upon it! He will not be moving in until about September. I believe he intends to alter it a great deal.'

'Who is John Ruskin? Is he famous?'

'My dear girl, don't you –' He broke off at the sight of her eagerness, and his expression became gentle: 'No – why should you indeed.'

And he spoke to her of John Ruskin and other names which would one day mean so much to her; of places and people, and art and literature.

Jealous of the man's attention, Thomas scowled at her from the bar, and Nana Annie, too, was concentrating on them. Rosaleen could see from the way she was knitting, and chewing on her lips that she was straining to hear what was being said; and she resented both of them.

But she was mollified again by the refined tones of her stranger as he talked, inspired by his enthusiasm, and although she didn't comprehend the significance of the 'Brotherhood' or the 'Pre-Raphaelites', she understood it to represent something fine: a band of artists seeking truth in art. She knew nothing of art, but she was enthralled by her companion – sat motionless and absorbed as he talked.

'The shawl you wear tied round your hips –' he leaned forward and fingered the fabric briefly.

'I made it,' Rosaleen said slightly defiantly, believing he was about to be critical.

'Well that is art,' he explained.

'My shawl – *art*?' She gave a peal of laughter. 'Why sir, I fashioned this when I was a child. I dyed the yarn and wove it. My father calls it my Joseph shawl on account of its colours.'

'That does not prevent it being art. Can you read?'

'Why yes, sir. I love to read. I can't imagine what it'd be like not to.'

'Well art is akin to reading, in that it is something you learn to understand and value. And the more you learn, the more you

41

appreciate. And the more you appreciate, the more you want to learn . . . So it goes on.'

Enlightened, she plied him with questions, repeatedly looking at her shawl anew, trying to see art in it.

He smiled kindly at her keenness. 'I shall tell the Professor to call at your inn.'

'The Professor?'

'John Ruskin. He is known as the Professor because of his links with Oxford University.'

'You *know* him?' Rosaleen's eyes widened.

'I know him very well.'

'Where do you come from, sir?'

'I am a nomad.'

'A nomad?' She looked puzzled, imagining Romanies.

'Yes – I wander. I explore.'

She laughed – and caught her father's eye again. He glared back.

'Aw sir, you're not a nomad!'

'There are many kinds of nomad, Rosaleen,' he said seriously. 'I consider myself one. Others consider me an eccentric.'

She was unsure of him – whether or not he was joking. There was a glint in his hang-dog eyes. She asked: 'Where will you travel to tomorrow?'

'To the borders.'

'Just you and your horse?'

'Just myself and Edgar.'

'Edgar?'

'My horse!'

'What a peculiar name for a horse.'

'Oh, I don't know. I think he looks like an Edgar. It is better than Dobbin or Blossom, I fancy. How exquisitely beautiful you are, Rosaleen.'

This greatly embarrassed her. Nana Annie's chin lifted more sharply and her long needle stabbed the wool. Thomas, rolling another barrel into place, did not hear.

'I expect you do not even know how exquisitely beautiful you are,' the man continued cheerfully.

42

She was discomforted; men lusted after her, and old women patted her head – but seldom did anyone tell her: 'You are beautiful.' She did not live in that kind of society.

'I've never really considered it, sir,' she answered after a pause, rubbing her forehead distractedly.

'No, I thought not.' He continued to study her. 'And you have beauty of character also – but I see I am disturbing you. How old are you, Rosaleen?'

'Eighteen, sir.'

'Rosaleen, my name is Frederick.'

'And your surname, sir?'

'Rosaleen,' he reproached her, 'I do not know yours, why must you know mine?'

'Ruddock, sir. Mine is Ruddock.'

'Ruddock. R–R–R-uddock,' he repeated, rolling the Rs.

'And yours, sir?'

'I refuse to tell you. If I do, then you'll not use my Christian name, and I prefer that you call me Frederick. Friedrich, should you prefer. My mother was Austrian.' And that was all he told her about himself.

The inn remained quiet that night. Outside it rained as though it had never rained before, hurling itself upon the ground, beating against the window-panes.

The hours passed. Nana Annie went to her bed, Robbie to his – accustomed now to sleeping on his own and to the leaping shadows. Her father had no one to talk to and no work left to be done, and he watched Frederick and Rosaleen speaking words he could not hear properly, talking anyway of things which would have bewildered him. His daughter's face was animated. He felt rejected.

Rosaleen knew how lonely he felt, but this night was her night. She saw him hesitate at the doorway, knowing he longed for her to detain him, but she would not, and clenched her lips against a fleeting urge to call to him. She heard Thomas go upstairs to his room with a defeated tread, and felt mingled regret and relief.

They remained downstairs for perhaps a half-hour, talking

and drinking strong sweet cider; she was the disciple of Frederick's stories. Eventually he said with a sigh: 'Much as I enjoy talking with you, I think I should retire now. I intend to rise early.'

'And if it is still raining?'

'Then, my dear girl, I shall accept it like a Buddhist.'

'What do you mean?'

'Well perhaps you know that Buddhism is a teaching practised in the East? It preaches an attitude of acceptance in life so that one is in harmony with day-to-day happenings, both good and bad. Perhaps you are a Buddhist, Rosaleen.'

She glanced at him to see if he were teasing her, but as before she could not tell. She replied politely, 'I think not, sir. I am a Christian.'

'Ah, that must be another discussion. And I wish you would call me Frederick, if not Friedrich.'

She laughed and followed him from the lounge, extinguishing the candles. Outside his room Rosaleen felt a sweeping dissatisfaction. He had entranced her – a few eloquent tales, a clever wit, a brief escape from her routine – then he would leave her with the repetition of her life.

The moment lent her recklessness, and with a beating heart she asked, 'Sir, will you bed me?' She heard the soft words as though they were not her own.

She so startled him that he stammered in return. 'Rosaleen – do you – are you – do you know what you are saying?'

'Oh yes, Frederick.'

The use of his name crumbled any resolve he might have had, and he went with her to her room – up the old staircase, she with her thoughts, he with his. From the other attic room came the dual sounds of the maid and cook snoring.

Rosaleen and Frederick faced each other in the candlelight; she was painfully nervous, and turning away from him unfastened her shawl, unbuttoned her blouse and bent to remove her shoes and red stockings. She then stepped out of her skirt and blue-striped underpetticoat and pulled off her chemise and drawers. Lastly she unpinned her hair and shook it free. She stood unmoving, with her back to him as he undressed, dreading to see him and shivering in apprehension.

'Please turn round and face me, Rosaleen,' Frederick whispered.

Nakedness which had been so natural to her no longer seemed to be. She had seen an erect penis before – Robbie's little one in the mornings, once her father's when she had scrubbed his back in the tub – but Frederick's arousal was because of *her*, and she was afraid of this thing that proclaimed its right over her.

Frederick stared at her, then laid her tenderly on the iron bed. Widow Cromby's bed. And Rosaleen had to stifle an almost hysterical laugh at the thought.

He stroked her; he caressed her; but she was tense and unmoved. Perhaps because she had propositioned him he presumed her not to be a virgin, and as he forced his way into her he realized his mistake:

'Oh you – silly – girl –' Then – 'Oh God it's been so long,' as he helplessly ejaculated.

'It's all right, Frederick,' she comforted him afterwards, when he repeatedly apologized. 'It were my idea. You didn't force me. It were my idea. Don't take on so.'

For a while they remained lying there, sticky and entwined and isolated. Rosaleen's mind felt numbed, and she was suddenly weary and wanted him to leave her. She had thought that if they made love she would link herself to his magical life, but she had felt only remoteness.

At her insistence he left to go to his own room. She went over to her window with its elevated view and stared from it until light hovered around the bareness of the lake: it looked a lonely place at this time in the morning when the sky meeting its flat darkness was only faintly infused with rouged streaks. If she narrowed her eyes she could just discern the even darker shapes of fishing boats dotted about – small inverted humps. Rosaleen watched the changing light with the casual dismissiveness of one who has woken to the same scene every day for years. She contemplated returning to bed, but its tousled state deterred her and she decided instead to wash and dress – soon it would be time to do so anyway.

She poured cold water from the pitcher into the basin and soaped herself quickly, wincing both from cold and from pain as the lather stung the soreness between her legs. She dried herself briskly, put on fresh underclothes and the same skirt and blouse as before. Peering into the dimly-lit mirror she wound up her hair, holding the pins between her teeth. Her face was both pale and dark in the shadows and her eyes were huge and disturbed.

To her reflection she said out loud, in a rueful voice: 'What did you expect then? But I had to . . .'

She returned to the window and in the dawn light she saw Frederick setting off on Edgar; she felt wistful rather than sad, and no remorse for what she had done.

'Ros'leen, Ros'leen – get up now, will you?'

'All right, Father. I'm already dressed.'

What point in answering a man who could not hear?

And she went downstairs to start her day in the same way she had a thousand other days.

⊸§ Three §⊷

THE RESTLESS SPIRIT

I did not realize how ordinary was my life –
Then I listened to words as gentle and inspired as a fine day.

'What happened to your fancy man then, tiny lass?' chided Nana
Annie. 'Your Nana might be three-quarter blind, but her hearing ain't departed yet. An old woman doesn't sleep sound. Them
were two sets of steps I heard climbing the attic stairs last night.'
Her sharp voice was shrill with indignation.

Rosaleen answered her levelly: 'You must have heard wrong,
Nana.'

And later her father, still saddened by her treatment of him,
reproached: 'You was flirting last night, Ros'leen.'

'No more'n usual, Father.'

'You was. I saw you, didn't I?' he shouted. 'The pair of you
like a couple of bloody birds.'

And in return she at last raised her voice, not because of his
deafness, but in an extraordinary tide of bitterness against him.

It was sheep-shearing time – late this year because of the
prolonged cold wet weather. Then with typical abruptness the
region was swept by gusts of warmth, the clouds dispersed, and
summer declared itself.

The sheep were gathered together from the hillsides – men
and dogs working together. The human cries and barking and
bleating could be heard for several days, and the excited black
and white forms of the dogs be seen tearing about in their efforts
to round up the scattered Herdwicks and Swaledales. They were
then carted off to be clipped, returning to the slopes pot-bellied,

47

skinned-looking creatures with stripes along their backs. Sheep-shearing was a serious business, and in the evenings the farmers would hold parties to celebrate, and Clipping-time Pudding would be served. Made of rice, dried fruits and sugar, it would be richly spread with bone marrow . . .

There were many who celebrated at the Coachman's Inn, and they included the farmer to whom Thomas had sold his land sixteen years previously. The inn was packed that night, and Rosaleen heard the man remark, 'I see you're taking plenty of money then, Mr Ruddock' – shouting above the general hubbub into Thomas's good ear.

Clearing the glasses and tankards from a table, Rosaleen stopped to listen. Her father was beaming in reply. He crowed, 'If I'd stuck t'sheep like you said I should've done, I'd never have had th'inn now. It were fate working its pattern. The oats failing were fate at play.'

'An omen,' came Nana Annie's thin screech from the corner. 'It were an omen.'

Nobody took any notice of her nowadays – sitting in her corner, a heap of bones knitting and chewing away. But she missed not a thing.

Rosaleen smiled to herself and was about to turn away again when she heard herself mentioned. The farmer continued, 'You're lucky with your daughter.' He gesticulated in her direction, and proceeded as though she were invisible, 'She courting yet?'

Rosaleen's body tensed as she awaited Thomas's reply. She saw her father's face darken.

'My Ros'leen ain't interested in boys. She's no time for 'em. Looks after me, she does.' He turned away and presented his right ear, and anything further said was lost to him.

She remained, caught in the midst of her actions, frozen within the confines of his words.

After her brief liaison with Frederick, Rosaleen had become restive and discontented, for although she had not felt sexually attracted towards him, she had liked him and he had brought to her existence an awareness of other, enriching things beyond her

48

immediate environment. All the local boys seemed now to her uncouth yokels, and she recalled Frederick's cultured ways with longing.

'What does it mean that Wordsworth once lived nearby?' she thought. 'Who do I know besides Robbie who's interested in poetry or the finer things? It is all hard work and shabbiness . . .'

Vibrant and vital, she felt that vitality dying and imagined herself as a drab hen with clipped wings; and whereas she had once been happy in her work, now she begrudged every chore. The constraints of her life pressed in upon her and her father became increasingly possessive.

She overheard him confiding to Nana Annie: 'She ain't been th'same since that gentleman rode by for the night – the one she was flirting with.'

'It's her age,' Nana consoled him. 'Moods is common to all lasses her age. You mustn't worry, son. She's a good girl, my tiny lass is. I'm old, but I understand a lass's moods.'

'She reads too much. Whenever she's a moment spare she's alone off walking – with a book . . .'

Rosaleen returned to her duties; she could not bear to listen further.

The vicar's wife gave her packages quite regularly now – books on geography or history or religion, the occasional novel – and she received them greedily.

'What do you want with all them boring books?' her father asked suspiciously one day when he saw her unwrapping the latest batch.

'But I don't find them boring, Father,' she said, and then, trying to convey her enthusiasm, thinking perhaps by doing so he might understand her better, she thrust a couple of books under his nose. 'See – they tell you all 'bout the world – places far away and people who lived before us.'

He glanced down disinterestedly at the illustrations and meaningless words, and then back at her with puzzlement. 'Well, I can't see why you should bother yourself with places far away or with people long-since dead. You live *here*, with people all around you. Life's here, lass. Around you.'

Robbie had become Rosaleen's confidant. He was very tall for his age, and spindly-thin. Over the years his phobias had subsided, but he was still serious and loved to write poetry. He read to Rosaleen in his unbroken voice: poems about eagles building nests on clouds of factory smoke because the mountains could not be found . . . Or of the jealous murder of one tailor by another; of the miner whose tea tasted of soot; the shepherd with a dead ewe draped like a scarf about his neck; or a traveller swallowed by the sands of Grange-on-the-Sands. Robbie saw lyricism in everything.

They lay on a grassy bank by Tarn Hows – that small isolated piece of water surrounded by tree-clad craggy hills beyond which the Langdales rose majestically. Tarn Hows lay only a couple of miles from Altwood Ground, and was one of Rosaleen's favourite places to come to, to think. Just to *be*.

She said to Robbie, 'You should have read your poems to Frederick. He'd have been interested.'

'Frederick?'

'You know – the traveller who stopped by that night.'

'The man with the flute?'

'Yes. Oh Robbie, he told me so many beautiful things. I cannot stop thinking of them . . . He spoke to me 'bout art and about people who follow religion in art. I didn't understand at first – and then it became clear. He told me my shawl was art! I laughed at that – imagine my shawl being art! He talked so fine, Robbie. You'd have liked his talk and his tales. And he told me about the new owner of Brantwood; his name's John Ruskin.'

'But I've heard of John Ruskin, Ros'leen! He's an artist besides a writer and a philosopher. He's ever so clever –'

'How've you heard of him, Robbie?' She sat up, hugging her knees together in excitement.

'Vicar was telling us at school th'other day. He read pieces to us written by John Ruskin.'

'But why didn't you *tell* me, Robbie?'

'Well I didn't know it were he that'd bought Brantwood.'

'But Vicar must've *said*.'

'But I didn't *hear* him say it, Ros'leen.'

50

'You're always in such a daze, Robbie mankin, and it were such an important thing to hear.'

'I'm sorry, Ros'leen.' He looked crestfallen, and she patted his arm.

'I suppose it's not your fault. But you must try a bit harder not to dream so. What else did Vicar say?'

'Nothing so's I recall. But I remember sommat Ruskin wrote. I remember it because I wrote it down and learned it, for I thought it so very fine.'

Robbie cleared his throat, and sitting-up straight-backed, recited: '"Man is the sun of the world, more than the real sun. The fire of his wonderful heart is the only light and heat worth gauge or measure. Where he is – are the tropics; where he is not, the ice world."'

'But Robbie, that is so, so beautiful. Oh how I *long* to meet him.'

'Perhaps you will if he's to move to Brantwood.'

'I shall make it happen, Robbie. Though what I could talk to him about I don't know.'

'You used not to care about such things – such people, Ros'leen.'

'It were Frederick who made me think about things differently. There was a light in his eyes when he spoke. There's more to life than drabness and work, Robbie.'

'But don't you see all the nice things any more, Ros'leen? You were happy before. You said the countryside was your own. You loved it. You said so. Ros'leen, you said you did . . . And it's not all drabness. There's market-days and fairs, and sports-day at Grasmere, and dancing and singing sometimes at the inn. And we care 'bout each other. It's not all bad, Ros'leen. You never used to think so before.' His voice had risen in panic.

When had her pleasure waned – that pleasure she felt in almost everything she did and saw? Frederick's appearance had only precipitated her change of attitude.

She could not explain. She took his hand and massaged its bony knuckles and tried to answer him.

'I know all you say. But the trouble is I've seen it all my life,

51

Robbie. I want to see sommat else now. It's as though . . . You see I've images in my head. Mother used to say I was over-imaginative; well perhaps it's because I am that I need to see other things.'

'It were you that taught me everything 'bout this place, Ros'leen. Don't you find it beautiful any more?'

'But of course I do, Robbie, for it *is* beautiful. But it's one kind of beauty. It's outside of us. There's beauty of other kinds. Is it wrong to want to explore those too? Mankin – see the little hillocks round the tarn – go on, look . . .'

His gaze followed her index finger which pointed.

'And now keep looking. Now look beyond the hillocks – at the Langdales. And there are further fells beyond those, and land stretching to the coast, and the sea after that, and then other coasts . . . Understand, Robbie. You like poetry. Surely you understand!'

She was almost weeping in her frustration to make him appreciate her viewpoint. He was her ally, and these feelings were so new and bewildering for her that she needed his moral support.

But although Robbie might have written poetry, he was only twelve, and since he was a toddler he had looked to his sister for consistency and strength; that she was wavering now threw him into turmoil. He did not want to understand her, because to do so would encourage her to pursue ideas which excluded him. He stared at her, shaking his head from side to side, restraining his tears.

Eventually he said through tight lips, 'Well I'll never move from here. It's home.'

Rosaleen thought, 'How like Father he sounds.' She said, 'Well, I'll do so. I have to.'

'But we *need* you, Ros'leen.'

'Robbie, that's the trouble. Everyone's always needed me. I love you all, but I've spent my life being needed and I'm weary of it. And Father won't get extra help. I don't want to be needed the whole time.'

'Don't shout at me, Ros'leen. It's not my fault.'

It all became too much for him and the tears fell. The hardness in her dissolved: this was her Robbie. She cuddled him to her.

'Aw mankin – don't take on so. Here – let me dab your eyes.' She took a corner of her shawl and reached up to blot his face. Some Canada geese appeared overhead and alighted on the water.

'You won't leave, Ros'leen. Promise me.' His expression was beseeching.

'Robbie, that's not fair. You mustn't ask me to make promises like that. You're growing up so fast now – why, see how ridiculously tall you are! And you've finished school this month for good; why – you'll be a young man before long. Robbie, don't fret so.'

'Father doesn't like me. He'd be awful with you gone.'

'That's not true, Robbie. For sure he loves you. He's impatient sometimes, that's all. You're too timid with him. You must face up to him.'

'He thinks I'm sissy. He says as much. He hates my poetry.'

He almost choked as he spoke, imagining himself without his sister's protection. She reached over and stroked his face, soothing his furrowed forehead.

'He doesn't understand it, that's all it is, Robbie. He doesn't like me reading books either. He doesn't like what he can't understand; it frightens him. He's just a bit lost, Robbie. He's soft-hearted really.'

'I wish I was you, Ros'leen.'

'Why, my mankin?'

'You're so brave. There's nothing frightens you. Ros'leen – I couldn't even wring a chicken's neck.'

'I'm not sure that's brave, Robbie. Brutal more'n like. It doesn't give me pleasure . . . But they're chickens and we're humans, and that's the way it is.'

'If you went I'd have to kill them.' He looked pale at the thought.

'Yes I expect you would,' Rosaleen answered. 'And just like I did, you'd get used to it. Just the same as you got used to being on your own with the shadows in your room at night. Just the

53

same as I got used to sleeping with the ghost of an old woman in my bed.' She added with sad tenderness, 'It's all part of growing up, so they say, mankin.'

Summer – temperamental as it had been – drew to a close with the clapping of thunder, a deluge of rain and high winds that drove away the rain as the days shortened into early autumn.

Then it was a time of riches – the picking of blackberries from the hedgerows, and making of elderberry wine – and memories of Flora scolding Rosaleen for her greed, and of the worms that had been her reward . . . Purple fingers engrained around the nails; and the making of jellies and conserves.

The men and boys harvested the bracken from the slopes, scything it in short sharp movements, then heaping it on to the sleds which were more practical for the hills and did not overturn like wheeled vehicles. The bracken was used for animal bedding.

In the valleys the reapers worked in the fields, bending and swinging rhythmically – men and boys and women, their heads bound in scarves. And at the end of the day's work there followed a hefty drinking session in the local inn. Some farmers ploughed immediately and the big placid horses could be seen dragging the ploughs behind them, trudging up and down, a routine act of fidelity – churning the field so that the yellow stubble was lost to the brown earth.

On several occasions during the months since her encounter with Frederick, Rosaleen had in secret walked to Brantwood and stood outside, gazing through the windows at all the alterations and building-work taking place. From within came the sounds of banging and sawing and hammering, whilst outside men cleared the woods at the back and heaped branches on to immense bonfires. Dozens of little paths were revealed, but more wonderful than anything was the making of a tennis court.

She watched the activity with a yearning so strong it was as though her whole being keened towards the house; she felt drawn to it, to the kind of life it would breathe when it was occupied. Her appetite had been whetted – uselessly so, for she knew how remote was the chance that she would ever be closer to it all than on these secret occasions when she came to stare and dream. She was convinced the traveller Frederick had forgotten her – and she had jeopardized her own position by her forwardness; by bedding him. She had only her own impulsiveness to blame.

That last Sunday of September was the Harvest Festival, and the little church of St Andrew's could barely accommodate its swollen congregation. The children had clean faces and the girls wore ribbons in their hair; many of the women were attired in their clothes newly bought from the second-hand market that week especially for the occasion.

Rosaleen had cut Robbie's hair, and her father's, but he refused to have his beard trimmed and it hung down on to his great chest. His body had lost its lean spareness, and too much of his own beer had resulted in an expanding girth which could barely be contained by his waistcoat, to which Rosaleen had sewn gleaming new buttons.

She teased him: 'See, Father, you're looking like one of your own barrels.'

And he replied good-humouredly: 'Where's your respect, lass? Whoever heard of an innkeeper without a good gut on him?'

Nana Annie wore new striped stockings to church, and Robbie new trousers. Rosaleen had dyed her over-skirt a bright pink and her ruffled petticoat beneath it a sky-blue, and she had found a pretty blue bonnet at the second-hand market that matched her petticoat. Around her shoulders, fastened with a paste brooch, she wore her Joseph shawl. Beneath the bonnet the front of her hair was swept up, whilst the back hung loose in curls.

Thomas and Robbie walked to the village and Rosaleen took Nana Annie in the cart: Nana Annie – hunched and hideous, and huddling close like a bedraggled bird.

'You're a good lass really,' she said, stroking and caressing the girl's arm. 'I understand a lass's moods, I do . . . Oh I was the same age as you – it don't seem so long ago. Once the lads used to swivel their heads t'look at me.' And in her nearly blind eyes was a flash of girlish longing.

In church, when all the other voices were raised in harmony, Nana Annie jutted her chin and opened her toothless mouth and emitted a witch-like screech which could be heard at raucous variance with the other voices. Smothering her laughter Rosaleen looked around her – and became aware of a young man staring at her. He stood next to a refined-looking middle-aged gentleman. The younger one whispered something to his companion, and then they both turned to stare. Embarrassed, she looked away.

The service ended after psalm a hundred and fifty, and then there was general social exchange and the distribution of produce. Rosaleen saw the two men slip away, and felt a sense of disappointment: their presence amidst the working-class congregation, most of whom she knew, had added a piquancy and touch of mystery.

A few days later she was mucking out the three sties, sorting the clean bedding from the dirty and heaping the soiled stuff on to the wooden skip. She worked quickly, but her nose wrinkled in disgust, and the pungent smell of the dung pervaded the sackcloth she wore to protect her clothing. Her hair was entirely concealed by a cotton scarf tied like a turban, and she wore stout boots – which now slithered in the mud. Rain fell in a steady mist as, graceful in her movements, Rosaleen bent and sorted and threw on to the skip – and patted the two laconic piebald sows, but not the boar.

Something compelled her to look up. A young man stood watching her, leaning against the remains of a dry-stone wall; he was laughing. She recognized him instantly.

'Why you're –'

'That's right. I saw you in church on Sunday. Lawrence Hilliard at your service, Miss Ruddock – popularly known as Laurie.' He vaulted the wall neatly and sprang frog-like at her feet, sliding in the mess.

She laughed, standing with her hands on her hips. 'And is Lawrence Hilliard supposed to mean sommat to me?'

'I doubt it, more's the pity,' he replied in a sing-song tone, 'but perhaps John Ruskin is.'

'John Ruskin!' She clapped her hands together.

'I am his assistant, his friend, provider of amusement, and everything else which is indispensable to a man such as he. I am also an actor.' He struck a self-important pose.

'How did you know my name?'

'Frederick Walton told Mr Ruskin about you. He wishes to meet you, and extends an invitation to dinner for a week's time – although I might suggest you wear something a little more becoming when you come to Brantwood . . .'

So Frederick had not forgotten her. Despite what had happened, he remembered; and she felt a flush of gratitude towards him.

When she told her father, he said, 'What do you want mixing with people like that for? 'Sides, I need you at the inn.'

'Father, Tuesday nights are quiet. 'Sides, you've got Robbie.'

'Lot of use he is. I don't want you to go, Ros'leen.'

There was fear in his voice. He felt threatened; and she saw only that he was trying to prevent her from doing something she passionately wanted to do.

'I'm going, Father. It's not harming anyone if I go.' She faced him stubbornly, her fists clenched.

'People like them – above our station, Ros'leen – what d'they want with you?'

'Nothing, Father. They want nothing from me. Can someone not just be kind for kindness' sake?'

'Well I don't want you to go,' he shouted.

'Well I do, Father,' she shouted back in her frustration.

They stared at each other defiantly, and then her mood dissolved as she recognized his fear for what it was.

'Aw Father, don't take on so. It's only supper. It's only a meal. Don't take on so, Father.' She tugged his beard and hugged him, filled with love for him and pity for all his uncertainties.

Thomas capitulated. 'I spoil you. I shouldn't ought to let you. Your mother always said I spoiled you. But you're my lass – what can I do?' His eyes gleamed – wet and devoted.

Nana Annie chided her a little: 'Miss Hoity-toity, eh? Becoming quite the Miss Hoity-toity . . .' And she cackled nastily.

Rosaleen bought a cherry-red woollen dress from the old-clothes market at Ulverston, and tailored it to her size, edging the tight-fitting bodice with pink satin ribbon and covering the buttons in the same satin. The skirt was draped and drawn back in the latest fashion over a dress-improver, and under it she wore deep red stockings and her brown worn, but well-polished, boots.

And now that the time had come, after all her longing to visit Brantwood properly and meet this Mr Ruskin, she was afraid to do so. That evening she left the safety of the inn – left behind Nana Annie knitting in her corner, the ribald laughter of two drunken shepherds who joked loudly with Thomas and did not perceive his inattention. She lit her lantern and went her way, shivering with apprehension and doubts.

'Oh I'm so nervous. Oh I'm so nervous. Oh but I'm so nervous.'

The walk seemed to take an age, but she arrived – stood by the door, away from it slightly, as her mother had taught her it was good manners to do, and waited in the evening's half-light for someone to come. The trees cast dark patches of shade on the yellow paintwork, and in the corners of the portico cobwebs shone silver.

Laurie answered her knock, and his eyes glinted merrily as he showed her into the spacious hall, already lit with candles. On the marble table lay a man's soft hat, thick gloves and a chopper.

Laurie explained, 'He's been chopping wood. Mr Ruskin's forever chopping wood. I daresay he finds it therapeutic.'

He led Rosaleen into the red and green drawing-room where four other people were already gathered, one of them a woman, and the man who came forward to greet her was the man who had sat beside Laurie in church. John Ruskin. He was tall and lean with a high-bridged nose and small indented chin; his light-brown hair was grey-streaked and his mild blue eyes showed that he was a man who knew what it was to suffer. It was a fine-featured and sensitive face.

'It is good of you to come, Rosaleen.' He shook her hand and smilingly gripped her arm to reassure her, noting her frightened expression.

Her reply stuck in her throat and momentarily she felt over-whelmed – by the grand room, the fact she was the centre of attention suddenly, by John Ruskin himself.

'What am I doing here?' she thought wildly.

Ruskin propelled her towards the other guests. 'Let me introduce you –'

'Good evening, Rosaleen.'

Frederick came towards her and grasped her hand tightly. She was so glad, surprisingly glad, to see him.

'Hello sir.' She smiled in her pleasure at seeing his crumpled face and downward eyes.

'Frederick,' he reprimanded. 'Or Friedrich.' His mouth twitched humorously.

'Oh Frederick, don't be so pompous,' laughed the woman in the group.

He whispered in Rosaleen's ear: 'Are you talking to me or are you angry?'

She whispered back: 'Angry – why should I be angry?'

The others looked on with curiosity. Ruskin continued his introductions: 'Rosaleen, this is Joan Severn, my very special cousin, and this is her husband Arthur. He is a fine water-colourist. Now do not redden, Arthur! Mr and Mrs Severn will be living here much of the time. A rather arty lot it might be said.'

The introductions were over and with them any formality was dispelled. Rosaleen wandered about the room, enchanted and inquisitive, touching and looking at objects and furniture and pictures. She determined to note everything so that she might recall it whenever she wished. There was such an eclectic assort-ment: a collection of shells in a display cabinet was flanked by a table crowded with valuable porcelain. A magnificent desk and filing cabinet was open to reveal all its compartments. Ruskin's

own beautifully executed water-colours and architectural drawings hung beside Turners.

That name held no significance for her then. 'But I shall learn,'
she thought as she stared at the pictures, delighting in their
varied styles and colours.

Then she saw the amused expressions of the others, and was
immediately conscious that she had been rude. She gave a little
gasp with the realization. 'Oh – I'm so sorry . . . Do you mind if I
look around?' she asked her host.

'But of course not, my dear.'

'I have longed to see this house!' Her voice rang out fervently.

'Then it is yours to see,' Ruskin told her gravely.

She rushed from object to object, then room to room. John
Ruskin followed her at a more leisurely pace.

In the study he explained, 'I had this wallpaper copied from
Marco Marziate's circumcision painting that hangs in the
National Gallery.'

Who was Marziate? What did circumcision mean? What was
the National Gallery? Rosaleen was angered by her own ignorance. She read whenever she could and still, it seemed, she was
ignorant.

'. . . And these are all Turners. It was through Turner I came to
love art. He knew my father and I greatly esteemed him, and
when, years ago, he fought for recognition, I believe I aided him.
He has influenced me – I cannot say otherwise. See how he uses
colour.'

She looked at the paintings through his enamoured eyes.

A pair of globes stood at opposite ends of the room and he
span one of them before sitting down on the window seat.
Rosaleen stood near him and tried to see out of the window: it
was too dark, but she could imagine the view. Ruskin watched
her with a faint smile that seemed to contain an element of
sadness.

'Where do you work?' she asked shyly. 'I mean, in which
room?'

'Well, I paint in the cottage in the grounds. The previous
owner, Linton, used it for his printing of radical newspapers. I

60

do my writing in this room – at that table by the fire. But as you know I've not been here long . . .' He patted the seat. 'Come sit beside me.'

She did so, and turned earnestly to him. 'I wish I understood about art. I'd never thought of it before – not until I met Frederick. Now it seems such a beautiful thing and I wish I knew about it.'

'Well, it is only beautiful if life is meaningful, for it depicts life. And tell me, Rosaleen,' he asked gently, 'why is art important to you?'

She could not believe he took her seriously, but when she scanned his face for falsity, she saw only compassion. She tried to articulate what she felt, but her reasoning was as yet flimsy: 'My days are ordinary, sir, as you'd expect. Yet all the while I go about my duties – cleaning, serving and a hundred other things – my mind soars into the distance. I want more – even if it's only to see a different view . . .'

She paused, dissatisfied with her answer. She had conveyed nothing of her listlessness, or her longing for knowledge. She added, 'Sir, I like to learn.'

'And the idea of art excites you?'

'Yes – only I've not explained myself well.' She looked away, dismal, and her shoulders slumped.

'I think you have explained yourself admirably,' he consoled her. 'But my dear, to learn about art and its many facets could take for ever. Art encompasses many, many things. However –' He held up his hand when her face fell, '– we shall arrange a further meeting. Several meetings. And I shall endeavour to show you all I can. It would give me great pleasure. Would you like that?'

'I should so like it, sir, but I'm not sure my father would permit me. He needs me at the inn.'

'You have needs also, and your own desires, have you not?'

He understood! How clear it was when he said that – and how often Rosaleen had thought similarly and been ashamed to voice it.

61

'I've never seen so many books,' she commented; they flanked the marble fireplace.

'You have not seen the inside of many houses then.'

'Well I wouldn't have, would I, sir?' she answered wryly.

He smiled at the quickness of her response, and for the first time Rosaleen noticed the scar on his upper lip, caused, she later discovered, by a dog biting him as a child.

He said, 'Well, the situation can be remedied. I can lend you some books.'

'The Vicar's wife gives me books from time to time. My brother Robbie used to bring them back from school for me. I daresay she'll forget now he's left. But there's always so little time for reading, sir. My day doesn't finish sometimes till long-gone midnight. And then I'm up again around half-past five.'

'Poor young Rosaleen. It is not easy. But you will find time. One does for things one really wishes. And your brother – tell me about him.'

'Robbie's twelve, sir, and almost as tall as yourself. He likes poetry, and Father bullies him rather. Robbie's sensitive. One sharp word and the tears bubble in his eyes. He learned about you at school, sir. He quoted sommat you wrote. I thought it so beautiful.'

'Did you now! What did he quote you, can you remember?'

She gave her gruff little laugh, pleased with herself that she remembered, and looking directly at him recited: '"Man is the sun of the world, more than the real sun. The fire of his wonderful heart –"'

Ruskin stared at her in surprise, his eyes bright. He continued with her: '"– Is the only light and heat worth gauge or measure. Where he is – are the tropics; where he is not, the ice world." Ah, and it is true, Rosaleen. But sometimes we forget.'

He looked past her into sadness.

Then with an abrupt change of mood he stood up and said cheerfully, 'Now it is time for dinner I suspect. The others will wonder why we have absconded for so long. But before you leave tonight I shall give you some books to read, and perhaps you will find time to look through them.'

The atmosphere of informality extended over the mealtime. Ruskin announced, 'I shall make a new dining-room one day. This room is too small and dark and has no views.'

'Brantwood seems to be sprouting in all directions,' Frederick commented. 'In Thomas Woodville's day it was a mere cottage!'

'A house depends on its views,' Ruskin replied defensively.

'You are indeed an unconventional architect,' Arthur Severn said.

'Are you an architect?' Rosaleen asked, and everyone laughed.

Laurie answered, 'When it suits him. And when it does not he dons one of his other hats, and in the face of criticism can truthfully answer, "But I am an artist" – to the critic of his architecture, or "a writer", to the critic of his art, or "a philosopher", to the critic of his writing. John Ruskin has an answer to all critics. But he criticizes all!'

There was light applause, and more laughter. Frederick held up his hand. 'While on the subject of architecture amongst other things, may I remind you all what someone famous wrote? "Design in architecture is not a matter of perfect proportion. First the architect must look to nature –"'

'Why – John himself wrote that!' exclaimed Joan Severn, a puzzled expression on her pleasant face.

'Frederick knows,' her husband told her kindly. 'He is being effete as usual.'

'I am never effete. I was merely demonstrating a point!'

After dessert and sherry they went into the drawing-room once more where their host read aloud passages from his own writings, and then they gathered round the piano and sang whilst Joan Severn played the accompaniment.

'Frederick must play his flute!' Arthur Severn said.

'Oh very well.' Frederick sounded grudging, but he was quick enough to stand up and produce his flute. He played melodies which were hauntingly sweet, and then he played *Greensleeves* to which Joan Severn sang softly in a rich warm voice.

Curled up in a large chair, Rosaleen – muted from music and culture and wine – fought against the urge to cry. She sighed instead. The sigh went through her body.

Later, when the coachman drove her back to the inn in the brougham, Frederick came with her.

'So, my little Rosaleen,' he asked, 'was it all that you expected?'

'Oh yes – and more besides. I was afraid beforehand it would be so grand.'

'And you are not disappointed that it is not so?'

'Oh no. How could I be? And Mr Ruskin was so kind. But although he laughs and smiles he seems unhappy, doesn't he? There's a loneliness about him, a look of pain.'

'You are a perceptive girl, aren't you? John Ruskin's a complex man, Rosaleen. He has had a full life in which he has explored the cultural avenues of religion, philosophy, art and architecture and literature, striving to form a link between them – and he has given his soul to each along the way. He has enriched others and been enriched in his turn, but he has endured repeated disappointment. It is inevitable – his ideals have been so great. Despite his achievements he is confused and uncertain of himself.'

'It's like one man trying to sweep up a forest of fallen leaves in a gale,' Rosaleen said sadly.

'It is indeed like that, and most men would not therefore attempt the task.'

'Is he ever content?'

'Who knows? Perhaps he will find peace of mind here at Brantwood, where he may look from his window and see before him the perfection of the mountains falling into the water. What are they called?'

'Old Man, Swirl How, Wetherlam.'

'Even the names must soothe a troubled mind . . . But you do not know his most serious problem.'

'What is that?'

'Perhaps I should not tell you; but yes, I think I shall. John Ruskin is in love with a girl by the name of Rose La Touche. At twenty-three she is thirty years younger than he is, and he has been in love with her since she was thirteen. She is his "Rosie-Posie", and he is her "Mr Crumpet", and he is as besotted as a man might be. But the relationship must surely be the most bizarre one could come across, for they have years when they do not see one another and only write of their love, which is forbidden by Rose's parents – who incidentally were once friends of Ruskin . . . And to make matters worse, at the root of the disparities is that age-old bone of contention, religion. At twenty-three, Rose is now old enough to defy her parents, should she so wish, but it seems that she has formed her own conclusions. And yet another twist is that Ruskin's ex-wife, Effie – now married to the artist John Millais – claims he was sexually incapable, and would be no use to Rose. If this was disproven, then the annulment of her marriage to Ruskin would be invalid, her marriage to Millais an act of bigamy, and her children by him illegitimate . . .'

'Oh the poor man, no wonder he is unhappy. But what's happening now?'

'Rose refuses to have anything more to do with him. We shall see. Personally I doubt it is the end.

'Rosaleen – what I have told you, only a few close friends know. I told you because you are compassionate and will not judge, and because I can see that Ruskin is drawn to you. He is a true gentleman, Rosaleen, and will only respect you. He likes the company of young people – he likes the purity of their bodies and their minds . . . You will not repeat what I've told you?'

'Who am I to repeat it to, Frederick?'

'It is only that he must not become the target for gossip in these parts. He is as fine a man as one could hope to meet, Rosaleen, but is subject to prolonged and recurring bouts of depression. I hope that he finds Brantwood will understand his elations and his sorrows. He has tried to put the world to rights. That he has not succeeded is his grief.'

Frederick fell silent. The brougham rattled and clattered and turned up the track which led to the Coachman's Inn.

Rosaleen felt an impulse to lay her hand on his. She did so, tentatively. 'You love him,' she said softly.

'He is like that,' Frederick answered. 'He inspires love and loyalty in his friends.'

He laid his free hand on their combined hands, and their brief ensuing spell of silence was warm and companionable.

They were nearly back. Frederick said, 'Rosaleen, I must ask you – why did you want me to make love to you that night? I have thought about it and felt so bad.'

'You must not. It were me that asked you . . . I just – felt like it at the time.'

She could not explain to him that she had wanted to link her life to his, to cling on to his stories. She did not want it to seem as though she had exploited him.

'No more, no less? That simple?' He sounded aghast.

'That simple!' She laughed uneasily at his bewilderment, aware that perhaps by her admission his opinion of her was lowered: in protecting his feelings she had risked her own reputation.

'I was a virgin,' she longed to remind him.

But Frederick had recovered and was bemoaning his own inadequacies: 'And I let you down. I was hopeless and am ashamed . . . Still we shall not speak of that now. So –' He took her face between his hands and tilted it to see into her eyes, ' – and now you are my friend?'

'I hope so, Frederick.' She looked back at him seriously.

He released his hold. 'I hope so also. You are a most rare being, Rosaleen.'

'Aw Frederick, I'm just ordinary.'

'No,' he insisted. 'That you are not. And time will tell. And now I believe we have arrived . . .'

The candle was still alight in Robbie's room. Rosaleen could see its glow through the half-open door as she passed.

'Are you awake, mankin?'

'Yes. I couldn't sleep for thinking of you. How was it?'

She sat on his bed by the lump of his legs. His face was pale, and in the strange light his freckles made irregular patches on the paleness.

'It were wonderful, Robbie. And see all the books he's loaned me. So many . . .'

*

The visits became regular and there was little her father could say because John Ruskin patronized his inn and sometimes brought other friends, but he tried to prise details from her and there was dread in his eyes. She did not want to see it because it stood in her way. She became secretive to avoid hurting him, and in turn his doubts made him demanding and overbearing and his moods became increasingly unpredictable.

'Ros'leen, you haven't washed these tankards proper . . . Ros'leen, go to smithie's and take pony t'be shod.'

'Can't it wait 'til tomorrow, Father? I already went twice to the village today. I'm in the middle of doing laundry, Father, and there's so much more t'do.'

'No it can't wait,' he bellowed. 'Are you too busy to remember your duties? You should've checked his feet.'

'That's not my job, Father,' she defended herself.

'I'll take him, Father,' Robbie whispered.

'What'd you say? Speak up lad. Don't you know by now I can't hear proper?'

'I said I could go to smithie's.'

'And I said I wanted your sister t'go . . .'

Sometimes he was repentant and humble afterwards: 'Aw lass, I didn't mean t'be harsh on you. You know how much I care for you.'

But at some stage almost every day his voice was heard raised in anger, and when it was not, his face was melancholy and his gaze followed his daughter about reproachfully. He could not understand what had happened to the child he had known.

He burdened her with yet more duties, vainly hoping to keep her so occupied she would have no time for ulterior thoughts. But the more he attempted to confine her, the more Rosaleen fled; and the more she sought her freedom, the more he raged. He saw no reason to contain himself, for John Ruskin hardly used the inn now she visited Brantwood so regularly.

Nana Annie tried to taint her pleasure by maligning the innocence of those occasions:

'Dirty ol' man. He's taken a shine to you. Can't you see it? He wants to bed you. He'll soon be wanting payment for all his trouble.'

'It's not like that, Nana.'

'Oh tiny lass, you're not daft in the head are you? No man does sommat for nowt with a pretty lass.'

Rosaleen recoiled. Inside her was the withering of her pleasure. She told herself, 'He is in love with Rose La Touche'; and recalling her conversation with Frederick, strove to retain the purity of her friendship with Ruskin. She trusted men, and of them all he was the most honourable.

Brantwood and its occupants offered her tranquillity and gentility – and more. It offered her a continuation of the education she had reluctantly relinquished when she had left school. Brantwood was no longer merely a house: it was knowledge, ever-expanding and infinite. What had once been dauntingly new became familiar, and as she learned, so she craved to learn more.

Besides Turner there were other artists whose names she knew now; but it was the Pre-Raphaelites she most admired. Their paintings captivated her with their depth of colour, richness of style and perfect detail. It was Ruskin who had pioneered their cause, but since Millais had married his ex-wife Effie, and he had quarrelled with Rossetti, only Edward Burne-Jones remained a close friend.

Sometimes when Rosaleen visited she would be the sole guest; then, after showing her the latest improvements to the house, Ruskin usually led her into the study where he would bring out books about art, and they would pore over them together, Rosaleen attentive to his every word and opinion. Afterwards he might take her on a tour of the grounds where – surrounded by swirling leaves – they would sit by the beck on his stone seat in the woods, and he would tell her of his philosophies and his changing outlooks on religion.

The last time, in a fit of boyishness, he had tied a scarf around her neck and run with her to where he kept his little boat named *Jumping Jenny*. He rowed her half-way across Coniston Water, and together they watched the changing sky and the different shades cast on the fells.

'I know of nowhere else with skies like it,' Ruskin said.

'And I, sir,' Rosaleen replied, 'know of nowhere else.'

He looked at her keenly. 'I understand you a little now I think, Rosaleen. I connect you with this place, and to me you seem a part of it, in rare harmony with it; but that is to attribute to you no finer instincts, and those you have in plenty. You have a mind which will not be happy unless it explores —'

'And for that I must move away,' she completed for him in a matter-of-fact tone.

He nodded, saying nothing.

Later, when they parted, he gave her as usual a fresh book to replace the one she had returned to him. He held on to her hand as they said goodbye.

'I have only just come to this haven,' he mused. 'It is strange to imagine someone would wish to escape it.'

'It'll be here when I return, sir. Unchanged and ever-changing.'

He smiled. 'How well I comprehend you.'

But her father did not, and when she returned that afternoon, having been absent for more than four hours, his unbridled rage rang throughout the Coachman's Inn. They were beyond appeasing one another, and she went up to her room and changed her clothes ready for work.

One evening in November Rosaleen was invited to dinner at Brantwood. Besides Joan and Arthur Severn there was another couple, and she was introduced.

'Rosaleen, this is a very close friend of mine, Mr Edward Burne Jones, and this is his wife, Georgiana Burne-Jones.'

She shook their proffered hands, momentarily enveloped by shyness, and then she burst out, 'How do you do? Oh sir, I do admire your paintings.'

And with the introduction Rosaleen's life changed.

⏗ Four ⏘

THE ADVENTURESS

I inhaled deeply and I was away,
Parted from my innocence for ever.

There was a day in December when Rosaleen made her decision.
She had quarrelled with her father, rebuking him mildly for his
treatment of Robbie, and he had turned his temper furiously on
her. Without another word she had left the inn.

She had walked for hours – to Tilberthwaite – thinking and
walking, the only human being in that lonely craggy place, and
on a day which was as cold as any so far that winter. She had
wanted solitude. She climbed quite high and sat by the cascading
waterfall.

'What a watery place I live in!' she thought. 'Certainly one
wouldn't die of thirst here.'

And she lifted her heavy skirts, exposed her bottom to the
cold, and urinated – adding to the rivulets of water running
through crevices in the ground. Only the sheep looked on,
staring disinterestedly with their marble eyes.

The Herdwicks sheltered from the elements in the protective
shade of shallow basins in the hills. A lone ram stumbled near
her, and she saw that one curly horn had been ripped off, tearing
away the flesh so that half the face was exposed and the skin
flapped loose. Rosaleen always carried a small knife in the pocket
of her top skirt, and now she whipped it out and grabbed the
ram, pinioning it, as shepherds did, while it was on its knees.
Swiftly she sliced off the loose skin and spat on the raw exposed
flesh to soothe it. It was all she could do.

The animal was quiescent throughout its ordeal and Rosaleen

pondered on the fact it hadn't uttered a sound. She thought: 'They feel pain differently from us. It hasn't the same meaning.'

She sat down once more; tried to forget the horror of the ram's face. An intermittent East wind made her shiver and she wrapped her cloak about her shoulders.

'What'll I do?' The question repeated itself and tiredly she lay back on the damp rocky ground, her head aching with tension.

'They'll be so sad . . . Father, Robbie, Nana Annie. I'll be sad. But I'll come back sometimes. Maybe after a while I'll come back for good. Am I wicked to go? But my mind's fit to burst with longing to see different things . . . Father could get help at the inn. Nancy's girl would come. It's not my fault he's so stubborn . . . His temper'll take a turn for the worse no doubt. Nana Annie'll go on as she always has – knitting and eavesdropping and preaching about omens . . . Robbie – he'll pine like a dog, but it won't harm him to stand on his own feet . . . They'll manage. It's only I feel so bad . . .'

After a while her tension eased; all deliberate thought seeped away and her mind emptied. She knew a beautiful lightness of body.

She passed the day immersed in meditation, and when the afternoon was darkening towards its end she heard the excited barking of sheepdogs and turned to see an old straight-backed shepherd wearing a collarless shirt and braces, and beside him a chattering little boy who came up to his waist. They were hand in hand. The dogs were weaving in and out of the sheep – one so ancient its legs were bowed and large bald patches showed amongst the knotted fur. The other dog was young, learning his trade from the senior one – his replacement. The old man and the boy; the old dog and the puppy . . . Rosaleen felt a reaching out towards them; she was touched by the significance of the simple scene. One day when the child was an adult he would reflect on this moment and recall the tall white-haired man who had held his hand and taught him his work.

They took no notice of her and their aloneness seemed remarkable to her, stirring the same nerve of sensitivity as did the isolation of the crags now veiled in mist, the sounds of ever-falling water, and the staring of the glassy-eyed sheep.

She got up slowly and made her way back.

Thomas shouted, 'Where've you been? I've been proper frenzied with worry.'

'I've been walking, Father, only walking.'

'All day?'

'Yes.'

'And no books with you?' He studied her anxiously to see if she might have one hidden on her person.

'No Father.'

'What did you want with just walking 'bout?'

'I just wanted to be on my own, Father.'

He looked sorrowful then. 'I was afraid . . .' He came to her and hugged her close to the comforting bulk of his body, and she remembered how it had once been.

'Aw lass, I'm sorry if I lost my temper. I didn't mean anything before. I was in a proper mood this morning. The beer had turned . . . There's a leak in the roof . . . Pony's lame. You'll be my lass again, eh?'

'Of course, Father.'

'And you're not t'go walking off like that and coming back when it's dark if I don't know where you've gone.'

Later that night, in his room, Robbie stated dully, 'You've decided, haven't you? You've made up your mind.'

'Yes, I shall go, Robbie mankin. After Christmas.'

'Oh Ros'leen . . .'

'Hush – don't cry. No Robbie, you really mustn't cry.'

'Can I come with you?'

'No.'

'I'd not get in the way, I'd –'

'No Robbie.'

'I knew you wouldn't let me . . . Will you write to me?'

'I've not gone yet!'

'No, but when you have.'

'Aw Robbie, of course I'll write to you.'

'And I t'you. And I'll send you poems.'

72

'That'll be lovely. I'll treasure them. Now go t'sleep, my mankin. You get so tired. You grew too quickly – like a beanstalk! It's not all so bad. And I've not gone yet.'

It was an evening in early February, 1873. Thick snow lay whitely outside, and all about was that unnatural silence that went with it. The inn was empty of guests and Thomas and Rosaleen were alone in the kitchen, except for the replacement mongrel who lay where its predecessor had used to lie, under the table.

Thomas threw another log on to the fire with more aggression than usual, and when he spoke his voice was harsh.

'What d'you mean you're going from home?'

'Father, I'm – going to London.'

She spoke hesitantly and caught his right ear, and he swung round angrily.

'You're tormenting me now, are you? Don't you know by now I can't hear in that ear?'

'Father, be calm. I wasn't doing it on purpose. You know that. Now sit down and hear me, will you? You mustn't take on so.'

He remained standing, towering above his daughter, antagonized by her calmness.

'You don't tell *me* how t'be, lass. You remember who you're speaking to. Now tell me 'gain what you said before.'

'I'm going to London, Father. Into service with Mr Burne-Jones's family.'

'And who be Mr Burne-Jones?'

'He's an artist friend of Mr Ruskin, Father.'

'I might've known it were through him. He's ruined you. You've been spoiled by him and his smart ideas. All them books. I knew there was going t'be trouble soon as I saw you with all them books. And you disappearing to the big house all the time. I should've put a stop to it before now.'

'I wouldn't have heeded you, Father.'

'And how's that a way t'talk to your father? I should've locked you in your room.'

'It wouldn't have done any good, Father.'

Thomas clenched his fists in frustration at her defiance. This was a new Rosaleen, and he was at a loss to know how he should deal with her.

'Well, I ain't letting you go no place, lass. Go t'your room. I've nowt further t'say on the matter. Go to your room, Ros'leen.'

She should have known when to leave him alone. Having stated her intention, it only remained for her actually to depart at a later stage. Instead she stood her ground, intent upon making her point to an already chastened man.

'I'm not going to my room, Father. I want you please t'listen to me.'

'I've heard enough, lass. I've had plenty of your lip . . .' He paced the room, his flowing bright hair and beard making him look like a mad warrior. 'I got one half-decent ear and I heard enough. You're not going t'London, and that's final. What do you want with going there? How can you think of leaving all of us, Ros'leen? Shame on you. How can you leave all this?'

He gesticulated wildly to beyond the window where the snow glowed, stark, against the black sky.

His finger shook, and Rosaleen was sad for it, but she answered in a steady voice, 'I've seen it all my life, Father. I need sommat different now. It doesn't mean I don't care about you because I want to discover other things beyond here. Mr Ruskin's shown me there's so much else to see . . .'

She tried to take his arm in conciliation, but the mention of Ruskin's name again was the catalyst which inflamed her father's wounded mood.

He shook off her arm and pushed her to the ground roughly. 'You dare t'mention his name again!' he roared. 'A man who poisons my daughter's head with his words and notions, who takes her away from her responsibilities –'

She got to her feet, as indignant now as he. 'Father, I'm done with my responsibilities. You've got them too, you know. You have responsibilities too. Since I was fourteen it's been me that's kept the place going. I do more'n my fair share here.'

'You do nowt more'n any loving daughter ought t'do.'

'I've never had thanks from you, Father.'

'What – a daughter expects thanks from her father for doing

74

her duty? That's ripe, that is. What thanks do I get for giving you a roof over your head? You're a spoiled hussy, that's what's wrong with you. A spoiled hussy,' he bellowed.

Stung, she shouted, 'Father, that's a wicked thing to say. And it isn't true. I'm not a hussy.'

'I've seen th'way you've been of late – coming in all hours with prettily dressed gentlemen.'

'It doesn't mean a thing. They're my friends.'

'Friends,' he roared derisively. 'What 'bout family then? You'd desert your family for "friends" would you? Your friends've poisoned you.'

'It's you who's poisoned, Father. Since Mother died –'

'You'll not speak of your mother now.' Thomas stood threateningly over her, red-faced and blazing-eyed, but Rosaleen continued heedless, her temper as aroused as his.

'After Mother died you became unreasonable, Father. You won't listen to anyone. You storm about expecting miracles and complaining all th'time, and it's been up to me to try and keep the peace. Well I've had it, Father. I've had it with responsibilities and with being needed every minute of the day. I'm young, Father. Have you ever thought what it's like for me stuck here, longing to do other things, but unable to? No you haven't, because you've turned into a foul old man with feelings for none but yourself.'

'You're an ungrateful lass, you are. You haven't got no pride running after gentlemen like what I've seen. You're worse 'n a bitch on heat. You're not a decent lass no more – forgetting your duties and family and putting a bunch of strangers before both. London –' He spat the word. 'City of smoke and whores more'n like. And you're no different th'way you're acting.'

She ran at him then – charging like a miniature bull furiously into the barrel of his body, beating him with her fists, and he swung his hand with his full strength twice across her face. She fell to the floor and lay there, her hatred of him masking her pain.

'I've never laid a finger on you before now,' Thomas shouted – perhaps to excuse himself – 'I never thought as I'd need to. Well I ain't sorry now. Little hussy.'

'I'm going, Father.' Rosaleen struggled to her feet. 'I've had enough. You're a proper tyrant.'

'Good riddance then. And don't come grovelling back. Thomas Ruddock doesn't forgive easy, Ros'leen. Get out of my inn now, before I strike you again. You're no daughter. Get out will you . . .'

She stumbled up to her attic room to pack – a few essential possessions and clothes, tying them together in a sheet . . . noticing her childhood loom suddenly and remembering. Bye-bye Widow Cromby's bed . . .

She went into Nana Annie's room and smelled her acrid breath. 'I'm leaving, Nana.'

'Where you going, tiny lass?' The old lady was groggy with sleep. Her hair was in a skinny grey pigtail down her back.

'I'm going t'London.'

'Not t'night you ain't surely?'

'No. I'll stay at Brantwood tonight.'

'You've lost your mind, child.'

'No Nana. I want my own life, that's all.'

'Self-indulgence I call it. You don't know when you're well off. And how'll your father cope?'

'He can get a girl – two girls even. Nancy's daughter was willing. She'd not want much wage and she could have my room.' Rosaleen tried to justify herself. 'You must see, surely, Nana.'

'Well I see I'll miss you, tiny lass. Times is surely changing when a lass sees fit to skuttle off like that. You've broke my heart.'

'I'm sorry Nana.'

'Give your Nana a kiss, tiny lass. I dare say we'll get by. It's not me as won't forgive you. I was young once, and like I say, times is changing. You was always a stubborn mite with a mind of your own.'

Rosaleen felt a wave of love for the old lady, and bent and kissed the disintegrating flesh of her cheek.

Her grandmother said as she left the room: 'I ain't afraid for you. You've got a good head, 'spite everything. Don't be swayed by pretty words, tiny lass. Remember that.'

Then into Robbie's room, where the door was ajar as usual and candles glowed.

'I heard it all,' the boy said, sucking in his breath and exhaling in admiration. 'I wouldn't have dared say what you did.'

'He made me angry. I'm not sorry,' Rosaleen replied in a tight voice.

'He *hit* you! I can see even in this light. Oh Ros'leen – you're all bruised and marked. Oh I *hate* him.'

She said nothing, biting her sore, cut lip; making it bleed again.

'Oh Ros'leen,' Robbie repeated, sighing a juddering sigh.

Poor Robbie with his tortured face! Rosaleen's resolve crumpled seeing it, and she could have stayed just to prevent his desolation. But he said bravely, 'You really have to go, don't you?'

'Yes mankin. If you can bear it.' She crouched on her haunches at his side and searched his eyes for assurance.

'I'll miss you.'

'And I'll miss you.'

'Aren't you sad?' he cried out, suddenly impassioned.

'Aw Robbie, of course I'm sad.'

He nodded with a poet's understanding at the paradox: she was sad, yet she was choosing to leave.

'Now you'll see to things nicely when I'm gone, won't you? And remember not to whisper in Father's right ear, but to holler in his left . . .'

'Ros'leen . . .' The tears poured down his thin cheeks and she stroked them away.

'Robbie mankin, don't make it harder . . . I wish I had sommat t'give you, sommat tiny even, that's mine. But I've nothing. I could give you a button off my skirt though, couldn't I? You could look at it and think of me.' So saying, she wrenched a button from her skirt and pressed it into his cold hand. She felt a tear drop on to her hand, and kissing him again, left before she too broke down and cried.

The door to the kitchen was open as she left and Thomas was

slumped at the table, vulnerable. Rosaleen hesitated, feeling herself relent, but her father looked up and scowled.

'Get out o' my inn, will you. I don't want you here. You're an ungrateful hussy. Get out and don't come running back, for you'll not be welcome. And I'm not sorry as I struck you.'

And that was how they parted.

Rosaleen trudged towards Brantwood, her path illuminated by the demi-moon and the snow. On her right glimpsed between the ghostly shapes of trees made magical and strange, the lake glinted black. Her feet sank in the snow's depth, becoming drenched, and her face smarted. Her lips were numb and swollen and within her she wept. She felt forlorn and displaced as she slipped and slithered her way along the road carrying her bundle.

When at last she arrived and stood back from the familiar doorstep, she was suddenly afraid that nobody would answer her knock. The place was in darkness and her spirits sank with defeat. She waited a moment, her body wilting in dejection, and was about to raise the knocker once more when she heard footsteps – and there was Joan Severn – holding her hands up in shock at the sight of Rosaleen and hustling her into the warmth exclaiming, 'Oh your face, your poor pretty face!' And then, 'Oh your poor darling feet, how wet they are!'

Rosaleen sat in the study unresisting whilst Mrs Severn removed her sodden boots and set them by the still-glowing fire. She was dazed now that she was here, and could not connect herself with the previous events – with that girl who had quarrelled violently with the man she had loved all her life and then been beaten by him; with the lonely white walk to Brantwood.

Dully she watched Joan Severn leave the room and return within a few minutes – chattering all the while – with some salted water and a sponge with which to bathe Rosaleen's bruises.

'. . . This might hurt your poor face. Be brave . . . John is in Oxford for the week –' Dab, dab; wincing herself as Rosaleen winced. 'Arthur is in the cottage drawing – how, in candlelight, I

78

do not know. Laurie is in London, also for the week, and the servants are asleep. I was reading and was about to retire. I am only so thankful I was around to hear you knock . . . Oh my dear, you must be in *such* pain, I can scarcely bear to look.'

She continued to bathe Rosaleen's face as tenderly as possible, then blotted the puffy flesh dry and spread soothing ointment on it.

'It is surprising how quickly skin heals,' she comforted the silent Rosaleen. 'In a day or so the swelling will go down and you will feel better. Perhaps you should have a little brandy for your shock?'

This was said doubtfully, but when Rosaleen nodded Joan Severn immediately fetched a decanter and poured a small quantity into a glass. She handed it to her guest gingerly. Rosaleen took a couple of swallows. She'd never had brandy before, and it spread warmth down her gullet, and seemed, even after only those two gulps, to restore some sense to her.

The other woman, who was heavily pregnant with her first child, studied her anxiously. 'Is that the tiniest bit better, dear? Tell me – what happened?'

'Father struck me.'

'Oh how terrible. But why?'

'I told him I was leaving to go to London with the Burne-Joneses,' and we quarrelled. I'll not forgive him.'

Then her feeling of detachment gave way to an inner grief that she would not release. Trapped, it settled in her soul.

Joan Severn spoke to her of forgiveness, of generosity and Christianity; and Rosaleen sat mutely in her chair not hearing a word, thinking only of her father's ignorance and selfishness. She could discount the years when he had lavished love upon her. Poor Thomas, who had doted on his daughter to excess and then depended on her in the extreme; he had hastened that very thing which had frightened him. She had left him. She had read her books despite him; collaborated with people of her choice in spite of him. He had driven her away.

Rosaleen stayed at Brantwood for three days, nursed by Mrs Severn who, although only in her mid-twenties, seemed a mature and mother-like figure. She made Rosaleen sit in one place by the fire during the day, and every few hours would sponge her face and re-apply the ointment. She tried to interest the girl in things and showed her Turner's sketchbook of 1845 which John Ruskin had in his possession. This contained a series of water-colours of the Channel he had done, and they astounded Rosaleen with their lack of form or structure as she had come to know them.

'I don't understand them,' she cried almost angrily — and bitterly disappointed. 'Why, they're just squiggles of colour.'

'John continually defends them,' his cousin said, smiling in a bewildered way herself. 'For my part I am no longer sure, and neither is Arthur. Do they not perhaps hint at an overall effect?'

Rosaleen looked again and saw nothing to enlighten her. These casual strokes of colour did not accord with her idea of art. She shook her head stubbornly. 'I like his pictures of Italy.'

And Joan Severn, seeing that Rosaleen was becoming upset, removed the sketchbook.

What she didn't realize was that Rosaleen felt inadequate: if Turner had painted these pictures they must be good, yet she did not like them. That made her a failure. Just when she thought she was beginning to understand certain aspects of art, she discovered she understood nothing.

Joan Severn spoke to her of other matters. She told Rosaleen of her year spent nursing old Mrs Ruskin, John Ruskin's mother, and then of her meeting with some people named La Touche and staying with them in Ireland . . . Rosaleen was suddenly alert.

'I was engaged briefly to Percy La Touche,' Joan confided. 'But after initially being swept off my feet I discovered he was too involved with superficial pleasures for my liking. I broke the engagement and shortly afterwards met dear Arthur. And now our first child is due any day.'

'Does Percy La Touche have a sister?' Rosaleen burst out unthinkingly.

'He has two sisters. Ah — I see you have heard about lovely Rose . . .'

Rosaleen looked embarrassed.

Joan continued, unruffled, but conclusive in her manner: 'Yes dear, Rose is Percy's sister. Now, it is time we tended to your face once more – and incidentally it looks a little better to me.'

During those three days Rosaleen was continually afraid her father would come for her, that he would try to drag her home. Or perhaps he thought she was already in London. She was not due to go to London for several days yet, but so anxious was she that Thomas would arrive at any time that Joan Severn sent word to the Burne-Joneses that their new maid-servant would be coming imminently.

'I hope we are doing the right thing,' she said to Rosaleen. 'I feel that I am interfering in a private problem.'

For the first time Rosaleen realized the predicament in which she had placed this generous-hearted lady. Impulsively she hugged her. 'I'm sorry . . . You've been so kind and I've been thoughtless. I just didn't know where to turn when I left home.'

'But you did the right thing, the only thing,' Joan Severn assured her, stroking Rosaleen's hair. 'It is only that in my heart I feel perhaps you should try and repair your differences with your father before going to London. I am sure he must repent his violence.'

'He may, Mrs Severn. But you don't know him – he'll only repent if I stay. He'll not hear of my going.'

'How sad it all is! What a terrible situation.'

'Please don't concern yourself over me. I shall be fine. I have to lead *my* life . . .'

The following morning Rosaleen left early for London, her bruises concealed by a veiled hat which Joan Severn had given her. Outside was an isolated white world which locked away the mountains and anything else friendly or familiar. The lake was shrouded in mist and from it came the lonely honk of a goose.

'How sad it should be like this,' she thought. 'No last impression of Old Man rearing up, no mystical lights cast on the water; how appropriate the bleakness.'

The journey to Ulverston station was slow for the snow

collected in balls in the horses' hooves, causing them to slip, and Rosaleen was jolted to and fro as the brougham was rocked from side to side and the wheels struggled to turn. But eventually the coachman deposited her and she stood on the almost deserted platform with her bundle beside her. She was weary from a poor night's sleep and her face was still sore; she was also fearful of leaving behind everything she had ever known. The overcast sky from which wafted the odd flake of snow further oppressed her. A young man also waited on the platform and Rosaleen's heart sank when she saw him; she knew him a little and disliked him. He was coarse and loutish, a quarry worker who had used the Coachman's Inn frequently once in the hope of attracting her attention. He had not taken rejection easily.

'Why, I do believe it's Ros'leen Ruddock hiding behind that fancy hat,' he said loudly. 'Why, Ros'leen, I scarce rec'gnized you.' He seemed to sneer as he spoke.

Rosaleen smiled wanly and turned her head away. Now the whole area would be talking . . .

'Is that bruising t'your face?'

'Bruising? No – it must be the early light. And it's not your business.'

'I was only asking. No need to get hoity. It's them people you mix with now. Th'whole village is talking 'bout it . . . I could swear as that's bruising. Where're you off to then this time o' morning?'

'It's not your business,' Rosaleen said again.

'I only asked, didn't I? Going t'meet a lover I'll be betting.'

'I am not!' She was riled into a reply. 'I'm going t'London if you must know. To rest with relatives.'

'I didn't know as you'd family there.'

'Well, you wouldn't would you?'

'Aren't you interested in where I'm going?'

'No.'

He told her anyway, with pride in his voice: 'I'm going to St Anne's t'stay with my sister. I've a nephew just born.' For a moment Rosaleen warmed towards him, then he added, 'Know a nice inn there. We could have us a bit o' fun.'

'I said – I'm not interested.'

'Here – let me see your face.'

He grabbed her by the elbow and lifted her veil. 'Ah!' he gloated triumphantly. 'I knew it were bruising. You've run from home, haven't you? Your father's had a go, hasn't he? His temper's famed from Coniston to Kendal. Lost good custom he has. So his precious lass got it at last then. Well I can't say as you didn't have it coming, Ros'leen. Too grand by far you thought yourself. Always too grand by far.'

'Let go of my arm.'

'I could throw you on th'track.'

'You wouldn't dare.'

He let go of her slowly and she was overcome by weakness. She rubbed her arm where he had gripped it and twisted it slightly. Then with relief she saw the ballooning steam of the train and heard it before the engine itself came into sight.

. . . Ros'leen Ruddock left home . . . Her father struck her . . . Deserved it I say . . . She imagined them gossiping and surmising about her.

'I'm glad I'm going. Everyone always wants t'know what the other's doing. They never care to find out the truth behind anything. It all becomes so distorted.'

The train halted and she climbed into a different carriage to the young man's, and then for safe measure walked through to another and sat in a compartment already occupied by a man and woman.

She looked out on to the platform: half expected – hoped – to see her father suddenly appear; catch sight of him from the window searching for her. And when he saw her his ruddy face would be rent by that special smile he had used to bestow on her. But of course he did not appear, and the steam swished in a compressed hiss from the engine, and with an abrupt jolt they were off, swaying and rattling the long journey to London. Behind her veil Rosaleen's puffed eyes shed their first and only tears.

The train became an extension of her surroundings, a thoughtless line streaking through the white and grey countryside like a sharp-cutting knife, stopping at towns which were familiar and unfamiliar to her – and then off again, slowly at first so that with its laboured procession Rosaleen's mind was leaden, and as it gathered speed, her mind became light and vacuous.

Then in its typical and unforeseen way there came a jagged split in the thick sky, and first an expanse of blue appeared and then abruptly the rest of the sky cleared, and her mountains were revealed. She leaned with her nose pressed to the window, her mouth breathing rings of warm damp condensation on the cold glass, longing for what was already in the past.

The countryside flattened out again – as though someone had taken an iron and ironed out the hills – and they stopped at Cartmel and passed the sands, which made her think of Robbie and his strange poems, and then she thought of Frederick, and of everything which had led her to be sitting in the train with her discoloured face, her body moving without contradiction to the movements of the carriage.

As 'her countryside' disappeared she felt a sense of misgiving. All around her now were the hideous signs of industry – chimneys and factories, giant kilns, mineworks, great steel contraptions, and dense blackened clouds the size of cathedrals mushrooming into the sky. And then after interminable stops and several train changes at ugly stations in dismal towns, there was a re-emergence of open views and a gentler countryside, and her optimism returned.

By the time the train drew into Paddington dusk had fallen, and for some while Rosaleen had not been able to decipher much from her surroundings, besides rows of terraced houses and an aura of poverty no different to the outskirts of any town; but this first dim and glamourless impression of London did not deter her. She was enchanted by the ambiguity: here in the city lay her unpredictable future.

She had told her father: 'I'm going into service with Mr Burne-Jones's family.' But she had only disclosed a part.

The idea had evolved slowly, and when the possibilities had dawned on her she had become increasingly excited. She studied the pictures at Brantwood and the books John Ruskin lent her, with their coloured reproductions, paying particular attention to the models, and then she had considered her own appearance.

'I'm not so bad . . . maybe it's as they say.'

She had rubbed the smoky toilet mirror and moved it about to see each part of herself revealed bit by bit, surveying herself objectively — features, neck, narrow child-like shoulders, the sweep of her breasts. She saw that she was slender, that her flesh was rounded where it was important, and that she was white-skinned without a single freckle. She had stared hard into her lilac eyes with their thin black rims and thick dark lashes, and thought again: 'I'm not so bad.' And then: 'I shall become an artist's model.'

And she had gone outside to clean out the pigs.

᭙ Five ᭙

THE MODEL

I'll try not to think of Lancashire,
London is where I live now,
Though I left behind my family,
A loom and a widow's bed.

The Burne-Joneses lived in North End Road, in semi-rural
Fulham, an area of meadows interspersed with residential
streets. Their Georgian house was called the Grange and was
surrounded by lush lawns and fruit trees. It was a harmonious
and homely place, decorated with the deep crushed-fruit colours
of William Morris, and was furnished with painted Gothic-style
pieces and contemporary chairs and tables besides numerous
hard-seated sofas.

Rosaleen had taken a cab from the station, paid for with
money lent her by Joan Severn, and arrived at the Grange shortly
after half-past seven – waif-like with her bruised face, her
apprehension, her tiredness, and her bundle of clothes. The
family greeted her and made her welcome: Mr and Mrs Burne-
Jones and their two young children, Philip and Margaret. Mrs
Burne-Jones took Rosaleen's hand in a concerned manner,
insisting she retire to bed immediately and entrusting her to the
care of the housekeeper, whose room she was to share.

Mrs Maddox was a hugely proportioned woman whose
hawk-like eyes missed no trick, and whose chins merged in tiers
without definition into the solid column of her neck. Beneath
her cap were concealed bald patches, caused, she later confided
to Rosaleen, by nerves. But despite her formidable appearance
and manner there was a streak of softness in the woman which

drew her to small defenceless creatures and to the beauty she herself lacked. Once she found a person upon whom to lavish her protection, Mrs Maddox latched on with a rare and fierce loyalty.

That night she fussed Rosaleen like a new-born baby, tucking her in to the bed beside her own and laying cold compresses on her inflamed eyelids. Under the soothing touch of her big callused hands, lulled by her croaking voice which attempted to sing nursery rhymes, Rosaleen became the babe Mrs Maddox willed her to be, and drifted into comforting sleep. The house-keeper then quickly prepared herself for bed, turned off the gas light, and fell asleep herself immediately, contented with her new foundling.

The following day Mrs Maddox introduced Rosaleen to the other servants. Apart from themselves there were the under-housemaid – who was in a lowlier position than Rosaleen – the butler, the nanny – who did not class herself as a servant – the cook and the kitchen-maid. They all shook hands with her formally, staring a little at her yellowing bruises.

'A house of few servants,' said Mrs Maddox, pausing for effect as everyone turned to her respectfully, for she was the over-lord of the lower hierarchy, 'but it is a merry house, and the master and mistress are kind and generous people.'

The others nodded solemnly in assent. Mrs Maddox then took Rosaleen aside and carefully explained her duties to her: as upper-housemaid she must be up and dressed by six-fifteen each morning to sweep the floor of the parlour, clean out the fireplace of that room and the library, blacken those same grates and polish the surrounds before making the new fires. She would then lay the table for breakfast in the parlour where she was to serve Mr and Mrs Burne-Jones, but the two children breakfasted upstairs in the nursery with their nanny. After cleaning away once more she had then to dust the furniture, books and ornaments in the parlour and library, whilst the under-housemaid tended entirely to the upper floors, emptying slops, making beds and dusting the contents of the rooms, with the exception of the nursery. That same maid then worked her way downstairs, polishing the banisters and brushing the stairs. The two girls shared the brushing of all the downstairs carpets, but the under-housemaid cleaned the remaining reception rooms, and, together with the kitchen-maid, cared for the servants' quarters. This was how the work was divided, and when she had related it all, Mrs Maddox took a deep breath and assessed Rosaleen for her reaction. She was surprised when the girl laughed.

'Back home I did the work of several people,' she explained. 'This isn't half what I did there.' And thought to herself: 'And besides – it's only a means to an end.'

Two weeks passed, and if a sudden vision of her old life flashed before her Rosaleen tried to banish it, concentrating especially hard on the task in hand: an image of her father's face, aged and pained with reproach – polish it away; Nana Annie stumbling over objects in her semi-dark world, or sitting forgotten in her window-seat – sweep her beneath the carpet; Robbie, timid, vague Robbie – what could she do with him? Lancashire lay in her past already and she told herself only her future was valid. But no amount of reasoning could still her subconscious; the memories flooded in at their convenience, and her anger with her father was now tempered with guilt.

On alternate Sundays Rosaleen was permitted to go to church, and one afternoon a fortnight she was free to do as she wished. That first afternoon she went out with the under-housemaid.

'A silly girl, that Marie,' Mrs Maddox told Rosaleen beforehand. 'Nothing in her head except clothes and men. The one she can't afford and the other'll never afford her. I wouldn't be surprised if she's loose, the way she talks sometimes. And such a gossip you've never heard! But she'll show you London anyway. And if you're taking money with you, keep it close to your person. There're pick-pockets everywhere, nimble as fleas.'

They took an omnibus into the centre of town; Rosaleen was overawed by the sheer enormity and bustle of the city.

'Where are its boundaries?' she asked Marie in amazement. 'It seems to spread and straggle for ever!'

'Don't ask me,' came the reply with a shrug. 'I just hop on an omnibus and take it for what it is. So how do you like the Grange then?'

'I like it well enough, thank you,' Rosaleen replied politely.

'I could tell you a thing or two . . . Goings on and such-like. Did you know Mr Burne-Jones doesn't sleep with his wife in the same room?' She waited for Rosaleen's response. None came. 'They say he's got a mistress,' the girl continued, and waited again. 'Hey – aren't you interested?' she asked, disgruntled.

'No.'

'Well hark at that! I'd've thought you'd want t'know.'

She was a tallish girl of about Rosaleen's age with bulging dark eyes which she blackened, and a coarse laugh, and she told Rosaleen haughtily, jealous of the other's superior status over her, and resentful of her disinclination to gossip:

'One day I'm going to become a lady's maid. That way you get all the pretty clothes when your mistress wearies of them . . . maybe I'll marry a soldier one day. I do so like their uniforms . . .'

Then her voice changed and lost its supercilious note: 'Oh look at those two young men going into that public house there – they're giving us the eye. Let's go in. Th'one on the right's quite nice. I think it's me he's eyeing . . . 'Course you've got pretty hair and all, but it isn't everyone as likes red hair, and it does make dressing-up a problem. I'm lucky – with my colouring I don't have no problems. And I've French blood in me . . .'

She dragged Rosaleen into the public house, and sure enough the two men came over and sat with them. Rosaleen scarcely spoke. Instead she observed: the way the other girl flirted and made her bulging eyes appear more prominent by opening them as wide as possible, obviously believing they looked appealing; the way her foot was pressing against that of the man of her choice . . . The way both men responded to her, having given up trying, in their crude way, to illicit a reaction from Rosaleen.

She would have liked to have left, but was afraid to do so; and instead she sat for a couple of hours growing bored – and when the images came to her she could not fight them. Beside her Marie and the men were giggling and talking suggestively, but they were now incidental, and she saw instead herself as a child with her father crossing Coniston Water on the gondola; she saw Old Man wreathed in light; and Tarn Hows – a heron picking its way to the water's edge. And Ruskin's eyes looked into hers, astute – understanding why she wanted to leave, but trying to dissuade her, because he knew that this was where it all was . . .

'I knew it was me they liked,' Marie said on the way back. 'Well you're glum, aren't you? Are you in a sulk because they didn't fancy you then?'

After that Rosaleen spent her fortnightly afternoons on her own. She longed for those afternoons when she wrapped herself against the cold and took the omnibus into town. There were so many choices: she could walk in the various parks where sometimes a band would be playing on the bandstand, or a group of amateur touring players performing; or stroll down a smart street lined with trees in blossom, and gaze at the shops with their elegant windows; or simply admire the theatre provided by the fashionable ladies and gentlemen walking about. But most of all she preferred to visit art exhibitions, whether at galleries such as the National – where she would gaze at masterpieces by Rubens, Botticelli, Canaletto, Poussin and countless other great names – or at small roadside shows where the pictures would be strung across the street like washing.

There were occasions besides her official free time when Mrs Burne-Jones would impulsively say to her, 'Rosaleen dear, the house is agleam and you have nothing further to do. You may spend the next couple of hours as you will.'

Then she would walk the family dog across the pastures of Fulham, or – if Mrs Maddox were not about – would lie on her bed reading, referring constantly to her dictionary to research the meanings of new words. And now whenever the images came to her she repeated out loud like a litany, 'Life is a forward movement. Life is stages. Life is a *forward* movement . . .'

Once Mrs Maddox came in when Rosaleen, in tearful mood, was muttering this to herself.

'Are you all right, dear?' she asked anxiously.

'Oh yes, Mrs Maddox,' Rosaleen assured her, blushing. 'It's just my prayers. I was saying my prayers.'

She quickly adjusted to her routine, and to the routine of the household, and little foibles of her employers became known to her: that Mr Burne-Jones had a horror of obesity and would leave any meat on his plate if it had the slightest trace of fat; that sometimes he sulked when forced to attend society functions; that his wife referred to him as 'Ned' in private . . .

But after several months had passed Rosaleen grew listless, and recalled that evening she had spent at Brantwood in the company of the Burne-Joneses. Then she had been socially their equal – a fellow guest of John Ruskin; now she was a servant in their house. She had not come to London to be a servant.

Once when she was particularly dispirited, she thought: 'Everything's beyond my reach – the books I dust on the shelves and long to read, Thackeray, Scott, Dickens; the pictures I daren't gaze upon for more than a moment, in case it looks as though I'm snooping; the people I see coming and going and whose conversations I may not listen to . . . Am I to remain nothing but a housemaid? Perhaps I should've stayed back home. Perhaps I *have* thought myself too grand . . .'

It was the end of May, 1873, and in the library Rosaleen was polishing the furniture, when Edward Burne-Jones came in and sat down with a large book. He opened it, but did not read, and instead watched her as she worked. Self-conscious under his scrutiny, she felt her neck reddening and rubbed the beeswax harder into the table-top.

He closed his book with a bang and she started. He was a man of good humour, and she chided him: 'Sir – you're making me nervous. First you stare at me as though I've snakes growing from my head, then you bang about so!'

'How do you know about Medusa, Rosaleen?'

'I've read books on mythology, sir.'

'At school?'

'Oh no sir. We didn't learn that kind of thing at school. But after I'd left the Vicar's wife lent me books. And Mr Ruskin – he did also.'

'You like to read?'

'Yes, sir – anything I can lay my hands on.' She smiled hesitantly and fiddled with her cap. 'Especially about art. And I like to learn new words. I've a dictionary of my own and I look things up. I learn at least two new words a day,' she added proudly.

'You astound me, Rosaleen.'

'Why is that, sir?'

He had a habit of resting his chin on his hands, and now he did so as he tried to explain. 'Well, your education was incomplete – if you will forgive me saying so – but you are naturally intelligent; you are articulate and have an excellent vocabulary. Without encouragement you have striven to learn by yourself. That is remarkable and praiseworthy. You have an inquiring mind; but there is more besides – I sense a resilience, a will to succeed; although what it is you wish to succeed at, I cannot tell, and even you may not yet know . . . Most interesting. Yes, definitely most interesting . . .'

He fell silent, and Rosaleen waited for him to continue. When he did not she resumed her polishing again, more self-conscious than ever as her employer watched her contemplatively.

After a few moments he said, 'Rosaleen, what you are doing looks most tedious. I should like you to stop shining that cabinet which is already buffed to its ultimate, and accompany me to my studio.'

'Why, sir?'

'Why? Why – so I may paint you. Is it not obvious?'

Her moment had arrived, and with her heart beating fast, Rosaleen followed him – past his wife's sitting-room from where came the sounds of the piano, and into the place of his work. So this was it – the laboratory of his art; and upon entering it she felt immediately gratified for it was all that she had envisaged, with its happy chaos coupled with business-like purpose.

Medium in size and North-facing, as was favoured by artists since Leonardo da Vinci who claimed that the light coming from the North was more constant, it comprised dozens of haphazardly stacked boards and canvases. Shelves were cluttered with bottles of colours and other fluids, tubes of paint and brushes and books – and more sketches propped one in front of the other.

Rosaleen caught sight of herself in a cheval mirror which stood beside a chaise-longue; she was paler than usual and wide-eyed, and she thought how unflattering was the starched formality of her servant's attire. She looked away hurriedly and her attention was caught by several unfinished works resting upon easels. One was huge, and divided into three panels.

'What is it?' she asked, looking at the drawn outlines of nude figures in different poses – a woman sitting pensively, men wrestling or fleeing in panic, other women huddled together in a corner.

'Ah – I began that quite a few months ago. It is called *Venus Discordia* and depicts the fall of Troy. The figure you are looking at is Venus who watches the tragedy unfold . . . I would have to tell you the whole story and now there is not time. But I am beginning to regret having undertaken a picture on such a vast scale. It will be years before it is completed and sometimes I cannot see it happening.'

'And the other two pictures?' Rosaleen moved quickly on to a pair of easels close together, afraid of losing his attention.

'Ah! That is my favourite: *Laus Veneris*. I haven't long begun it, but as you can see it is in oils. I am going to use red and deep royal-blue as my predominant colours and add plenty of gold. It will be a lavish picture.'

'The woman reclining – she looks so sad, so beautiful . . .'

'That is Venus once more! And is she not a little like yourself with her luxuriant red hair – russet, I prefer to call it – and languid eyes? . . . Are you blushing now, Rosaleen! In this instance Venus is the absolver of the sins of a repentant wandering knight. The idea is based on an old German legend called *Tannhäuser*.'

Rosaleen stared a moment longer at the figures of women grouped around a music stand – marvelling at the depth of expression in their faces, the grace of their bodies, and at the detail drawn in, waiting to be painted. The whole made up a beautiful design and the word which came to Rosaleen's mind was 'draughtsmanship'. It was a word recently added to her vocabulary. She moved over to the third canvas.

'And this?' she asked, pointing to it, single-minded in her desire to glean from Burne-Jones all the knowledge she could.

'This one – and what should I do if I had a dozen unfinished works set up, would I have to explain each one in turn to you? – this one has a nice little story attached to it. It is called *Le Chant d'Amour* after an old Breton song my wife plays. I first did a series of water-colours using the theme, and then decorated the inside of a piano-lid with it! Pianos are such ugly things, I find. This, as you see, is painted in oils and depicts a knight listening to a beautiful young woman playing a rather delicate little organ, whilst Love, sitting rather languorously, don't you think, attends to the bellows.'

'Why are their faces always so sad?'

'Why, why? Rosaleen, you are quite as bad as my wife's nephew, young Rudyard Kipling, who seems to spend more time here than in his own house. Every time he visits he demands – yes demands – to be shown my studio. And then I must answer a barrage of questions.'

'But you haven't answered mine, sir!'

'Relentless child. Are their faces sad? I do not think I intended them to look sad. Grave, yes. Or serene. I have wanted to portray an inner beauty and purity – but perhaps I have merely succeeded in making them sad.'

'What kind of painting do you prefer, sir?' Rosaleen asked, having wandered to a different part of the studio, and glancing now at the many and various-sized sketch-books and water-colours carefully stacked.

'If you mean the medium I prefer, then I think I must answer water-colour. Water-colour and body-colour. It is so sensitive . . ' He twiddled with the straggly ends of his light-brown beard. '. . . However, if you mean what subject matter do I prefer, then that is harder to answer. Once I painted mostly subjects of a religious nature, but now, like my colleagues, I have become freer in my style and have discovered the pleasures of interpreting mythology; and there again I enjoy painting portraits – talking of which I have brought you here for that specific purpose! You have diverted me for long enough, young lady, although I much appreciate your keenness to learn. However, you are in my studio not so that you might admire its chaos or that I may instruct you in the way I paint, but in order that I might do your portrait. Rosaleen – when you arrived you wore a shawl. I have seen you wear it also when you go out. Will you fetch it please – I think the colours most effective.'

Frederick had told her, 'Your shawl is art,' and she laughed. Now she ran joyfully to fetch it from her room. Mrs Maddox was there fixing her cap over her bald patches, her chins and neck wobbling as she turned her head.

'You coming in all excited – what's happened then?'

'He's going to paint me!' Rosaleen cried, twirling the bewildered woman around so that her cap fell off. 'He's so famous, so great a man, and he's going to paint *me*!'

'Who – the *master*?'

'Yes!'

'Well I never! What a to-do! Wait till I tell the others downstairs. And won't that Marie be jealous? Well I never!'

However, when Rosaleen returned to the studio with her Joseph shawl slung over her shoulder she was quite unprepared for Edward Burne-Jones's next request:

'Please would you strip and drape yourself in that shawl,' he ordered her as casually as he would request a pot of tea.

She had not considered this aspect of modelling, and her lips parted in dismay. She clutched her body self-consciously, and made no move to obey him. For a moment he looked mystified, then his brow cleared and he threw back his head and laughed.

'Oh my dear girl, if you knew how many naked women I, as an

old man of forty, have looked at – and am ashamed of how little it means to me! Well at the very least strip to your underclothes then.'

Feeling stiff and clumsy, Rosaleen undressed – the dark cotton dress with its small crinolene, the white apron, the thick grey stockings – and stood in her shabby chemise and drawers, threadbare from so much bleaching. She hugged herself coyly while Burne-Jones slipped down the straps to bare her shoulders, and then unpinned her hair, fluffing it about until he was satisfied and murmuring to himself all the time.

Finally he was happy and he settled her on the chaise-longue. 'Now the first thing you must do is relax,' he told her cheerfully, draping her shawl about her arms, but leaving her shoulders naked, and adjusting her hair yet again. 'You understand a little of art I believe,' he flattered her. 'It cannot be achieved without the co-operation of the model. Now please turn partially towards the mirror, and as I have already said – you *must* relax – yet remain still. Think of whatever you will.'

Rosaleen watched him fix a sheet of paper to a board and rest the board on the pegs of his easel. She was already becoming used to her state of partial undress.

'How long will you be before you start to paint it?' she asked.

'Oh heavens, Rosaleen – there are often a series of several sketches before one progresses to painting. Are you so impatient?'

'Impatience is one of my weaknesses, sir.' She smiled disarmingly.

'Well now you must be still.' He took a pencil from the table and proceeded to do strange tricks with it, holding it before him at different angles, positioning his thumb, and apparently measuring the air before making marks upon the paper.

'What are you doing?'

'I am judging perspective.'

It was a word she understood, having read of its importance, and this small point of comprehension drew her to the artist so that she was suddenly overwhelmed with pride to be lying there under his scrutiny. No longer was he Mr Burne-Jones, her employer, a man with a peculiar sense of humour and a tendency to grumpiness. This man was the Famous Artist, Edward Burne-Jones, member of the élite Pre-Raphaelite Brotherhood. He had ceased to be a mere man.

Rosaleen became aware of her body – stretched her muscles and felt them elongate. She was a sleek cat, wallowing in self-generated contentment, soothed by the sounds about her: the Master's pencil scraping faintly against the paper; his heavy breathing as he concentrated his attention on her; the branches of a tree scratching the window. Rosaleen became a part of a pattern, and soon it was as if she were not there, so light was her body; and she was engulfed by this lightness. Her mind wandered to the letter she had received from Robbie that morning. It had read:

Dear Rosaleen,
   You've written only twice and I four times – this is the fifth. You promised you would write to me often. I have not much news. Today's the first mild day since before winter and now I'm sitting by Tarn Hows where we sat months ago and you told me you thought you'd leave. Even as I sit, the funny craggy hills peer out through the mist and the dark conifers are as if shielded by the smoke of a bonfire. You used to like Tarn Hows. I wish you had not gone. Everything is changed since you've gone, and there's no joy.
   The inn is quieter too – none of the lads from the mines bother now you're not here. Perhaps Father worries because it's quiet, but he doesn't say, and he just broods. Word's spread he hit you – everyone in the village seems to know that 'Rosaleen Ruddock's eye was blackened the day she left home', and there's some are siding with you, and others who say you shouldn't have gone. It's not for them to judge, is it though? There's one or two local lads who've pestered me for news about you, but I tell them I don't have any, and now they've taken to jeering when they see me. I don't care. Nancy's girl started here a few days ago and business was a bit busier last night. I suppose she's quite

pretty – though not like you – and she flirts an awful lot. Maybe the lads from the mines'll come back now she's here. I don't care.

Yesterday I went to market with Father – we bought a couple of ewes and he muttered sommat about 'breeding a few sheep'. But he doesn't know what he wants. He goes about as usual, but speaks less than ever, and when he does it's only to rant. He doesn't mind how he looks now, and I think it'll not be long before his beard'll reach his belly (which is as huge as a cow in calf). I detest him. And I'll not forgive him for striking you. Two days ago I was opening a window to release a trapped fly, but before I could, he took hold of the insect and squeezed it – clack – to death in front of me. He wished it were me he was doing it to. I could tell. I de*test* him.

I am thinking I shall go to Kendal and maybe look for a job there. I like Kendal better than Ulverston; it's a merrier place. For sure I can't bear it here much longer. And Nana Annie sits like an enchantress casting spells, knit-knitting all day and drinking cider – sucking it – and talking about you; talking about everyone she used to know years ago who are all dead. She sees omens more'n ever now. I wrote a poem about her – about everything, but you wouldn't like it so I've not sent it to you. It's a sad poem. Please write. I run to the post each day in hope of a letter from you and it's never there . . .

'Oh . . .'

'What is it, my dear, are you uncomfortable?' Mr Burne-Jones set down his pencil and looked anxiously at Rosaleen. There were tears in her eyes, but she had not realized she had uttered a sound.

'No, sir. I was day-dreaming, that's all. May I see?'

'Goodness, what is there to see yet, except a few lines which could be a map of Europe?'

She lay back once more and composed her reply to her brother.

Dear Robbie,

I'm sorry — I know I promised to write often and months have passed and I've only written twice. Are you feeling better? Your letter has worried me so badly that to tell the truth I feel inclined to get on the next train back. What an outpouring! But Robbie, I know that for the moment I must stay in London. It isn't an easy choice for me, and I wish you could understand this, but it is the only choice, because back home I had reached my limits, and here there are none. Do you see? One day you'll realize why I went, and that it was not a question of being in the most beautiful place on earth; it is an inner thing, not an outer thing. But I am not clever with words like you; I can't write poetry, and I can't really express what I mean . . .

Robbie, one thing I know — you *cannot* go looking for a job now. Why, you're still a couple of months from your thirteenth birthday, and there's not much a lad your age could do besides working down a mine or in a factory or helping in another inn. You don't want that. And you'd be swallowed alive in Kendal on your own. Be patient. Wait till you're fourteen. Anyway, perhaps things will look up now Nancy's girl's started. Please don't make me feel too bad for leaving. I'd done my share, Robbie, and believed you were grown enough to cope. Indeed, I know you are.

I'm happy here. There's not much free time, but my duties are not too many and I'm well-treated, and when I do get off I'm away like a bird. And I've seen so many different things and am continually learning. You know how I love to learn. The Burne-Joneses are kind, informal folk, and visitors come and go all day. Once the famous Mr Rossetti visited, and I wound myself into a proper state of excitement. But after opening the front door to him (the butler was busy at the time), I was not summoned to serve. And Mr William Morris often visits with his wife and comes each Sunday for breakfast. He is a designer who works in business with Mr Burne-Jones, and she is tall and dark and very lovely — from a working-class background, would you believe! She's famed as an artist's model, but mostly models for Rossetti. I would not truthfully say she is as beautiful in the flesh as the pictures he paints of her.

Sometimes when I serve tea I can drag it out as long as a quarter of an hour and hear so many snippets! Oh how I wish I could be allowed to listen in properly. The Grange is a lovely house – not as fine as Brantwood, and of course there are no views, but the place is nicely decorated, even though the chairs are mostly uncomfortable.

Mr Ruskin visited once. I was so happy to see him, but I wasn't permitted to join them in the drawing-room, and he – being the kind, humble man that he is – came to see me in the servants' quarters. But to tell the truth it were a bit awkward with him there, for I couldn't speak with him in the old way. Well, I'm a servant here and I was a guest in his home.

But now I must tell you the most exciting news yet! Mr Burne-Jones is doing a portrait of me, and I lie here for hours and I can as near feel the pencil as though it were drawing on my own body!

Dearest Robbie – I so hope that by the time you get this letter you will be feeling a bit better. And be nice to Nana Annie. Tell her I send her my love – that her 'tiny lass' is happy.

Has spring come yet? I envisage it all suddenly, clear and bold, and the image quite makes me catch my breath. Dear mankin, I remember you every day, even though I'm bad at writing letters, and when I'm in church, or when I say my prayers at night, I ask God to take care of you. For sure He will. You're a good lad. Now you mustn't be gloomy, for I love you. And don't let Father distress you . . .

It took a couple of months of numerous sketches and countless sittings before Edward Burne-Jones was satisfied with his picture of Rosaleen, then finally one day he sought her out and with typically oblique humour asked, 'So young lady, do you think it time perhaps to confront your own image?'

'You mean —?' She was in the midst of clearing away breakfast, and held a pile of plates in her arms. She stared at him.

'Come and judge for yourself.'

Rosaleen followed him to his studio – longing to rush ahead into the room. The palms of her hands were clammy in anticipation and she wiped them on her skirt.

Standing next to the draped easel Burne-Jones teased her, 'You know, Rosaleen, some models never see the completed works. In fact many works are not completed.'

'Aw sir, you wouldn't do it to me!'

'No,' he laughed, patting her on the back. 'I would not. You may unveil it then. But carefully.'

Tentatively she lifted the sheet of calico, wondering if there were further tricks in store for her – but when she peeled back the fabric, there she was. Rosaleen gazed, incredulous, at the luscious creature on the chaise-longue: she reclined with her profile slightly turned, sensuous and languid, her eyes far-seeing.

This was how he saw her; as Rossetti and Millais had seen Elizabeth Siddal and Hunt had seen Annie Miller.

Her shawl was picked out in great detail, its colours captured in purples and greens, maroons and blues. The cheval mirror reflected her light auburn hair which was swept to one side over her shoulder, and the skin of her back seemed so iridescent she longed to touch the picture.

'It's really me. I can't believe it's me!'

'Well for sure it is not Maud down the street! And for your interest I used water-colour and body-colour so thickly it has almost the texture of oils. I am sometimes criticized for this method, and actually resigned from the Old Water-colour Society on account of quarrels relating to it . . . A bunch of buffoons I was dealing with . . . No!' he cried, grabbing Rosaleen's hand as it was about to trace the outline of herself. 'You must not touch it!'

It was already July, and in the close-knit art world in which everyone knew the other, word travelled fast: Edward Burne-Jones had a new model.

During the course of the day it was usual for different people to call without prior arrangement, and there were sometimes large impromptu gatherings for tea; but now Rosaleen would be summoned to make an appearance, becoming briefly the focus of their attention: brooding Rossetti; fair Millais; the leonine-looking Spencer Stanhope; bushy-bearded Holman Hunt; intense-looking George Price-Boyce, the landscape artist and friend of Rossetti; and many other names she had dimly heard of, and others not at all.

For those few moments Rosaleen was petted and fussed – and expected to say little whilst they complimented Burne-Jones on his 'find'. Then she was dismissed from the room.

To begin with she was flattered, so awestruck that she was content to be at the beck and call of her master, but soon, when the novelty wore thin she became increasingly resentful of her menial status and of Burne-Jones's proprietorial attitude. Once when Rossetti had asked to paint her, Rosaleen listened to her employer claim her as his own.

'She is my model,' he said in an arrogant tone. 'I shall not have her made public property.'

And she felt the same withering within she had used to have when her father had tried to impose boundaries on her life.

'I'm nobody's property,' she thought angrily, catching Burne-Jones's eye and not returning his cheerful look. 'I belong to myself. Why is it men are so possessive? Are a woman's feelings not to be considered? Well I'll not remain here. I'll not be owned. And in truth – what have I done but preen myself and sit for a pretty picture. What is clever in that?'

It was amidst all this liveliness, and shortly after Rosaleen heard that Edward Burne-Jones was planning a long trip in Italy – which of course meant she would again be nothing more than a housemaid – that Frederick reappeared one wet afternoon. Rosaleen saw him from the window on Edgar, watched him dismount and drop the reins, whilst the giant horse stood with his head drooping placidly. The butler led Edgar away, and Frederick disappeared inside the house.

'Oh how good it is to see him . . .' Rosaleen ran into the

hallway where Frederick was brushing the rain from his clothes. He was rather bedraggled from the downpour and his flute protruded from his pocket.

'You always bring rain with you, Frederick.' She leaned casually against the wall by him.

'Rosaleen!'

He held her at arm's length and kissed her hand. 'One must observe protocol,' he said in a mock-serious tone. 'It does not do to be over-effusive in a public place . . . How strange to see you in a different context. I shall identify you for ever with the Lake District. But you are unchanged, I am glad to see – I can tell from your eyes. Candid as ever. I have been hearing many things, Rosaleen. Come and enlighten me.'

'Frederick – I cannot just do as I please. I must wait to be called.'

'My dear girl, surely you are allowed to speak with an old friend without permission! Very well, then I shall arrange to have you called! Though goodness knows I cannot believe that Burne-Jones has degraded you to this extent.'

'He has not,' Rosaleen replied fiercely, wishing both to defend her employer and retain her self-esteem.

'Hush – I have not come here to exasperate you, but to say hello, so I shall do as you wish.'

She was permitted an hour to talk with Frederick, and in the privacy of the parlour she told him all that had been happening, including her recent dissatisfaction.

'Am I so ungrateful?' she asked him.

'Not in the least. But you are too intelligent to be a servant.'

'I had hoped to be a model,' she confided, 'but now Mr Burne-Jones is going to Italy, and he has told his colleagues they must not use me. It is as though I belong to him.'

'Would you like to be more independent?'

She answered hesitantly, 'If I could live . . . But I've no money . . .' And was afraid to return his look, in case it seemed as though she were enlisting his support.

'That is of no consequence,' he replied dismissively. 'Now answer me, Rosaleen.'

'I should like to go,' she said, looking directly at him then. 'I no longer feel free.'

'Oh my Rosaleen – nobody is free.'

'You are.'

'That is not so. I tried to cultivate my freedom, but I have my shackles.'

'What kind?'

'Regrets, dear girl.' He stared into the distance for effect. 'But that is by-the-by.'

'You say things so lightly sometimes, Frederick, that I've no way of telling when you're serious. What are your regrets?'

'When we know each other better, then perhaps I shall bare my soul to you. Meanwhile – what say you to moving in with me? Now don't look askance – it is most upsetting and uncomplimentary – I have far too much room and promise not to intrude on you when I am around, which is not so very often. There is a most amiable couple I employ to look after the place, also the odd parrot or two, and a couple of cats the last time I was home.'

'When was that?'

'Oh . . .' He looked vague. 'A month or so I suppose.'

'You are forever travelling.'

'I told you I was a nomad and you did not believe me.'

Rosaleen laughed. 'Where've you been this time?'

'Scotland.'

'Scotland! All the way on old Edgar?'

'Edgar is *not* old. He merely looks it. He even looked old as a foal.'

Rosaleen shook her head fondly. 'Aw Frederick, you do say such funny things, and always with those serious brown eyes.'

'And what is wrong with my eyes?'

'They're like a dog's!' She grinned delightedly.

He laughed. 'But tell me, are you not the tiniest bit flattered that I have visited you even before I have been home?'

'Is that true?'

'Yes, I promise. Well, to be fair I did not journey from

Scotland all in one day. I stopped off at Brantwood and heard about your fame.'

'Aw Frederick, you know I'm not famous.' Impulsively she hugged him. His body felt stocky and solid.

'I believe you are glad to see me, Rosaleen Ruddock.'

'Just a shade glad.'

'Joan Severn told me of your quarrel with your father.'

'It were nothing, Frederick.'

'He was, of course, mortified at your leaving.'

'I won't speak of him, Frederick.' She lifted her chin defiantly.

'Very well – and you have no need to be defensive. Now, tell me, will you move in with me?'

'And – we are only friends?'

'Nothing else, more's my chagrin.' He took her hand, gently massaging its scarlet roughness. She felt disquieted under his gaze.

'People will talk, you know,' he continued, smiling mischievously. 'Their tongues will wag – tattle-tattle – and they will assume that you are my mistress.'

'Let them! I do not give a jot for talk,' Rosaleen said loftily. 'Besides – those people who matter don't talk.'

'What a profound person you are. So, sweet Rosaleen – I take it that you have decided to accept my invitation.'

'You have never told me what you do, why you spend so much time travelling.'

'Why, Rosaleen! Are you about to care more how I spend my days than what constitutes my soul? Such inquisition should be confined only to the most tedious of soirées. Look into my dog-like eyes – are they not to be trusted?'

'*They* are . . .' She raised her eyebrows in consideration. 'But are you?'

⤙ Six ⤚

PLATONIC FRIENDS

If I should confide my fears to you
I shall not expect you to fall in love
With my vulnerability.

Towards the end of July Rosaleen moved into Frederick's house. Hidden by a high wall, it was a tall, pale-pink building in a tiny lane in Chelsea. A cobbled courtyard led to the coachhouse and stables. To the rear was a long narrow garden, informally laid and dominated by a weeping willow.

Rosaleen was enchanted. 'How pretty it is! And is that Edgar I can see in there?' She peered into the stables.

'Well I only have one horse! I suppose it is rather a waste with three other stables and the coachhouse, but there you are.'

'Who looks after him – cleans his stable?'

'I do when I'm around. And when I'm not and I have to leave him here, then I hire a man to tend to him.'

'You look after him *yourself*?'

'But of course, and why not? Edgar is my friend.'

'People of your kind have a groom.'

'I belong to no "kind",' Frederick told her, sounding faintly annoyed. 'It gives me considerable pleasure to care for Edgar myself. Why Rosaleen, I do believe I've succeeded in surprising you.'

'You have.'

'I like my life unencumbered. I am not often at home and the house is well-cared for by dear Mrs MacDonald who is house-keeper-cum-cook. Her husband is the butler, and there's a housemaid who is a little mad and a little deaf, but most efficient and thorough. You see – I enjoy the humdrum as much as I enjoy the ludicrous airs we must occasionally assume. What a constant delight life is with its contrasts.'

The summer warmth was on their faces. Beyond the wall was the irregular line of other roofs and the leafy tops of trees. From somewhere a starling stuttered in outbursts. Beside her, Rosaleen's bundle of possessions seemed as forlorn as discarded laundry, and a picture flashed across her mind of Nana Annie's old windswept cottage on the Banks, the allotments overhung by dismal lines of washing. She felt a fleeting estrangement from her immediate environment – a pang of nostalgia for her home – and drew her shawl about her.

Inside they were greeted by Mr and Mrs MacDonald – both small and grey, their faces creased in smiles. A cockatoo perched on the woman's shoulder and regarded Rosaleen with beady suspicious eyes, lunging at her with its beak.

Frederick introduced them: 'Mr and Mrs Mac – this is Rosaleen. Is she not a delight?'

'Aw Frederick, don't embarrass me.' She nudged his elbow with her own.

'But dearie he's reet,' Mrs MacDonald said. 'And I'm happy to meet you. I've heard ever such a lot about you.' The cockatoo lunged again, and she reprimanded it: 'Now behave, Henry. That's awful rude.'

She showed Rosaleen to her room which, although small, was beautifully decorated, with walls papered in a pink candy-stripe, and flower-patterned festooned blinds. A crochet spread covered the brass bed and upon it were scattered lace cushions. Two tabby cats lay on the rise of the pillows.

Rosaleen stroked them and felt the purring start as a vibrating line down their backs.

'What a lovely room. I've never slept in such a lovely room.'

'Sir Frederick had it done especially. You should have seen him. He was so excited!'

'*Sir* Frederick?'

'Och yes. You didna know then?'

'He never said.'

'No, he wouldn't of his own accord. He likes to seem a bit of a mystery you know. But between you and me there's not too much mystery about any man after a while.'

Rosaleen changed into the red dress she had worn for her first dinner at Brantwood, and joined Frederick in the parlour. 'You never told me you were a "sir",' she reproached him.

'A sir? Oh great Scot – a "sir"! *That* kind of "sir". Oh I see. How terribly funny. Now what relevance is it to our relationship, Rosaleen?'

'That's not the point.'

'But it *is* the point,' he argued.

She thought for a moment. 'You're determined I shall like you for what you appear to be.'

'I am as I appear to be. And I insist on being liked or disliked on *that* basis, and not because I am a "sir"!'

'Well, it's about time you told me sommat about yourself, Sir Frederick Walton!'

He laughed. 'Very well – and what would you like to know first, the gruesome or the mundane?'

'The gruesome.'

He rubbed his hands in a Machiavellian way and bared his teeth. 'Grr! The gruesome it shall be! Come and see my lair . . .'

They went up a single flight of stairs and he pointed casually to an open doorway revealing a room decorated in masculine style.

'That is my room . . . And here is my den!' He flung open the door next to his bedroom with a dramatic gesture.

Rosaleen peered in – and gasped in horror, for wherever she looked her eyes alighted upon skeletons or skulls or jars filled with strange organs and substances.

'Of course I would not have shown you had I believed you to be in the least squeamish.'

'Are they real?' she asked, entering the room cautiously.

'The skeletons? But of course, my dear girl.'

A pedestal desk was in the centre of the room, and upon it were scores of sheets of paper covered with drawings or with untidy writing, and as her gaze travelled about she observed that the books lining the shelves were nearly all of a medical or scientific nature.

'You're a doctor!' she exclaimed triumphantly, relieved that she had not, after all, wandered into the house of a maniac.

'Yes, I am a doctor. But now I do not practise. Instead I dabble in research here and there and lecture when I feel so inclined or when invited. Hence I have all my macabre friends whom you have just met.'

'They were not once your patients then?'

'Hah! I appreciate your humour, Rosaleen.'

'And the jars – what are in them?'

'Foetuses and things.'

'*Foetuses?*'

'Yes . . .' He shrugged and looked vague. 'And other nasties. I pickle them!'

'Aw Frederick, I don't believe you.'

'But I don't jest. It preserves them.'

'Aagh.'

'That is a most unfeminine sound, Rosaleen.'

Back in the parlour once more all was genteel as Mrs MacDonald served them tea.

'How funny it all is,' Rosaleen thought, 'me sitting here as though I were a lady of station, and taking it quite for granted.'

'Rosaleen,' Frederick said between mouthfuls of cake, 'I think we should discuss your future.'

'My future?'

'My goodness, you look quite stricken! Yes, your future. What do you want to do with it?'

She was taken aback. 'I hadn't considered . . . I don't know, Frederick . . . I want to model for artists. But that won't earn my wages, will it? And how will I pay you for living here? . . .' Her voice tailed away uncertainly.

Frederick took her hand. 'My dear, I did not raise the subject to throw you into turmoil, but to be constructive. If you wish to model then we must let it be known that you have left Burne-Jones's service and are here. It is as simple as that.'

'And – the money?'

'That too is simple. So simple in fact that we shall forget about it. So insult me on that score no longer.'

That summer was warm and giving, and Rosaleen took each day as it happened and lived it with intensity, revelling in her freedom – the freedom to be as she wished; selfish, guiltless freedom.

Frederick would rise early, tend to Edgar and then put on his dressing-gown, and Rosaleen became accustomed to him drifting about in his paisley silk robe until midday. They breakfasted together with the ease of old acquaintances, drinking coffee outside if the weather permitted, in the shady seclusion of the courtyard. Often friends dropped by and breakfast would extend late into the morning, then Frederick might go into his den of skeletons, and Rosaleen would be left to entertain the visitors.

Thomas Carlyle, the Scottish writer, visited sometimes, a crusty, elderly man who awed her with his intellect and lack of small talk, and she dreaded being left alone with him, for they sat in silence until Frederick's reappearance. Known as the Sage of Chelsea, Carlyle lived in Cheyne Walk, locked away from the noise of neighbours and tinkling pianos and hubbub of domestic animals – a sad figure whose moroseness was only lightened when he was editing his late wife's writings. But he and Frederick conversed for hours, and Rosaleen had even seen Carlyle smile.

There were many other guests besides: writers, musicians, some artists, although Frederick was only on the fringe of the Pre-Raphaelite set, and that because of his friendship with Ruskin. Most of the people he knew were socialist-minded academics, and several were atheists like himself. Rosaleen was the eavesdropper on their provocative conversations; she loved to listen to their discussions of Karl Marx and communism; of Darwin's theories in relation to Genesis; of the role of the Church; the power of literature; the outdated penal system; the necessity for trades unions as advocated by John Ruskin . . .

She would listen to these sessions, attentively quiet, offering no comment, and uncaring that they might consider her stupid; but she took note of everything discussed, and later debated the issues in her own mind.

One morning, when Rosaleen had been with Frederick for about three weeks, the front door bell jangled, and she answered it to find Dante Gabriel Rossetti standing there. She immediately recognized his heavy, Italian face.

He greeted her perfunctorily, with typical arrogance, and said directly, 'Sir Frederick Walton called upon me the other day and told me you were here. I have come to see you. I teach a class of students twice a week and should like to use you as a model.'

And so it started. Frederick saddled Edgar and left on his wanderings, believing Rosaleen safely settled, and she began her 'career'.

She would go to Rossetti's house in Cheyne Walk, and once in the studio – in a state of partial undress, or at the other extreme draped with velvet, furs and jewels – would remain achingly still for a couple of hours at a time, with only an occasional rest. She would assume endless poses – sitting, reclining, sprawling, standing, pretending to play an instrument or brush her hair – and became used to the constant scrutiny of the students. No longer hindered by modesty she was as much the observer as the observed.

The students were so intense and engrossed, absorbing Rossetti's words, his techniques, his knowledge, and his very self; and in his presence they were humble – respectful of his criticism, his sudden vacillating moods, his non-committal silences. But afterwards, when they had left his house, they would be like hounds at a fox. Rosaleen would join a group of them at a coffee house in the King's Road, or they would return to someone's room, and then the attacks would begin. They were cruel, these boys who talked behind their great master's back with the impertinent disrespect of those who have achieved nothing and are still too young to know they are unlikely to.

'. . . Rossetti has had his day.'

'. . . There is nothing original about his art. He and his

colleagues are merely attempting what the Italians did a great deal better centuries ago.'

Rosaleen sat listening to all this bravura, knowing that less than an hour before she had watched them struggling to emulate their teacher. She thought how poor they were by comparison, and only by behaving grandly after class was over could they boost their flagging morales. Yet these same students were the first to boast to outsiders: 'I have the great Dante Gabriel Rossetti as a master.'

'He is deranged,' someone said. 'Ever since Elizabeth Siddal died he has become increasingly depressive. It even affects his eyesight.'

Another said: 'They are all deranged. William Morris is constantly glum as he gets older, and he and Rossetti feud all the time nowadays. Rossetti's passion for Jane does not help. Burne-Jones appears amiable but hides his gloom behind a jester's mask of humour. And as for Ruskin – well, he is a psychotic –'

At the mention of Ruskin's name spoken so disparagingly, Rosaleen could no longer keep quiet.

'It's not *true*,' she objected furiously. 'These are great men you so jauntily destroy. And as for Mr Ruskin – he wants to bring culture and education within reach of ordinary folk, but he is forever thwarted. You mightn't believe in what he's doing – but what right do you have to sneer at a man for only wanting to do good?'

Her impassioned voice fell on their silence. Then on her left came: 'Phew!' And somebody said: 'I didn't know she could talk.' Everyone laughed.

One student teased: 'If you are not nice to us, Rosaleen, we shall paint you with drooping breasts and a long nose.' The conversation became bantering, and her outburst was forgotten. Initially several of them had attempted to seduce her, but she had rebuffed them with quick-witted repartee and they had not persuaded her into their beds. They were, after all, no different to the boys back home.

Rosaleen attended three classes a week now – two with Rossetti and another with a little-known artist who scraped a living solely by teaching art. She became used to the unique smells of a studio; the sharp smell of turpentine and more cloying odour of paint; the smell of bodies as the students, concentrating hard, sweated freely. Now she appreciated the long procedure of producing a picture – which in the end might be subjected to pitiless criticism – and felt a tenderness towards those aspiring artists who revelled their way through life, some poor, some privileged, but united under the umbrella of art. She would listen to the soft scraping of pencils or charcoal, the faint swilling of brushes in solvents; to the muted murmurs in the room, and – posing under their detached gaze – could be as drunk as if she had imbibed mulled wine. Her body offered itself chastely to them.

The months passed. Frederick would arrive and disappear again in a clatter of Edgar's hoofs, and Rosaleen explored London. She learned the names of monuments and statues, buildings and bridges, and the history behind them. She went to afternoon concerts, to fine-furniture auctions, or to Covent Garden Market. And if the weather were fine she might walk to Hyde Park to watch the riders and stare at the lines of elegant carriages. Children's cries would reverberate and the air be redolent with an indefinable quality. And Rosaleen would fling herself on to the grass and stare up at the sky, losing herself in reverie.

Sometimes she walked along the river by Cheyne Walk to see the barges pulling their loads, the bargemen shouting to one another; or she would watch a pavement-artist painting. His cheeks would be hollow and she'd stoop and gently place a coin in his cap. In the King's Road a cheeky boot-black volunteered to shine her boots in return for a favour. In Mayfair an old man bought her a rose and pinned it to her blouse – then left her. Its scent drifted intermittently to her nostrils . . .

Once she saw a dancing bear; but her smile died when she noticed his poor tattered fur and sunken eyes, the ridiculous steps of his cumbersome body. Nobody else perceived these things. The little crowd clustered around clapping and cheering and chanting, throwing farthings into the grimy hat the tamer held out, whilst the bear dragged his chains and danced on wearily. He had been trained on hot coals.

'My mother sat at home and embroidered all day,' Frederick commented when Rosaleen told him how she spent her time.

'That's sad.'

'Yes, I suppose it was. And she had no other children to fuss.'

'What did she do with all her embroidery?'

'Nothing, as I recall. They were mostly useless squares. And when she developed rheumatism she could do nothing at all. She became quite embittered. But it is not expected that a well-bred woman should do anything.'

'I'm glad I am not well-bred.'

Rosaleen was content; yet at nights her mind, ungoverned, was invaded by dreams of what she had left behind. She was there again – wood-fairy child – cosseted by her parents, holding Robbie's timid hand and embraced by her countryside.

Robbie's letters disturbed her. He wrote like a lamenting lover: 'I am despairing . . . When will you return? . . . When shall I see you?'

She wrote back: 'Do not despair . . . I have no plans to return . . . I do not know when you shall see me . . . Be patient, Robbie' – to soften the harshness. Once she added, 'Give my love to Father.' But she crossed it out heavily.

It was mild mid-September, an early-morning lemon sky. Rosaleen and Frederick sat having breakfast in the courtyard. Frederick was dressed for travelling.

'Do you think of your home?' he asked her.

'Sometimes.'

'But do you *miss* it? You never say, you strange girl. You are so self-contained.'

'Well, I don't hanker after what I've left behind. There'd be no point to that.'

'Stranger still. You are so positive, so certain of issues.'

She did not answer. The issues were simple so long as she did not have to reflect on them too profoundly. She thought of the litany she had used to repeat almost every evening to give herself strength.

He persisted: 'You leave your home and with it everything you trust and know. For what, Rosaleen? What is it you *want*?'

'I don't rightly know, Frederick. Is it important? Does there have to be a reason for everything? I am nineteen now, and there are so many things to do and to see and to visit – those are my "reason", if you like.'

'Oh how you bewilder me! I understand my skeletons better I think. I am only envious of you, Rosaleen.'

Rosaleen was astounded. 'Frederick! How can you be envious of me? What do you mean?'

'I envy you because you are nineteen and yet do not search, whilst I am thirty and I search.' He sounded almost anguished.

'What do you search for, Frederick?'

'The same thing as any man. Peace of mind.'

'Aw Frederick . . .'

She couldn't console him so she took his hand in hers and stroked it.

'Aw Frederick,' he copied her, smiling ruefully. 'You do not say "aw" so often nowadays. In fact I fear you are becoming sophisticated and I would not wish that to be my doing. Rosaleen, you need some new clothes. Let me buy you some.'

'You just said you did not wish me to become sophisticated.'

'But you *need* new clothes.'

'I'm fine the way I am, Frederick.'

'You are stubborn.'

'I've got nothing to give you in return.'

For the first time Rosaleen saw him react angrily.

'What – you mean unless you sleep with me I cannot buy you anything? You would accept gifts if you were my mistress, yet you will not as my friend. That is truly a shame. Well, I have news for you. There is to be an important exhibition at Sutton House in Park Lane in two weeks, on October the third. Burne-Jones is exhibiting and Whistler and Rossetti – what a motley trio – and you must surely attend. But you have nothing to wear.'

'Why must I surely attend?'

'Because, dear Rosaleen, Edward Burne-Jones is showing his portrait of you.'

'Oh – oh . . .'

'Ah – she is lost for words at last.'

He rode off soon after and turned back and smiled as she stood by the gates. Whatever it had been, it had passed and his displeasure with her was over. His smile stayed with her.

Frederick had still not returned by the morning of October 3rd, and Rosaleen was desolate. She had been looking forward to the exhibition with longing and impatience.

'I shall go out for a walk,' she told her reflection in the mirror in her room. 'No matter. It's really not so great a matter.'

But it was, and her steps dragged like an old woman's and she thought how grey and dirty the Thames was.

'What am I doing here? What allegiance do I have to this place – and with Robbie, Nana Annie . . . Father, miles away?'

'Rosaleen – what a surprise!'

It was William and Jane Morris – she tall and still beautiful in her maturity, though her beauty was of a dark and intense kind. Her arm was linked to her husband.

'You are shuffling along like a tramp!' she continued. 'Are you distressed?'

'No, not in the least.'

William Morris said kindly, 'Now that must be untrue. Nobody shuffles like that who is not distressed. Would you care to join us? We were only taking a stroll before returning to Rossetti's house.'

'No – thank you all the same. I must be returning.'

'Well, we shall see you tonight,' Jane said. 'I have heard you will be quite in the limelight. I shall be most jealous.' And she laughed, showing strong white teeth, with the confidence of a woman who believes she has no rival.

'But there are lines about her eyes and mouth,' Rosaleen thought uncharitably. 'And her eyebrows are too thick.'

Drearily she returned to the house – and heard sounds from

116

the stable; the peaceful blowing and munching sounds of Edgar eating his food.

Frederick was back.

'Oh I'm so *glad* you're home.'

'Don't tell me you missed me.'

'No. I was only so sad to miss the occasion tonight.' But this was not the entire truth.

'You really are without tact, Rosaleen. You have quite distressed me – raising my hopes and then sending them crashing again.'

'Don't tease so.'

'Very well, although you cannot of course be certain I was teasing. Now in a few moments I shall hear all your news and tell you mine, but first let me show you one or two things.'

He took her hand and led her into the parlour. It was a dark day and Mrs MacDonald had already turned on the lamps, and the fire blazed and snapped. A butler's tray was laid with tea for two.

'On the chesterfield you will see several boxes. Why don't you open them?'

They were expensive-looking boxes – Rosaleen could see that – done up with satin ribbon. She looked at Frederick suspiciously.

'Go on,' he encouraged.

She opened the first box tentatively, carefully unfastening the silky ribbon, picking the tiny knot.

'You would think it was full of asps the way you are progressing,' he grumbled.

'Hush Frederick, let me be. Anyway it is open now.'

Lying in its bed of soft paper was a white organdie evening gown. She stared at it.

'Hold it against you.'

'It's never for *me*!'

'It isn't? My goodness, girl, who else do you suppose it is for? Now do as you're told and hold it against you. I wish to see it.'

She laughed delightedly and pressed the mass of billowing white to her. The pearl-trimmed bodice was designed to be worn off the shoulders, and the sleeves were frothy balloons finishing at the elbow. Lilac ribbon roses outlined the deep V of the waist and neck, the scallops of the overskirt and the ruffles of the sleeves.

'Frederick . . .'

'You like it then.'

'I scarcely know what t'say.'

'Open the other boxes then. Incidentally the lilac matches your eyes. I thought that a cunning touch, although I say so myself.'

The next one contained a lilac velvet hooded cape, entirely lined with white silk and fastening round the throat with white silk tassels. When Rosaleen put it on she swirled it about her – ran around the room with it twirling whilst Frederick watched, smiling.

'You look like something from a painting by Tissot.'

She stopped twirling, breathless. 'Who is Tissot?'

'James Tissot is a French artist forced to live in London at the moment as his political beliefs are not popular in France. He is young – in his twenties – but he was well-established in his country before he left a couple of years ago. Now, shall you open the other boxes?'

. . . There were white gloves fastened with lilac roses, lilac satin slippers, white silk stockings, undergarments, and lilac ribbon for her hair. Boxes and paper were strewn everywhere, and Rosaleen sat on the floor amidst the mess, slightly dazed, holding first this garment then that one to her – pulling on the gloves, and then peeling them off carefully.

'I should keep them on,' she said ruefully. 'They hide my red hands. It's interesting to think that inside such dainty gloves are such ugly hands.'

'They are not ugly,' Frederick contradicted her, pouring the tea into cups. 'They are most serviceable hands.'

'That doesn't prevent their ugliness. No matter –' She got up and sat by him. 'Tell me about tonight.'

'What must I tell you?'

'Everything. Who owns Sutton House? Will there be a great

many guests? Tell me about Whistler – I've not heard of him. Is John Ruskin going t'be there? And is Gabriel Rossetti really in love with Jane Morris like I've heard –'

'Enough, enough!' He held up his hand laughing. 'Pax. I shall tell you all you want to know.'

He passed Rosaleen her cup of tea. She took a sip and nursed the cup in her hands, looking at him expectantly.

'Sutton House is owned by Lord Henry Taggart-Laughton,' Frederick told her. 'He is an exceedingly rich, stodgy old widower with one son and three ugly daughters, and as a staunch supporter of the arts, regularly holds exhibitions. He is also a personal friend of the Prime Minister, so Gladstone will probably be there tonight.'

'Goodness.'

'Oh he will be just one of a line-up of "distinguished" guests. There will be between four and five hundred people including dukes and duchesses and earls and counts and various other assorted bits from the aristocracy all over the world. Everyone connected with art will be there and many who are not. I *believe* John Ruskin might be there, but I cannot be sure. He is a man who does as his mood tells him.

'Whistler – what can I tell you about him? He is an American . . . He painted a portrait of Thomas Carlyle recently and I believe that is to be shown. Whistler is a miniature dandy with a very varied talent and style, and a penchant for beautiful red-haired girls.'

'Now you're teasing, Frederick.'

'Say "Aw Frederick". No, I am not, as it happens. It is actually true. His titian-haired mistress for many years – and also his model – was a young Irish beauty by the name of Jo. She called herself Mrs Abbott for decency's sake. There have been a succession of redheads since Jo – who incidentally is left holding the baby of one of his other mistresses . . . But all this is in the open, and everyone seems happy with the arrangements. You will immediately recognize Whistler by his dapper little figure and the thick white lock of hair he carefully separates from the rest which is black. As a man I cannot comment other than to say that beneath his outrageousness I believe beats a profound heart.

'As for Rossetti and Jane Morris – I dislike gossip and hearsay and will not encourage either in you. However, since you asked – I have heard that Rossetti has long been infatuated with Mrs Morris and tried to resist his passion because of his friendship with the lady's husband. I have also *heard* that of late and due perhaps to William Morris's moods, Jane returns his passion. I have *also* heard that aside from teaching Rossetti barely paints nowadays and has vowed never to paint Jane Morris again. But I cannot believe that to be true. Rosaleen – all these intrigues are just part of artists' lives, and most of the Pre-Raphaelite group are a God-fearing bunch. There! Are you satisfied?'

'Yes thank you! And thank you for all the gifts. I have not done so, and you are so thoughtful and kind.'

She kissed him on the cheek and he gripped her momentarily. She drew away, embarrassed, and the look they exchanged was weighty with awkwardness.

It was a crisp, dry evening, and dusk had fallen when they arrived at Sutton House shortly after half-past six. Carriages stretched down part of Park Lane and into Brook Street, and when the driver took Rosaleen's hand to help her down her cloak spread gloriously around her.

... The Coniston lass come from the sticks ... Our Ros'leen ... 'You've got a wise head on your shoulders, tiny lass ...'

She linked her arm through Frederick's and joined the grand throng, the trailing rustling skirts and cloaks, and beside her Frederick's cane tapped with the other canes, and his silk top hat was lost amidst all the others.

'I'm nervous.'

'I am beside you.'

'Everybody is so very fine.'

'And what are you?'

'Yes, but it is an illusion. It's only the clothes. I open my mouth and I'm still me.'

'Rosaleen, if you talk like that we shall go directly home. You *are* you. Never forget.'

'You'll not desert me half-way through?'

'Not unless you wish me to.'

Sutton House was a four-storeyed white, bow-fronted mansion with striped awnings adorning the lower windows, and a pair of tall bay trees like sentries either side of the massive entrance. Two footmen in full livery stood just outside on the upper step, and two more inside, who took cloaks and hats and passed them on to maids. Rosaleen felt lost amongst so many people – diminutive and swamped.

She gazed at the crystal chandelier swaying gently and jingling; at the black-and-white chequered floor; and she thought: 'We could play chess . . .' She knew how to play chess. Frederick had taught her.

'Rosaleen, don't look so afraid.'

'I'm not . . . Why are we waiting?'

'Because we have to be formally announced.' They stood in a queue of silk and bustles and animated voices, waiting for the introductions.

'There is Mr Gladstone ahead in the queue!' She spotted his old cadaverous face and penetrating eyes.

'His days are numbered.'

'Why?'

'Disraeli will win the next election if Gladstone does not retire first.'

'But that is a *pity*.'

'Yes, in that I am a liberal. But we need someone younger. England is full of old men; stale thinkers without an advanced idea in their heads. It is only a pity Disraeli is not a liberal . . .'

'. . . Your name, sir – and the young lady's.' The master of ceremonies bowed from his height.

'Sir Frederick Walton and Miss R. Ruddock.'

'What a name!' Rosaleen thought, suddenly longing to erupt into nervous laughter. 'You can almost see the red-cheeked farmer's wife, and smell the pig shit on her husband's boots.'

'Hold your head erect.'

She swept proudly through the parted double doors – all five feet of her – leaning on Frederick's arm, into the most magnificent, immense room she had ever seen or imagined. Panelled walls were covered with paintings, and rows of crystal chandeliers dipped and glittered, suspended from ceilings with intricately painted and gilded cornices, their moulded fruit and leaves picked out in different colours. The parquet floor – or such of it as was visible between the hundreds of feet – was highly polished and shone like pouring honey. How many servants had bent for hours on callused sore knees over that floor?

Lord Taggart-Laughton shook their hands. His gaze lingered on Rosaleen and saliva oozed on his fat lower lip.

'I have seen your portrait. Exquisite. Quite exquisite.'

'Thank you . . . M'Lord.' Was that correct, she wondered?

His three ugly daughters were beside him. How should one address them? Should she have curtseyed to the old man? She averted her eyes from the giant mole on the middle daughter's nose and murmured something inconsequential – before passing on with Frederick. A footman offered her a glass of champagne from a salver and she grabbed it, drinking it as quickly as if it had been water.

Frederick took her arm and they wove their way through the dazzling crowd. Everyone was taller than her. She seemed to have shrunk, like Alice. 'Drink me, drink me' – perhaps she would disappear into the ground.

'Look there is John Ruskin,' Frederick said, and Rosaleen saw him amongst the heads, looking gaunt and aged since the last time they had met. They went over to him and Ruskin kissed her hand and kept it held in his gentle clasp.

'How lovely it is to see you, my dear, and how very lovely you look. Well, little Rosaleen, this is a special occasion indeed. How do you feel seeing a picture of yourself hanging amongst the others for all to view?'

'I have not seen it yet tonight, sir.'

'But it is quite the finest portrait here!'

'Sir – you're biased.'

'No my dear. I am at all times objective, and I am accused for it. Gabriel Rossetti resents my outspokenness, yet I helped establish him. They will lap up the praise and recoil from the criticism,' he said bitterly.

Rosaleen waited a few respectful seconds, then asked, 'Sir, what news from Lancashire?' She was impatient to hear – and disappointed by his reply.

'I have not been at Brantwood for a while. I have been teaching at Oxford at the drawing school I established there. I have also been involving myself with a publishing enterprise with George Allen. And of course I have been crusading as usual. It makes me tired nowadays. It is always so deflating.'

'Then why do you do it?'

'That is of course a most reasonable question! I can only answer that it is a compulsion, my dear – an obsessive interest in the human character, and an inherent belief in man's basic goodness and his potential.'

'But you can't force a man, sir, any more than you can a stubborn animal. Take my father for instance – there'd be nothing you could do with him. He wouldn't have it. He's suspicious of what he doesn't already know.'

'Ah, but learning is a progressive thing through the generations. He sent you to school. You have learned on his behalf.'

'But sir – respectfully – I know plenty of local lads back home who went to school who weren't interested. And there'd be nothing you could do would make them so.'

Frederick said, 'I think Rosaleen has a fairer understanding of human nature than most people I know.'

'Frederick, don't tease.'

'I am not, my dear. At least, if it is not an understanding it is a philosophical acceptance.'

She gave a dismissive shrug, and turned back to John Ruskin, her expression earnest.

'Mr Ruskin sir, when will you return to Coniston?'

'I am going back at the weekend.'

'Oh sir, will you do sommat for me? I'd be so glad of it.'

Frederick looked at her curiously.

'My dear – anything,' Ruskin said.

'Will you check on my brother Robbie for me? Make sure he's not in trouble. I've heard nothing from him for more'n three weeks now and I'm worried. He kept talking of going to Kendal, and he's too young. He's only thirteen.'

'I shall check for you, Rosaleen. I promise I'll not forget. Now you stop worrying. I am certain nothing will have befallen him.'

'Why did you not tell me about Robbie?' Frederick asked in a disgruntled tone when they were by themselves.

'There was no need. What could you do about it?'

'But you could have told me at any rate – shared your worry.'

'But it wouldn't have solved anything, Frederick.'

His eyes were puzzled and hurt.

Amongst the crowd Rosaleen saw other faces she recognized: Edward Burne-Jones – back from Italy especially – and his wife; the aquiline features of George Price-Boyce; Spencer Stanhope; and Thomas Carlyle – talking to a small foppish-looking man.

'Is that Whistler?' she asked Frederick.

'Yes.'

'He is so effeminate.'

'He is rather, isn't he? But believe me he is entirely hetero-sexual! Now – perhaps it is time we viewed the paintings. Are you not longing to see yourself framed and in pride of place?'

And there she was, beside Jane Morris – more creamy-skinned and redder-haired and lilac-eyed, and much, much more delicate.

She stood and paid homage to herself, a little half-grin on her face at the ridiculous impossibility that this was she.

'The very incarnation.'

Rosaleen turned. The speaker smiled down at her with roguish amusement.

She looked up at him and was ensnared.

❧ Seven ❧

INFATUATION

Then I left on a crest of infatuation;
Discarded my friend, my sense, for a whim of recklessness.

In the fraction of a second's silence which followed the young
man's words, it seemed to Rosaleen that time was suspended and
during it she became another person.

'Hello Tags,' Frederick said without enthusiasm.

'Hello Freddie, how extremely good to see you. Will you
introduce me please? I believe the young lady must have a name
besides "The Joseph Shawl".'

'Miss Rosaleen Ruddock – the Honourable Edward Taggart-
Laughton,' Frederick intoned dully.

Rosaleen recovered her senses. 'Oh you must be the son of –'

'And you must be the daughter of Mr Ruddock,' he interrupted her.

She laughed – and saw that Frederick was about to walk
away.

'Where are you going?'

'I wish to speak to someone I have just seen – are you
coming?'

'I –'

'I shall look after her for a while,' Tags told him. 'We shall
study the pictures. Why Frederick, you do not even have a
catalogue.'

'I have no need.'

He walked away and Rosaleen watched his departing back,
surprised by his abruptness.

Edward Taggart-Laughton still smiled.

'What is so funny?'

'You are! Burne-Jones's picture is remarkable for its likeness to you, but it depicts your beauty in that typically ethereal style of his, which is quite intimidating, when really you are rather quaint.'

'I am not quaint!'

'You are so adorably tiny one longs to stoop and pat you! I am not insulting you, you realize. Where are you from?'

'Lancashire.'

'My ancestors came from that county.'

'And were dukes no doubt.'

'No doubt. And no doubt your ancestors were not. But I do not see that need concern us. Whereabouts in Lancashire?'

'I come from Coniston.'

'Ah – that is where John Ruskin has hibernated to, is it not? My father is a great admirer of Mr Ruskin. I have heard that the Lake District is one of the few places in England left undefiled. Is it true?'

'Well it is true of where I live, but I can't answer for the rest of England.'

'You are a realist! That is a quality one finds in few women. Now shall we slip away from the crowd? You may tell me about Coniston and the lakes and mountains, and I shall close my eyes and imagine it all.'

Rosaleen hesitated – and looking around for Frederick felt an instant's panic that he was not to be seen. She turned uncertainly to Taggart-Laughton again, and he gave a slight nod in the direction of the door. They went into the library – a much smaller room whose pine-clad walls and simple bracket lights lent it a cosiness. A pair of leather chesterfields faced each other with a library table in between, and they sat simultaneously and without thought beside each other on one of them.

'I wish I might lie stretched out with my head in your lap,' the young man said.

She made no reply, and he sighed at what he took to be her refusal, unaware how she longed to have his head in her lap, to stroke his smooth skin and fine features.

'So then, Rosaleen, speak to me of your countryside.'

'It is wild . . . It's very lovely, very lonely . . . How can I tell you?' She could not take her eyes from his.

'*Try* to tell me.'

'It makes me sad to remember it . . .'

'What are you thinking?' He touched her forehead gently.

'How best to begin . . .'

When they returned to the ballroom they found they had missed the speeches and that many of the guests had already filtered into the dining-room for the buffet banquet. There was no sign of Frederick, and with fewer people about they could view the paintings without being continually jostled. Tags commented on the various works:

'Rossetti paints strength. See the strength in his painting, the boldness of style even when his subject is allegorical. And his painting of Jane Morris in her most pensive mood – still there is a forcefulness. And have you observed the similarity in each of his models? He depicts their mouths with identical shapes, the upper-lip lifted and bowed, the small area of flesh between nose and lip deeply emphasized. Rossetti does not paint much nowadays. Between bouts of depression and bouts of sightlessness and bouts of passion for the lovely Jane he sometimes brandishes a brush. I was surprised my father selected his works for this evening. Most of these paintings are old ones in private ownership.'

'I sit for Rossetti's classes twice a week.'

'I wish I were a student and could gaze upon you! Now you look perturbed. Why?'

'You were flattering me.'

'And of course I was! What is so wrong with that?'

'I don't trust it. It reminds me of a snake – insidious.'

'Hah!' He gave a snort of laughter. 'But one must be light-hearted about these things! Very well – I shall allude no more to your perfect beauty and dwell instead on your quaintness. Now tell me about Rossetti. What is he like to work with?'

'He is silent and moody – one could almost forget he is there, and then he will suddenly leap and storm because sommat's not right, and the class will be all aquiver –'

'Say that again.'

'What?'

'Sommat.'

'No.'

'Oh *do*.'

'No.'

'But I like it.'

'Well I shall not say it merely to please you. I am not some performing animal.' And along with other words it disappeared from her vocabulary.

Tags resumed his little lecture: '. . . Now Whistler is unusual in that he appears to have no fixed style. Whistler is a versatile artist –'

'You are talking about me, sir?' an American voice enquired.

Whistler had approached with the softness of a cat, and Tags introduced Rosaleen to him.

Whistler said, 'I was admiring your portrait, Miss Ruddock. It is truly a miracle of exquisiteness. Mr Burne-Jones has almost done justice to you.'

'Steady, old man,' warned Tags. 'Not so effusive. Miss Ruddock dislikes flattery. You are liable to get your head bitten off.'

'I refuse to believe it. All women like to be flattered, and most especially when it is true!'

'Miss Ruddock, I am learning, is not most women. Now, Mr Whistler, I should so like to hear about yourself. This painting –'

Whistler was delighted to speak of himself and his art. 'It is of my mother. I am devoted to her. I wanted to paint this portrait simply in grey and black as I did Thomas Carlyle. I wanted to depict her goodness. She had been ill and her patience was very great, as I rubbed out and rubbed out again every attempt I made at her picture! However, I think I am pleased eventually with the portrait. I have used the oil paint thinly – barely at all in places, particularly where the head-dress is concerned so that it might appear transparent.

'This one is very different. It is the first of what I intend as a series called "Moonlights". I am fascinated by the river, and painted this study in blue and green from Cheyne Walk where the stretch of water is more tranquil, but still dotted with boats and barges. I do so enjoy the irregularity of the veiled buildings across the bank – it is incredible how their daytime ugliness is transformed . . . I prepared the canvas with a red ground and this brought out the blue, and of course darkened the tone of the whole thing. I poured on liquid paint – and would you believe I painted this on the floor to stop the paint running – then I dragged and streaked my brush across the canvas to effect the sky –'

'I cannot say it appeals to me, sir.' John Ruskin had arrived on the scene and was appraising the work critically.

'Why is that, sir?' Whistler asked pleasantly.

'It is amateurish,' Ruskin retorted bluntly.

Rosaleen was astounded by his rudeness.

'Is that so?' Whistler's voice lost its amiability.

'Yes. I find it little more than a sketch.'

'And I begin to find you insulting.'

They continued to wrangle, oblivious to the other two, and Taggart-Laughton, turning to Rosaleen, said quietly, 'Let us leave them. Shall we eat? We can return later to the paintings.'

He took her hand and studied its redness without commenting, before leading her into the dining-hall, a room at least as large as the ballroom. Here long white-clothed tables were set with silver and candelabras and flower-arrangements, and in between, the food was arrayed in a lavish and mouth-watering display which had Rosaleen agog.

There were boars' heads garnished with aspic jelly, and fowls covered with mayonnaise; decorated tongues and cold meat pies, galantines of veal and game, and lobster salads. And the desserts! Tiered dishes held fruit jellies and iced cakes, pastries, tartlets, custards and meringues, charlotte russes and various flavoured creams . . .

But more amazing than the food was the sight of the guests: a moment ago genteel and sophisticated, they were now reduced to voracious clamouring vultures. Rosaleen watched astonished as beautiful women tore at bones, and refined men filled their mouths and then spoke, so that food spilled out and splattered their whiskers. Dignity went to the winds as people queued and jostled for second and third helpings.

Through the throng Rosaleen spotted Frederick, seated on a flimsy gilded chair beside a man and woman. Tags was talking to someone and Rosaleen made her way towards Frederick, her plate modestly heaped.

'You disappeared,' she said to him, to alleviate her conscience.

'I thought three was a crowd . . . Rosaleen, this is Mr and Mrs John Millais.'

Effie Millais – who had been married to John Ruskin when she had met the artist and whom Ruskin referred to as a 'demanding social climber'. Now she was a demure-looking middle-aged woman, but one could see the vestiges of an earlier beauty.

'How do you do? I am pleased to meet you.' Rosaleen shook their hands in turn.

Millais said, 'We met briefly at Edward Burne-Jones's. I have been hearing much about you from Sir Frederick here, whom I have not previously had the pleasure of meeting.'

'I dread to think what he has been telling you, sir.'

He smiled. 'Believe me, the remarks were most complimentary. Will you not sit down and join us?'

'So my dear – are you enjoying yourself?' Frederick asked – on a slightly sarcastic note, Rosaleen thought. But she answered equably:

'Oh I am. It is all most interesting. And I've just seen Mr Ruskin. I left him and Mr Whistler quarrelling.'

And then, looking stricken, she recalled Effie.

The latter said mildly, 'My former husband quarrels regularly. It is just one of his less endearing habits.'

'I'm sorry – I was not thinking. It weren't for me to comment, anyway.'

'*Wasn't*, Rosaleen. It *wasn't* for me to comment.'

'You always creep up unexpectedly,' she accused Tags, pleased however, by his reappearance.

Taggart-Laughton gave a small bow. 'I did not mean to eavesdrop, but I thought you had abandoned me.'

'She would do better to do so, Tags,' Frederick parried without humour. And Rosaleen glanced at him, not understanding his antagonism.

Tags ignored Frederick. 'Tell me, Mr Millais, do you not consider Miss Ruddock here a most perfect subject to paint? I have been assessing her from each angle and can find only symmetry!' Rosaleen had a bone caught in her throat and could not interrupt.

Millais said, 'I had been going to ask Miss Ruddock if she would sit for me.'

Rosaleen coughed, and the bone dislodged itself. 'I should love to sit for you,' she told Millais.

'Good, then we will make arrangements.'

Edward Burne-Jones approached the little group, looking hot and flustered.

'Greetings, everybody . . . Damnably warm isn't it? Too many people by half. Well, Rosaleen, perhaps you are a little proud of our mutual accomplishment? May I borrow her from you, good people? Rosaleen, there are many who wish to meet the mystery model who has ravished their eyes. Will you do me the honour of coming with me?'

This time she was no servant. This time, resplendent in the dress Frederick had bought for her, people noticed her when she was introduced, and their tone was not patronizing. It was no trivial thing to have one's portrait painted by Edward Burne-Jones and hung in Sutton House next to a portrait of Jane Morris.

'Has it sold yet?' someone asked.

'Yes,' Burne-Jones answered.

'Who to?' Rosaleen asked.

'My dear, these things are very discreet!'

'For how much?' another enquired.

'The asking price, I believe,' he replied.

'Come now, Edward – why so evasive? Five hundred guineas? A thousand? Fifteen hundred? I would not be surprised if it fetched that.'

'I dislike talking about money . . .'

As they went from group to group Rosaleen noticed that the women watched her through narrowed eyes, and was disquieted. Burne-Jones scanned the room across the sea of heads:

'There is Monsieur Fantin-Latour, the French painter and lithographer. He is a friend of Whistler's, so that explains his presence. And there is old Thomas Landseer – elder brother of the recently late and not so lamented Sir Edwin – you know, he of the wide-eyed animals and the lions in Trafalgar Square. Thomas, who must be almost eighty, is an engraver, and takes himself a good deal less seriously than his brother. He is talking to Frederic George Stephens – surely the uppermost art critic today. He is the critic for the *Athenaeum*, amongst other journals, and is a perfectly amiable chap when he is not pulling one apart! He does not talk a great deal, but he has depth of soul. By the by, you look enchanting in that dress.'

'You look proper enchanting all dressed-up like that,' her father had said to her once on the way to church. 'All the lads'll be after you,' he had added aggressively . . .

Eventually Burne-Jones left her on her own and Rosaleen sought out Frederick, who was in the ballroom talking to a woman. She was tall and reed-thin, with dramatic dark colouring and passionate eyes. They were quarrelling.

'It is scandalous,' the woman was saying in a shrill voice.

'My dear Leonora, I scarcely think it is your business,' Frederick told her coldly.

'Everybody is talking.'

'And when have I cared for such wasted breath? . . . Rosaleen – you are returned. Meet Baroness Leonora von Hoffnung.'

'I have no wish to meet this *person*. Why – I have heard she cannot even speak properly.'

'Come, Leonora, that is quite sufficient. Where are your manners?'

Rosaleen's disbelief became mortification. While she had

paraded in her finery had they all been sniggering behind their hands? It was what she had dreaded – and then forgotten. Oh her vanity! In that moment the whole evening was abruptly negated, and she minded their derision more than she would have thought possible.

She heard Nana Annie's voice chastising her: 'What are they to you, tiny lass? Have you grown soft in the South? You'll be tripping over them pretty lilac ribbons next . . .'

Rosaleen stuck out her chin and retaliated in strong dialect. 'She ain't got no manners, Frederick. Manners is sommat you're born with. There's folk 'bout who ain't got no manners more'n our pigs back 'ome.'

Frederick looked at her askance, then burst out laughing, and Rosaleen, still trembling inwardly with humiliation, joined in.

The Baroness's voice was high with indignation. 'I fail to see what is amusing. Where did you dredge her up from, Frederick? She is just a peasant in expensive clothes – bought by you no doubt. You are a fool. I do not associate with fools.' She flounced off.

'Oh that was good theatre!' Frederick said, still chuckling. 'But damn the woman. She had no right.'

'Is it true that they are saying things about me?' Rosaleen's voice was very small; her face was utterly crestfallen.

'Dearest Rosaleen – a very few might be, but they do not signify. Remember what you said to me – and it is true: those that matter – those people who are valuable – would not consider talking so idly. It is their problem, if they are limited, and one must treat the issue in that way.'

Rosaleen, who had never had any enemy and could not comprehend what she had done now to make one, asked, 'Frederick, why was the Baroness so malevolent towards me?'

'Shall I tell you? Yes I shall . . . Because in a moment of madness, my dear, about four years ago, I promised to marry her. The old Baron – whom she had married for money – had died the previous year, and we were introduced. She is not unattractive you might say; she is highly intelligent, and her spirit appealed to me. We became engaged and for some months there was a relationship between us that alternated between passion on both our parts and intense dislike on mine. The latter claimed victory, and one morning I awoke and questioned my sanity.

'The Baroness was definitely not pleased . . . And that is that particular story. You will not admire me for it, I daresay. I was accused of being a cad – and a lot more besides, but I have no regrets in that direction. Indeed the more I see of her, the more I feel an overwhelming relief at my narrow escape. One of the better by-products of the episode is that terrified mothers keep their tedious daughters away from my disreputable clutches!'

'But Frederick, you did the right thing. She is an evil woman. B'sides – she shouldn't have married the Baron for his money.'

'Oh my dear Rosaleen, there is nothing unusual in that. It happens all the time in society, and is considered a fair exchange: a woman's youth and beauty in return for a title and wealth. And speaking of wealth – here comes the Honourable Edward Taggart-Laughton himself.' His tone was sarcastic. 'Beware of him, Rosaleen. I have known him for years. He is too charming and not to be trusted . . . Hello Tags, we are just taking our leave.'

'Now that is a great pity.'

'Be that as it may . . .'

They were so different to look at. Tags – handsome, slender – was still a boy, with constant laughter in his light-blue eyes. His black hair curled as irrepressibly as his smile, and his complexion was unfurrowed by the weight of troubles.

Beside him Frederick was like a cob next to a thoroughbred. He was shorter and more powerfully built with his strong neck, burly shoulders and chest, and he exuded muscular fitness. His fair hair was sun-streaked and very fine, lying flat to his head, and his skin, where it was not hidden by his beard, was rough and ruddy in texture.

He stood now in an aggressive stance – had become humourless in Tags's presence; dry as a nut.

Tags asked, 'Am I about to lose my quaint little friend?'

'It would seem so,' Frederick replied.

'However – not for long! She is residing with you, Frederick, is she not?'

And Rosaleen, anticipating another rebuff from Frederick, interrupted, 'I can answer for myself.'

'My apologies –' Tags gave her a conciliatory smile, '– of course you must answer for yourself – I shall visit you at the good Sir Frederick's if that will be convenient.'

'You may not be welcome, sir,' Frederick told him curtly.

'Frederick –' Rosaleen glared at him.

But Tags spoke across her. 'I shall take that risk. Rosaleen may surely decide for herself.' He winked cheerfully at her and left before Frederick could discourage him further.

'How could you behave in such a way?' she demanded of Frederick as they walked to their carriage.

'I told you. He is not to be trusted.'

'And are you my guardian? What business is it of yours if he wishes to see me?'

'I am looking after your interests.'

Inside the carriage they did not speak, and the atmosphere on the way home was tense.

Back in her room with its especially chosen décor, she undressed. The dress, the slippers, the cape, the silk underwear, the gloves – mementoes of Frederick's caring generosity – lay in a heap on the love-seat. There was a poignancy about them, and she felt sad.

The gibbous moon shone palely into the room. The moon had used to shine into her uncurtained attic room and sometimes she had imagined it assumed Nana Annie's face. Now she fell asleep intending to dream of Tags, but another dream came to her: that Robbie could not be found. He was floating somewhere unseen – the lake? The clouds? The sands of Cartmel? And his voice was calling: 'I'm *here*, Ros'leen. *Here*,' with the frustration of one who knew that the other was looking in the wrong place. 'I'm *here*!' The frustration became pleading despair. The clouds tumbled into flat water to become giant waves, and Thomas was drowning. Rosaleen stood watching her father helplessly from the bank with her feet trapped in bracken whilst Robbie in

Jumping Jenny tried to row and reach him. But the boat did not move and Rosaleen's feet were the roots of the trees and she was growing from the earth. Her father became Robbie and he disappeared under the rolling lake which was transformed into miles of sand . . .

'Robbie . . . Robbie. *Robbie.*'

'Hush, it is all right. Dearest girl, it is all right.' Frederick was crouching beside the bed in his nightshirt, holding a candle. His face, rumpled from sleep, was reassuring.

She sat up, breathing quickly, still partially immersed in her nightmare. 'I dreamed – it were so muddled . . . I couldn't find Robbie . . . Then it were father drowning . . . and then Robbie again . . .'

'You're crying.' He rocked her in his arms and she lay, compliant, being rocked, rocking with him. He climbed into bed beside her and continued to stroke and hold her, murmuring banalities until, curled against his solidness as she had used to be with Robbie, she fell asleep again.

When Rosaleen awoke Frederick was gone, and she thought perhaps it had been part of her dream. Later Mrs MacDonald told her he had departed early that morning on Edgar, on his travels again. His flute had jutted from his pocket and he had been in a particularly cheery mood.

Frederick was away until the end of October, and during his absence Rosaleen sat for her classes, socialized, and was invited to 'evenings', as they were known in the art world. There she would have glimpses of artists' turbulent lives, ruled by petty jealousies and feuds; where one minute a man would die for a friend and the next be prepared to kill him; where scorn was reserved for a colleague's painting, not his lowly background; where a quarrel would arise from just how much oil should be mixed with pigment . . . Rosaleen was fascinated.

Meanwhile, she was being courted by Edward Taggart-Laughton. He had announced himself a couple of days after the exhibition with a bouquet of flowers, and had called most days since. Their times together were varied: drives in Hyde Park; a trip to Hampstead; visits to exhibitions, to the music-hall, the theatre – and the opera. He took her to see Mozart's *Magic Flute*, performed by the Royal Italian Opera, and when Papageno made his appearance Rosaleen immediately recalled her first meeting with Frederick:

'I shall be Papageno, and you shall be Papagena.'

Tags courted her lavishly and persuasively, and when she had worn her red dress on the third consecutive occasion, he insisted on taking her shopping.

She was stubborn. 'I cannot accept gifts from you.'

'And I cannot accept the prospect of your red dress on a fourth occasion.'

'Don't you like it?' She was hurt.

'Naturally I like it, my quaint lass, but all I am pleading for is a change.'

'Then I shall go to market and find something. Or at least buy some cloth to make something.'

'Rosaleen, you did not say "sommat". This calls for a celebration!'

They went to Bond Street, and Tags – remarkably, not bored and seeming to thoroughly enjoy himself – sat patiently in a series of shops whilst she swivelled and pivoted, and was pinned and tucked and unpinned. He shook his head or nodded, obligingly interested in all the feminine goings-on.

On the way out of the shop, armed only with some of their purchases, for most items required alteration, he said to her, 'Now Rosaleen, you will not put your Joseph shawl over your new dresses will you?'

'Yes Tags, I shall.'

'But you cannot. It will destroy the style.'

'I have my own style. I like my shawl.'

Patchwork of her past . . . And where was Robbie? She had heard nothing, and John Ruskin's letter had only increased her anxiety, although that had not been his intention.

. . . I have tried to find Robbie, but without success. I have been to the inn and seen your father who was, as you might imagine, not overly joyous to see me and attempted to shut the door in my face. However Laurie was with me and had his foot in the way and your father was bound to let us in! He was reluctant to impart any information to us, but it would seem that Robbie has left home and run off to Kendal. Your father appears unconcerned and has no intention of seeking him.

However, you must not think the worst. Kendal is a reputable town and I daresay your brother has found himself a job and decent lodgings. There is probably nothing more sinister in his inattention to letter-writing than fear of rebuke from you. I shall see if I can do some detective work in Kendal, but meanwhile please refrain from your anxiety.

It was most pleasant to see you at Sutton House the other evening, and of course looking so particularly splendid. I apologize for the quarrel between Whistler and myself, with you in the midst, but the little fellow has always antagonized me, and I cannot abide sloppy work. The audacity of the man for daring to exhibit such rubbish incensed me.

Now be happy and feel fulfilled. Do not forget, should you wish to return to the Lakes and need a temporary home, that Brantwood awaits you. Never forget your roots, Rosaleen. All else is transient. Mr and Mrs Severn send their kind wishes to join mine. And please convey my best wishes to Frederick. He is a good man . . .

Silently Rosaleen called for Robbie. She thought that surely her anxiety would be transmitted across the distance and seek him out. She strained to hear his reply; but none was forthcoming.

She thought perhaps she should go home – envisaging how it would be now, nearing November, with autumn hues and low damp cloud; and the sudden appearance of the sun, so that a sheep standing solitary on a rock would be lit in a halo of light like the golden calf . . . But she was reluctant to return, fearful of confronting her father, fearful of the general deterioration which might have taken place and which would preclude her leaving again. These fears were as strong as her fears for her brother.

Tags said, 'I shall come with you.'

'You?'

'Yes, that very same. Why not?'

A dozen reasons why not. 'No Tags, but thank you.'

'You will go on your own?'

'Yes. I shall wait a while longer, and then I'll go to seek him.'

'You are a stubborn spirit. You know that of course.'

'I was always like it. Nana told me it were because of my hair.'

'*Was. Was* because of your hair. Rosaleen, I have a proposition to make – one I think would be most amusing and pleasant for both of us. I should like you to become my mistress. I could teach you to speak properly and you could teach me your philosophies! Think what a fine time we would have.'

Frederick arrived back the following afternoon, his face ruddy with health and good humour. He had travelled to Plymouth and lectured there, before going on to St Ives to visit relatives. He sat beside her and warmed his feet before the fire, having removed his shoes.

'You would love Cornwall, Rosaleen. I shall take you. It is as wild as where you come from – but there is the sea, rushing into hidden coves, hurling itself round rocky headlands . . . We shall buy you a horse and we can go together. A friend for Edgar. A mare perhaps. She could be called Ethel. Edgar and Ethel! What an adventure it will be.'

She faced his happiness and knew she was going to ruin it. 'How lovely that sounds.'

'Are you glad I am returned, tell me?'

'Of course I'm glad, Frederick.' But she had been wrapped in Tags's arms and planned to go to him that evening after she had told Frederick.

He frowned. 'Something has happened in my absence.'

She looked down, crossed and recrossed her legs.

'Rosaleen – you hesitate. And you seem remote.'

'Aw Frederick, I'm not remote.'

'Better! I actually get an "Aw Frederick". But I am not as unperceptive as you might believe, and I think, Rosaleen, that you and I know each other sufficiently well to be direct. Something has changed about you – please tell me.'

She braced herself. 'Tags and I are going to live together.'

He sat heavily on the chair he had been leaning against. 'You *cannot* be serious.'

A familiar anger prickled her. 'I am.'

'I see. When did all this happen? I cannot think you know the gentleman very well to make such an important decision.'

'No less well than I knew you when I made another important decision.'

'*Touché* . . . Rosaleen, let us not quarrel.'

'Dear Frederick, of course I've no wish to quarrel. We like each other so well, and I feel bad about leaving . . . But it was your suggestion that I come here, and you gave me to think I was free to come and go as I please.'

'Well, and that is true. You know it.'

'Then why do you challenge what I do?'

'Because Tags will hurt you, Rosaleen.'

'How do you know?'

'Because he would have proposed marriage otherwise. I know him. I know you. You matter to me. What you do matters to me.' He looked so unhappy, his eyes so downcast, that Rosaleen adjusted her position and rested her head on his knee.

'I shall be all right, Frederick. And I can leave him if it does not work.'

He shook her head from his knee. 'And then what?' he demanded. 'From person to person, place to place?'

'What do you wish me to do if I'm unhappy with him – stay there?' Rosaleen raised her voice also.

'No, that is not what I wish. Look, Rosaleen, why don't you find your way slowly – go out with the chap by all means, but use here as a base for your self-discovery. I promise I shall not hinder you at all. You are just so impetuous.'

'I know what I am doing.'

'But you do not.'

'You're only jealous. I think you don't want me to go because you are piqued with jealousy.'

'Maybe I am, but that has truly no bearing on what I say or why I do not want you to go. It is *you* I am thinking of – not myself and my wretched feelings. I do not wish to see you hurt.'

'Well you will not then, for I shan't be here. I'll be with Tags.'

She left the room to prepare her packing: too much to tie in a bundle this time. Instead she packed everything carefully in all the boxes she had kept, using the tissue paper she had hoarded. She took the boxes downstairs into the hall, unaided by Frederick who watched stony-faced.

'I shall arrange a cab,' he said, and left abruptly, and when the cab arrived to fetch her he was nowhere to be seen; but typically, he had pre-paid her fare.

By now Rosaleen's temper had calmed and she longed to see him, to apologize and express her remorse; to hug him, and to explain: that she cared deeply for him, was grateful to him, and – that Tags mattered more?

She waited, increasingly dispirited. Outside the driver paced up and down impatiently.

Mrs MacDonald said, 'He won't return, dearie. When he's morose like that he'll be gone for hours.'

So Rosaleen left. She had behaved shamefully. And towards Frederick of all people.

❧ Eight ❧

THE MISTRESS

I did not demand that it would last for ever –
Only a little longer.

Edward Taggart-Laughton lived in rented accommodation in a smart semi-detached villa in a Knightsbridge square. As Rosaleen's carriage drew up she saw him standing out-side, in a nonchalant pose, his face hidden from view, and was disquieted by this impersonal impression. Then he swung round, and she was cheered by the pleasure in his expression.

For that first half-hour or so of her arrival he was awkward, almost gauche; he was, after all, only twenty-two years old and his bachelor's existence was about to end. For all his bravado he was not experienced with women, and he was uncertain how he should welcome his new mistress into his home. His cheeks were flushed, and he talked rapidly, not waiting for any comment between his remarks . . .

'This is the drawing-room – I have not furnished it as I should like, because I had not expected to be here for long. It is uncomfortably big anyhow, and I only use it when I entertain on a large scale, which is seldom, as I prefer to go out . . . Oh I have not yet offered you a drink, would you like a drink? Have I told you that you look charming – Oh I must not compliment you . . . Next we have the dining-room – rather gloomy, do you not think? I should like to decorate it in the Japanese style – it is all the rage . . . In case you wonder about servants I have a valet for myself, and two housemaids and a cook – who also supervises the maids. I have given them all the night off – pushed them out,

so to speak, in order to have you to myself . . . Lord, Rosaleen –
I am as nervous as a cat.'

'I know. I was as bad until I saw the state you were in!'

'And that is meant to console me? Oh, by the way I have hired
a maid for you, and she will unpack your boxes in the morning.'

'Oh Tags, I cannot have a *maid*.'

'Why not? Every lady has a maid. I thought you would like a
maid.'

'But I am not a lady.'

'What poppycock – you are my own, special, quaint lady.'

'But what would a maid *do*?'

'Oh I don't know . . . Run your bath –'

'There is a proper *bath*?'

'Certainly. There is a bathroom with running water, and a
tiled floor. The floor is rather cold underfoot.'

'Oh I have never seen a real bath!'

'You see it will have been worth coming here even for the
experience of the bath alone.'

'I shall use it twice a day. I'll spend all day in it, soaping myself
and soaking it off.'

'I shall soap you. All over. That will be my job.'

'And the maid – what else'll she do, besides running my
bath?'

'Well – she will prepare your clothes and dress your hair and
mend and iron and bring you anything you require, and check
your laundry –'

'But I can do all that for myself.'

'But you are not expected to.'

'But I *want* to.'

They stared at each other in dismay. Tags had decided how it
should be, and now Rosaleen had disrupted his plans and his
confidence momentarily deserted him.

Then he brightened. 'Let us not disagree over such a silly
issue. I thought you would want one, but if you do not – why,
what difference to me? I shall dismiss her! Now come here to me
and stop looking as though I have a devil's horns either side of
my head.'

That night on his immense Elizabethan four-poster bed Rosaleen became his mistress. Until then Rosaleen had regarded her body with casual dismissal: a useful vessel of purpose which must be fed and clothed in order to respond to the demands made of it. She had not experienced erotic longings or fantasies, and that single time with Frederick had left her emotionally untouched and physically unaroused. But with Tags she discovered a self she had not imagined; she became acutely aware of her sexuality, luxuriating in this exciting body that was hers. They were insatiable; they played; they were children and her love for him was a child's love. What a novelty this thing was for them both – and they enjoyed their eroticism with healthy gusto and an almost innocent pleasure.

The disturbed nights took their toll on her appearance: she was having tea with John and Effie Millais after a sitting, and John observed the dark stains beneath her eyes.

'You look a little tired, Rosaleen. Is Frederick not caring for you properly?' he teased.

'I am no longer with Frederick, John. I live with Edward Taggart-Laughton now.'

'With Tags? But Frederick – ?' He looked bewildered.

She could discern Effie's disapproval by the set of her head. 'I was never Frederick's mistress, you know.'

'Oh, I thought you were.'

'Yes, I expect many people did.'

'You were – his lodger then?' Effie enquired, trying to establish Rosaleen in a role with which she could feel comfortable. She had apparently forgotten that her own past was not unblemished.

'Not really. Frederick and I are – were – are friends. That is all.'

'Oh,' Effie exclaimed. And John Millais looked discomforted.

Rosaleen left soon after that, unsure what had happened, whether their disappointment was in her, or whether their embarrassment was at themselves because of their error. She felt disturbed by their reaction – that people she liked might be critical of her.

Two weeks elapsed and still she had heard nothing from

Robbie, despite having written home enclosing her new address, and she could no longer defer the prospect of returning.

'Perhaps he is remaining silent in order to entice you back.'

'No Tags, Robbie would not do that. He's not devious.'

'So what do you think has happened?'

'Oh I wish I knew. I only know he left the Coachman's and has perhaps gone to Kendal, and in that case he'll not have my address here . . . But he had Frederick's address, and Frederick would have forwarded me any mail . . . Oh I'm so worried, it's been almost a couple of months now. I shall go home. Monday next week I shall go.'

She dreaded to return: to find that her father still raged – or worse, was beaten; to find that they had suffered and were continuing to do so; to discover that Nana Annie's sight had completely failed; that business had plummeted and the servants had gone, and the inn was falling into disrepair; afraid that without her they could not function; fearing that the power of her own countryside would draw her to it. And she saw her new life retreat like a defeated army.

'You are so silent, what are you thinking?'

'Only about going home. I shall set off on Monday, like I said.'

'So that is that. What can I say? You will not let me accompany you. So have a teeny drink now and be a little merry. Today is only Wednesday and to be glum is to be boring.'

'Oh Tags, drinking doesn't solve anything. You drink at all times.'

'Do I detect disapproval?'

'What you do is your affair.'

'Quite so. An apt observation.'

She prayed that night for Robbie; that he might be safe; that he might let her know of his safety so that she need not go home.

In his most rational voice Frederick had said, 'Now Rosaleen, you know God does not really exist.' And had proceeded to expound on this theory methodically and with a chilling logic which profoundly perturbed her, for until then she had not questioned His existence, and like all others from similarly rural areas accepted that He played a part in their daily lives.

Since that conversation she had been uneasy in her prayers, aware that her feelings were based only on instinct and what she had been told, whereas Frederick's viewpoint was intellectual and reasoned . . .

Tags reached for her under the sheets, and automatically she spread her legs. She was as dry as a virgin, and he hurt her; and all the time he was thrusting and sighing, oblivious to the change in her, she felt alone. Afterwards, when he lay asleep and she awake, she questioned what she was doing lying beside a boy who grew bored when the laughter stopped.

The next morning the sun streamed through the parlour window. Tags's glass of whisky was the colour of topaz.

'There is a young gentleman to see you, Miss,' the house-keeper announced to Rosaleen with disapproval in her voice.

'For *me*?'

. . . And there he stood, in crumpled trousers inches too short, his boots encrusted with soil; gangling and shamefaced, and his hair on end: Robbie – bringing with the impact of his arrival myriad memories, and tears to her eyes.

'Mankin, oh Robbie mankin . . . Where have you been? I've been half mad with worry.'

Hugging his long bony form to her, Rosaleen smelt his unwashed sourness, but was too glad to see him to care.

Tags watched with the detached air of an amused onlooker. 'I take it this is the erring wanderer.'

'Oh I'm sorry. This is Robbie. Robbie – this is Tags.' She wondered whether she should have been more formal.

'Robbie, I am truly delighted to meet you,' Tags greeted him amiably, and took Robbie's dangling right hand, shaking it enthusiastically.

And perhaps he was glad: here was a chance to display his tolerance; not only had he taken a working-class mistress, but now he extended his hospitality towards her brother and, most importantly, he would make sure everybody knew what he had done and then revel in the malicious whispers.

'How do you do, sir,' Robbie enquired politely.

'Tags. I am Tags to everyone. Now I think perhaps it politic to leave you . . .'

His face shone with benevolence. He replenished his glass of whisky and disappeared with it in his hand.

Rosaleen and Robbie sat on the big settee.

'You smell ripe, Robbie!'

'Do I? I can't smell it myself.' His voice was becoming a man's – veering between croaks and squeaks.

'When did you last wash?'

'Aw Ros'leen – how can I remember a thing like that?'

'Why didn't you write? Mankin, where have you *been*?'

'I kept thinking – I'll do well. I'll show her I can do well on my own and then I'll write and tell her . . . Only that didn't happen, and there weren't any point in writing with nothing good t'say.'

'Wasn't.'

'What?'

'It's "wasn't", not "weren't", Robbie. There *wasn't* . . . No matter. Oh but tell me, from the beginning.'

'I got your address from Sir Frederick. I went there first of all this morning –'

'You were fortunate he was there. But I'd have thought he'd have made you take a bath before going any further.'

'Well he wanted me to. But I was in a hurry to see you. He's ever so nice, Ros'leen. Why did you leave? And the picture of you is really good. I couldn't believe it when I saw it hanging there.'

'What picture?'

'You know. Your picture. The one you wrote to me about.'

'Gracious! So it was Frederick who bought it. Oh how sad I am knowing that.'

'Why? He likes it. He was telling me 'bout it.'

'That only makes me more remorseful! You see I wasn't nice to Frederick in the end and he was only ever good to me. He never told me about the picture. Where is it hanging?'

'In the parlour, above the fireplace.'

'He had a painting of Edgar, his horse, there before. I have replaced Edgar. That is honour indeed!'

147

'Well anyway . . . I left home some weeks ago – maybe six weeks, two months –'

'You're always so vague, Robbie.'

'But it isn't important, Ros'leen . . . I couldn't bear it a moment longer. Father's become rough and violent and the inn's dirty, and the customers only come on account of Isobel – you know – Nancy's girl. The old housemaid's gone and another's taken her place. She's got most of her teeth missing. I think Father beds her.'

Rosaleen's heart sank as she digested this information, which was not so different to what she had envisaged. She asked, 'And Nana? What news of her?'

'She's the same. She doesn't change. Oh she had a dream 'bout you once. You were washing someone and the pail was filled with blood. She said it were an omen. She misses you, and she weeps a little. B'sides that she's the same.'

'Does Father ever mention me?'

He hesitated. 'No, Ros'leen.'

'Oh. I was just wondering. Go on with your tale.'

'So I left the Coachman's and went to Kendal like I said I wanted – and you didn't want me to go, so I didn't tell you. I wanted to come and see you then, but I'd no money saved . . . I went to work in Lancashire Screw-Bolt Works where they make bolts and rivets and ironwork. They've got lots of machinery, Ros'leen, and it were exciting to start with. Then after a bit I grew bored. All I'd do all day was stand by this machine feeding metal tubes down a sort of relaying belt, and check that they were chopped in the right places. It were ever so boring. So I left. I was sleeping in a lodging house then, it weren't too bad really . . .

'And then I tried to get a job with the newspaper – you know, the *Kendal Gazette*. I'd have done anything there. But they didn't want me. So I went into Ye Old Fleece in Highgate, and they took me on there.'

'What did you do?'

'A bit of everything. Served customers, cleaned boots. Scrubbed floors and polished . . . And it weren't too bad at first . . .'

'*Wasn't.*'

'Aw Ros'leen – don't get at me. You used t'speak like me before.'

'Well it's not the right way.'

'Who says?'

Who did say? 'Everybody. It's grammar. It's the way it is written. When you write your poetry you write it properly.'

'Writing it's one thing. Saying it's another. There's no point in pretending t'be what we're not, Ros'leen. We're ord'nary folk.'

'You never used to argue, Robbie.'

'Well you never used to criticize me, Ros'leen. Not with silly things anyway.'

'Oh mankin, I'm sorry. Of course you are right. Go on with your story.'

'Some money went missing . . . It weren't me. Ros'leen, I swear it weren't me.' He became agitated.

'Hush Robbie, of course it wasn't you. I know that.'

'They thought it were – me being new and all. A policeman came and snapped handcuffs on me. It were dreadful. The landlord – he wouldn't believe anything I said, and suddenly there was a big crowd gathering, and they were talking and pointing at me and staring. The policeman led me away.'

He twisted about in his distress and Rosaleen took his hands and unclenched them. She said, 'I wish I'd been there. I'd have given the landlord a piece of my tongue. He wouldn't have accused you with me there.'

'As like as not. But you weren't there, Ros'leen.' His remark wounded her with its reproach, and she thought that if Robbie grew up to be cynical it would be because of her.

'What happened then?'

'I spent the night in jail.'

'No! They'd no right.'

'But they did it just the same. There was a man with no legs in the cell. He'd stole some jewellery. Imagine shoving a man with no legs in prison, Ros'leen. It's a cruel thing t'do. He had little stumps which finished in shrivelled knobs and went blue with cold. They'd taken away his crutches and he couldn't get about

149

or do things for himself. I helped him on to the slop. There were a drunk too, and a man who'd wounded another in a brawl. He said it were self-defence. We were all in the cell together. It smelt proper bad, and I couldn't eat – a kind of poddish it were – for my belly'd turned. They left the slop in there brimming over.'

'But can they keep a lad your age in jail?'

'I don't know. But anyway they didn't know my age. You see I'd lied to the landlord to get the job. Anyway, I was out the following morning, as they caught the lad that really did it. Someone overheard him boasting to a friend.'

'Oh Robbie, Robbie . . .'

There was nothing to say which could compensate him for what he had endured, and she hugged his foul-smelling body to her and thought how lonely he must have felt since her departure.

Muffled in her arms he continued, 'I'd no money. I'd saved a couple of shillings, but somehow it'd gone, and I'd nowhere to stay meanwhile, and no means of getting t'you without money. So I left Kendal. I took the Windermere road without any plan in my head, then I came to a village sign. I followed it and came to a farm. They needed a willing hand and in return I could sleep in the barn and be fed. They were good folk. I was there a week, and th'last day we harvested the bracken. They gave me two shillings and threepence and a food pack to be on my way. I took the train for part of the journey and got picked up by cart or a kind traveller for the remainder. I walked plenty also. It took almost three days. But I made it, didn't I?'

He broke away from her, his dirty, freckled and weary face lit by a proud smile. And he was every bit entitled to his pride. Rosaleen's timid brother had proved his resourcefulness and courage.

'Robbie – I think it is time you took a bath.'

'Ros'leen – you're crying.'

'Well, what do you think, mankin?'

After a while the three of them felt the strain of being together. Tags lent Robbie clothes and attempted to be jovial, Robbie tried to fit in and seem worldly, and Rosaleen became tense trying to be loving towards both of them when each demanded her time and affection and was jealous of the other.

Tags felt that Robbie was in the way; his benevolence had been short-lived. 'I do not want him with us the whole time,' he said sulkily when they were about to set out for a ball.

'But we are going by ourselves tonight.'

'The first time in twelve days, and that is only because of course he could not go to a ball. Why must he constantly latch on to us?'

'Because he is my brother.'

'I took you in. I did not expect the entire family. When is your father arriving? Oh, and there's a Nana somewhere isn't there? Nana Annie, that's it. How quaint.'

'He won't be here much longer, Tags. He only came to find me.'

'Well he must leave soon – or else he can stay, but stop imposing himself on us everywhere, and establish some independence for himself. Does that not seem fair?'

He was trying to be reasonable, and Rosaleen had to agree it was fair. They left for the ball, where she watched Tags lose himself in whisky and abandon her to making social chat with people she knew spoke disparagingly about her once her back was turned, and to dance with young men who considered her easy prey.

When they left Tags vomited in the street. He swayed and clutched his stomach and retched, and afterwards was, as usual, morose.

'I am selfish and bad . . . I love you . . . Don't leave me . . . Life is disagreeable to me, you know . . . I am a rebel, Rosaleen. A rebel at heart . . .'

He remained in bed the entire next day, suffering from a self-inflicted headache and stomach disorder, and Rosaleen and Robbie went out on their own. She took him sight-seeing, and later, when they walked in St James's Park in the drizzling rain, she took the opportunity to ask him his plans.

'What are you going to do, Robbie?'

'I don't know, Ros'leen. But I know I shan't remain in London. It isn't a place that I can feel comfortable in. I don't know how you can be happy here.'

'But I am.'

'I know.' For a few seconds there was a significant silence between them. His 'I know' still rang in the air, accusatory.

'So where will you go?' she asked, taking his arm to try and re-establish contact, and feeling him respond.

'Back to Lancashire. I miss the lakes. I miss the fells. I miss the bleakness b'sides the beauty. I'll find sommat t'do.'

'Robbie, I'm not letting you leave until I know you are sorted. I shall write to Mr Ruskin. Just wait a while. Let me write to him and see if he can place you.'

Within a week she received a letter in reply to hers: '. . . But of course young Robbie must come and work here. Rest assured he will be well-looked after and given a responsible job to do . . .'

A couple of days later she said goodbye to her brother at the station. He looked healthy and relaxed, his face was scrubbed and his hair well-behaved, and about him was a new air of assurance. Rosaleen sensed his relief that he was going back and tried not to feel hurt. The courses of their lives had diverged.

She issued last-minute instructions: 'You must visit the inn — just to let them know you are safe. Give them — give Nana Annie my love, and you've nothing to fear from Father now, Robbie. You've grown up. Give Nana this.' It was a shawl she'd bought at market.

'And you, Ros'leen? Won't you come back one day?'

'One day I shall.'

'And what about you and Tags? You squabble so much, and he drinks. Why don't you leave him and go back to Frederick?'

Could this be the same Robbie, who now offered her advice?

'Frederick and I were friends, Robbie, that is all. And I love Tags. You don't know him — it was difficult being the three of us.'

'He'll hurt you. I know it.'

Rosaleen touched his cheek, felt its young man's down with a rueful pang. 'I harbour no illusions about Tags,' she said.

She waved to him, his blurred face straining through the open window, until the train was gone from sight.

When she returned to Knightsbridge the valet informed her Tags had gone to his club; to drink and gamble, no doubt. He was a curious boy, she thought – more complex than other people realized. He had been brought up to treat life one way and strove to treat it another; and although he was clever and cultured he preferred to cultivate his image as a rebel, the black sheep of the family, when in fact he was nothing of the sort. Tags's was not a strong enough character to sustain the part he tried to play. But he read his socialist journals assiduously and attended liberal meetings, and flaunted his views in much the same way as he flaunted Rosaleen – in order to shock. Yet his bouts of extravagance and inherent selfishness mocked his idealism, and recognizing his own inconsistencies Tags drank and gambled; because both these things were simple and gratifying.

That afternoon Rosaleen was visited by his middle sister, Evelyn. The other two sisters had already visited on separate occasions and by coincidence Tags was out both times. Or was it coincidence? This afternoon was no different to the others: Evelyn came wrapped in her morality to judge Rosaleen, and Rosaleen poured out tea prettily and made conversation. She enquired of the other's embroidery, the book she was reading, the piano music she preferred. They spoke of the opera and balls and of other safe subjects, and Rosaleen tried to keep her eyes from drifting towards the mole on the young woman's nose.

But Evelyn was no more appeased than her sisters. It was as if Rosaleen was a courtesan who had baited their brother; a nothing from nowhere whose intention was to destroy the family reputation; a Lady of the Camellias.

However, their opinion did not trouble Rosaleen any more than the opinion of Tags's father, who had also paid her a surprise visit. The old man might have been Gladstone's friend, but he lusted after her with no highbrow thought in his mind. He dribbled from the corner of his mouth, and when he asked her to stop seeing his son in return for payment he laid his hand on her knee.

'I do not want money from you, sir.'

'Then why are you with my son?'

'I enjoy being with him.'

'He'll not get a penny from me if he stays with you. You will not receive a penny if he marries you.'

'I know that, sir. I want nothing from him.'

The family had nothing to fear in any case. Tags had told her at the outset that their relationship could not last.

'My inheritance is conditional upon my marrying into a suitable family,' he had informed her. 'It is no meagre sum to which I refer, you understand.'

'Yes I understand,' she replied.

'And now you are offended.'

'No – just bemused by the new things I learn each day.'

'And will you stay with me knowing what I have told you?'

'Yes.'

'Of course you could always remain my mistress.'

'No, Tags. I shan't ever take second place.'

Through Tags Rosaleen became known, and much in demand as an artist's model. The little money she earned she sent to her father, with a brief note someone else would have to read. Perhaps the money might be useful to him, but really it was her way of trying to make amends. But she had no acknowledgement from him and no way of knowing whether he had received the gift.

1873 staggered to a close; over a year since she had been home. The new year came in and ceased to be new, and Disraeli joined forces with Gladstone to form a coalition government.

Tags gambled and drank. They bickered and Tags sulked, but in between quarrels they loved and rejoiced.

He took her to Paris in late spring where they partied and were entertained and explored the city – the wide boulevards, cobbled lanes and hidden alleys. They walked in the Tuileries and listened to music there, sitting in the shade of trees. They took cab rides in the Champs-Élysées, ate at restaurants or sat on the pavement outside little cafés . . . But it was Montmartre he knew would interest her – that small rural area surrounded by vineyards and windmills, and comprising a warren of tiny winding and steeply climbing roads, with the ancient church of St Pierre high on a hill.

'This is where many artists live,' Tags said, as they drank coffee outside the Café Guerbois, 'and it is at this café that a band of artists regularly meet. They have been dubbed the Impression-ists by a journalist called Leroy: Renoir, Manet, Sisley, Cézanne – and others besides.'

'How do you know all this?'

'I have read about them. I have seen and admired their work. Besides – I am quite simply a knowledgeable fellow!'

'And most immodest.'

'But you love me!'

'In a way.'

'You really are a most unobliging girl, Rosaleen. You will not give a fellow even a little encouragement.'

'Please tell me more about these Impressionists.'

'Well I can tell you they always paint out of doors – Renoir even paints from his little boat; I can tell you they spend hours studying the natural light for its different reflections; that they paint an immediate *impression* of what they see – for instance a crowd *is* blurred, is it not? We do not notice details . . . How-ever, I can do better than tell you all this. There is a first exhibition of their work at the studio of a photographer called Nadar. They have organized it themselves since the Salon rejected them. I shall take you to the exhibition and you can draw your own conclusions.'

Rosaleen was enraptured. It was art as she had never imagined it – vivid and light and so different to the styles of painting she had come to know and understand: the Pre-Raphaelites, or the Old Masters. Here in vibrant colours were people who breathed, scenes which lived, flowers she longed to pluck. She wanted to visit the places of these pictures.

They were in Paris for about a fortnight and Rosaleen awoke to each day with a feeling of excitement. She would lie gazing at the reflections in the room whilst Tags slept on beside her, elegant even in his sleep, and she relished those private moments of thought, in which her mind was already sharply alive.

The nights too held their pleasures, of another kind. Then, with the window open on to the Paris sounds and the street light streaming in, they made love with as much zest as they had done during the first weeks of their relationship, and afterwards slept the untroubled sleep of satisfaction.

They returned to England at the beginning of June on a particularly windy day. The Channel was rough and Rosaleen was sick, which revolted Tags although she reminded him of the many times he had been sick after excessive drinking. They returned to London, tired and irritable and barely speaking, and almost as soon as they were home things changed.

He began to go out without her. 'It is not possible for you to come,' he would say – knowing she would not ask for an explanation. The valet would hand him his top-hat and cane with a conspiratorial look in his eye and Tags would swagger off, leaving Rosaleen alone except for the hostile servants.

She was no meek and whining creature – if this was what Tags wished then he was free to do as he pleased. She went out by herself also – to gatherings of artists, and evening exhibitions, and once to Herne Hill to visit Joan and Arthur Severn when they were in London. She thought often of Frederick – wondered how he was, where he was, but she never saw him at the places she went to, and although she would scan the room eagerly for sight of him, he was never there.

Tags frequently returned from his excursions drunk. He would climb into bed beside Rosaleen and attempt to make love, but his penis was flaccid, and he became tearful at his impotence. She could only feel pity for him then; for Tags was confused and she was sorry for his confusion, whatever its cause. So she cradled his head and agreed with him that the room rocked and the bed pitched, and that no, these were not figments of his imagination. She consoled him for his inept efforts at love-making, and then when he was asleep, rolled him on to his side from on top of her body.

His anger was more difficult to cope with: not knowing its origins she had no means of defending herself from it. So after a while she would leave the room rather than try to rationalize. In between, there were times when all was almost well – a flash of affection, of the old rapport, of attraction; a loving look, a teasing remark. But these times were increasingly rare. Tags was trying to shut her out.

In September, not quite a year after they had met, he told her he was going to marry. Rosaleen knew her slightly: an insipidly pretty fair-haired girl from an old aristocratic family with a frail appearance and a face which would always be virginal. Rosaleen remembered her as being inclined to fainting.

She did not question his decision – after all, he had always been honest with her – but she was sorry because she knew he would not be happy and that he would probably become both a compulsive gambler and an alcoholic. She was sorry for his weakness and that he would be disappointed in himself. He had only played at rebellion. She was sorry, also, for herself.

She left when he was out, because she did not want to endure the falsity of parting, the spurious promises; and because she knew he would try to give her money, which she would find hard to refuse; and because she was afraid she might cry.

She did not take the jewellery he had given her, but she took the clothes and the small trunk he had bought her for Paris. She struggled with it down the stairs, gave the valet a note for Tags, and went outside into the square.

She was fortunate to see a vacant hansom cab immediately. She hailed it and climbed in – before realizing she had no idea where she wanted it to take her.

Nine

ALONE

Ah Ros'leen – so much for your fine ambition, lass,
It would not have taken you far on your own.

Rosaleen alighted from the cab on the other side of Battersea
Bridge. Across the river were Cheyne Walk and Chelsea, which
Whistler had painted in the sweetness of evening light. Now it
was grey, and dampness rose from the water. Behind the factories and warehouses and gasworks were ugly rows of identical
brick terraces like those she had seen from the train the day she
had travelled to London. She was no longer enchanted – read no
romance into the glumness about her. It was all monotony, and
the people's faces bore testimony to it – devoid of joy.

She had become spoiled during the last year and a half,
accustomed to luxury and gentility, and it was the first time since
her arrival that she had been truly on her own. The trunk was
heavy and her arm ached from lugging its weight and from the
awkwardness of the boxes. Rosaleen felt lonelier than she had
ever been, trudging along without direction.

In one of the bleak little streets there was a wooden board
outside a small semi-detached house with 'Room to let'
scrawled on it. She knocked on the door, and a short stout man
opened it. His dyed black hair was brushed back from a pro-
tuberant forehead, and an abundance of equally black whiskers
partially smothered his jowled cheeks. He was chewing on a raw
onion, and Rosaleen could smell his breath from where she
stood.

'What do you want?' he demanded, surveying her through
small puffy eyes with an expression which made her glad she was

158

wearing nothing more elaborate than her red dress and Joseph shawl.

'You have a room –' she began timidly.

'Oh yes.' His attitude changed. 'Do come in, miss.'

She followed him inside to a small shadowy hallway where the wallpaper hung in shreds, and the tiled floor was chipped. The smell of his breath did not override the stale smell of urine.

'So you want a room?' His voice was surprisingly cultured.

She hesitated – stared at the peeling walls and dirty paintwork, sniffed the foul smells – and closed her eyes against it all for a second, before replying, 'Yes.'

'It's a basement room . . .' He watched her intently, and licked his teeth to clear the remnants of onion away. 'You're on your own?'

'Yes.'

'You're not up to anything irregular, are you?'

'No!' she answered indignantly.

'That's good . . . That's good,' he repeated in soothing tones and gave her a long look. She averted her eyes. 'I am on my own also. We shall see . . . We shall see.'

'How much were you wanting for the room?' Rosaleen enquired, not liking the turn of conversation.

'That's what I appreciate – a lady who comes right to the point. Though you're not quite a lady are you, if you know what I mean?' His look was sly.

She felt the heat burning her cheeks pink, and without a word turned to go.

'Wait!' He caught her by the arm. 'No offence meant. It's only my humour you see. You need a room. I have a room.'

'How much is it?' Rosaleen asked again.

'Say half a crown a week, and that's cheap as you will agree.'

'I should like to see it.'

He began to bluster: 'Well it isn't a palace, I mean what can you expect for a half-crown? And these days it is very hard to find a room. I should know. When I was on the stage and looking for accommodation –'

'I'd really like to see it.'

There was a small doorway in the hall and slippery stone steps led from it to the basement room. The door to it had warped and opened with difficulty. Within the room was twilight dark and what scant light there was filtered through a draughty prison-like window which revealed the pavement and the legs of passers-by. The room was pervaded by a dank odour and was little more than a hole in the ground, with minimal furnishings – a sagging bed, a lopsided table with pitcher and basin and a cracked toilet mirror upon it, and a small pine linen press with no doors. Beside the bed was a chamber pot. This too was chipped, and on the floor next to it was a kettle and burner. Cobwebs hung at the corners of the ceiling.

She wanted to flee this awful place and wash it from her body, to dip her face into a stream and splash the water over herself. She was not new to poverty or hard conditions, but where she came from one could escape it – one could open the door of the lowliest hovel and run free and inhale the air. At home the folk were scrupulously clean. This was squalor, and her skin felt tainted by the dirt, the damp and the grime of it all.

Rosaleen was besieged by doubts: what did she hope to achieve by staying in London? Certainly it was not this. So far she had proved only that she could not really survive on her own, that she was dependent on others for her comforts.

She thought of the lakes with unbearable yearning: 'I could go home now. There's nothing to stop me.' And she knew fleeting elation. Her feet were light.

'Where's your resolve, tiny lass?' Nana Annie's voice was shrill and taunting in her ear, and she knew she would not return home, defeated like this. Her sense of purpose was strengthened by the decision. Only she was responsible for her actions.

The man was shuffling his feet restlessly, his strong breath coming in sharp bursts.

'It's dreadful,' she told him firmly.

'I said it was not a palace.'

'I wouldn't put chickens in it.'

'It's cheap.'

'That it's not. It is not worth half what you are asking.'

'Look miss, this isn't a charity institution. Go find yourself a lodging house then if you want something cheap. Twopence a day is the rate, and no privacy.'

'So I must pay an extra shilling and fourpence for privacy? Or does the dirt cost extra?'

From what depths did her courage come to speak to him in this manner? For she was weary and forlorn, and defenceless too; a very small person alone with a disagreeable man, and apparently no one else about who would hear an incidental scream. She could not imagine that the feet walking past would even hesitate in their step.

'I admire your audacity, dear, I must say.' He drew himself up theatrically to his full height, and sleeked back his hair. Looking at her shrewdly he said, 'Perhaps we can strike a bargain between us. What say you to two shillings and twopence? And I shall have the room cleaned for you by this afternoon.'

'Thank you, but it's still too dear. Two shillings – and the room cleaned.'

'Payable in advance then . . .'

October was a gloomy month, and autumn was early – murky and thick, and wet underfoot. Its cold dampness permeated Rosaleen's cell, and her body never knew warmth.

They had an unspoken truce, she and her landlord. He did not bother her so long as she was in a position of strength, and she learned how to manage him and keep him at bay. But whenever he spoke to her it was with innuendo, and sometimes he would attempt to touch her – a finger would run down her spine or stroke her hair, an arm would encompass her waist – before she leaped back. She would face him without a word, and his hand would drop to his side and his eyes slide downwards like a scolded child.

He was forever chewing onions. He claimed they helped his catarrh and digestion, but Rosaleen doubted this because in the mornings she could hear him continually clearing his throat and spitting, followed by loud coughing; and then came the belching – explosions which reverberated through the floorboards. His corset could not have aided his digestion either. She saw him in it once, his flesh compressed into it like potted meat, the hairs of his chest sprouting above.

He had once been an actor, and now he peppered his sentences with pathetic reminders. 'When I was on stage . . .' he would say, or 'When I played Macbeth . . .', or 'The audience loved it when . . .' He blamed a weak heart for destroying a promising career, he told Rosaleen in a moment of confidence, and it was not for her to question his delusions.

Three doors down the road was a small shop which sold provisions and haberdashery, and whenever Rosaleen went in there the spinster who owned it narrowed her small lashless eyes and immediately busied herself. She believed Rosaleen was having an affair with the landlord – possibly it was he who had perpetrated this rumour – and soon others in the street stared with unfriendly expressions whenever she passed. At first Rosaleen had nodded and smiled to everyone, but their blank responses drove the smile from her face and she felt her spontaneity shrivel. She was aggrieved at their hostility, and pushed further into her depression.

'At the end of the day it is kindness and friendship which matter,' she thought. But no one bothered with her, and women brushed facelessly past with children clinging to their hips. What did they have to look forward to, she wondered, these poor disapproving people with their suspicions and their husbands who drank their earnings? What a dreary antagonistic place.

Rosaleen became thin. With only the kettle and burner she was restricted in what she could prepare in the way of food, and fruit was expensive. Money, or its lack, was a constant worry, and nowadays she walked all the way to her classes: from Battersea to Chelsea, from Battersea to Kensington, from Battersea to Victoria. She was used to walking.

No gold-rimmed invitations came her way now. Nobody knew where she was. Sometimes she thought of Tags with affection and without recrimination; often she thought of Frederick. She was too ashamed to contact any friends – indeed who were they? Her misfortune was hers alone.

Millais had become a friend. She sat for him regularly now that Rossetti was in Florence. He enquired where she lived.

'South of the river,' she answered vaguely.

'That is most obscure, Rosaleen! Whereabouts?'

'Battersea.'

He nodded and let the matter drop. She looked forward to going to Millais's, as after their sessions she was always given tea. She ate cut sandwiches and little cakes, and drank thirstily; it was a weekly reminder that civility existed. She returned to her room with her shrunken stomach replete.

Premature autumn made way for premature winter. It was early November and snow showers fell, before gales drove them away again. In the early mornings the roofs of Battersea were white with frost, and the inside of her rattling window was fringed with it. It was impossible to keep warm.

'Penny for the guy . . .'

'I don't have a penny . . .'

Who cared about her or wondered what had happened to the red-haired lass from up North who had invaded 'society' and then abruptly disappeared?

'Gone back to her pig farm,' she could imagine the Baroness von Hoffnung might jeer.

And those who were more avant-garde, belonging to the artistic circles or the intellectual set, who had found her a novelty and had welcomed her as such – perhaps they had been curious at first. 'Does she no longer come to any Evenings?' someone might ask.

'No, she appears to have disappeared from the face of the earth . . .'

And Tags, bored with his fiancée's bland face and fainting fits, drinking so as to forget his jaded ideals – did he miss her? She had been as ephemeral as a moth.

She existed. More than that could not be said. She cooked eggs in her kettle and ate bread dipped in dripping; she melted old candles together and used one of her dresses as a curtain to try and block the draught. She slept in her clothes and was still cold, and when she washed she had no way of drying herself properly. Water had to be fetched from a pump at the top of the street. There was a queue in the mornings and the women all talked amongst themselves and ignored her. It was absurd how she longed for their approval: a single generous-hearted smile, the slightest gesture of kindliness would have filled her with joy, and she felt utterly deprived of any feeling of caring. When her turn came to fill her pail, it seemed all eyes were upon her, pouring out animosity. Silently she concentrated on pumping out the cloudy brown water . . .

She knew she must extricate herself, but did not know how to set about it. With no money, where else besides a lodging house could she go? She began to understand how girls resorted to prostitution out of desperation, and in her mind she saw them in hopeful rows, her own face amongst them.

Above her, her landlord lived in comparative comfort and did not attempt to alleviate her hardship. Only in return for a 'favour' would he have lent an extra blanket or given her some candles, and Rosaleen could no longer hide her disgust of him. Occasionally he came downstairs to gloat over her discomfort; he could not forgive her for repelling his advances, and the only way he could take his revenge was by deprivation, and watching to see if her strength wavered.

'It would cost him nothing to make my life more agreeable,' she thought bitterly. 'But he wants to see me defeated in the hope I shall come begging. Well I'll not do that.'

Youths of Robbie's age played in the street. They formed groups, and sometimes would not let her pass. Linking arms to make a barricade, they would call out rudely or chant lewd rhymes, and she was intimidated by their combined physical power and ignorance, and by the latent violence in their expressions. Twice she had dodged quickly under the bridge of their arms and escaped, but she dreaded seeing them . . .

She was afraid to go out – to face the spinster in her shop where buying provisions was an ordeal, to queue at the pump, to confront the gang of youths . . . And she was loath to remain indoors, in her dank room underground.

Then at the beginning of December Millais told her he and

Effie were going away. As he spoke Rosaleen thought that her face must have visibly paled; but she wished them both a pleasant trip.

It was growing dark when she left. Kensington was animated and colourful and the wheels of carriages made a colossal sound on the cobbles. There was a festive feel in the air, and Rosaleen felt herself a wan little mouse, pallid amongst such liveliness. The words sang in her head: 'No fees from Millais, no fees from Millais . . . have an enjoyable trip . . . No fees from Millais.'

The following day she walked in Battersea Park for something to do. There was a fair, and the sounds of the hurdy-gurdy mingled with the noise of the crowds and the jolly playing of a band. She wandered about the stalls and side-shows and stroked the organ-grinder's monkey, then she stopped at the Punch and Judy show.

'Naughty Mr Punch,' cried the children in unison as Mr Punch whacked Judy over the head.

'Ain't no different from any other man,' a woman standing by Rosaleen observed. 'And them little boys watching'll soon learn the same habits.'

'. . . Have yer knives sharpened,' called the knife-grinder.

'. . . Muffins, fresh muffins.'

'. . . Chestnuts, pipin' hot ch-e-e-e-st-nuts.'

Once she would have enjoyed looking at everything, but now she was detached from it all, engulfed by heaviness. The day was milder than some that had preceded it, but the ground was still wet and penetrated the worn soles of her shoes. She began to shiver, and felt impounded by the noise about her.

She decided to return to her room, and on the way back was accosted by an old hag. Rosaleen had noticed her before, and realized she was trailing her.

'What a pretty pale little girl, what pretty hair.'

The woman reached her hand out from her ragged skirts to stroke her hair – and Rosaleen saw then the scissors in her hand and realized, horrified, her intention. She reacted quickly – jerking her arm away, so that the old woman fell backwards, her skirts billowing about her. The scissors flew to the ground.

'Bad things'll happen to you!' she called after Rosaleen as she fled. 'You wait an' see if they don't.'

Rosaleen ran back, her heart pumping fast, overcome by terror and hopelessness. Her despair was everyone else's – the beggar-woman who sold hair to survive; the gang of youths who only knew joy when they had a victim to taunt; the spinster in her shop; her landlord – and a million others.

She lay on her bed shivering and trying to breathe normally, and she fell asleep. She had a dream which for years after she recalled because of its vividness: it was of a small exotic bird with luminous green plumage. The bird had flown into a conservatory whose doors were slightly ajar, and having circled a couple of times it flew arrow-like through the gap. It then came in again and repeated its circuit, before flying out once more. This procedure happened again and again, the bird never missing the gap or flapping against the glass the way birds in a panic do. It always flew, wings pinned back and arrow-straight, through the gap in the doorway. During the dream Rosaleen knew a beautiful lightness of spirit, as though by toying with its freedom the bird communicated a message to her: that despite the obstacles in its path it was ultimately in control.

The next day she became ill. She could barely move and a cough racked her chest. She missed her class, and could only lie on her bed coughing, alternately sweating and shivering. She got up solely to use the chamber pot. She slept fitfully throughout the day. The following morning her landlord came to investigate. He knocked on the door, which she kept bolted for her protection.

'What is it?' she called, in between coughing.

'I wish to speak with you.'

'I'm ill. I'm lying in bed.'

'Well come and open the door. I don't know why you keep it bolted anyway. I wish to speak with you,' he said again.

She got up to undo the bolt, pulling her Joseph shawl closer about her in an effort to make herself decent and conceal the holes in her skimpy chemise and drawers.

'What's all this then?' he said, pushing his way in.

He was in his bullying mood. He assumed different moods to suit the occasion; it was the only chance of acting he had, Rosaleen realized.

'What's all this then?' he repeated, as usual chewing on an onion. 'You're behind with the rent you know.'

She had no strength to argue. 'I'll pay you next week I promise. I have no money this week.'

'I want it this week. We had an agreement.'

'But I *can't*.'

His breath made her feel nauseous and she leaned against the wall and was seized by a coughing fit. When it was over his mood had changed to one of concern; but his concern was as slimy as a slug's trail.

'You are ill, my dear.'

'I said I was.'

'You need warmth. You need looking after.'

She did not reply and sat on the edge of the bed, shivering, her eyes focusing and unfocusing on details – the lump on his left temple, the bulbous shape of his nose, the hairs in his nostrils – and then away again. He did not matter. She did not matter. Nothing mattered.

Outside she heard a voice call, 'Christmas soon. What cheer are they talking 'bout, I ask you?' Feet moved on, trudging slowly by.

Her landlord floated back into focus and Rosaleen noticed the red veins on his cheeks and the rim of grey hairline before the blue-black. He faded once more and she lay back and closed her eyes.

'The rent you owe me – we could forget about it, my dear. You could be warm, have medicine.' His voice was distant; barely a ripple intruding upon the privacy of her drowsiness.

'I'm tired . . .'

'You'll think about it? We could be happy. You could be warm . . .'

'Yes.'

The hand lingered and left her respectfully alone. 'You sleep now.'

He shut the door behind him. She did as she was bid and slept, awaking – how much later? – to raised voices.

'You can't go in there.'

'Oh but I can.'

'This is private property. My property. You have no right –'

There was a hiatus in the interchange for a few seconds, and then the landlord's voice: 'Well I suppose since you have been so generous you can go in. What do I mind?'

The door creaked as it opened and a man tiptoed inside. Rosaleen heard his steps and did not dare open her eyes for fear of disillusion. She felt the raging heat of her body and the sweat on her skin; was aware that her heart beat furiously – and held her breath as he came closer.

'Rosaleen. Dear girl – what pit have you got yourself into this time?'

At last she released her breath and opened her eyes to see Frederick. She clung to him, tears rushing down her cheeks to mingle with the bubbles from her nostrils, and he lifted her face and gently wiped it with her bright red handkerchief.

'Oh dear girl, what a place – *what* a place! Are you well enough to get up? I have a cab waiting outside.'

'My clothes, my belongings –'

'I shall return later to fetch then. Don't fret. Lean on me, dear girl . . . Oh Rosaleen, you are so *thin*, so ill, what has happened? No – don't answer. Just lean on me.'

When she left the landlord looked truly dejected. 'I never meant anything, you know,' he said in the hallway. 'I just hoped – well, with my appearance I could not think of another way.'

Rosaleen felt sudden pity for him, standing lost in his hallway with the tattered wallpaper and cracked floor. On an impulse she kissed his cheek – then, leaning heavily against Frederick, she allowed herself to be led away.

She was ill with severe bronchitis for the rest of the month, and for the first week and a half veered between reality and mild delirium. In the candy-striped bedroom Mrs MacDonald plumped her pillows, spoon-fed her with warm gruel, and sponged her face, whilst Frederick administered medicaments. She was conscious of day becoming night and then day again, but there was no form to them. Snow fell outside, and she would stare at its patterns on the window-panes before drifting into sleep once more. It was all she wanted to do. When she was awake there was in her a residue of sorrow she could not discard.

Frederick read her stories – fairy-tales by Hans Christian Andersen and the brothers Grimm. She lay there immersed in the plights of Thumbelina or the adventures of the Tin Soldier, soothed by the sight of Frederick sitting on the edge of the bed, and she regressed into a dependent and feeble child with no inclination to regain her strength, only to be cosseted and lulled by tender voices for ever.

But she did regain her strength, and with her recovery came curiosity.

'How did you find me?' she asked Frederick.

'It was not easy. Your brother wrote to me saying he was disturbed by the tone of your letters and did I know where you were since you had not kept him abreast of your whereabouts after parting with Tags – and did I not tell you that was doomed? However I shall not lecture you – Robbie knew little other than your landlord was a failed actor with dyed black hair and that you lived in sight of the gasworks. Which gasworks I had no idea! I thought you might still be sitting for Millais and so I enquired of him.

'"Battersea," he told me. "It was all she would reveal. Most suspicious I think; and she looks drawn and thin. But I could get nothing out of her."

'I rebuked him a little then, for not investigating further, and then embarked on a little detective work to find you.'

'How did you do that?'

'It took a couple of weeks. I asked around. Fortunately you are a distinctive-looking girl. I must have been down every street within visibility of the gasworks asking if anyone knew a man who let rooms who had been an actor and dyed his hair black, or if anyone had seen a beautiful, very diminutive girl with hair a golden red. I was led on wild-goose chases, but eventually was led to the right place. *What* a place. What people – so dreary.'

'I have not thanked you for your trouble. Thank you. Thank God for you.'

'Trouble!' He made an impatient gesture. 'I was *worried*, Rosaleen. Do not speak of trouble.'

'I –'

'I know what you are thinking – that you are in my debt, that you are again trapped. No worry – when you are fully recovered I shall help you find somewhere to live. Somewhere decent. Never let me see you living like that again. There was no need.'

'I had no money.'

'You had friends.'

'I could not ask them.'

'Did not Tags give you money?'

'I am certain he would have done, but I left without seeing him. I did not want anything from him.'

'Oh you silly girl – but now you will accept my help.'

'I shall repay you, Frederick.'

'I have no doubt, my dear.'

He seemed older, more serious. Rosaleen noticed a faint lingering tan to his complexion.

'Have you been travelling?'

'Yes. For over half a year. I returned a couple of months ago.'

'You were gone that long? On Edgar?'

'No, oh no!' He laughed loudly, which cheered her. 'Even Edgar could not make Greece and Egypt!'

'So far? What were you doing?'

'Exploring, observing, listening – and digging. I dabbled in a little archaeology which was amusing; unearthed the occasional stone which had once been a part of someone's drawing-room! I had a flirtation with the Sphinx, was suitably awed by the Pyramids and stunned by the Nile, and then I thought it time I came home.'

'Why were you gone so long?'

'Why not? I had no ties here,' he answered sharply.

She nodded and covered his hand with hers.

Something troubled her which she needed to confide to him. It preyed upon her mind. 'I'd have lain with him you know, Frederick. I was that disheartened I would have succumbed to him and lain with him. And I'd have ended up on the streets. Why not, when you think of it? I would have debased myself with him – why not with others? It would have been easy.'

'Do not talk of it.'

'But that is how it happens.'

'But it did *not*.'

'But it could have. And I must face it, and myself knowing it.'

He reflected a moment: 'Then face it. Face it squarely – and then leave it behind for good.'

In January of that new year, 1875, Frederick found her lodgings: a furnished apartment on the ground floor of a pretty house in Holland Street, off Kensington Church Street.

Rosaleen said to him, 'All I do is take from you.'

'I do not see it like that.'

'Well I do. One day I hope I can do something for you.'

'You could marry me.'

'Oh Frederick! . . . Of course you're teasing.'

'Of course. And I do so miss your "aw"s.'

Ever conscientious he remained in London long enough to see her settled in, and as she had used to, she accompanied him to social events. People said, 'Where have you been? We missed seeing you . . .'

At a restaurant in Mayfair they met the Baroness von Hoffnung. Surrounded by friends, she remarked, 'So you have crawled back – and had elocution lessons by the sound of it. However, an expert can always tell a false gem.'

'It takes no expert', Rosaleen retorted, 'to see that you are one.'

The Baroness would have slapped her had not Frederick caught her hand and reprimanded her quietly, 'Enough, Leonora.'

There were tears of humiliation in her eyes. 'I have had sufficient from this little trollop,' she said furiously. 'I thought,

Frederick, that you had come to your senses. Oh I promise I shall get my own back . . .'

'I took her out for dinner a couple of times recently,' Frederick confessed later. 'I don't know what possessed me.'

'She is still in love with you.'

'She is in love only with herself, Rosaleen.'

'Well I suppose that is better than being in love with no one!'

They both laughed, and forgot the incident.

Rosaleen started modelling again, re-establishing contact with the artistic circle in which she had previously mixed. However, even as she enjoyed the renewed comfort and privilege of her life, there was always at the back of her mind the thought that left to her own devices she would be living in degradation.

'Bury that memory,' Frederick said.

'I cannot. I am constantly aware that I have not managed on my own.'

'Nobody does. You will always find that along the route someone has offered assistance, however slight.'

Frederick departed on one of his trips, leaving Rosaleen with sufficient money, and she wrote to Robbie at John Ruskin's. In reply to her letter some goods were delivered to her address a couple of weeks later: her loom, her spinning wheel and several bags of fleece.

How nostalgic she felt when she saw the loom and spinning wheel! How the memories came flooding back – and her father's initials and her name still boldly carved there. Suddenly she longed to see them again – Thomas and Nana Annie and Robbie. She thirsted for her countryside, to watch low cloud break up unexpectedly and witness the revelation of a crag bathed in ochre, as though it were the sun itself.

She plunged her hands into a bag of soft fleece and remembered.

So she set up her little business as she had long ago, when she was a twelve-year-old child. In her spacious bedroom she spun the fleece and soaked the yarn overnight in different vessels filled with dyes. Then she wove the uneven colours and finally fashioned the fabric into shawls. Joseph shawls. It did not take long before she had a little industry going. Her landlady was her first customer, and then friends of hers, and friends of theirs. Jane Morris bought two, and soon all the other women from the same circle were placing orders. Rosaleen could hardly make the shawls quickly enough, and was continually writing to Robbie for more fleece. When Frederick returned she was proudly able to pay him three guineas, and retain a little money for herself.

In June she sent Robbie a silk cravat for his birthday, and he wrote to thank her – and told her that the previous month Rose La Touche had died.

> . . . Mr Ruskin saw her for the last time in February. Now she is dead. Laurie said her mind had gone. It was he who told me the news, to explain the Professor's mood of silence. Rosaleen, I have never seen a man so morose. In between bouts of reading he stares out of the window with a tragic expression in his eyes, and his lips moving in silent conversation. Even Mrs Severn seems unable to revive him, although last night she mentioned that he was fractionally better and was showing a renewed interest in his religious books. He is so very fine a man, Ros'leen, and I am certainly fortunate to work for him – he reads my poems and is always candid in his views. I could weep for his grief . . .

Summer 1875 was memorable. At last Rosaleen felt some pride in herself; that she was able to earn a living – albeit a moderate one – without enlisting help. She was beholden to nobody.

She thought: 'It was Father who taught me one cannot be secure in security provided by another. I shall provide it for myself from now.'

'. . . Rosaleen – dance with me.'
'. . . Rosaleen – let me paint you.'
'. . . Miss Ruddock, what is your opinion of Darwin's theories?'

She was fêted; danced into the night – and returned on her

own. She felt ready to go home for a few days, to announce herself: 'Here I am, Father. It has been so long, can we not forgive one another? Once you took me to school in the cart and I'd bounce up and down on the feed sacks . . . You'd take me in the gondola . . . You called me your little darlin' – do you recall that? . . . Nana Annie – it's your tiny lass back . . .'

But she did not return, because that summer Frederick introduced her to Kate Hardwick.

❧ Ten ❧

A BROTHER AND SISTER

*We strive to reach the golden plane of love
As though it is the cure for life's every inconsistency.*

It was a fine August day, and in the courtyard of Frederick's
house he sat with Rosaleen having lunch. From the stable came
the sound of Edgar snorting down his nostrils and then moving
about, and there was a slight breeze blowing gusts of warmth,
carrying with them the faint smell of horse.

Rosaleen stretched out her legs which were bare of shoes and
stockings. There was a tranquil, rather dreamy expression on her
face; the mixed odours in the air were redolent of home. 'I
thought about returning to the lakes for a few days,' she said.

'What a good idea – but before you do there is someone very
special I should like you to meet.'

Rosaleen was immediately interested, thinking that at last
Frederick had found himself a lady friend. She smiled knowingly. 'Who is that?'

'Hah!' he pounced. 'I see by your expression you have come to
the wrong conclusion! Although once I did fancy I was a little in
love with her . . . No, this is a distant cousin of mine by the name
of Kate Hardwick. She is about twenty-five years old and I think
you will get along famously. I shall introduce you.'

'You have not mentioned her before.'

'She and her brother live in St Ives in Cornwall. It was them I
was visiting whilst Tags was busy luring you away.'

'Frederick, I prefer not to discuss that.'

'No – but incidentally I heard he was married a fortnight ago
. . . That is by-the-by. Kate and her brother Oliver are in

175

London, living like lords for a month in a distant uncle's Belgravia mansion whilst Oliver is exhibiting some pictures. He is an artist . . . More than that I shall not tell you. I shall let Kate tell you herself.'

'Why do you think we will get on well?'

'Because I know you both – a little anyway, before you glare at me for my presumption.'

'So Tags married,' Rosaleen mused. She thought: 'I was good enough to be his mistress, if not his wife, but not good enough even to warrant an invitation . . .' A small sigh escaped her.

'Are you jealous?'

'No, truthfully not that.' She tilted the parasol so that it shaded her a little more from the sun, and they were quiet for a few moments – the easy quiet of companionship. Then Rosaleen recalled a remark Frederick had once made.

'Frederick – ages ago you told me you had regrets. What are they?'

He looked astonished, then smiled dismissively. 'I fear I was being melodramatic, my dear.'

'I fear you were not, Frederick!'

He gave a delighted laugh and clapped his hands together. 'Please tell me.'

'My goodness, you are in an insistent mood. Regrets . . .' His tone became serious. 'I regret my lack of courage; I regret that I toy with ideas and ideals without carrying them through; I regret that I can only enjoy the state of genius vicariously; I regret that I did not become a surgeon; I regret my self-imposed bachelorhood; I regret the poor in this country and do nothing about it; I regret I was a bad son and did not see my mother before she died . . . And yet I pass for an honourable man, which I surely cannot be! There you have it. And there are others, to be buried safely from surface thought. Like that one can pass for happy – most of the time.'

His face was gloomy, and after waiting a few suitable seconds, Rosaleen said, 'Out of the whole lot I have sifted out only two which can be taken seriously.'

'And what are they?' His eyes brightened.

'That you did not become a surgeon, and that you did not see your mother before she died. The one is surely not too late to rectify. The other is sad. But you did not know she would die.'

'Oh wise lass. But before you are too stern – as you remember, I did not wish to divulge my regrets in the first place. You dragged them from me, and now I am rebuked for airing matters I should have preferred not to. That, if you do not mind me saying so, is a typically female trait. Enough. We will have a post-lunch cognac to celebrate.'

'What are we celebrating?'

'My bachelorhood, which I have after all decided is a worthy state.' He poured them each a brandy, and went over to the hammock and sat down. He patted the cushion beside him. 'Come.'

They sat together letting the hammock roll to and fro of its own accord. Rosaleen felt pleasantly muzzy. 'Frederick, will you play the flute for me?'

He regarded her affectionately. 'How demanding you are today. However – yes I shall.' He took it from his pocket, polished the mouthpiece on his sleeve, and put it to his lips. The reedy sounds combined with those other summer sounds around them.

Two days later he visited her accompanied by a young woman. 'Rosaleen – this is Kate Hardwick. Kate, this is Rosaleen Ruddock.' So saying, he left them.

'He really is a strange man at times,' Rosaleen commented, staring at the doorway of her sitting-room as though he might reappear.

'There he goes on Edgar,' said Kate, her nose pressed to the tall sash window. Her voice was softly Cornish.

Turning, they faced one another simultaneously and smiled, assessing each other in a swift embracing gaze: Kate tall, thin, with mousy-colouring, given to lavish gestures with her long-fingered hands. In the high-cheekboned gauntness of her face it was her eyes one noticed, not for any particular beauty in shade or shape, but for a steadiness in their expression, a light that came from within her.

177

Kate's first impression of Rosaleen was no different to everyone else's: she saw a small exquisite creature; but she sensed also those qualities which contributed to Rosaleen's character: inner fortitude, directness and perception.

Kate was the first to drop her eyes and speak. 'I hope I am not intruding . . .' She gesticulated with a sweeping action of her hands around the room, which was in its usual disarray with shawls draped everywhere.

Rosaleen laughed her gruff laugh. 'You most certainly are not. The place is always like this. I leave the shawls out as a kind of display. I make them and sell them.'

'Frederick told me. You are talented.'

'Oh no. They're not hard to do. Sit down, Miss —'

'Kate. You must call me Kate of course.'

'And you must call me Rosaleen. I detest my surname anyway.'

'Why?' Kate asked, edging herself on to a settee.

'Because it makes me think of coarse-skinned farmers' wives.' She lit the wick of the burner for the tea kettle and rested the kettle on top.

'But farmers' wives always conjure up such jolly images, don't you think?' Kate asked.

'The ones I know are overworked and exhausted,' Rosaleen stated. 'They have callused hands and harsh voices.'

'You're from up North?'

'From Lancashire. A small lakeland area not many have heard of.'

'But I have.'

'Frederick told you?'

'Yes. And my brother Oliver visited there once to paint. He told me of its beauty.'

'Yes it is beautiful. And you are from Cornwall . . . How funny: I am from one of the northernmost points and you from the southern, and now we have met.'

'And will become friends, I know,' Kate said, a little shyly.

Rosaleen confided, 'I have never had a friend before.' She poured out the tea carefully and passed the cup to her guest.

'Why is that?'

Why was it? She reflected that as a child there had been no need; as a girl no time; as a young woman the opportunity had not arisen. She explained this to Kate.

The other nodded in understanding. 'I have not had a friend for a long time either,' she told Rosaleen. 'My mother died when I was fourteen –'

'Why that is when my mother died too,' Rosaleen interrupted.

Kate smiled gently, her teeth white and even. She continued, 'We lived in Penzance – my father was a doctor – and I was brought up by a governess. My brother was living away from home studying art. He is twelve years my senior. I had a few friends up till then, but it is interesting how outsiders cannot cope with the embarrassment of bereavement. People do not know what to say, how to react; it is easier not to have to trouble themselves, is it not? And then of course they are filled with guilt at their selfishness and so strive to avoid that very person who stirs all these feelings . . . So my friends dwindled, and the one who at least made a semblance of effort died shortly after. But there was my dear father to comfort, who was suddenly and through no fault of his own as friendless as I . . . I turned inwards. I wrote poetry, stories –'

'My brother Robbie writes poetry, although he is very young yet. Do you write poetry now?'

'A little. But mostly articles and books. I am a writer. In a very small way,' she added with a dismissive laugh.

'But that is so interesting.'

'It is certainly better than wasting all day at needlepoint and gossip!'

'Oh I am so pleased you think as I do. So few women do.'

'Women are not expected to think, that is the problem. But I believe there must be many women dissatisfied with their lives. It's only that they can do nothing about it, and have to accept their circumstances.'

'It is unjust. I have often thought about these issues.'

'What is just?' Kate sighed. 'We all subjugate ourselves to something or someone.'

'We, meaning women?'

'Definitely women more than men. Most definitely women subjugate themselves to the demands of men. But increasingly nowadays men subjugate themselves to ambition. At least women do not have to do that.'

'I should prefer it,' Rosaleen said.

'Would you really? You are braver than me then.'

'I should rather remain on my own than lose that self which is me, to any man. At least ambition would be my own and therefore within my control.'

'I doubt it. It seems to be the other way round often.'

They fell silent, thoughtful. Then Rosaleen said, 'I interrupted you earlier. You were telling me about when your father died – how you turned to writing.'

'Oh dear, I was not intending to relay my life-story – only to explain why I had no friends!' Her fingers fiddled with her fine hair which had loosened from its knot at the base of her neck.

'But I am *interested*,' Rosaleen assured her, leaning forward and touching Kate's arm, feeling the thinness of it through the fine muslin of her sleeve.

'Very well, you have persuaded me. When I was eighteen my father died. Oliver inherited the house and he became my guardian. I love and respect my brother – but he is very jealous and dominating. He sold the house without consulting me and announced that we were going to live in France for six months. The trouble was I had a suitor at the time.'

Rosaleen was appalled. 'So what did you do?'

'It was a problem,' Kate said placidly. 'Oliver told me – rightly – that I could not be by myself in Penzance for six months, and that my suitor – his name was Claudius, an odd name, but his father is a Latin scholar – would wait for me.'

'Did you protest?'

'A little. But he is a hard man to argue with. You will meet him, I hope. And of course I was flattered in a way to accompany him – I had always so idolized him. He made it sound exciting and I succumbed. Well I had no option, for otherwise he would have been disagreeable.'

'I don't think I care for your brother.'

'But you *would*. You will meet him and see. It is only he is so demanding in his love, and when he makes plans he is carried away like a child with enthusiasm and cannot bear dissent. This was to him a little adventure . . . So we went to France for six months. We rented a house in the hills near Marseilles and he painted and I began my first novel; it was idyllic in a way and we became extremely close. I grew to understand him so well, to know that — yes — he is a difficult man, more than I had ever suspected, but to care for him despite it. I looked after him, after the house. We had no maid . . . I wrote to Claudius. Perhaps he resented my ability to live without him, or my praise for my brother. Perhaps I was becoming too much of a Bohemian. I told him I wore an old skirt and bare feet and that my legs were tanned brown; perhaps he envisaged a peasant woman . . . His letters became fewer and stopped. And then after almost five months came a single short note: breaking off our engagement and announcing his intention to marry someone else.' She shrugged. 'One is philosophical about these things. If he did not want me, I certainly did not want him.

'Oliver bought a cottage in St Ives, which is a fishing village near Penzance. It was a fisherman's hovel, but we have decorated it and have lived there together since. I have no close friends really — I have little in common with the other women, but Oliver lives with a French girl named Marie, whom I tolerate rather than like, and there are a few other writers and artists who have chosen to live in that area for its beauty. But they are mostly men and form a "clique" with Oliver. There is one couple with whom we are close — Colin and Talwyn. He is an artist and Oliver's greatest friend, and Talwyn . . . She is his mistress and is extraordinarily beautiful, but she is subnormal.'

'What do you mean? To what extent is she subnormal?'

'She is wonderful and loving and sweet, but has the ways of a small child. And she has the terrible fears and phobias and obsessions of a child also. Occasionally they manifest themselves in rages — but not often.'

181

'But how can Colin tolerate this? If he is a normal intelligent man, what can he find in common with her mentally?'

'Colin is certainly clever and normal. But he is a very strange man – an idealist, a Romantic, a "seeker of truth and purity", to quote himself. In Talwyn – which incidentally means "Fair one", he sees truth and purity in her insanity. He sees it as the most basic and essential honesty, untarnished by the regulations we have imposed upon ourselves as normal adults. Whatever his strange thinking, he loves her wholeheartedly, and cares for her devotedly . . . And now I have spoken enough. Will you tell me about yourself? I am only so glad Frederick brought us together.'

Much later they stood together in Kensington Church Street waiting for a cab. The rain was heavy and neither girl had an umbrella.

'When shall I see you?' Rosaleen asked, suddenly desolate.

'Tomorrow morning?' Kate called as the cab moved off with a clatter.

Her hand could be seen, a dark outline waving . . . Rosaleen walked back slowly, glancing up now and then to reciprocate a 'hello', or to nod to a passer-by whom she knew; somebody turning into a shop or a house or into the tavern.

Back in her own place once more she sat in the rocking chair by the French doors which looked on to the tiny square of garden. There were lupins in bloom and in a vase on a small occasional table. A few petals were scattered on the wood, and a drop of water – fat and wobbling slightly – on the waxed surface.

'I shall make my next batch of shawls in the colours of summer flowers. I'll give one to Kate . . .' Rock, rock, rock. The mirror on the wall caught the light curtains and the windows dotted with rain; it caught the still-life painting and the table with the lupins; it caught Rosaleen in her chair, rocking – captured the peacefulness in her face.

'I didn't know how I longed for a friend, another woman to speak to,' she thought. 'To know someone thinks the same, to feel the tenderness of friendship, is beautiful. I have missed it, without realizing.' She remembered that she had intended to go home, remembered her imagined conversations. She jettisoned those thoughts now, deferring them yet again. Family must make way for a friend.

They saw each other on three consecutive days, and on the third day Kate invited Rosaleen to visit where she was staying.

'Come and dine with us this evening. We are staying in this palatial establishment belonging to some great uncle we barely know. The walls are smothered with the heads of poor dead beasts of every description. It is desperately cold so we make fires even though it is summer. You will meet Oliver.'

Rosaleen was apprehensive as she stood outside the large house with its fine proportions and shuttered windows. She realized she would be viewing her friend in a new context, and dreaded that they might feel strained in another environment and with the presence of other people. She was so unused to having a friend, so afraid of losing her . . .

A maid opened the door and Rosaleen followed her into a big room – a library – where three people were caught in different poses, their faces turned, expectant: Kate, wearing a severe blouse and black skirt, with her back to the fire warming herself; her brother, barely visible and slumped in a low chair with one leg draped over its arm; a girl perched prettily on the other arm.

For a fraction of a second that is how Rosaleen observed them, and then the three stood to attention and Kate came over and gracefully kissed her cheek before introducing her. Rosaleen saw in her friend's eyes the same tension she felt, and glad of it, squeezed her arm.

The other two made no move. They stood beside each other, almost at the far end of the room, aloof, waiting for Rosaleen and Kate to come to them. Rosaleen noticed the way the girl glanced a couple of times at her lover for guidance. Over the fireplace was a mounted stag's head and on the floor a tiger skin, positioned so that it appeared to be about to devour their feet. Kate's brother stood just aside from the tiger's head, a tall and wide-shouldered man with a shock of prematurely grey hair brushed back from a fine broad forehead. His tanned face was strong and sensuous and except for a clipped dark moustache was clean-shaven.

Rosaleen, about to shake hands, tripped over the tiger's head.

'Its teeth will devour you. You must be careful.'

'I knew his voice would be deep,' she thought, flustered by his penetrating eyes.

'And this is Marie.'

Marie – fair and blue-eyed – attempted a smile. She looked away from Rosaleen almost immediately and back to her lover, linking her arm through his and giving a needless little trill of laughter. It peeled in the air and stopped. Rosaleen noticed Oliver pull his arm away and saw the little intake of breath from Marie . . .

They went into the dining-room for dinner, a little female-dominated quartet clustered around one end of the enormous table. A butler poured wine into the silver goblets, and as he did so Marie gave another little trill. Rosaleen saw Oliver glare at her. Kate was wearing what Rosaleen now recognized as her 'wryly amused expression'. When the maid had served them with food and left, and the butler had disappeared, Kate said to her brother, 'Oliver – you must admit it's funny.'

'What is?'

'Oh come now, dear,' she chided him lovingly. 'Us – with all these servants and living like royalty, when in St Ives we are pure Bohemians.'

'It is a good show here,' he admitted.

'I promise my brother is not always so stuffy and formal,' Kate told Rosaleen gaily, her cheeks flushed from tension and alcohol.

He ignored her. 'I daresay you are used to servants,' he said rather sarcastically to Rosaleen.

'Surely you can tell by my accent that is not the case,' she replied. 'In fact I *was* a servant.' She held her work-worn hands defiantly before her and he stared at them without a word.

'Lotions, *ma chérie*,' offered Marie brightly. 'You must rub the lotions on them.'

'Nothing works,' Rosaleen told her.

'I shall not sit at the table and talk about lotions,' Oliver said rudely.

'Well what will you then?' Rosaleen burst out.

'Oh dear . . .' murmured Kate, appealing to both of them with her eyes.

'Rosaleen, would you like some more wine?' Oliver asked, suddenly civil.

'Yes please.'

'And how did you come to be a servant?'

'I was born to it. Lowly, humble . . .'

'I was not mocking this time.'

'Neither was I.'

Kate interceded. 'Rosaleen is from Coniston in the Lake District, dear —'

'I know that. It is the one thing you told me. But it does not explain —'

'I saw no need to give you Rosaleen's life history before you accepted her in this house — which is not ours,' she added by way of rebuke.

'No of course not. I would not expect you to. I was merely being polite and expressing interest —'

'I shall furnish you with the details of my life, Oliver,' Rosaleen said sharply. Her fists were clenched on her lap. 'My father is an illiterate innkeeper, and when my mother died I took over all the duties. I helped look after the inn, my father, my brother, my Nana, the chickens, the pigs, the well, the kitchen, the cleaning, the cooking. He could afford extra help but wouldn't hire anyone because he had me. I loved to learn and to read and he tried to prevent me because he feared that too much knowledge would be bad for me. I loved my father but I began to resent him . . . And then I met Frederick — he stopped by the inn — and he introduced me to John Ruskin —'

'John *Ruskin* —'

'Hush Oliver,' Kate reprimanded him.

'— for whom my younger brother now works. Through John Ruskin I became interested in art . . .' She paused, aware of everybody's gaze upon her, but more particularly of Oliver's.

185

She calmed down, wiped her eyes roughly and found her eyelashes spiked with unshed tears. She began to speak again quietly. 'He showed me books, pictures, objects. We talked for many hours about many topics and all my restlessness disappeared when I was with him. I saw then that it was caused by the limitations of my life, and understood how much more existed that I *wanted* to experience. I longed to become involved in the world of art . . . so when Ruskin introduced me to Edward Burne-Jones, I came to London, to Fulham, as a servant in his house and then became a model for him and later Rossetti and Millais. I left Burne-Jones and – other things happened – and eventually with Frederick's help, I rented my apartment from where I now run a tiny business making Joseph shawls.'

'Making what?'

'Like I wear round my hips.'

'You *made* that?'

'Yes.'

'I told you Rosaleen made shawls, Oliver.'

'But not like that. That is art.'

Rosaleen laughed then.

'Why are you laughing?' Oliver asked.

'Because Frederick said that the very first time I met him. He tried to explain the meaning of art to me and used my shawl as an analogy. I laughed at him then too.'

'You have had an interesting life, Rosaleen.' Oliver sounded formal once more.

She shrugged. 'I have not thought of it like that. Most of it seemed full of drudgery and little else to tell the truth. And the last two years – well there is nothing clever in modelling is there? Now to do a painting is another thing. To commit one's skills to canvas or paper – that is admirable.'

'How would you define art, Rosaleen?'

She thought quickly. 'I think art must be the refinement of self-expression.' She regarded him steadily and he returned her look with narrowed eyes.

'I like that definition,' he said softly and continued to hold her gaze.

After dinner, back in the library, Rosaleen handed Kate the parcel she had brought with her.

'For *me*?' Kate asked. Rosaleen nodded.

The others watched as she unpicked the wrapping. There was a subtle change in the room now; Marie no longer sat close to Oliver. She was huddled uncertainly by the fire, whilst he was on the arm of the chair where she had previously sat. In the chair now was Rosaleen. Kate, sitting on a footstool, bridged the space between the chair and the fireplace.

She held up the shawl, with its delicate summer colours, and draped it around her head and shoulders. 'It is beautiful, dearest. Thank you.' She went over to her friend and hugged her.

Oliver watched them thoughtfully. He called across to Marie, 'You look very gloomy.'

'No, no I am happy,' – she said 'appee' – and gave one of her ripples of laughter.

Oliver accompanied Rosaleen home in a hired cab. When Kate suggested she come too he said, 'It is a cool evening' (which was untrue), 'and it is late. You will be tired. No, my dear, it is best I go on my own.'

'Shall I see you tomorrow, Rosaleen?' Kate said in the doorway.

'Yes. In the morning, before my sitting.'

In the carriage Rosaleen was conscious of Oliver's proximity – his warmth beside hers, his strength, his breathing, the slight smell of brandy on his breath. They were both silent until they approached the borders of Kensington.

'I wonder what he is thinking. He seems so forbidding . . . maybe that is his way. Kate says his views are rigid. Well I do not like that. I do not like the way he orders people. And Kate *does* subjugate herself to him. I shall say something.'

'Rosaleen –'

'Oliver –'

They both laughed self-consciously. 'You first,' he said.

'Dare I now?' she thought. That little self-conscious laugh had made so much difference. 'But the essence of things has not changed . . .'

187

'You are a long time,' he teased her. His voice was tender and his closeness tormented her. She thought he moved his arm fractionally towards hers.

'I – I – was going to ask why you must order people about so? Do you believe it is your prerogative to be autocratic? I was wondering why you feel it necessary to be condescending, even to your sister.'

He moved away and she felt a small constriction of sorrow within her.

'And you feel it *your* prerogative to judge me?' he answered. His voice, like his sister's, had a Cornish burr. He continued coldly, 'I think, if you ask Kate, you will find she answers she is happy. I suggest that before you set yourself up as a critic you make a lengthier study.'

'I have no need,' she said shortly. And they lapsed once more into silence, with a space of air between their bodies.

She remembered that he had been going to say something and that there had been warmth in his tone; remembered the slight pressure of his arm, the inclining of his head. She thought perhaps now she would lose Kate as a friend – would lose her anyway, she realized, when she returned to Cornwall. She shivered involuntarily.

'Are you cold?' Oliver asked.

'No,' she answered, wondering – was there an inflection of concern in his tone? – turning the three little words about in her head, adding different emphasis to each. Was his arm marginally nearer hers again and his head just the tiniest bit closer . . . ?

And then they arrived.

'Thank you. For your hospitality. For accompanying me.'

'It was a pleasure.'

Was he about to kiss her hand when she moved away shyly? Briefly her eyes acknowledged his in that awkward instant after she had retreated from him, and then he was gone.

She lay awake for most of the night, bothered, listless and dissatisfied – with herself, with Oliver, and with the evening in general.

The following morning Kate visited her, wearing her Joseph

shawl. They breakfasted together in the little garden.

'I was concerned you wouldn't come,' Rosaleen said.

Kate looked mystified. 'Why ever not, dearest?'

Rosaleen, already realizing her mistake, said dismally, 'I thought Oliver would prevent you.'

'But Rosaleen, you have got him wrong. He would not prevent me doing something important to me. He cares for me. It is only in minor issues he is dogmatic. In matters which involve my well-being he consults me.'

'And Claudius?'

'That was a long time ago,' Kate said. 'And he proved right, did he not? I could not be on my own at eighteen, and Claudius did not wait. He did not wait because of me, not because of Oliver. Dearest, Oliver has many faults of which I am aware – he is arrogant, overbearing, convinced always of his own rightness. The list goes on. But he would not knowingly deprive someone he loved of anything valuable to that person. I assure you his list of virtues at least balances his faults. And he is a good artist. Well I think he is, although I confess I am no expert. And you cannot imagine the encouragement he has given me in my writing.'

'You have not spoken of your writing to me.'

'There is not much to tell. And certainly not this minute for I have much other news!'

'What – since last night?'

'Especially since last night.'

Rosaleen poured some more coffee for each of them, and sipped from her cup. The sun was warm on their faces and cast foreshortened shadows on the ground so that they lay, dark and stunted. In the distance was the Kensington traffic. Nearer a single blackbird chortled energetically. The sounds were all abbreviated and separate from one another.

Kate said, 'We did not sleep a wink last night. Marie and Oliver quarrelled and continued to do so during the night and into this morning, when Marie finally left. I cannot say I blame her, although she began the quarrel. And although I always felt she was a silly girl there was some truth in what she said.'

'What *did* she say?'

'She accused Oliver of flirting with you. As soon as he returned she launched into one of her Gallic attacks, as Oliver refers to them.'

'Flirting with *me*? But nothing could be further from the truth. Your brother despises me.'

'Oh no, there you are wrong. I know my brother. Oliver's defences were fully engaged last night – why? Because he feared himself. He is his own worst enemy and that enemy is quite awesome.'

'But what did he fear?'

'Oh dearest, if you forgive me for saying it, you are being rather sightless. He feared his attraction to you. First he was prepared to resent you because any friend of mine would have to pass the test of approval as it were – is she good enough for my sister? – but this time it went beyond that. This time he had not reckoned with his own susceptibility. Marie immediately spotted the change in him, and as I said, although she began the quarrel, she was right in her reasoning. Oh Rosaleen – your face! I have never seen such amazement in anyone's face!'

'I think I am a little naïve,' Rosaleen smiled.

'May I tell you what you are?' Kate asked, waiting for Rosaleen's assent. 'I think you are not naïve, but you are unconcerned by your beauty and expect other people to be similarly unimpressed.'

It was of course true. But although she had no desire to exploit people by utilizing her obvious assets, her effect on others was the same as had she deliberately planned her tactics. She who admired talent and ability and the rewards of learning, herself attracted others in a way more befitting the frivolous Marie.

'I shall not continue with my modelling,' she thought. 'That in itself is vain. It was a means to an end, that is all. I shall find different ways in which to involve myself with art. I shall not be regarded as a "fairling".'

'Rosaleen, have I angered you?'

'No, I was thinking. What you said is true. And I do not like it, Kate.'

'But why? You are so fortunate. I am so plain in comparison.'

'You are not plain,' Rosaleen assured her stoutly.

'Whether I am or not is incidental. I have reconciled myself to my appearance, and you must also, Rosaleen – to the other extreme.'

'But I have done! I never even think about it.'

'That is the problem. You must think about it, and accept that because of the way you look you will always be singled out.'

'Oh Kate –'

'Yes dear?'

'Nothing. You have not finished telling me about Marie and Oliver.'

'Oh my goodness! Well, they accused each other of many things, some true, some fabricated, but meanwhile they were wading deeper into a mire. Then this morning, after several plates had been thrown and broken by Marie, Oliver told her that he was attracted to you and that she, Marie, was inconsequential to him.'

'But that was cruel.'

'Yes, it was true. He had been tiring of her for a long time and could not bring himself to hurt her. She provided him with the opening. However, it is harsh on her, and if I sound uncaring, it is only that I confess I was never very enamoured of her in the first place. Anyway she has left. She will return to Paris where her parents have a small *pension*.'

'They will accept her back, knowing of the life she led?'

'Oh she never told them the truth. Most certainly they would have disapproved. So dearest, that is the little saga. And my brother wishes to know what you think of him, before he approaches you. You see how uncertain he is of himself in reality!'

Rosaleen considered everything Kate had said. She thought of the cab journey the previous evening, the burning proximity of their bodies, their simultaneous 'Rosaleen –' 'Oliver –' followed by that self-conscious laugh. What had he been going to say? She thought of his immense body and imagined snuggling against it;

of the thick silver hair brushed back from his face, and the steady grey eyes – like Kate's, she realized now . . .

'Tell him . . . It is the same for me,' she said.

She sat nervously in her sitting-room waiting for him to arrive, imagining him in that room, his bulk filling one of the chairs. The grandfather clock in the corner of the room recorded his tardiness. Its ticking became infuriating to her, and she was first angry and then despondent. Then he arrived – breathless, his cravat askew.

'I apologize. You will think it was deliberate – I assure you it was not.'

'He is straightaway defensive,' Rosaleen observed. 'I see now what Kate means.'

'Sit down, please make yourself comfortable,' she told him, prepared now to be magnanimous. 'Your lateness doesn't matter.'

He stopped pacing, turning to her suddenly, and she was reminded of a proud stag. 'Frederick arrived as I was about to set off. He is so likeable I could not be curt. We talked for a while. It seems he has been dabbling recently in politics –'

'He has kept very quiet about it! I didn't think he was interested by politics.'

'He refers to his involvement as "non-political political interest"!'

'Oh that is a *typically* Frederick remark.'

'We spoke for a while. Then I explained I had to leave, and he enquired where I was going. I told him. "I see," he said in the most ominous tone, as though I had no right to call upon you . . . So here I am – and I should like to take you out for dinner if you will join me. I've a cab waiting outside.'

They went to the recently extended St James's Restaurant, which formed part of the famous concert hall and was situated in Piccadilly. A waiter showed them to their table. Rosaleen, walking beside Oliver, felt tinier than ever and she gave a small laugh.

'What is it?'

'I feel I have disappeared next to you! You are particularly tall and I am particularly small.'

'I am six foot three, I think.'

'And I am just five foot. How silly we must look together! No wonder people are staring.'

'They are staring because you are surely the loveliest creature they have seen. They are staring at your hair and eyes and your perfect body, and at the way the cream silk of your dress enhances your ivory skin.'

'Hush Oliver, you are speaking so loudly!'

'And I give not a damn.'

'Your table, sir,' said the waiter, whose ears had become red. He held the chair for Rosaleen and she slid into it.

'There is not a man here who does not wish you were his mistress,' Oliver continued unabashed and grinning almightily, whilst the waiter smoothed the napkin on to Rosaleen's lap, the back of his neck growing pink. Having settled them with menus and taken their orders for aperitifs he walked off as quickly as was polite.

'Oliver, for whose *benefit* was that?'

'I could not resist it. Although what I said was true. Now what will you have to eat? Let us be done with the ordering and then have all the time to talk.'

'Salmon. I should love to have salmon.'

'Then salmon it shall be. And I shall have lobster.'

'They are so ugly.'

'You mean you do not like them? But they are delicious.'

'I do not like to look upon them.'

'Will you mind if *I* have them?'

'Oh that is perfectly fine. It is only if it were on my own plate. I don't like their claws.'

'If I had claws I would clasp them about you . . . "And I would be the girdle About her dainty dainty waist, And her heart would beat against me, In sorrow and in rest: And I should know if it beat right, I'd clasp it round so close and tight."'

His foot was by hers under the table, just touching. Rosaleen felt a flush spread through her body.

'Who wrote that?' Her voice, always husky, was exaggeratedly so now.

'The Poet Laureate – Alfred Tennyson. It is from "The Miller's Daughter". There are other verses in the same vein. I shall save those for another time.'

Across the square table his eyes bored into hers so that she could not look away – was drawn to him and into him. They sat, wordless, staring, and it was into this atmosphere – reverberating with sexual tension – that the waiter returned with their cocktails and to take their order . . .

'Oliver,' Rosaleen said when the waiter had gone once more and they had resumed their eye-contact, 'this is really no good. We must at least speak a little.'

'Why? Because it is expected? Or because you are afraid to acknowledge physical attraction?'

The latter was true but she wanted to know him, how he thought and believed. She said this to him.

He made a dismissive gesture with his hand. 'There is time.'

'But there is not. Soon you return to Cornwall.'

'You could come with me.'

'Oh Oliver, you cannot say that after a few moments together.'

'I just have.'

'I did not even like you last night. Or at least, not to begin with.'

'I misjudged you,' he explained without apologizing. 'Kate had said little about you and I thought you would be of the usual type. I cannot stand the way girls give themselves airs and are taught it is obligatory to have hysterics and faint all over the place. They are indoctrinated by mothers and governesses with pious purity, and have the sole aim of finding rich husbands. Women are capable of far more intellectually than they are given credit for.'

'Well certainly I agree with you.'

'I encourage my sister to write. She submits articles to newspapers and journals and has written a couple of quite passable novels. But she has to use a pseudonym in order to publish the articles.'

'Why is that?'

'Because she was continually rejected as a woman. So she re-submitted them with the name of Karl Harper and they were immediately accepted.'

'It is so unfair. I read *Middlemarch* by George Eliot – alias Mary Ann Evans – about a year ago. I thought it a wonderful book.'

'She is a remarkable woman. A free-thinker. She was raised as a staunch Evangelist and then rejected it. Evangelism is dangerous.' When he made controversial statements Rosaleen noticed how he spoke louder, as though being deliberately provocative. Now several people turned.

'Why is it dangerous?' She kept her own voice low.

'Because it is repressive, and repression in itself is dangerous. It is unnatural and therefore harmful. The expectations are too high and the resultant stress placed on mere mortals becomes hard to bear.'

'Oliver, I think we should change the subject.'

He threw back his head and laughed deeply, gripping the edge of the table with his hands – which she saw were massive and broad. 'Why? Because of the outraged expressions on the faces of a few virtuous matrons you mean? Ah – you are saved from further embarrassment. Here is the food arrived.'

They were quiet for a while as they ate, Oliver cracking the legs of his lobster and sucking on them unselfconsciously. Watching him Rosaleen thought: 'If he was wrong in his impression of me, I was equally wrong in my assessment of him.'

He spoke to her then about his art – he was primarily a landscapist who followed the old school in style. But she gathered he had not achieved the success he wanted and he was resentful because of it, accusing the members of the Royal Academy of being 'an incestuous bunch of cronies'.

'Why incestuous?' she asked.

And he explained that he had meant it in the metaphorical sense because they were loath to consider artists whose names were not known to them already. Rosaleen could not gauge his objectivity, but she offered her support and sympathized with him over their 'fuddy-duddy limitations'. She thought how mercurial were his moods – one minute ebullient, the next almost morose.

In the cab home he sat with his arm around her.

'"And I would be the necklace, And all day long to fall and rise Upon her balmy bosom, With her laughter or her sighs, And I would lie so light, so light, I scarce should be unclasp'd at night."'

She leaned against his shoulder. 'It is so beautiful. Is it the same poem as before?'

'Yes.'

'How wonderful to write such words.'

He stroked her hair, and they did not speak again until they arrived at her place in Holland Street. Standing beside him at the little wrought-iron gate she was suddenly shy. 'Thank you for a lovely evening.'

'It was a lovely evening indeed . . . It need not end yet.'

For a second she hesitated, drawn again into his gaze, aware of the tingling spreading through her once more. 'No,' she said softly. 'Not so soon.'

He nodded faintly in accord. 'May I at least kiss you?'

'Yes.'

He bent down and she reached upwards. The kiss under the street light with the coach-driver looking on was brief, but it fired her sexuality, and she longed to pull his head to her so that their mouths were hard on one another and their tongues like coiled snakes. She longed to lie with him . . .

'You must go.'

'Can I see you tomorrow, and the next day, and the one after, and the following?'

She laughed and pushed him lightheartedly away. 'Yes. Now go.'

'I love you.'

'It is too soon to say that.'

'No it is not.'

She went to bed but was unable to sleep. She was pent up with physical tension and erotic imaginings; felt herself aflame with them. Absently she stroked her own body – up and down underneath her nightgown. She felt smooth and sleek. Her nipples were hard. She was moist.

'What am I doing?' she thought, shocked, as her fingers began to massage the softness between her legs. She leaped out of bed and lit a candle, and for the remainder of the night sat in the rocking chair reading by this little light, and looking out at the dark garden, until it became less dark, then hazy grey, then rose, and finally it was dawn.

On their third occasion together Oliver again declared his love for her and on the fourth Rosaleen declared hers for him. The following night he stayed with her. She marvelled at the magnificence of his muscular body with its dark curling hair on his chest and around his hugely erect penis. The hair on his legs was fine and straight, and she stroked their length, from the tips of his feet to his inner thighs.

'If I could paint I would paint you,' she said.

He turned her over on to her stomach, and kneeling over her ran the tips of his fingers, light like butterfly wings, down her spine, lingeringly stroking the small twin humps of her arched buttocks, reaching between her legs and finding her drenched . . . Adjusting his position so that his tongue replaced his hand. When at last he entered her she was so aroused her orgasm occurred almost immediately.

But to Rosaleen the most sublime thing of all was the fact that she loved him; that as he tenderly probed inside her, she was ever conscious it was him, Oliver – his eyes piercing hers, his body grinding upon hers. And as he went still deeper into her, it seemed there was not a part of them that was not embracing.

'I love you, love you, love you . . . I cannot stop saying it.'

'Do not then.'

Later he said, 'I want you to come back to Cornwall with me.'

'Are you asking or telling me?'

'Begging.'

She laughed. 'I always take pity on beggars.'

'You can be my assistant. I shall teach you everything I know about painting.'

When Rosaleen told Kate the following day, she was at first thrilled and then anxious. 'Dearest, it makes me so happy to think you will be with us, but I think it only fair to warn you that Oliver can be difficult.'

'I know. I have seen it.'

'No, far more seriously than you have seen. I am not being disloyal to him, for he is a wonderful man and I am devoted to him . . . Only he is inclined to the most frightful depressions, you cannot conceive.'

'I am certain I could cope with them, Kate. Besides, if he is happy with me perhaps he will not have these attacks.'

'Rosaleen, that will only have a bearing for a little while. It is something buried deep within him – a deep inner dissatisfaction. He seeks something beyond even his line of vision and becomes quite despairing that he cannot see it, let alone attain it. I would say he is a manic-depressive.'

'I love him, Kate.' Rosaleen's expression was fervent and she gripped her friend's hand. 'I am sure I can help him. And if I cannot, then I shall just have to suffer alongside him.'

'He is jealous and possessive.'

'Those things I know.'

'Then if you will not be dissuaded, I have been disloyal enough, and wish simply that everyone may be extremely happy . . .'

Two days before they were due to depart, Rosaleen went to see Frederick. She found him in the stable grooming Edgar. He wore only a shirt and braces above his breeches and sweated freely so that the shirt was stained dark in patches. Seeing him, a wave of fondness came over her.

'Hello Frederick.'

He turned, his expression hostile, and when he acknowledged her it was as though he could barely bring himself to greet her. With the dandy-brush in his hand he wiped his damp forehead roughly, pushing the lank hair from his eyes, and continued to groom Edgar.

'He knows,' she thought. 'Oh dear, he has taken it badly.'

She continued to watch whilst Frederick worked a shine on to his horse, strapping him energetically, whilst the dark stains on his shirt enlarged and merged. After several minutes of this, when it became apparent he would stay in the stable all day if necessary without offering a word, Rosaleen said, 'Frederick, can we talk?'

'Go ahead. I am not stopping you. Talk.'

'I mean somewhere – more convivial.'

He whirled round and she was stunned by his livid face. 'I find it most "convivial" here. What a trite word. Convivial.' He repeated it in a sneering tone.

'Please, Frederick.'

'What is it you desire to talk about? No –' He held up his hand as she was about to answer. 'I can guess perhaps. It is about joining a particular relation of mine in Cornwall, is it not?'

She nodded, her chin jutting defiantly.

'Well Rosaleen, you certainly move with speed, I'll say that.' He put the brushes and stable-rubber back into the wooden grooming box, and wiped his hands on his breeches. 'Now if you'll excuse me –'

'No Frederick.' She spoke gently, and caught his arm as he was about to brush past her.

He stopped, stared into the sweetness of her face, its familiarity, its concern for his feelings, and he gave a sigh that went through his entire body. His shoulders sagged and the anger went from him. He took her hand. 'Come inside then, and we will talk.'

She unpinned the flat little hat she wore low over the front of her forehead and removed her short tailored jacket, setting both on a chair. Her hair as usual was worn loose at the back and curled to a few inches short of her waist. Frederick watched each of her actions, her purposefulness, the natural grace of her movements. He thought: 'I do not want to lose her as a friend. I shall try to listen to her without impatience. It is, after all, as she is always at pains to remind me, her life. Ah but Rosaleen, your life is precious to me, and I fear you are abusing it.'

He took her hand again and said in as kind a voice as he could muster, 'I introduced you to the sister in good faith you would find in her a friend –'

'But I did!'

'Let me finish. And I am glad you did. But I was shortsighted in that I did not foresee what would happen with the brother.'

'How could you have done?'

'I suppose I could not have.'

'But what is so wrong? Are you not glad of my happiness?'

He could not believe that she did not realize his feelings for her; wondered fleetingly if it were a streak of perverse cruelty in her – dismissing the idea even as he thought it. He tried continually to be unselfish with her and to view issues from her – often impulsive – point of view.

'If I thought you would be happy, dear Rosaleen, I would be delighted.'

'And why do you not think I shall be happy?' Her eyes narrowed.

'I pray you will.'

'Oliver is your cousin. I thought you liked him. You visited him in Cornwall.'

'I like him immensely. I admire many aspects of his character.'

'I detect a "but".' She was relentless now that she had decided he was against her.

'Rosaleen, I have no wish to quarrel.'

'But you ooze disapproval, Frederick.'

'You must do what you wish. You have no need of my approval.'

But something in her had. 'You should have left me – untroubled – in Coniston. The raw country-girl, untouched by sophistication, ignorant . . .'

'You know you did not see yourself like that, Rosaleen. You were never ignorant. Innocent and unworldly yes, and what is wrong with that? Ignorant – no. And am I to blame myself – or even congratulate myself – for everything which has happened to you since leaving Coniston? Am I to blame myself you ever left?'

'You offered me snippets of culture as though they were

sweetmeats.' She was aggrieved and tears glistened in her eyes.

'All I did was crystallize the dissatisfaction you already felt, Rosaleen, and you know it. Now let us not have dissent. I care too deeply for you. Instead – here – let me wipe your eyes, and I shall wish you luck and come and visit you.'

'Do you really wish me luck?' Childlike, she lifted her face submissively to have it dabbed by him with a handkerchief.

'Yes, dear girl, that always.'

'And you really will visit?'

'I promise.'

'Frederick –' His eyes were so sad.

'Yes, dear girl?'

'I'm so sorry.'

Walking back to Holland Street, she realized she had asked him nothing about his politics.

Two days later, Rosaleen, Kate and Oliver set off for Cornwall.

❧ Eleven ❧

THE ARTIST

These ageing seekers of something elusive –
They do not see it is all they have.

The early autumn sun had not long been up, but for those engaged around the harbour the day was already old. Rosaleen walked from Norway Square down tiny cobbled Church Place, past the slums to the wharf. She stood outside the Blue Bell Inn – a noted rendezvous for smugglers – and watched all the activity. She never tired of it.

The tide was out, and pushed up on the beach were dozens of fishing boats – many of them long seine boats – with their nets drying over their sides. Some were still out at sea and she could see the men in them, standing attentive to the gestures of the huers who signalled from the cliff with 'bushes' when they sighted a shoal of pilchards, and cried 'Hevva!' – meaning 'found'.

On the beach bare-footed urchins dug for bait; fish-bulkers, mostly women, arranged pilchards in layers of salt, building up the tiers until the wall of fish became so high they could no longer reach. Men fastened dog-fish to frames ready to be skinned; men and women worked together, packing pilchards in hogsheads for storage on Smeaton's Pier, from where they would later be shipped abroad; horses with bowed heads waited to have their carts filled . . .

An old jouster approached, bent under the weight of her basket heaped with fresh fish, and Rosaleen moved to let her pass. Briefly the woman stared at her – the small pale face framed by the vivid hair, worn loose now and blowing a little. 'Pretty chile,' she murmured. Then lowering her eyes she shuffled on.

Rosaleen suddenly felt the chill in the air and rearranged her Joseph shawl to cover her head. 'How colourful it all is,' she reflected. 'A medley of bustle and sound. And wherever I turn something is happening. Oh there are so many diverse aspects to life and I long to see them all.'

Life in St Ives revolved around the pilchard industry and tin-mining. The place stank. It stank not only of fish, but of sewage. Everybody brought their slops to empty on the harbour front, and parents in better-off families forbade their children to play there.

'A malodorous town,' a visiting bishop once observed, while the vicar said the stench was so terrific it could stop the church clock. Rosaleen herself had at first been sickened by the smell, but now was as used to it as she was to the poverty and tumble-down hovels of many of the people. The inhabitants were divided into two distinct categories: those whose children wore shoes, and those whose children did not; and the latter grovelled in the sand for worms, or helped load up the carts, swam unconcerned in the harbour water, and went home to their one room which housed numerous other siblings and a few chickens besides.

A month after her arrival, she noticed only the quaintness of the place – the impossibly tiny streets with names like Pudding Bag Lane, and Chy an Chy, leading artery-like one into the other and clambering steeply, interspersed by alleyways and cottages huddled one almost on top of another, linked by crooked steps and lines of washing. And by contrast there was Treganna Hill, with its fine architecture and fresh air – a road so steep that horses pulling loads were exchanged for fresh ones half-way up.

People knew Rosaleen now, and their faces when they greeted her were friendly – the beaten faces of fishermen under oiled sou'westers, the wreathed faces of women who were old when they were thirty-five. When they spoke to her she was even able to understand some of their dialect, so that she no longer gawped idiotically, as when the old woman in the provisions shop in Fore Street had told her she was a 'geet beet with pretty hull'.

'What on earth did she mean?' Rosaleen asked Kate – who laughed and told her, '"Geet beet" means great beauty, and "hull" is hair!'

Norway House was a pretty white-washed building with steps up to the front door and two stables incorporated beneath – home to a sturdy black pony which the blacksmith in Pudding Bag Lane looked after whenever Oliver was away. Downstairs the house was devoted to a dining-room, spacious sitting-room and good-sized kitchen and scullery, while upstairs there were three bedrooms, one of which was occupied by Kate, another by Oliver and Rosaleen, and the smallest was used for storage and also by Rosaleen for making her shawls. From the landing a staircase led to the attic studio – wonderfully light and spacious and with views over the higgledy rooftops towards that part of the harbour where the larger boats were hauled up, their masts tall and the rigging as intricate as cobwebs. In between the masts could be glimpsed the sea; it opened out beyond the harbour, edged by the coast of Hayle a few miles away.

Oliver was working on a painting depicting Porthmeor beach during a storm – dark figures watched from the island as the *Covent Garden* lifeboat was rowed out to rescue men from a ketch in distress.

'The accident happened about six months ago,' he told Rosaleen who studied it thoughtfully.

She tried to envisage the drama. 'Was anyone killed?'

'Fourteen men. You grow accustomed to it. Each week bodies are washed ashore. Often they're smugglers who've been taking one risk too many.'

'There's so much talk of smuggling here.'

'So much goes on, that is why! It is simple to organize. For instance, the men out fishing for mackerel will meet the Dutch boats several miles out and bring back perfume and spirits and twists of tobacco they'll hide in their boots. Once word got round the excise men had decided to clamp down, so everybody hid their bounty in pits dug on the island. Only, when they went to retrieve it, it had disappeared. Someone had been spying on them!'

'It is a different world here.'

'That it is. But are you happy?'

'You know I am.'

'By night my mistress. By day my assistant. A perfect arrangement!'

'I don't know which I enjoy more! But certainly I have learned a great deal about painting and the effort which goes into the preparation beforehand. I'd no idea so much was entailed.'

'Did you think one just went into a shop and bought everything ready prepared?'

'I suppose that is what I must have thought.'

She sat by him sometimes watching him paint. He was painstaking and had infinite patience – a quality he didn't demonstrate in other areas of his life. Working mostly with fine brushes, he tended to use sombre colours which Rosaleen thought a shame; and there was an exactness about his style which somehow made his pictures lack depth. 'I cannot see joy in them,' Rosaleen thought. 'Although I am certain they must be good . . .'

He taught her how to grind colours, mixing linseed oil with pigment on a marble slab, grinding it with a muller, adding saponified beeswax to prevent separation, and then scraping the prepared paint from the slab into tubes made from bladders. He explained to her about earth colours and minerals, and that she must not inhale the white paint as it contained lead and was toxic. He demonstrated drawing in chalk and how to hold charcoal in a porte-fusain; showed her how to prepare a canvas by taking the fabric and stretching it taut over a wooden frame, nailing it to this and then sealing it with four coats of rabbit-skin glue which she made from granules soaked overnight in water and strained and warmed up the following day. Once the canvas was sealed it was then painted with primer – a matt base usually of grey or pink, and left to dry for a month.

Rosaleen could do all these things on her own, and without being asked made sure the various jars, bottles and tubes were kept full. She knew the correct way to hold a pallet with the thumb in the hole and spare brushes sticking through the aperture; she learned how to transfer the idea of a small sketch to a large canvas by squaring up; that white should be used thickly and dark colours thinly . . .

'In fact about the only thing I have not taught you to do is to paint,' Oliver said one day.

He said it jocularly; fondly; as an impossibility. But as he said it Rosaleen's heart quickened and she thought: 'Oh how I should like to try.'

But she was sure he would ridicule her. The thought left her and she forgot it.

Rosaleen adapted to her new life as she had always adapted. She would awaken in the morning before either Kate or Oliver, pad downstairs to the kitchen to wash, go back upstairs to dress, swiftly and quietly, and then – out of the house on her lone walks. She would go to the harbour, or Porthmeor beach, or Porthgwidden, or maybe, as a surprise for Kate, to fetch water from the St Ias well on the Island; that summer was so dry their own water-butt was empty. There was always something going on, on the Island. The women laid their laundry out to dry, and close by the fishermen mended their filthy nets. Inevitably the one encroached on the other. Straying pigs were also a threat, and men and pigs alike would incur the wrath of the women. 'Lummox,' they would cry without discrimination. 'Buzzahead!' Both words which Rosaleen now knew meant 'fool'.

By the time she returned to the house, her cheeks cold and pink, the others would be up; she helped Kate prepare breakfast and then they all sat and ate in the kitchen – silent, because Oliver did not speak early in the mornings, nor could he bear anyone about him to do so. Occasionally the girls would catch each other's eye and fight the urge to laugh. After breakfast, if they felt like it, they might clean the house, or shop for provisions, but there was no formality to the day and nobody was bothered by a little dust, or having at the last minute to rush out and buy a sack of potatoes or take their bowl to fill with treacle. It was Oliver whose mood dictated the day – whether or not he would paint;

whether they would take the pony and cart for a pleasure-ride; whether they would go to Penzance; whether he was morose and expected the other two to sit around the house in commiserative gloom; whether to visit friends – in particular Colin and Talwyn.

Colin and Talwyn lived in the Barnoon area of St Ives, high up and with views to Porthm r beach. They made a strange couple: Talwyn tall, voluptuous and with the white skin, black eyes and hair of her Spanish ancestors, incongruously clutching her wooden 'Joanie' doll; Colin shorter than her and stout, pale and academic-looking, his expression severe behind his glasses, and with a tendency to purse his mouth thoughtfully before answering a question. When he did answer he seemed incapable of offering a direct reply; it always had to be qualified and usually managed to be ambiguous while trying to appear profound.

He had plucked Talwyn the year previously from the streets of Penzance, where she had hung around the port offering herself indiscriminately to sailors. She had been doing it since she was ten.

'She is untouched by it,' Colin said once, his hand on Talwyn's shoulder proprietorially. 'She is as innocent as an animal who has no consideration for the act it instinctively commits, and does not know the meaning of falsity or hypocrisy. She is God's child.'

God's child, curled up by his feet on the floor, stared blankly ahead with no understanding of what he was saying. She would murmur to herself or to her doll and occasionally chuckle, leaning against Colin's leg and clasping it to her, wrapping her arms about it, closing her eyes and rocking.

'She is so peaceful living within the confines of her mind,' he continued, regarding her dark shining head adoringly. 'And her fears – who knows what she sees? I envy that vision of hers which is beyond my perimeter.'

'What nonsense he talks,' Rosaleen thought. 'He loves her because she is a pliable instrument in his hands. It is this old issue of the male need for ownership. Only he carries it a stage further. Who does he trick with his odd philosophies? Surely only himself. No – he tricks Oliver too . . . How can he be taken in so? Oh what a "lummox"! Hear how he is carried away by his own theories!'

Later, in bed with Oliver and absently stroking his stomach and pulling the soft hairs, she said carefully, 'I thought Talwyn and Colin an unusual couple.'

'Talwyn is the result of two generations of cousins inter-marrying,' he told her. 'She was raped by her father and intro-duced to prostitution by her mother. She uses her own body as easily as Kate gestures with her hands.'

'I was not criticizing her, Oliver. I'm sorry for the poor thing –'

He didn't let her finish her sentence but became angry, lifting her hand and moving away slightly. 'That is an ignorant remark and demonstrates just the point which you have misunderstood, and why Colin is so perceptive. She has no need of your pity. She is content as she is, unaffected by the things that go on about her and by the world's cares.'

'Oh Oliver, how do you know what affects her. You are being as absurd as Colin is.'

'And you are limited in your views. You are unenlightened.'

'You say those things whenever a person doesn't accord with you!'

'I say them when I am right.'

'Colin enjoys Talwyn's dependency on him, don't you see? He is smitten by this shadowy ideal he has of truth and purity, but he is far too garrulous to be genuine.'

'I will not have you attacking my friends.'

This she understood, and ceased her quarrel with him. 'I am sure he is an excellent artist,' she tried to mollify him, snuggling up close, and because their relationship was still so new he could only respond.

'He has done wonderful works of Talwyn. And he sculpts also.' His hand reached for her breasts.

'I am bored with discussing them.' She disappeared under the sheet.

*

The four of them met at least twice a week at either house. Colin had a maid who prepared meals, but at Norway House Kate and Rosaleen shared the task. Rosaleen learned how to make local dishes such as tatie cake, squab pie – made with veal and herbs – and sago plum pudding. She cooked scrowlers for Oliver, splitting the pilchards and cooking them quickly with plenty of salt until the smell became too strong to bear – this meant they were ready, and wrinkling her nose in disgust she lifted the pan from the heat. She became adept with the primitive cloam oven and experimented with baking; and learned, too, to make herby beer. She, Kate and Talwyn would gather ingredients for it from the wayside: nettles, yarrow and dandelion leaves. Talwyn would cling devotedly to Kate's hand whilst the other clutched her Joanie doll, and she would sing nursery rhymes and old Cornish tunes as she walked, her voice as sweet as a child's. Then her attention would wander. 'Look – cherries,' she exclaimed on a walk one morning.

'No Talwyn. Those are poisonous berries.'

'I like berries.'

'Yes darling, but *these* berries will hurt your tummy.'

If the women were busy in the kitchen the men would go to one of the taverns and drink scrumpy, returning in jovial spirits, ambling in with linked arms and loud voices, and smacking the women heartily on their rumps. Food would be taken informally in the kitchen, with a jug of herby beer set on the table and plenty of fresh-baked bread. After the meal the high spirits would give way to a more serious mood and the usual discussions would begin – those inconclusive and repetitious soul-searching conversations which both men seemed to find so essential to their well-being.

Perhaps once a fortnight they met with other friends – if they did not bump into them accidentally in the streets in-between – and these occasions passed in the same way, but with more people; intense, shaggy-bearded individuals who believed passionately in the theories they expounded.

'I have never met such a bunch of ageing seekers,' Rosaleen commented to Kate. 'And you know what Colin answered when

I asked him what he sought? "Something fine," he answered in that mock-profound way he has. And then he pursed his lips, paused for effect and repeated it! Kate, I had to restrain myself from bursting into laughter. And you know how humourless he is. He would not have forgiven me.'

'It is because they have not yet attained their artistic aims. Everything else is a substitute. It is what I meant that time about being a slave to ambition. It does not have to be material ambition.'

'I find it so tedious – all their talk of life's meaning.'

'It is taken rather to an extreme,' Kate agreed.

'What is taken to an extreme?' Oliver came into the kitchen.

'Nothing,' Rosaleen answered busying herself immediately.

'Something must be,' he argued irritably, following her about as she put crockery away in cupboards and hung up pans.

'Did you know Tamara from the Red Lion hid smuggled goods beneath her dress yesterday and pretended to be with child when the excise men arrived?' Kate said brightly.

'She didn't!' cried Rosaleen, stopping what she was doing to hear the tale.

'I asked you a question, Kate,' Oliver said, catching his sister by the arm.

'Dearest, Rosaleen and I were talking amongst ourselves and I don't recall what we were saying.'

But he was in morose humour. 'I dislike feeling excluded.'

'Nobody is excluding you, Oliver.' Rosaleen tried to kiss him, but some inner blackness had seized him and he thrust her away roughly.

'Then do not treat me like an imbecile and pretend you have forgotten what you were saying.' His face was distorted with rage.

'Really, dear, it was not of importance,' Kate said in soothing tones.

Rosaleen, silent and ashen, waited.

'So tell me,' he insisted.

'You are being so obstinate, Oliver – making something out of nothing. We were merely discussing our opinions.'

'What opinions?'

Rosaleen became angry. 'Oliver, you are being utterly unreasonable. Kate and I are entitled to discuss our opinions in private on whatever we like.'

'Yes, but you are hiding something from me. I sense it.'

For the first time she was aware of his deep-rooted insecurity, and was shocked.

'I *will* have an answer,' he roared.

'How has it happened?' Rosaleen wondered, staring bewildered at him. 'An hour ago we were having breakfast. He goes to his studio and comes down like this. What thoughts occurred to him up there as he battled with his painting?'

Kate said quietly, 'We were discussing our views on the purpose of life.'

'And what are they?'

'We had not got that far,' Rosaleen said. 'You came down.'

'So tell me now.' His smile was twisted.

Rosaleen answered quietly, 'I hold no views. We were created and now we must get on with living as best we can. That is all.'

'But it is *not* all.' He slumped into a chair and leaned his elbows on the table, his expression agonized.

'Oliver –' Her heart went out to him, and tears of pity were in her eyes. Tentatively she touched his cheek.

'Leave me.' He got up and blundered from the room. They heard him trudging upstairs.

'Oh dear – you see I did warn you,' Kate looked hopelessly at Rosaleen.

'I know. It – was just a surprise.'

'It could last a while. I don't know what brought it on. The slightest thing could have done. It cannot be predicted.'

'I feel so hopeless, Kate. I feel I have failed him. I was certain this would not happen if he was content in our relationship.'

'Dearest, it is no deficiency in you. You can contribute in a major way to that contentment, but it is never the entirety. You know that. One's happiness is dependent on several components.'

'I thought he was so strong.'

'Oliver? He is not in the least strong. Why do you think he is so possessive, so demanding, so jealous? These traits are because of his self-doubts.'

'Kate, I must go out and walk a little.'

'Darling – do not be sad.'

She took the coastal track following Hain Walk, over Porthminster Point, to Carbis Bay. In the background were the tin-mines, their chimneys reminiscent of castle turrets: Wheal Providence, and St Ives Consols, and Trelyon Consols. A small group of bal-maidens and children, whose job it was to sort the rocks and minerals, passed her. They were smoking and laughing. One of them coughed raspingly.

Rosaleen descended from the cliff to the beach. She wore the clogs of the local people and they were heavy and awkward. The day was blustery, and she wrapped her cloak closer about her, pulling its hood over her head, and stood watching the sea; the gap between the huge waves rolling in and hitting the shore was like a giant intake of breath. On the damp sand were dotted little worm spirals, and seaweed lay scattered like dark dead fish or was pushed into piles. The wind drove into her face and stung colour into her cheeks. She could see the lighthouse off Godrevy Point – a lonely symbol rising high on its rock, surrounded by immense Atlantic waves and foam. Rosaleen remained looking out to sea for a while longer, then climbed the path to the cliff once more, continuing until she came to Carrack Gladden, or Hawks Point as it was known. She made her way across the meadow with its wild briar and hazel-bushes – and there concealed amongst all the growth, close to the edge of the cliff, was the ancient 'fairy' well. She crouched beside it looking into it, recalling the legends she had heard, and about her the wind howled, whipping her hair across her face. She stood up once more, invigorated, holding her arms wide as if to embrace the wildness, her cloak flapping open and her skirts pressing against her legs. She did not see the old woman until she was right beside her, and started at her appearance.

'Don't take fright, maiden. Let me geek you.'

She was wizen-faced and clad in layers of rags and bleached

sacks. Her light-blue eyes surveyed Rosaleen. 'Come, maiden.'

She was barefooted and Rosaleen followed the tiny figure past the upturned boats, which had been made into dwelling places, through a thicket, and into a small clearing. Here was a tumble-down hut where the woman obviously lived as a hermit. A fire was blazing and some meat cooking in a pot suspended over it. Rosaleen recognized the smell as hedgehog.

The woman removed the pot from the flames and tore the meat with her hands. She gave Rosaleen a chunk after blowing on it. Rosaleen took it questioningly and the woman nodded, smiling, showing yellow stumps of teeth, her bright eyes lost in her apple-cheeks.

'Is't good?'

It was surprisingly so. 'Yes. Thank you.' She smiled back shyly.

The woman laid her hand on Rosaleen's arm in acknowledgement – she had fingers missing – and took some meat for herself, chomping noisily and sucking. When she had finished she offered Rosaleen more, but she refused it: there was so little, and she worried that she would be depriving the woman. She patted her stomach to indicate she was full.

'Gus on with 'ee!' The woman laughed, but didn't press her. Instead she took Rosaleen's right hand and studied it carefully, frowning a little, tilting it this way and that to examine it from all angles.

'Tha'll not stay in Cornwall. There's bloodshed afore 'ee.' She peered into Rosaleen's troubled face and touched it with a mutilated finger. 'Tha'll be goin' afield . . . bright colours . . . Tha'll be wed and have a chile – a maiden wi yalla hull . . . Don't geek downcast. Life'll be fair to 'ee . . .'

Rosaleen walked back. She felt peaceful and no longer re-proached herself that she had failed Oliver. She dismissed the hermit's predictions as an old woman's ramblings, and only much later recalled Robbie's description of Nana Annie's dream.

*

Winter came, mild but wet, and a bank of sandbags was built along the wharf to keep back the water. The pilchard industry ground to a halt and fishermen exchanged their oilskins for miner's garb for the next few months.

In a haphazard way the days had a routine; Kate wrote articles for the *St Ives Penny Post* and started a new novel, Oliver painted, Rosaleen assisted him or made her Joseph shawls which she sold in Penzance. Oliver's moods came and went and Rosaleen suffered with him each time, once going so far as to lie beside him on the floor for the best part of a day, cradling his head as he cried silent tears and refused to move. 'I am here, my love, I am here,' she assured him when he moaned to her not to leave him.

'What is it you fear?' she asked him gently when it was over and she was curled against him in bed that night.

'I fear my inadequacies,' he answered. 'I feel as though I am trapped within myself. I cannot convey what I should like to put *meaningfully* on to canvas.'

It was what she had noticed almost immediately but had hoped she was wrong. She held him tighter, wishing only to fill him with strength and belief in himself. 'Why can't you feel free when you paint?'

'Because I am a perfectionist. I'm continually bothered by detail.'

'Do you have other concerns besides your art?'

He gave a bitter little laugh. 'A hundred of them. I am thirty-eight now and it bothers me increasingly that time is passing, and I have fewer years in which to take risks. When you are young the unknown is exciting. As you grow older it is daunting. Sometimes I am seized with panic that I shall die unfulfilled. And I have a horror of death. Unlike Colin I have no great belief in the hereafter. I need to achieve something before I am ready to contemplate it.'

He was so tortured. 'And love?' she enquired. 'You have not mentioned it. Are not the rewards of commitment to another human being to be compared with the rewards of achievement?'

'Of course they are – but only in part. Since we are merely

marking time to be snuffed out again we must look for other truths.'

'What kind of truths?' she cried, frustrated by the ambiguous conversation and flinging herself away from him. 'I see Colin often enough. He believes in "truth" apparently – and is the rudest man I know. He is rude to everybody with the exception of Talwyn. Although I suppose that means he is true to himself!'

'Please come back into my arms. Don't be angry. I do not want you to be dragged down with me . . . You know, when I first met you I saw a small hesitant girl and all I wanted was to protect you.'

'I do not need protecting,' she protested. 'From what, anyway?'

But he was so humble that Rosaleen was contrite; all she had intended was to offer solace. But she saw simplicity as the key to tranquillity, and was against the constant analyses to which Oliver and his clique subjected themselves. She realized that although they considered they were on a higher plane than others, their arrogance was bluff, and their art no more innovative than their beliefs.

After his depressions Oliver would become fearful he was driving Rosaleen away, and reacted in two ways; one was to adopt a mood of great gaiety, the other was to be obsessively jealous – because he doubted that her love for him could have survived.

'You were flaunting yourself at the tavern last night,' he accused her one morning, sounding like Thomas had used to.

'Oliver, I was *not*.'

'With Stuart Colefax. As soon as he told you he was an author you adopted that expression you more usually see on a dog. You hung on to his every word.'

'Oh what poppycock, Oliver.'

And Kate who was sitting at the kitchen table trying to write, looked up to defend her friend. 'Oliver, Rosaleen conducted herself most properly.'

'Of course I did,' Rosaleen snapped. 'He was telling me about the St Ives Institution Literary Association of which he is a

215

member. And actually he was suggesting Kate should join. I hardly call that flaunting myself – which is something I have never done.' She started to walk from the room.

'Where are you going?'

'To the beach,' she called over her shoulder.

'By yourself?'

'Oh *Oliver*.'

'I love you so much,' he said a few nights later. 'I am terrified you will leave me.'

'I love you too. I'll not leave you.'

But increasingly he tried to confine her, and then, early in the new year of 1876, just when his possessiveness was becoming intolerable, he and Kate had to visit their late father's spinster sister in Bristol. She was dying. For the first time in four months Rosaleen found herself on her own.

The little house seemed plunged into an unnatural quiet which she found most odd, and it was a few minutes before she realized how glad she was to be alone. She sat pensive, in the kitchen, brewed some coffee, and ate an orange – chewing slowly, and stretching out her legs under the table; then she went upstairs to check on the yarn she was dyeing. She unfolded a shawl and stroked its softness . . . 'Your shawl is art . . .' 'I wonder how he is?' she thought. 'He said he would visit . . . And I still cannot think of it as art!'

On an impulse she went up to Oliver's studio. There was a washed brightness in the room as outside the sun tried to penetrate a watery haze. All was, as usual, orderly within, and Rosaleen wandered about looking at and touching items now familiar to her. She gazed at the stacked canvases dispassionately – completed and unfinished works – and was disappointed she could not marvel at them or connect them with the man she loved. Beside them were several other canvases, unused but prepared, and Rosaleen took the smallest of them and ran her fingers lightly over it. A tremor of excitement rippled through her. 'I wonder – oh I'd so love to try – what is to prevent me?'

She clasped the canvas with one hand whilst she put the other to her mouth as if to muffle her excitement. Then she could no longer restrain herself, and ran to the shelves and cupboards where she knew everything was kept. After adjusting the easel she set the canvas on it and the implements upon a table beside it and sat on the stool. She was putting a charcoal stick in a porte-fusain when she realized she did not know what to draw.

'How irritating it is,' she reflected. 'My fingers itch to be started and I have no subject matter!'

Through the window she could see two small boys crouched on the harbour beach playing with what looked like a piece of driftwood. 'They shall be my subject,' she thought, smiling to herself at the sight of them; 'except I shall imagine they are playing on rocks, and small pools of water left by the tide will lap at their feet.'

Rosaleen stared for a moment longer at the engrossed figures, trying to see the positioning of their limbs, the curves of their bodies. They were too distant, but she felt she instinctively knew, and after a brief hesitation tentatively drew the curve of one of the boy's backs. After those first cautious strokes she became emboldened, used to the springiness of the canvas, and sketched rapidly, recalling Robbie as a young child, the hollow at the nape of his neck, the ridge of his spine, how his clothes hung on him in some places and clung in others. Tenderly she remembered the way his unruly hair grew, and how enormous his feet were – shooting like boats from the skinny stalks of his ankles; and as she remembered, the figure she was drawing became her brother.

She exchanged a pencil for the charcoal and drew in details – their features, a gull perched on a rock, the beginnings of a distant schooner – as rapt as the two boys who had inspired her. Having spent so many hours posing herself, when all there was to do was reflect or observe those who observed her, it seemed natural she should understand every line of the body, and she drew joyfully and freely so that several hours passed without her realizing. It was only when her fingers became stiff with cold that she stopped, aware how icy the room was. Her teeth were chattering slightly, although that was partly in excitement – and reluctantly she broke off to light a fire. She blew on the small flames to make them spread swiftly and held her hands over them to warm her numbed fingers. Then she returned to the easel and surveyed her effort.

'I believe I can *draw*,' she thought, laughing out loud in happiness . . .

Rosaleen worked until the light failed, then tidied everything ready for the following morning when she would begin painting. She set the guard in front of the fire and left the house to have some scrumpy and something to eat at the Blue Bell Inn; she was ravenous, and with Oliver away she could do as she pleased and talk with whomever she wished . . .

The following morning found her back in the studio as soon as the light was up, and this time she immediately lit a fire. She rummaged in a cupboard and found a few tubes of paints already made up, and took a burnt umber to use for underpainting. This was something Oliver always did and it involved mixing the paint to a thin consistency with turpentine before applying it quickly to those areas drawn in, using a rag to wipe over wherever a light effect was desired. Rosaleen was glad when this was accomplished, but before she could start painting in earnest she had to grind more colours and select her brushes. She chose hog's hair filberts and sable rounds, the former for the large expanses of background and the latter for the more detailed work.

She wondered: 'Where should I start – with the background or the figures? Oh but I'd like to try painting the one who resembles Robbie.'

Taking the palette in her left hand and holding it with the brushes as Oliver had shown her, she dipped one into blue, an expression of concentration on her face and the tip of her tongue between her teeth . . .

She did not hear the knock on the front door much later, or the footsteps up the stairs; only when the door opened did Rosaleen turn, startled. Frederick stood there, ruddy complexioned and wearing a tweed riding cloak.

'Frederick!'

'Rosaleen!'

They were equally astonished: Rosaleen shocked out of that private state in which she had been immersed; Frederick surprised at seeing her apparently turned artist. She stumbled to her feet to greet him.

'Dearest girl – but let me see what you're doing.'

'No, Frederick, it is –'

'Tut Rosaleen, since when did you have need of embarrassment with me?' He went over to the easel and regarded her picture with its lovingly-drawn figures.

She took his silence as criticism and felt wretched with shame. 'I have only begun to paint it,' she stammered, 'and am experimenting still with colours . . . It's for my amusement, that is all . . . Kate and Oliver are away –'

'Rosaleen, you are *good*.'

Her face relaxed then and broke into a relieved smile. She sat down on the stool. 'Am I *really*?'

'I do believe you are. With practice I am certain you will be. You could join the ranks of Henrietta Ward and Rosa Brett!'

'Who are they?'

'Oh dear. They are extremely talented artists – one the sister of John Brett, the other the wife of Edward Matthew Ward. Because they are women they do not get the recognition they deserve. However, they are excellent at their craft. Mrs Ward paints largely historical subjects, whilst Rosa Brett is influenced by the Pre-Raphaelites. For many years she used the name of Rosarius, for obvious reasons, until her brother persuaded her to declare her identity . . . But how exciting all this is! I tell you what – I've settled Edgar in the spare stable, and I could do with some good beer. Can you tear yourself away? I can hear your news over a pint.'

They went to Betsy 'Chilloff's beer shop, so-called because old Betsy who owned the place always asked her customers if they wanted some spirit in their beer to take 'the chill off'.

Lizzie Tin-Drawers was in there gossiping, leaning on the counter, tankard in hand. Her husband had given her the nick-name when he'd first met her as a pretty bal-maiden. Now pregnant with their eleventh child it was difficult to believe she'd ever been pretty. She had a small child with her, gripping her legs fiercely with one hand, while in the other dangled a dried herring. He threw it at Frederick.

'That ain't nice, Harry. If you ain't careful I'll be clouting your chacks. Why hello, Ros'leen . . .' She stared at Frederick curiously, shifting her bulk and resting her fist on her immense hip.

Rosaleen could imagine the way her mind was working. 'Now who's that she's with?' she would be thinking. 'What's she up to whilst her man's afield?'

Rosaleen knew that she and the 'artist lot' were objects of curiosity anyway, incongruously placed amongst the small community. She smiled disarmingly. 'Hello Lizzie – Betsy. This is a cousin of Mr Hardwick's unexpectedly arrived from London. We were wanting a spot of beer.'

Old Betsy immediately busied herself, moving around on rheumaticky legs, pouring ale into two tankards. The smell of it was everywhere – ripe, slightly sour, wholesome, and Rosaleen inhaled it appreciatively.

'Will you be having a drop of spirit in it t'take the chill off then?' Betsy asked predictably.

Rosaleen turned inquiringly to Frederick. His eyes were gleaming merrily and his foot tapped against an empty barrel as if to some private rhythm. 'As much as you can spare, Betsy.'

'Why, I remember you, sir!' the old woman said as she poured good measures of whisky into the tankards, her creased face beaming in recognition. 'You're the gentleman as plays the flute so prettily. You wouldn't play it now would you, sir?'

'Well I do happen to have it with me.'

'Oh sir – stand by the nice warm slab and play a tune for us.'

'Let me take a sip of your excellent brew first, Betsy.'

He took a couple of long swallows then went over to the range, or the slab as Betsy called it, and leaned a little against it in a relaxed pose. Rosaleen stood with the other two women and the child, disgruntled, pushed the fish about on the counter.

Frederick began to play, his bright brown gaze regarding the three women, and as his eye caught Rosaleen's she felt a wave of tenderness for him. 'He is surely a dear friend,' she thought. 'I would not be without him.'

Her body swayed to his lilting melodies as did old Betsy's and huge Lizzie Tin-Drawers', and the child ceased playing with his dried herring to gape at them with their arms about each other rocking moist-eyed to the man's music.

By the time Frederick and Rosaleen arrived back at Norway House darkness had set in. They lit candles and threw more logs on the fire and sat companionably in front of it on the hearth-rug. Rosaleen leaned against Frederick and yawned loudly.

'Are you tired, dear girl?' He put his arm round her.

'A little. But pleasantly so.'

'And generally happy.'

'Yes. And although Oliver is not an easy man I love him very much.'

'I realize that.'

'I wish I could help him. I am superfluous and useless when he has his attacks.'

'You must harden your heart and tell yourself it is not your concern.'

'I know.'

'Now speak to me of your painting. You will take it up seriously of course.'

'Do you think I could?' She turned eagerly to him. The dark and light of the room cast shadows on her skin, resting in the hollows of her face and emphasizing its delicacy. Her eyes were alert, and the lashes, too, were shadowed on her cheekbones.

Frederick touched her face briefly; her skin was glowing, and he felt in him that familiar longing. He said, 'I know you could. You must work at it every day; be adventurous – which I know you will. If you were in London you could attend a school, although I am not so sure these places do not detract from a pupil's originality.'

'I wonder how Oliver will react.' Rosaleen huddled her knees in sudden anxiety.

'My guess is that he will react very favourably. He has been most supportive to Kate.'

'I hope you are right. I can't explain to you how it is when I draw and paint . . . I feel as though I am in complete harmony with myself. Even if what I am doing is poor, I am blissfully content doing it.'

'And I am delighted for you.'

'You are very dear, Frederick. But you have not told me your news! And are you still dabbling with politics?'

He laughed and scratched his beard. 'Oh dear, how things become distorted! I am not interested in politics, as you know. However I do take an interest in human suffering, of which there is tragically an abundance in London, and all I am doing is lobbying for better working conditions, medical aid, more aid for the old and infirm, more funds for medical research.'

'How are you doing that?'

'In short – I am making a thorough nuisance of myself, my dear.'

'Oh Frederick!'

'"Aw Frederick" – those days seem a long way off. How refined you have become.'

'I am not!'

'Are you insulted at my compliment?'

'Well I am sitting here in a loose calico robe, my old shawl, thick stockings and clogs – and you tell me I am refined! It does not quite tally, Frederick.'

'Your mind, dear girl; you have a refined mind. And you look especially exquisite in your Bohemian attire with your hair tumbling loose, highlighted by the flames of the fire.'

'Frederick, you're embarrassing me.'

'Very well. I'll say no more.'

'So what have you been doing? Who have you been seeing?'

'I've been spending rather too much time in London – which is why I thought it an excellent idea to visit you – what with writing letters to politicians and papers, dragging money from the reluctant pockets of rich men, and trying to establish a small organization of people with similar outlooks to myself. My view is that we spend too much money abroad – in our blasted colonies for instance, pandering to the tastes of our attachés there and on the defence of those colonies, half of which we surely don't want. Instead that money could be spent at home. England is rich at the expense of her own poor. And no – I have not become a Radical overnight, only a little more aware . . . Anyway, besides all that I have done little of interest. I suppose I should tell you – why is it that when I'm with you I am compelled to confide everything to you? – that I see the dreaded Baroness from time to time.'

'Von Hoffnung?'

'Yes, the very same I am afraid. I do not really like her, Rosaleen, and she continually opposes my ideals, but she *is* most stimulating, and I cannot say she is unattractive. A man has his needs . . . Before you attack me I must tell you I have no love for her, but some fondness. I know she is cunning, malicious, vicious-tempered, a fearful snob and all the rest, but she has on her side none of the boring hypocrisies of other women. She is not timid of stating her mind, can be amusing, is clever and articulate . . . And I need a woman in my bed, Rosaleen. There you have it. Are you horrified?'

'But no. Why should I be? Perhaps now we are on a more equal footing with our love affairs.'

But she minded, and could not say why that was.

Frederick sat in the studio while she painted, reading a book or writing notes. He never interfered and rarely commented, leaving her to explore without hindrance, so that she could nearly forget he was there – yet was pleasantly conscious of his presence. He had been at Norway House for five days and was talking of leaving within the next couple of days, when Oliver and Kate returned.

'Why, Frederick!' Kate greeted him, hugging him.

Oliver, however, was less effusive. Rosaleen watched the shadow cross his face. 'How long have you been here?'

'Five days,' Frederick replied equably.

'Five *days!* What – alone with Rosaleen?'

'Oh dearest, don't be so absurd,' Rosaleen chided him. 'Here, kiss me hello at least and let me tell you what has been happening . . . Oh – what of your aunt?'

'She died,' Oliver answered shortly.

'Yes but we have come into quite a large sum of money,' Kate said gaily, 'and the poor thing was really not in the least an amiable person –'

'And we have several plans what to do with the money,' Oliver interrupted, apparently forgetting his resentment towards Frederick.

Rosaleen thought: 'Thank goodness there is not going to be a scene.'

It was Frederick who told them about Rosaleen's painting and led them up to the studio. Rosaleen hovered behind, embarrassed, watching from the doorway: Kate's delighted reaction; Oliver's taciturnity. He called her: 'Rosaleen, come here.'

'As if I was a dog,' she thought, going over to him reluctantly.

She waited, dreading – and then he almost lifted her off the ground into his arms. 'I am so proud of you, my darling. I cannot tell you how *very* proud. I shall give you your own part of the studio and help you all I can. You will be an artist, Rosaleen.'

'Dearest Robbie – a quick note written by candlelight while the rest of the house sleeps. I cannot, however, for the most marvellous thing has happened: I have discovered I can paint. Even Oliver says I can. Robbie – I am going to be an artist.'

❧ Twelve ❧

THE TRAGEDY

I had a dear friend once –
But we picnicked in a poppy-field.

St Ives was alive once more with the calls and cries around the harbour. Summer approached, and in Norway House Kate sat writing at the kitchen table. A ribbon of light filtered through the small window near her and caught her pallor, shone through the dishevelled wisps of her fine hair. She sighed as she wrote and gazed intermittently through the window with troubled eyes, dangling her pen absently in the air and seeking inspiration from the empty space.

In the attic studio Rosaleen and Oliver painted in their separate corners. Rosaleen's face was tense. 'I'm still not satisfied,' she muttered.

'Believe me, it needed more brown. Cobbles are *not* blue.'

'But why does it have to be so *exact*? It's too gloomy. There was a radiance before. Even the Pre-Raphaelites whom you so admire use white ground.'

'Rosaleen, you must learn to trust my judgement.'

'What have you got to show for your judgement?' The disloyal thought frightened her, and she said nothing, resuming her painting of Bethesda Hill – a cobbled lane that was little more than a passage descending steeply to the harbour.

In the past few months since she had been painting, and as Oliver exerted more influence over her, the freedom she had initially enjoyed was being replaced by the same concise style as his own. She longed sometimes to splurge outrageous colour across the canvas, and fought constantly against her growing frustration; but she was his pupil, and could not match her instincts against his experience.

'The picture lacks dimension,' she complained after a few minutes.

'It does not. It is as it should be.'

'It looks like an architect's illustration.'

Nowadays she seemed frequently to be in an irritable humour, blaming him for removing her joy and her sense of adventure; and because she had her own dissatisfactions she had less patience with his bouts of melancholia. Once she had even shouted at him to pull himself together. Then, off – on a lone walk, hands in the pockets of her short coat. During it, calmed by the bracing air and gentle wind, she wondered: 'What is happening to me? I am becoming a shrew! I am as tedious as they are with my moods.'

Repentant, she returned.

'I have never met an artist who is not moody,' Kate told her.

'But I cannot accept that! Why should I suddenly be a different person from the one three or four months ago?'

'When you are learning something new, surely it is normal to endure doubt?'

'Perhaps you are right, yet –'

'What, dearest?'

'He is trying to inhibit my style, Kate, to take away my individuality. All the wonderment has gone for me . . . But I am horribly ungrateful in return for his kindness, and of course, Oliver is an excellent artist.'

But Rosaleen was no longer convinced of the truth of her own praise.

One wet afternoon in early June, when Oliver and Kate were in Penzance, she wrote to Frederick:

My dear Frederick –

Almost five months have passed since you visited here in January, and I had a sudden impulse to write to you! I wonder how you are keeping, and whether you are still

involving yourself in 'non-politics'? No doubt you have
been travelling also – you and dear (old) Edgar. No – I am
not insulting him; I am fully aware, as you told me, that he
only *looks* old . . .

Why am I writing to you? I think simply because I need
to air my sentiments and cannot do so to Oliver, nor even to
Kate, as I would feel disloyal. So here I am, about to
unburden myself to you, dear Frederick, whom I think of
often and with great affection . . .

Concerning my painting: I feel I am progressing
nowhere, and although I remind myself that in order to
improve one must suffer frustration and irritation –
nevertheless I am unconvinced those impulses are being
channelled in the right direction. I know my fault is
impatience, but I become increasingly uncertain that I am
following the right path.

Dare I be honest? I am growing disenchanted with that
school of art which first so enamoured me. I am beginning
to find it too stereotyped and self-indulgent, and although
there is no denying the genius and brilliance of the
Pre-Raphaelites, I find their works, despite their lavishness
of colour and splendour of composition, lack that freedom
which to me is the essence of everything. That word
'freedom': perhaps I have based my own life too much on it!
I believe you think I have!

But Frederick, in France there is a group of artists who
have been dubbed the Impressionists – I know you have
heard of them – and I think often, and with tremendous
excitement, about their painting.

Now you see why I could not speak of these matters to
Oliver, because despite his Bohemian attitudes he is
essentially a conventional artist. He fears new ideas, and will
always be a follower. To succeed as a follower one must be
exceptional. I am afraid that Oliver is not exceptional . . . So
how am I to progress?

Enough of that . . . life here in St Ives does not change
and I continue to be enchanted by everything I see and by

227

the characters I meet. We keep fairly busy, and sometimes see friends, but I still cannot really take to Colin. There is something unreal about him. In trying to be fundamental he succeeds in being the opposite. On balance Oliver and I are well together, though I cannot deny there are trying moments. Kate, bless her heart, is as good and precious as ever, and she has become like a sister to me. How lucky I am to have met her.

But I hope you will see us all shortly. For we are coming to London in a fortnight's time on June 18th, to stay in Oliver and Kate's uncle's mansion in Belgravia. Isn't it fortunate to have such an obliging uncle who makes himself scarce at just the right time? I am looking forward to it greatly – to being in London, and of course to seeing you, dearest Frederick. I believe that Robbie might be travelling down from Lancashire, so I am doubly excited. Goodness – how long ago it seems since I left home, and hasn't a lot happened? And there is surely more to happen yet. That is why I cannot return: I must go back in a position of strength and achievement. When I am confident of those two things, then I'll be able to resist the pull to remain there.

As regards that achievement – I am apprehensive how people will react to my paintings. I think perhaps it is conceit on my part which allows me to exhibit them. And as a woman it is doubly hard; I do not have the advantage like Elizabeth Siddal, of having been married to Rossetti. However, I do not envy her untimely end . . .

I am bringing with me to London the three pictures I have done, but that is against Oliver's wishes. He would prefer me to bring only two and exclude that first effort which you saw developing. However, despite the fact it may have many technical faults, it *does* have vibrance and liveliness, and looking at it one could tell I enjoyed doing it. But there again – to exhibit one's very first painting does rather seem to lack modesty!

How I ramble. I shall close now, and look forward

immensely to seeing you in two weeks' time – assuming you are not in some distant land.

Yours very affectionately,
Rosaleen.

The weather was unbearably hot and humid. Each day the temperature rose, and the reek of fish and sewage was everywhere; one could not avoid it – it permeated clothing, hair, skin and even closed windows . . . People moved about with lethargy and glazed eyes, and the queues at St Ias well for fresh water were long and tedious, unrelieved by gossip. Instead the waiting women shifted about irritably, exchanging the odd word, their appetite for juicy snippets quashed by the heat.

Rosaleen opened the window of the studio to let in some air – and shut it immediately, sniffing in disgust. 'I'll not be sorry to leave here,' she thought, 'not with this continuing. The only way to escape the smell is to walk along the headland or to one of the beaches . . .'

Her face was a light golden colour from her walks, and her hair was bleached a shade paler than usual.

'Golden child.' Oliver came up to her and traced the outline of her lips, a tender expression on his face. 'And such a sweet upturned child's mouth.'

'But not such a sweet child,' she replied lightly.

'Yes you are. I forget sometimes how young you are.'

'And you are about to sigh about your own old age and how you are beaten by time!'

'That's cruel.'

'Oh dearest, I was teasing. You know I was.' She reached up to kiss him; she loved the fullness of his lips and would nibble at them gently.

He held her to him and she nestled against him, inhaling his body's smells – sweat, paint, tobacco, and on his breath peppermint from a sweet he had been sucking. His hugeness encompassed her and made her feel safe, and she recalled having the same feeling as a child with her father.

'I worry about us,' Oliver said. 'I am besotted with you as I've never been with another woman, and I fear that I drive you away.'

'You are *kind* to me,' she assured him, hugging him fiercely. 'And I am not always appreciative or grateful.'

'I want neither of those things. I want your love.'

'You have that.'

'It will do us good to be in London.'

'I was thinking the same.'

They stayed by the window, their arms about each other, looking at the evening harbour, peaceful now; at the yellowing-reddening sky.

Kate called, 'Colin and Talwyn are here.' And instantly their moment together was curtailed as Oliver rushed from the room to welcome his friends.

'He is so easily impressed,' Rosaleen thought. 'And once I believed him to be so strong.' She went downstairs without enthusiasm.

'Hello Colin, Talwyn.'

'Er – good evening, Rosaleen.'

'Even a simple utterance like that requires premeditation . . . But she smiled through her annoyance and touched Talwyn's hand gently. The young woman didn't glance up in acknowledgement.

Rosaleen had become fond of her and asked, 'What's wrong, Talwyn? Aren't you pleased to see me?'

Colin answered for her. 'Her sensitivity is – er – disturbed by the heatwave. She is, as you know, susceptible to the least change in environment, be it –'

'Talwyn,' Rosaleen cut across him, speaking directly to the girl and crouching now at her side, 'would you like some herby beer? You helped me make it.'

'No.'

'Where's your Joanie doll, dear?' Kate asked.

At that Talwyn looked up. Her dark eyes poured out sorrow. 'I lost it. Joanie doll's gone away . . .'

'I told her we'd get another,' Colin said loudly, nodding sagely as if he'd made a profound statement.

'Don't want a new Joanie doll. Want my *old* Joanie doll,' Talwyn screamed out, standing up so suddenly and forcefully that Rosaleen was thrust aside.

She was shocked to hear a child's petulance intoned by a woman. Its innuendo changed, and Talwyn, standing in the middle of the room, seemed disproportionately tall and menacing.

Kate got up and went over to her. 'Dearest Talwyn, we'll try and find your Joanie doll – but if we cannot, then it means she is with God, and you must be glad of that, because you love God.'

Talwyn's face cleared immediately. 'I love God,' she repeated. 'And if Joanie doll's with God, will she be happy?'

'Yes dear, very. I promise you. Now will you come sit beside me?'

Talwyn – the epitome of ripe womanhood – was led docilely by Kate towards the settee.

But the matter was not quite finished with. 'Tomorrow, will you look for her? If she's not with God, will you?'

'Yes dear – oh goodness . . .' Her voice trailed off as she remembered they were travelling to London the next day.

'What?' asked Colin snappily, jealous that Kate had calmed Talwyn, where he had failed.

'Have you told her we are away for a month?'

'I thought it best not to. She reacted so badly last year.'

'Kate isn't going away? Kate *isn't*.' Talwyn rose to her feet once more and this time ran agitatedly from one person to the next, her clenched fists flailing.

'Hush darling. I'm coming back.' Kate was at her side, trying to comfort her; but Talwyn pushed her roughly away, wailing and shrieking incoherently.

Oliver spoke finally in a stiff tone. 'I think you'd better take her away, Colin. She is overwrought.'

'It is the heat,' he explained again, taking her arms and trying to pinion them as she spat at him and clawed with her fingers in the air.

They left, and the other three stood wordlessly watching the two figures, combatants now, disappearing down the lane, and heard the insane screeching long after.

Later, over supper in the kitchen, they were silent and thoughtful. Oliver said soberly, 'I have to admit that at times I question Colin's reasoning involving himself with Talwyn.'

Rosaleen didn't comment; she saw still the violence in Talwyn's contorted face and felt disquieted.

'I love her dearly and try to accept her for what she is,' Kate said. 'But when she acts as she did this evening I do not *know* what she is and am almost afraid of her.'

The next morning they left on their long journey to London – a journey that was strained and discordant because Rosaleen had insisted on bringing her first painting with her, and Oliver sulked at her defiant disregard of his opinion.

Weary and grimy from the heat and from travelling they arrived at the mansion in Belgravia when night had fallen. But the house was illuminated both outside and within, and servants rushed about taking their baggage and tending to their needs as soon as they set foot inside. From the walls the eyes of great felled beasts stared reproachfully, and a pair of suits of armour stood in the cool marbled hall. Rosaleen thought that if she had been a nervous type she would be intimidated by the echoing gloom which pervaded the place. They had a light meal laid out on butler's trays in the library and went directly to their rooms to bed.

Oliver muttered, 'I don't know why you brought that picture. You will never listen, will you?' And disgruntled, fell into immediate sleep, lying sprawled across the mattress and snoring loudly so that beside him Rosaleen became increasingly tense and wakeful.

'How disagreeable he is sometimes . . .' She looked at his dark outline dispassionately. 'I suppose I love him . . .'

The first few days were spent socializing – entertaining friends of Kate and Oliver whom Rosaleen had not previously met, and visiting others. Frederick visited the day after their arrival and Oliver showed him first his own paintings, about which he was courteous, and then Rosaleen's.

'She has improved, has she not?' he said proudly, his arm around her.

Frederick's reply was too quick and non-committal, Rosaleen thought; and as he continued to linger over her two pictures she examined his expression keenly. His face revealed little, but she knew him well and her heart sank. His cautious praise confirmed what she had feared. She turned away from him and fought back tears. And the more Oliver lauded her to Frederick, believing absolutely in what he said, the more pent up Rosaleen became.

'Why can't he see it?' she thought. 'Why *can't* he?'

She had a few minutes alone with Frederick later on, and confronted him immediately with the issue. 'You agree with what I wrote to you, don't you?'

He hesitated, then looked at her unhappily. 'Yes.'

'I knew,' she said in a small voice.

There were a few seconds of brooding silence. 'I don't know what to do,' she continued. 'I feel – despairing.'

'Don't. Have you brought your first painting with you?'

'Yes. We quarrelled over that.'

'I am glad you brought it. It is your ammunition.'

'My ammunition?'

'When it is complimented and perhaps sold, and the others are disregarded, then he will realize and leave you to your own devices.'

'I hope you are right . . . And yet I need guidance.'

'But not from Oliver.'

'. . . No. Oh I feel so disloyal.'

'You are not disloyal. You are, as ever, realistic. And Rosaleen – without wishing to sound condescending – you are young. You have plenty of time.'

She shrugged impatiently, and then asked tremulously, 'Are they very bad, the other two?'

'I am no expert,' he answered. 'I would not say they are bad. Possibly they are even quite good, for they are accurate and nicely executed. But they are uninspired and I find them flat and without substance.'

'Do you think them technically superior to my first effort?'

'Rosaleen, Rosaleen . . . As I say, I am no expert and you put me in a spot! Possibly they are "technically superior", but that is not the most important thing. If you could combine the effervescence of your first picture with your subsequent knowledge, then you would soon progress in giant leaps. Now be encouraged.'

She laid her head against his chest. 'How sensible you are, and how I value our friendship.'

Frederick closed his eyes tightly and paused, his hands half-raised, before letting them fall to tenderly cup her head. 'And how I value it,' he said.

John Ruskin called the following afternoon. With him was Robbie. Rosaleen had not seen him for over two and a half years and he had just had his sixteenth birthday. He was even taller, but his frame had filled out and any trace of gawkiness was gone, replaced instead by muscular litheness. He was neatly dressed, his newly-cut hair lay respectably flat, and beneath his freckles his face was ruddy and firmly padded with flesh.

She felt a sense of shock. 'He is a young man . . . He looks like Father, despite the colouring.'

'Rosaleen.' The deep voice was a shock also, and when he came forward to embrace her his skin was rough and masculine.

'I can't believe it,' she kept repeating, half laughing, half crying. 'Let me look at you. I can't believe it.'

'He does a good day's work, Rosaleen,' John Ruskin said, looking fondly at the brother and sister. 'You'd be proud of him. But you have not changed, Rosaleen . . . And these are your friends.'

Introductions were exchanged and Oliver clasped the famous man's hand, his clear eyes gazing at the other admiringly. 'I am truly honoured to meet you, sir. I have the utmost respect for your many accomplishments and achievements.'

'Thank you, you are most kind.' Ruskin smiled – but his face was gaunt and strained about the mouth. Rosaleen knew he had been travelling extensively since Rose La Touche's death; and

Robbie had written in his letters that when in England he still gave regular lectures, wrote his books, researched, sketched and organized exhibitions.

'He looks ill,' she thought, saddened. 'And his eyes have a weariness about them.'

Kate said gaily, 'Well, now that we have introduced ourselves, are we going to stay amongst all these poor severed heads in the hallway, or shall we adjourn to the library?'

Oliver brought Rosaleen's paintings out again, and although she knew he was well-intentioned, she thought how mistaken was his pride in her, and cringed with shame, tensing herself in preparation for Ruskin's criticism.

'But Rosaleen, these are splendid attempts,' she heard him say – and looked up slowly, disbelievingly. 'Most interesting to see your development,' he continued, glancing from one to the other, as Oliver stood paternally by her, his face glowing on her behalf. 'This last one, the one of the two boys –'

Oliver tried to interrupt: 'Actually sir that is her –'

'– is quite lovely. It has all the boldness I would expect from you.'

Oliver fell silent and Rosaleen felt him slump a little next to her.

'And – the other two?' she asked quietly.

'They are well-drafted and precisely done, to be sure, and certainly not to be ashamed of. But they are not atmospheric in the same way; they lack warmth. No, I think this new freedom of style you have discovered must be encouraged, and that you must further your technique within those realms . . .'

Oliver and Kate went early to bed that night, the former subdued and sullen, and when Rosaleen tried to take his hand in understanding he had snatched himself away from contact with her. Ruskin had departed during the course of the evening and Rosaleen was left alone with Robbie.

'So mankin, how've you been?'

'Really fine, Rosaleen.'

Now that he sat beside her she was used to him again. The changes in him did not alter his essential character: he was still her mankin. She pulled him comfortably against her and stroked his coarse hair.

'Oh Robbie, how long ago it all seems.'

'What does, Rosaleen?' His voice was muffled by her closeness.

'Everything. Now sit up once more and speak to me of all that's been happening.'

He told her about his work at John Ruskin's; about Laurie Hilliard and Joan and Arthur Severn; described the alterations at Brantwood and Ruskin's continuing passion for the place; he recited a couple of his latest poems to her and told her, blushingly, that one had just been accepted by the *Kendal Gazette*.

'But that is wonderful!'

He blushed deeper still as he confided, 'I wrote it for a girl.'

She looked at him tenderly. 'Are you in love, Robbie?'

'I think so. She's seventeen and there's several lads after her, Rosaleen, she's so pretty. And they're all older than me. But it's me she cares for.'

'Well you're special, Robbie, that's why. You have grown up to be special.'

'She's the niece of the Vicar's wife come to stay since her parents have both died. And she's clever. She reads a lot and likes poetry. You'd like her, Rosaleen.'

'Of course I would, Robbie. Now stop looking so anguished!' She laughed chidingly.

'I miss her.' He swallowed; his Adam's apple slid up then down.

'It's not easy, is it, mankin? But you must bide your time. At your age it's the sensible thing to do.'

'I'll not have a change of heart,' he said, glancing at her defiantly.

And she soothed him, touching his arm lightly with her fingertips. 'I know you'll not. And why should you. But if you ever do then it'll be sweet to remember . . . Robbie – talk to me of home. Please tell me what news from there.'

'I was last there three weeks ago or more,' he told her. 'The inn's busy again now, what with Isobel – you know, Nancy's girl

– spreading her favours and everything. And Father – he's a bit better with me now. When I go there I sometimes lend a hand and he doesn't say much. But at least he doesn't rant at me so. He's not changed in his appearance – not to my eyes at any rate. He got rid of the maid he was bedding, and there's another replaced her – but not in his affections. She's old, this one. He talks about mother sometimes to me. At times I think he's lonely . . . Well I suppose he must be,' he added reflectively.

'And have you mentioned me to him ever? Does he know or care where I am or what I'm doing?'

'He'll not hear your name, Ros'leen.'

'That's a shame . . .' She sighed. 'Ah, poor Father. I ceased to blame him a long time ago. Not that there was much to blame him for really. It was more a matter of understanding one another . . . And Nana Annie?'

'Well like I wrote in my letter, she was poorly a month or so back, but she's herself again now. Though she drinks too much cider. She still talks about you – wonders how her tiny lass is faring, as she says. Her sight's completely gone now, though she says she can differentiate between light and dark. But she hobbles about as though she can see. Knows every nook of the inn she does. And her hearing's sharper than ever.'

'I'll write to her. You take the letter home with you and read it to her. I'll write to Father too – and if he's agreeable you could read it to him also.' Rosaleen was thoughtful, and then recalling a conversation with her brother years previously, smiled and asked, 'Tell me, mankin, did you ever have to wring the chickens' necks as you so dreaded?'

'Yes.' His mouth trembled babyishly. 'It was awful. I don't want to think of it. Just once. It all went wrong . . . It took ages. After that Father did it.'

'Well at least he had some compassion! Poor young Robbie.'

'But I'm not am I now, Rosaleen?'

'No, mankin, you're not and I'm proud of you.'

'I'm proud of you – with your painting and all. I love getting your letters; you can make me see everything. I can really picture it.'

237

'Well that is good.'

'Kate is so nice.'

'And Oliver?'

'I'm not sure.'

'I thought not.'

'But I like him rather better than Tags.'

She laughed and cuffed his ear. 'That at least is something. Perhaps in time you'll like him. He is a difficult man with whom to become acquainted.'

Robbie stayed a couple of days more, then left for Lancashire. Rosaleen gave him the letters for Nana Annie and Thomas at the station.

'Please read them,' she instructed.

'I shall do, but I don't hold much hope that Father'll want to hear his.' He stared at his sister with a flash of sorrow that he was leaving her. They hugged each other emotionally and he boarded the train. He disappeared for a few moments then reappeared at the window of a compartment. She called through it, 'What happened to that button I gave you when I left home – do you have it still?'

He rummaged in his jacket pocket and then flourished it to show her. 'You see,' he shouted above the guard's whistle and the squeal of the engine, 'I'll never lose it. It's my most precious thing.'

'Apart from a lock of your loved one's hair.'

'How did you know?'

'I didn't. I guessed.'

His cheeks were crimson and she leant forward to touch them through the open window. Then the train lurched forward and she was left touching empty air, gazing at his swivelled head, waving . . .

The heatwave endured and the next three weeks passed in visiting exhibitions, the theatre, going to concerts and to restaurants. On one occasion Frederick took them to dinner and had as his other guests the artists Edward and Henrietta Ward. She was in her mid-forties and her husband sixteen years older. They had met when she was just eleven when he had become her teacher and mentor; and by coincidence they had shared the same surname. Since that early age Henrietta had established herself as one of the few women artists to be regarded seriously, having first exhibited at the Royal Academy at the age of fourteen. Now, while the men talked among themselves, the three women conversed animatedly – about art, about the problems facing women involved in a field usually reserved for men. Here was a woman who knew the difficulties, Rosaleen thought; who had won battles and founded a reputation, so that now she accepted Royal commissions and taught various members of the royal family. Yet her reputation continued to be linked with that of her husband, and Rosaleen felt the old anger which rose in her whenever she considered the subordinate role women were obliged to play in society.

She reminisced: 'When I was a child I'd study the men drinking in my father's inn and think how lucky they were – always so assured. I liked them and was only too happy to serve them; but I envied them then and envy them more now. They are superior even when they are inferior.'

'My husband has been everything to my art,' Mrs Ward stated, quietly defensive. And added, 'And he has Ruskin's ideals, incorporating nature in art.'

'Your father is an artist also, is he not?' asked Kate hurriedly, anxious that Rosaleen might become too aggressive.

'Oh my father is an excellent painter and engraver. We are an entire family who brandishes brushes,' she joked.

'And your children?' Rosaleen asked.

'All eight of them? Oh dear – that would be too much,' the woman said drily.

'Will it improve, do you think?' Rosaleen looked at her with respect. 'The situation, I mean; so that women will be wholeheartedly accepted into the schools; so that women may paint the subjects of their choosing without being attacked by critics; so that they are not continually compared unfavourably with men?' She paused for breath and realized that her voice had been raised and her hands were clenched in tension. The men had stopped speaking to listen.

'You have some very valid points there, my dear,' said Henrietta Ward, smiling. 'You must pay me a visit at my home and studio in Upton Park, Slough, and we can speak at length. I would be most interested to continue our discussion.'

'And I too would be, and am grateful for your invitation – only we return to Cornwall next week.'

'And I am away from tomorrow for a few days. What a great pity. But when you next come to London – we shall certainly meet then, and I shall extend the invitation again.'

'Thank you kindly.'

'Not at all, my dear. I find you most refreshing.'

The following evening was the exhibition which would continue for five days, until they returned to Cornwall. It was held at a small gallery in Conduit Street belonging to a friend of Oliver's, and a number of slightly influential people had been invited: critics; potential patrons; artists; affluent men of business; a few members of the aristocracy.

'A mixed bunch,' Oliver said to the terrified Rosaleen as they were about to go inside – himself in surprisingly good humour. And he pushed her gently through the open entrance doors, she wishing it were over, and regretting having ever wielded a brush.

There were perhaps thirty people present and one of the first guests she recognized was Frederic George Stephens, writer, painter and art critic.

Rosaleen's spirits sank lower. 'Oh no – surely not him.'

By contrast she had never seen Oliver more elated or confident. He left her side – a thing he did not normally do – and she crept about mouse-like, appalled that the people in the room were all here to view – amongst other pictures – her paltry efforts. A flunky appeared with glasses of champagne and she took two pretending one was for someone else. When he had moved on she drank them in quick succession.

Pleasantly relaxed, she stood leaning slightly against a chair as far as possible from her pictures, and observed the activity about her, a little half-smile on her face: Kate was talking with a tall fair-haired man she knew to be a Liberal politician. She heard him say, 'It is a pity you live so far away – I should like to see you again.' And Kate's reply: 'I could always travel to London and stay with a relative.' 'Can I see you before you leave? Tomorrow?' And the expression of pleasure in Kate's eyes. And Oliver – talking to another artist, a fellow contributor to the exhibition. Oliver was loudly declaring his loyalty to the old school and although the other's response was inaudible Rosaleen could tell by his arrogant stance he was not in accord. She glanced at the other people – more men than women; some were there with total disregard for the paintings and had only attended because they had been lured by the prospect of plenty of champagne and a pleasant social occasion; others were there genuinely to view, and these types she watched carefully. They hesitated long over the work of Oliver's acquaintance and made notes, and Arnold Edgar, the gallery owner, was called over several times and wrote something in a book; they frowned over another artist's exhibits and looked taken aback . . . And then they came to Rosaleen's trio, alongside Oliver's pictures. She saw them scan her two later works with quick disinterest, and then stop at her first. Arnold Edgar was again called over and remained there to speak with a couple of gentlemen who glanced in her direction and then proceeded to stare at her.

A hand tapped her shoulder and she swung round.

'Miss Ruddock? Dear me – did I startle you? I believe we met briefly some years ago at an Exhibition at Sutton House, when you were the subject of a marvellous painting by Burne-Jones. I mean by that, *The Joseph Shawl*, of course. My name is Frederic George Stephens.' He smiled down at her, a thin man with fine eyes and a modest smile.

'I know. How do you do?'

'I am delighted to see you again and delighted too – and may I add somewhat surprised – by your change in career.'

She stood up straight and looked at him uncertainly.

'For how long have you been painting?'

'Since January of this year only.'

'Five months? Is that all? Really I am quite impressed. Yes quite . . .'

Oliver appeared with Frederick, who had arrived late. With

him was the Baroness von Hoffnung, and he looked shame-faced.

'Hello Rosaleen.' He bent to kiss her on the cheek and whispered in her ear, 'Sorry, she insisted.'

'Miss Ruddock, I see you have switched careers.' The Baroness curled her lips.

'I was just discussing that very thing with Miss Ruddock,' Frederic George Stephens said. 'And I was about to ask a few questions. You were saying you have done these paintings in the last five months?'

'Yes, Mr Stephens.'

'How very worthy. And how was the one depicting the boys placed?'

'It is my most recent picture,' she lied firmly, looking challeng-ingly at Oliver as she spoke and noticing his expression darken.

'Well then, you are to be commended. You have progressed and will surely continue to do so. And I believe it has sold already.'

'*Has* it?' She clapped her hands in excitement – then glanced suspiciously at Frederick.

'Do not look at me, dear girl. Not this time! It has been bought by a businessman for twenty-eight guineas solely on its merits.'

'Twenty-eight guineas!'

'Some of that is to go to Arnold Edgar as commission,' Oliver said flatly.

'Twenty-eight guineas!' Rosaleen repeated softly, ignoring him.

'My poor country-girl,' the Baroness said drily. 'Twenty-eight guineas is neither here nor there. It is hardly a sum over which to lose one's head.'

'It is a good price for a new artist's first sale,' Stephens contradicted her sharply. And turning to Rosaleen said gently, 'You will not find it an easy passage, Miss Ruddock. But persevere regardless, and I wish you good fortune . . . Mean-while, look out for the *Athenaeum* in four days' time. Now, if you will excuse me . . . Baroness, gentlemen . . .'

'Frederick, shall we take our leave now?' the Baroness asked, turning her head with a swift haughty movement and holding his arm ostentatiously.

He moved away from her. 'I wish to stay and talk with Rosaleen, Leonora.'

'Oh you are so famous now, you see, my dear, that your origins no longer matter,' she said to Rosaleen.

'Leonora –'

'I am taking my leave, Frederick.' Her supercilious gaze rested on the three of them, then, swirling her skirts around herself, she left.

'I apologize, Rosaleen. She forced her way into the hansom with me.'

'It isn't your fault. She doesn't bother me. I am too happy to let such a little thing concern me.'

'And I am proud of you. You must be too, Oliver.'

'Yes naturally,' he said shortly, but his hand, when Rosaleen took it in hers to restore their closeness, was cold and limp.

By the final day of the exhibition Rosaleen's other two pictures remained unsold, which neither surprised nor bothered her, but of his eight works Oliver had sold only one. Rosaleen was mortified on his behalf, feeling his pain, his slain pride.

'He will recover,' Kate told her.

'But he takes such rejection to heart. He says nothing of it and his sense of failure builds up inside him. You and I know how he is. He thinks everything pointless. I wish so much for his contentment, Kate.'

'I know, dear, and so does he.'

'It is not sufficient.'

The following day the weather broke and the deluge of rain which burst from an oppressive sky flooded roads and replenished rivers. That same day the three returned to Cornwall, and the journey back was as silent and weighty with solitary thought as the journey to London. Next to him Oliver's portfolio was a symbolic reminder that he was a failure. Opposite him his sister sat with a preoccupied expression, her face serene. She thought

243

perhaps she was in love. Rosaleen was on Oliver's right, by the window. Her hand rested lightly on her lover's knee, and the other hand clasped a copy of the *Athenaeum*. In it was Frederic George Stephens' article, and she was mentioned. He had said she showed 'promise', and 'demonstrated a sympathy with colour'.

Rosaleen hugged her pleasure to herself. From time to time it sent small ripples through her – and then, guilty, she would stroke and massage Oliver's leg gently to remind him she was there . . .

Summer months passed: July with its festivities – fairs, horse-racing, the five-yearly John Knill celebrations with the procession to Worvas Hill and then the dancing around the tall granite tower to the music of a fiddler; August; and then into early September. As the memory of Oliver's humiliation receded he gradually let slip the cloak of introversion he had wrapped morosely about himself. He ceased to condemn those who had not had the taste to appreciate his work, or to glare at Rosaleen every time she spoke, and fragile harmony was restored.

He no longer interfered with her painting and they worked peaceably together in their respective parts of the studio – with very little conversation and only the sounds of their creativity to be heard. There was harmony in their togetherness, she thought in a moment's awareness, when a fond glance between them had stimulated her consciousness; and she envisaged themselves as they might appear: the two of them immersed in their separate tasks, united by the single aim of interpreting art; united by their love. As an interloper she saw them stop to exchange a look of understanding, a comment – before picking up their brushes again; and she was enchanted. She thought: 'I'll look back on these times in years to come and remember them.'

Then swiftly following it came another thought: 'But in years to come won't we still be sharing our experiences? Why did I think that?'

The first week of that September Oliver announced that he

wanted to use his inheritance to move. 'I have had a thought,' he said over dinner one evening. 'And I hope you will both be happy with it, because I am so excited by my idea, and have already mentioned it to Colin, whose enthusiasm is no less than mine.'

Rosaleen tensed. Any plan which involved Colin held little appeal to her. But Oliver's expression was so lit with happiness she could have begrudged him nothing.

'I feel I have purpose at last,' he prefaced what was to follow.

And she thought: 'After such a statement how can he expect Kate or I to disagree with any proposal he makes?'

'My idea is that we sell Norway House and buy a large country house – a farmhouse perhaps – somewhere we could be virtually self-sufficient. Colin and Talwyn would move in with us and Colin and I would start an art school. There would be enough space to accommodate three or four pupils if necessary.'

'Well!' Kate exclaimed.

Rosaleen was silent. Her mind was churning.

'But what do you *think*?' he asked, impatient.

Kate said, 'We'd need help to run it – servants. We couldn't do it on our own.' She was dismayed, because her Liberal Member of Parliament had twice visited St Ives and made his intentions clear.

'I know that. But we've plenty of money and soon enough we'd be earning from our fees.'

'Well . . .' She said again, blushing and wondering whether it was too premature to say anything.

'Oh you are hopeless!' he accused her. 'Is that all you can say: *well* . . . ?' His face had darkened as he saw his idyll about to be crushed. 'Rosaleen?'

'It could be interesting,' she replied cautiously.

'And I thought you would both be so excited.' He looked at them with disgust. 'Instead you speak like uninspired puppets.'

'Oliver dearest – it is such a surprise, that is all.'

'That should not detract. And it's everything you wanted, Kate. You always craved space, the idea of your own kitchen garden, and chickens and pigs . . .'

'I did want all that before . . .'

'Before *what*?' He flung his arms wide in frustration. And then his attitude changed and he slumped in his chair like a disappointed boy. 'Of course if you are both against the idea I must respect your wishes and not try to persuade you.'

And then, at the sight of his defeat, both women immediately capitulated and rushed to his side – to fuss him, and assure him of the brilliance of his idea.

Kate thought: 'I wouldn't have to stay once it was established . . .'

Within minutes his enthusiasm was restored – and had even communicated itself to them, so that they were laughing together, and talking simultaneously, their arms about each other.

'I have news for you both,' he said, when the excitement had died down. 'I have planned to see a house with Colin tomorrow. It's ideally situated being not far from Penzance near Marazion. I thought perhaps we would drop off you two and Talwyn around Gulval; you could have a picnic somewhere and we'd return for you later. Rosaleen might even want to take her sketch-pad and water-colours – there are some fine views up there.'

The following day was warm, and the four of them were jocular in the little trap as Oliver drove them, bumping, along the dusty road from St Ives into the freshness of the open and wild countryside, its bracken and gorse-clad ruggedness reminding Rosaleen of Lancashire. As they approached Gulval the scenery became more muted and agricultural, and small lanes meandered cosily off the main road, surrounded by soft countryside. They turned down one of these lanes and came to a poppy-field. It was completely red.

'How beautiful,' Kate cried. 'Oliver, stop here. We can picnic here. What do you think, Rosaleen?'

'It's perfect. And we have passed a splendid view I could walk back to and paint afterwards.'

The women got out and the men drove off, waving cheerily. 'We'll return in about three hours,' Oliver called.

'That means four,' Kate said complacently. 'He is surely one of

the world's most unpunctual men . . . What a glorious spot . . .
Why, what's wrong, darling?'

Talwyn had shrunk back. Her face wore a look of horror
and her mouth hung open, quivering. She didn't answer
Kate's question, but pointed with a trembling finger to the
field.

'Talwyn?' Kate persisted gently. 'What is it?'

'It's bleeding,' she burst out, screaming the words. 'The field's
bleeding.' She clutched at her hair and tried to run. Kate and
Rosaleen held her.

'Hush Talwyn,' Rosaleen tried to comfort her. 'It's a field with
pretty flowers. They're red flowers. See – if you wait here I'll go
and pluck one to show you.'

'Will you, Talwyn?' Kate asked, stroking the girl's forehead as
she cowered against her.

She nodded, still with her head buried in Kate's sleeve. She
seemed Amazonian beside the other's thinness.

Rosaleen returned with three poppies. 'See Talwyn? Pretty
flowers. One for you, one for Kate and one for myself.'

Talwyn took it tentatively, fingering its dark centre and soft
petals and sniffing it suspiciously. 'Flower doesn't have pretty
smell.'

'But its petals are like velvet, dearest,' Kate soothed her. 'Soft
as your chacks.' She used the Cornish word for cheeks, and
rubbed her poppy lightly against Talwyn's face. 'Now,' she
said brightly, 'shall we go in the pretty field with all its
flowers and have our picnic? Rosaleen and I shall look after
you.'

They carried their things into the meadow, to a part shaded by
an elm tree through whose leaves were coins of blue and white
sky. Kate spread the rug, and blades of long silken grass
overlapped the edges. In the breeze the poppies waved a
little.

'Isn't it nice?' Rosaleen said.

They unpacked the hamper and sorted out the food – various
meats and a pie, tomatoes, cheeses, chutney, a tart and fruit.
Talwyn took a plate and piled it. Once she had been hungry and

she had not forgotten it. She ate greedily and broodingly, her agitation subdued by the food. The other two ate and talked between themselves.

'Oliver has this back-to-nature image fixed in his head,' Rosaleen remarked to her friend. 'I think that he envisages himself stripped to the waist, revealing that wonderful muscled torso of his glistening with sweat while he works the soil. And when he's not working the land he sees himself as a mentor to a class of admiring students.'

'And you? How do you see yourself?' Kate flicked her hair out of her eyes.

'I see myself going off on my own and painting,' Rosaleen said. 'Because otherwise I shall be at your dear brother's beck and call. What about you?'

'As an unpaid servant.' But she laughed lightly.

'What of your politician friend – Mr Bennett? Is that your concern?'

'It is early days yet to say much.'

'Perhaps. But anyway you're free to do as you wish. Remember that, Kate. I'll be here to mollify him . . . And you never know, his idea might work.' She lay back with her elbows cushioning her head and gazed at the discs of light between the elm's branches.

'I hope you are right. I hope for my brother's sake it works. He'll be unbearable if it doesn't. Are you better now, Talwyn dear?'

The young woman made no answer, but continued to tear at a chicken bone with her white teeth.

'Oh dear, she's in one of her moods,' murmured Kate.

'And I was wanting to go and paint that view I saw. It was so beautiful – overlooking Mount's Bay and with St Michael's Mount as clear as anything.'

'But of course you must go and paint it, dearest.'

'What about you – and Talwyn?'

'I shall tell Talwyn stories. I love to tell stories; and she can curl up against me whilst I do so. Would you like that, Talwyn – for me to tell you stories and stroke your forehead?'

The big black eyes looked up, vacuous, disturbed – and then away again. 'Yes.'

'You see? All will be well now. Off you go, Rosaleen – and we shall see you later.'

She took her portable easel, pad and box of watercolours and walked down the road . . . round the bend, and up a hill, until she found her 'view' again. She was quite high and the landscape was composed of sweeping hills divided into areas of pasture and undulating to the coast – and there was the wide curve of the bay, and like an island from a legend, St Michael's Mount rose in its midst.

Rosaleen set up her easel, and stood quite still, observing the magnificence around her. 'How can God not exist when there is this to prove it otherwise?' she thought.

She settled to her task, intending at a later stage to re-do the scene in oils. This was to be a preliminary sketch and it was only for convenience she used water-colours. She was happily engrossed and had been gone for about three-quarters of an hour when she heard cutting across the air, a distant almost unearthly cry. She stopped painting and listened, her senses alert, her head strained forward; but the unnerving cry was not repeated and she concluded that it had been a snared animal, or a vixen objecting to an ardent dog-fox . . .

For a few moments she was chilled by the sound, so that it rang out again in her ears, but then the gentleness of the countryside, the calmly grazing animals, and the infinite sea took hold of her again and once more she lifted her brush . . .

A further half an hour elapsed, then Rosaleen packed her things neatly, folded her easel and set off to join the others again. She was happy with her work and with her day, touched by the loveliness of the place; and as she walked along the lane she hummed, holding her head jauntily high and feeling the sun on her hair. When she came to the poppy-field she called gaily, 'Cooee, I'm back.' And then, since no answer came, she called again, 'Halloo – I'm back.'

There was no reply.

Suddenly and unaccountably she felt a sense of misgiving and

249

started to run, through the long grass and poppies towards the elm tree. There she was greeted by a scene of horror. Sprawled across the rug lay Kate, her eyes staring upwards and blood already drying around the corners of her open mouth and on her chin. There was blood on her Joseph shawl and everywhere else that Rosaleen looked – and there cowering beside Kate's body was Talwyn, still holding the cheese knife.

Rosaleen stumbled forward, clutching her mouth. Her gasps became more rapid until they became a single scream. She fell on to her knees near Talwyn, and hugging her arms about herself rocked to and fro. She didn't cry out again and muffled her fist fully into her mouth to prevent herself from making a further noise. For a while she remained like this, and then slowly withdrawing her fist she asked in a deadened tone, 'Why did you do it, Talwyn?'

The other girl had not moved and was still hunched up, shivering. She said, 'The field's bleeding. Don't like this field.'

So they were found by Oliver and Colin. The three of them similarly frozen into immobility; and the field was indeed bleeding.

✒ Thirteen ✑

THE AFTERMATH

Paint me a picture
And I'll play the flute.

The trap tore along the dusty lanes to Penzance, tossing its bloodied occupants back and forth. Colin drove, his expression fixed, unfathomable, cracking his whip every so often so that the pony would break into a cumbersome canter and dust flew up from the road.

No one spoke. There was nothing to say. The horror was already a part of them – absorbed into them. There was nothing to doubt or contradict, and Rosaleen's one scream and Oliver's wailing were already in the past. Kate's body lay between them, across their laps, and Rosaleen cradled her friend's head. Oliver stroked the white face with clumsy shaking fingers, and from time to time little whimpers escaped him. Seated beside her protector, Talwyn huddled her knees to her chin and thought – who knew what?

Rosaleen related the events to the policeman in a whisper. He told her to speak up, but then she ceased to be able even to whisper, and swayed on her feet. He caught her as she fell and propped her on a chair. She felt her tongue fill her mouth and her lips draw back, sucked in like an old woman's. She began to pant.

'Miss . . . Miss . . . Here's some water . . . Miss, you're all right.'

She began to scream, and she heard the succession of sounds ringing out from within a cave. Someone slapped her across the face and the screaming halted abruptly. She slumped in her chair.

Dimly she was aware of Talwyn – God's child – being led away in handcuffs, and of Colin's rough outburst in protest – she had never heard him speak so naturally – and then they were driving back to St Ives, the three of them – with the body covered by a blanket.

Colin helped them carry it into the cottage. A neighbour stood outside hanging her washing. 'What happened –' She was open-mouthed.

'Nothing, nothing,' Rosaleen cried, pushing the men inside and into the kitchen where Kate's long battered length was unwrapped and laid on top of the blanket on the floor.

Colin hovered about uncertainly. 'I don't suppose there is much I can do,' he said awkwardly.

'Yes – leave,' Oliver shouted. 'Your mad-woman killed her.' He gave a strangulated sound and made as if to hit his friend. Then his arms fell limply to his side. 'Leave,' he repeated brokenly.

Colin's eyes met Rosaleen's briefly, and he turned abruptly and left.

She filled a pail and washed Kate tenderly, dabbing the dried wounds as if she were alive. Oliver knelt by her, a diminished man, sobbing intermittently, muttering, 'Oh my God . . . Oh my God . . . Oh my God . . .'

Rosaleen could not cry. Her pain was the most intense she had known and she couldn't release it. She knew it would never ease. Dab. Gently wipe. It was all she could do: make as respectable as possible the body and face of the woman who had become her sister. The water turned quickly red and she emptied it outside, watched by the curious neighbour. As she carried the refilled pail back to the kitchen she stopped suddenly and put it down so heavily that water slopped over the edges; her body went rigid as the recollection came to her:

'Nana Annie's dream. She told Robbie about it. She saw it . . .'

She collected herself, retrieved the pail and returned to her gruesome task in the kitchen – as capable as she had been at her mother's deathbed; as she had been when she had scalded and skinned the newly-slaughtered pig; or when she had wrung the chickens' necks. It was simply a matter of detaching herself.

Kate was cremated a week later and the ashes filled a surprisingly small box.

'Is it all her life amounted to?' Rosaleen thought. 'How pathetic we are, I am, she was . . . All that kindness and love and beauty of soul reduced to powder in a little box.'

Fifteen or so people stood outside in the churchyard, buffeted by the wind and staring alternately at the charging grey clouds and the box, and each other; embarrassed, fumbling, shuffling. An odd assortment come to pay their respects to a gentle woman.

Rosaleen – straightbacked, hurting with her grief – nursed her thoughts. Oliver's accusations burned in her mind: 'Why did you leave them? . . . It was as much your fault . . . You heard a scream, why didn't you investigate? . . . I have to say I hold you partly responsible . . .'

She didn't defend herself, and, crippled with the awfulness of her guilt, sorrow and sense of loss, she could share her feelings with no one.

Oliver was an island – isolated and ravaged, he was one minute savage, and the next a child with a tortured face craving her love and a strength she did not have.

A little behind them stood Colin, chastened and stammering. He could not defend himself either. And beside him, stoic and pale, was the man Kate had been planning to marry. They would have been well-suited, Rosaleen thought – and looking at him she recalled Kate's radiance in her love. Several other friends were present – the cronies as she thought of them: the author Stuart Colefax, with whom Oliver had once accused her of flirting . . . And Betsy Chilloff, red-eyed next to huge, gawping Lizzie Tin-Drawers. There were a few other people – dark and drab beneath a windswept sky which carried on it the smells of St Ives . . .

Sleepless, tossing-turning nights saw in days which groaned with the weight of passing, days of growing alienation from one another. Rosaleen and Oliver exchanged looks which were pitying, or held blame, or sadness, or longing; they were fleeting looks which held no love and imparted no comfort. Sentences were begun and left unfinished, to hang unhappily in the air. In bed they would instinctively turn towards each other and perhaps touch lightly – and spring apart immediately. She would have snuggled against him, but he dreaded to relent, needing to dislike her because that helped counteract the despair. The days became weeks.

She said quietly to him once, 'I know why you are behaving as you are.' Whereupon he launched into a tirade, not wishing to be understood. His dreams were spent, he told her: the school, his memories. He had looked after Kate – been a father to her. And Rosaleen never disillusioned him by telling him his sister had been planning to marry.

She visited Talwyn in Bodmin, and found her crouched in the same position she had been in that fateful day, in a cell with five other women – drunks, thieves, a prostitute; a single slop was largely ignored and a rat scavenged around it, disregarded. Ragged and filthy, the women were alike with their pallor, smell and degradation. There was no further level to which to sink, other than to be hanged. No one knew yet what would befall Talwyn. She was another mad woman, another murderess who awaited trial. Nobody was in a hurry.

'Hello Talwyn.'

None of them reacted except the prostitute. 'Caw. Geek you,' she leered – and then looked quickly down and lapsed again into silence.

Talwyn stared at her vacantly. One eye was blackened and the cheek bruised. Her clothes were rent, and Rosaleen wondered: 'How many have had their way with her?'

'Have you seen Colin?'

At that Talwyn's expression lost its blankness and she shook her head, a tear sliding down her swollen cheek. To Rosaleen this was the worst kind of treachery: that he should have deserted her now. He had introduced her to a comfortable life, fed her, fattened her, protected her and loved her – and now abandoned her, bewildered, with her own madness.

'Talwyn – he will come and see you.' Rosaleen watched her struggle in her limited way to establish some sense in the jumbled compartments of her mind.

'How could Colin have said she is happy as she is?' she asked herself. 'She *knows* she is different.'

Talwyn cried out plaintively, 'Is Kate with God?'

'Yes dear,' Rosaleen answered gently, fighting back tears. She wrapped the other woman in her arms, and Talwyn drooped against her, suppliant.

'The field was bleeding. It was all red.'

'I know.'

'Time, miss.' The warden unfastened the gate and the metallic sound resounded down the corridor. For a minute there was nothing else but its finality. Then all the other sounds returned – moans, screams, coughing, laughter, raucous voices – and Talwyn's sudden despairing 'Ros*leen*.' Her fingers extended in a pleading gesture through the bars and Rosaleen touched them briefly.

'Oh *God*.' She stumbled from the prison into the air, and stood with her hands clutching her hair, breathing quickly.

When eventually she was calm once more the tragedy had acquired new meaning. She saw Kate's death clearly as something which had severed the fragile link of interwoven lives: Kate's Member of Parliament; Colin and Talwyn; Colin and Oliver; Oliver and Rosaleen herself . . . They had been expelled like seeds from a burst pod, as separate entities. Kate had sealed them together.

Rosaleen took the train back to Lelant and found a lift with a brewery cart to St Ives. There she visited Colin: that part of his face exposed between his glasses and his whiskers was grey-tinged and unhealthy.

'He is really suffering . . .' she thought. And all the bitter words which had been ready to erupt from her died on her tongue as she and Colin faced each other.

'I went to see Talwyn,' Rosaleen said finally.

His greyness became infused with crimson and she was filled with sudden pity for him.

'Won't you come in?' He wore a brightly-patterned, stained waistcoat undone over his shirt and she noticed that he had lost most of his stoutness. He gestured to a chair and she sat in it, in the small, dark sitting-room, waiting for him to speak, observing the works of art dotted about – mostly his own sculptures. 'They *are* good,' she thought. 'Perhaps I've misjudged him . . .'

He locked his hands together behind his head and looked anguished. 'I didn't know what to do for the best, where my loyalties lay . . . I've been biding time – hoping Oliver's attitude would change, and then I could go and see her.'

'Poor Colin.'

He glanced quickly at her – and then seeing the soft sadness in her face, wept quietly. She did not move, couldn't quite muster the strength to offer him comfort when she needed it herself and there was none.

'I am sorry – sorry as you cannot imagine,' Colin said between sobs.

'I know. But it was not your fault – and Oliver blames me too,' she added.

Colin rubbed his eyes behind his glasses and stared at her. '*You?*'

'Yes. I should not have left them.'

'But they've been alone together hundreds of times. Talwyn adores – adored – Kate.'

Rosaleen shrugged.

'I sometimes don't understand Oliver,' Colin said.

'Sometimes we none of us understand each other, Colin.'

'I resented you, you know. You intruded in our little circle. Marie was a nothing and no threat. I regarded you as an interloper.'

'I know.'

'I love Talwyn truly.' He gave a sigh that was emitted in short puffs. 'Whatever she might be – and I cannot any longer pretend to know her – I love her anyway.'

'Go and see her.'

'And Oliver?'

'Will not forgive you either way.'

256

'You loved Kate.'

'I loved her as much as anyone could her own sister.'

'And yet you are so brave.'

'. . . I don't want to be brave. It is only I know no other way . . .'

That evening she told Oliver she had seen both Talwyn and Colin.

'How could you?' he raged. 'My sister – your friend – was *murdered* by that creature. And she was his mistress. How can you be so unfeeling? How could you do such a thing?' He lunged towards her, and taking her by the shoulders shook her violently so that her teeth rattled. Rosaleen offered no resistance. Partly she was numbed with sorrow and exhaustion, and partly she welcomed his roughness as her punishment.

For the next few days they barely exchanged a word. They slept with a channel of space between them, they ate together in silence and painted in their separate corners . . . And then gradually she observed a change in Oliver; he ceased to attack or blame, but seemed possessed of a new mildness. She often found him immersed in a bible, and noticed a different light in his eye and a serenity of expression. And she felt herself further distanced from him with this change of mood which was private to him and excluded her with its remote gentleness.

One night, as she was about to go to bed, and after hours without speaking, Oliver said, 'Kate is somewhere I cannot conceive of – a place beyond the realms of my conception. Hers is the ultimate experience and for that I envy her.'

'Oh Oliver.' Rosaleen's exclamation was quietly despairing, and she shook her head dejectedly, trying to see in her lover something of his old self. But she saw only that strange light in his eyes which focused on an invisible horizon.

'He looks like a priest,' she thought. 'Kiss me please,' she whispered, stretching up to him, pursing her lips, and tugging at his shoulders to make him bend to her level.

He did so, gently. It was a priestly kiss. An act of kindness.

Tearfully she left him – up the stairs to their room, where she lay cold and shivering in bed waiting for his warmth beside her.

She continued to wait, dozing fitfully, and then, when he had still not appeared, dragged herself tiredly from the bed and went with a lighted candle downstairs to find him.

He was hanging from the central beam in the kitchen. The stool lay upturned, kicked to one side, and his dangling toes only missed the floor by a few inches.

For a moment she gazed, disbelieving – and then she was running from the house – running and retching and vomiting through the streets until she reached Colin's house . . .

In London the following evening, just returned from a trip to Tuscany, Frederick read the telegraph: 'Terrible double tragedy. Need you desperately. Please come as soon as possible. Rosaleen.' Twenty-four fours later he arrived and Rosaleen all but fell into his arms.

'Little Rosaleen . . . Little Rosaleen . . .'

After the funeral he helped her pack up her possessions and took her back to London with him.

Rosaleen, pale and white-lipped, swaying with the motion of the train, said in a voice barely above a whisper, 'I can't stay with you for ever . . . I don't know what to do.'

'Please Rosaleen – for a bit let me look after you. Just for a bit,' he repeated. 'You can paint there. There's a room doing nothing which can serve you temporarily.'

'I don't feel like painting.'

She didn't say anything further for a while, and then he saw that she was crying. He'd never seen her cry before – she was always so resilient – and her hurt was his own. They were alone in the compartment and he reached for her hand, kneading it and squeezing it, longing only to impart to her his love and pity.

At his house in Chelsea Frederick arranged her easel and materials, and stacked her canvases. Rosaleen was only an onlooker. Her movements were as slow as an invalid's and she dragged herself about, averting her eyes and speaking in a monotone.

'How long shall I stay here?' she asked when the room was ready. 'I cannot stay indefinitely.'

'No, not indefinitely, but a couple of months perhaps.'

'You've made the room so nice for me and I can't possibly paint.'

'Yes you can. You'll start tomorrow.'

'I don't have the urge.'

'The urge be damned. You get on with your painting.'

A tear slid down her face.

'Oh, my dear girl . . . I'm so sorry. I was only trying to chivvy.'

'I know . . .' She gave a huge intake of breath, and released it gradually, sniffing her tears away. 'And I shall start painting, only . . .'

'What, dearest girl?'

'I feel I shall never know happiness or a clear mind again.' Her voice broke.

'You will,' he assured her. 'Please believe me that you will.' His forehead creased with his concern for her, and he looked away, because absurdly he felt tears welling in his own eyes.

'I wish you were right,' she said, so quietly he could hardly hear. 'I don't know how to set about feeling happy; how to begin my life again or where to begin. The problem is I don't even want to.'

'You begin by being positive.'

'But I've lost my closest friend and my lover.' And then she cried out, 'And I blame myself.'

He held her close – a dispirited little form he wanted to cherish for the rest of his days. 'It is now the end of November. In the new year we could go to Paris. There – will that cheer you? Remain here until then. Build your strength, paint, learn to feel again – and then I shall take you to Paris, and you can meet the Impressionists as you have longed to.'

'. . . Dear Frederick.'

'. . . Dear Rosaleen.'

'Will you play the flute later for me?'

'I shall strike a bargain.'

The ghost of a smile twitched the corners of her lips. 'I'm not sure I trust your bargains.'

'This one is fair. Paint me a picture and I'll play the flute.'

He looked so earnest that she actually laughed. 'Hang-dog eyes.'

'Leave my eyes out of the discussion! Have we our bargain?'

'Yes.'

'I love you –' But he would not burden her by saying it out loud.

It was not until the end of March 1877 that they went to Paris; one reason was that Frederick was busy with his 'non-political activities', and the other was that he had heard the third Impressionist exhibition was to be held in April.

'It is too good an opportunity for you to miss,' he told her. 'And then when we return I suggest you look for an apartment and studio.'

Shortly before their trip he set off on Edgar for Oxford, and that afternoon the Baroness von Hoffnung paid a visit. Mrs MacDonald showed her into the 'studio', where Rosaleen, in a smock, and with her hair flowing loose, was painting. She looked up, startled.

The Baroness, wearing an elaborate peacock-blue velvet day dress, and with her black hair splendidly coiffed, regarded her superciliously, her lip curling. 'I see you are still daubing colours.'

Rosaleen lay down her palette and brushes. 'I am still painting,' she said.

'And how have you found it living on twenty-eight guineas a year?'

'Easier than you would living off two thousand eight hundred, I expect.' She looked steadily at the other woman, leaning against the easel, and inwardly trembling a little. She did not feel like having a confrontation.

'I choose to ignore that remark. I came to see Frederick, not you. I gather he is away.'

'He's in Oxford for a few days.'

'Holding Mr Ruskin's hand no doubt.'

'There is nothing kind about her,' Rosaleen thought. 'How can Frederick align himself with her?' 'Have you a message for him, Baroness?' She controlled the anger in her voice.

'I think not. When are you leaving these particular lodgings, Miss Ruddock? Or are you planning to remain *ad infinitum?*'

'No Baroness. When we return from Paris then I shall look for somewhere.' She looked innocent as she spoke, but well knew that the Baroness was ignorant of the proposed trip.

'Paris? What do you mean, Paris?' she asked her face dropping its guard for a moment.

She looked old in that instant, and Rosaleen wondered if perhaps she *was* in love with Frederick, and felt almost sorry for her.

'We are going to Paris for a month or so,' she explained carefully.

And at that the Baroness spluttered, raged and insulted. Rosaleen leaned more heavily against the easel. She was shocked by the vehemence of the other's hatred – was unused to having an enemy, having no malice herself.

'Baroness – there is nothing between Frederick and myself. We are merely friends.'

'*Friends!* What an earth can he find in common with a little slut like you?'

Rosaleen blanched. 'Would you leave please? I think it would be better for both of us.'

The Baroness's gaze swept mockingly round the room with its colourful clutter. 'One day you will realize you are out of your depth here, my dear.' And she turned and left, her expensive perfume lingering behind her.

Paris was recovering from winter when Rosaleen and Frederick arrived, and a general feeling of relief hung in the air at having shed the old season. Aproned women with plaits wound round their heads carried pails and brushes and swilled the pavements so that the gutters ran with soapy water. Enthusiasm replaced staleness, and shutters were scrubbed or painted, and brass polished. The aromatic smell of baking mingled with garlic and drifted from open windows, and in the kitchens chefs kneaded and pounded with renewed zest. Agitated French voices could be heard raised in conflict, and outside cafés street tables were laid with bright cloths, the waiters whistling cheerfully.

L'Hôtel Palais Royal was a gracious, early-nineteenth-century building converted from a private mansion into a small and luxurious hotel. Discreet and rose-tinted, it was situated in the arcaded Rue de Rivoli with its glove and handkerchief boutiques, fashion shops, book shops, pâtisseries – and Rumplemayer's tea room. Abutting the arcade and bordering the banks of the Seine were the Tuileries, with the trees in blossom and the sweet-citrus scent of mown grass. Pools and geometrically arranged shrubberies interspersed the colourful terraced flowerbeds, and men and women walked arm in arm along the neat paths . . .

Rosaleen, strolling with Frederick in the gardens their first morning said, 'It is so genteel – there is about it a haze of unreality so that it seems to belong to another world. The depression they say France still suffers after the Communards' revolt seems to have affected nothing.'

'How do you know about the Communards' revolt?'

She hesitated. 'Tags told me.' Frederick's hand on her arm did not tense, and she continued: 'He told me a little about the Franco-Prussian war, and how in early 1871 many of the wealthy fled from France, and that the poor people became rebellious.'

'That is true. But it is not all gloom in Paris, as you see. The French have a knack of keeping submerged life's unpleasantness, and there are new buildings – hospitals and schools and places of culture – being constructed the whole time. Paris is here to be gorged and guzzled and thoroughly enjoyed – and there is nobody better than the Frenchman at doing it!'

That evening over dinner in the Palais Royal restaurant, an elegant silk-walled room, Frederick asked Rosaleen, 'When you were in Paris with Tags did you go to the Café de la Nouvelle Athènes?'

She flushed faintly. 'No. We went to the Café Guerbois.'

'Well I have heard it is at the Nouvelle Athènes that Renoir and many other artists and writers meet nowadays. We shall go there – and to the Café Guerbois should you wish. But besides that I have friends who could prove useful. In particular the Charpentiers.'

He paused significantly, so that Rosaleen felt bound to ask, 'Who are they?' She was tired – seemed permanently so nowadays – and sitting across the table from Frederick with the candle flickering between them, confused memories and images flitted across her mind.

'Who are the Charpentiers?' she asked again, not sure she had asked it the first time.

'Oh Rosaleen –' Frederick said on a sigh. 'Can you not even feign a little interest, there's a good girl.'

'I am interested.' The tears sprang to her eyes. For years she had never cried. Now it seemed she did little else.

He leaned across and wiped the tears with his fingertips. 'The Charpentiers are an interesting couple,' he told her softly. 'Georges Charpentier is a publisher – but in a big way – his firm has handled Victor Hugo, Alexandre Dumas the Elder and Balzac, and now Zola – to name but a few. More relevant to you is that he is a friend of Renoir and champions the Impressionists' cause. His wife holds regular social occasions which Renoir and his band often attend.'

He looked hard at Rosaleen and was rewarded by the flash of interest which crossed her face. 'Is there a chance we could be invited, do you think? At the same time as Monsieur Renoir?'

He smiled. 'There is a good chance.'

Her expression brightened further. 'I should so love to meet Monsieur Renoir and to speak with him.'

The invitation came the next day, an informal card inviting 'Sir Frederick Walton and his partner' to a gathering of friends at the Charpentiers' house the following Tuesday afternoon.

Meanwhile during the next few days they played the part of tourists. They visited the Louvre – how changed during the centuries from its original concept as a compact twelfth-century fortress, now become an immense institution packed with masterpieces and hordes of people paying homage to them. They saw Napoleon's tomb in the Dôme, Place des Invalides;

attended a sale at the Druot auction rooms where the prices reached dizzy levels; had dinner in the superlative Grand Vefour restaurant . . . And sat outside the Café de la Nouvelle Athènes drinking red wine.

Frederick delighted in looking at Rosaleen. He watched her taking in the Montmartre scene unfolding before them and thought that if, as he had said, one was meant to gorge oneself on the splendours of Paris, then the city had certainly nourished her. Her skin glowed again, tinged a delicate peach on her cheeks, and her face had lost its gauntness and was once more padded with the soft contours of youth. Gone too were the dark circles beneath her eyes which had emphasized their haunted expression; now her eyes were usually bright. Only sometimes did he catch a reflective darkness in them.

'She seems nearly happy again,' he thought. 'That obsessive look has disappeared. She does not start at every sudden noise or become tearful at the slightest thing . . . It is all I want – her happiness.'

'What are you thinking?' she asked.

'About you . . . I was thinking how much improved you seemed, and I was watching you watching everything going on – and thanking God that at least you could notice it all again.'

She said nothing then, but shook her head with a tender expression and took his hand, and they continued to watch the activity together, bound by the warmth of the spring morning, the glow from the red wine, and the greater glow of their friendship. People got up and left their tables and others replaced them.

'There is Émile Zola!' Frederick announced, pointing to a handsome, dark-haired and lush-bearded man who was with a bald-headed companion. 'And the man with him,' he continued, 'is the Impressionist Paul Cézanne. Now that is curious.'

'Why?' Rosaleen stared at the famous pair, childishly excited at being so close to them.

'Because although Zola, as critic for L'Événement journal, pioneered their cause when the Salon rejected Impressionism, he now seems to be reconsidering his opinions and increasingly spurns the artists he first encouraged. I don't understand – one minute these people are vying, the next flinging their arms about each other! It is all too much! And Cézanne himself is a bit of a paradox in that he believes draughtsmanship to be of equal importance to painting itself. In this he differs from the other Impressionists; he likes to convey the permanence of things and not just a fleeting image. So he says – and yet to me as a layman his paintings seem a little sketch-like.'

'Will he be exhibiting at the exhibition?'

'Yes.'

'Oh I am so looking forward to it.'

'You don't know how happy that makes me, Rosaleen – to hear you say that you are looking forward to something again.'

'I never thought I'd be able to say it.'

'It is always a matter of time.'

They went to a concert that night at the Conservatoire, and the soloist in the second half of the performance was a final year violin student named Lorenzo Mellini. He was slight and boyish with a beatific expression and soft brown curls which shook as he played; and as she looked at him – his slender body one minute submissive and the next ferocious – Rosaleen felt herself un-accountably drawn to him. She knew nothing about music, although she enjoyed hearing it and thought this young man probably played well – but her liking for music had nothing to do with the inexplicable attraction she felt towards him. She would never know him, but she studied him intently as he played and continued to be drawn to him. The work came to an end and the audience clapped with moderate, although not outstanding, enthusiasm. The boy stood, outlined small and dark on the stage, claiming his dues, and smiling a little half-smile which seemed slightly superior as he gazed at the rows of heads. Then his eyes wandered lazily to the front row where they alighted on Rosaleen – and remained fixed, frowning slightly in puzzlement, before eventually lifting to survey the rest of the auditorium once more.

'I wish I could paint him,' she thought, as she gathered her things and Frederick helped her on with her cloak, oblivious to the incident.

They made their way from the hall and were immediately enveloped by the soft, bustling Paris night.

The Charpentiers lived at 11, Rue de Grenelle. Madame Marguerite Charpentier was a dark-haired woman with a pale soft face and a plump rolling chin. Her stoutness made her appear matronly even though she could not have been more than thirty years old, and her kind eyes and amiable expression masked an intellectual mind.

As Rosaleen and Frederick were shown into the hallway two pretty little girls with fluffy golden hair and short frilled dresses leaned over the banister to see what was going on. An enormous piebald dog with a studded collar sat between them, and each child had a plump hand upon its head. Rosaleen, handing her cropped jacket to the maid, glanced up and smiled as a shrill voice called, '*Mais qu'est-ce que vous faîtes là?*' And the sisters scuttled back to the nursery, the dog following lethargically.

In the light and spacious drawing-room Madame Charpentier greeted her visitors easily and introduced them to one another. Frederick and Rosaleen were the last to arrive, and already present were six guests: a handsome woman in her mid-thirties by the name of Berthe Morisot – an artist belonging to the Impressionist group and married to Édouard Manet's brother; the composer Gabriel Fauré; a French politician with a long nose and a longer name which Rosaleen immediately forgot; a journalist with sharp eyes and a dreadful stutter; the actress Jeanne Samary, a wasp-waisted and vivacious young woman; and finally – Pierre Auguste Renoir.

He was a compelling-looking man – thin of face, with fine brown hair brushed neatly behind small flat ears and a rather sparse beard and straggly moustache patchily covering his chin and firm mouth. There was an alert shrewdness in his expression, and his large brown eyes appraised Rosaleen as he gave a comic little bow. She met his gaze with a steadiness she did not feel.

Frederick said something to him in fluent French and Renoir's face broke into a wreathed smile. 'Ah – so you are an artist.' He regarded her kindly. 'We must talk. And you must speak also with Berthe Morisot. She is an artist *formidable*. You will please sit by my side? *Oh, mais vous êtes tellement jolie* . . . I am saying you are so pretty . . .'

She sat beside him, and patiently, in his halting English, he answered her many questions, smiling benevolently at her eagerness. He explained his beliefs to her, his ideals, and told her a little of his early years – his apprenticeship to a porcelain painter from the age of thirteen, and later his student days at the École Impériale et Spéciale des Beaux-Arts.

'But I was not academic, not a good student. In my entrance I was sixty-eighth out of eighty persons! I fight, fight, fight all my life. *Et maintenant* – I am still fighting! I have fortune in my friends. They believe in me – Georges Rivières who published the *Journaux d'art* which has taken up our cause . . . *Et* – the Charpentiers, so *sympathique* . . . Murer also. He has a restaurant where we eat and we bring him pictures for his kindness. *Vous voyez, jolie mademoiselle* – our art, it is different, and the public, she is afraid.'

Rosaleen said hesitantly, 'I love it for being different . . .' She was shy of him, despite his ordinariness. He made a gesture with his hands for her to continue, and she noticed the paint engrained around his nails.

'I find it more honest and unpretentious than anything I've seen – the colours, the sunlight, the freshness . . . I want to go to the places you paint, Monsieur Renoir.'

'Ah young lady, I wish everyone thought as you do. *Les critiques* – they do not like me.'

'But they will do!'

He smiled widely. 'You must visit my studio. I invite you. After the exhibition you will come – yes?'

'Yes. Of course, yes.'

Frederick, seated next to Marguerite Charpentier and Jeanne Samary, glanced at Rosaleen intermittently. He noticed her body's excited little movements, her gesticulations, her lively and continually changing facial expressions – and his heart went out to her. He knew an enormous joy seeing her like that. It filled him, selflessly. That she was happy completed his own happiness.

Later he joined her with Renoir and Berthe Morisot so that they made a group of four – discussing in a mixture of languages the frustrations of life as an artist, worse as an innovative artist; and surely worst of all, as an innovative *female* artist.

'You have before you very many problems, *chérie*,' the lovely Berthe Morisot told Rosaleen gravely, when she learned the other had only recently commenced her career. 'You must be strong.'

They all toasted each other with cups of *thé au citron*, and ate little biscuits dusted with icing sugar which were so light they crumbled in the mouth . . . Then Fauré noticed the flute peeping from Frederick's tweed jacket, and the remainder of the afternoon was given to music and stimulating talk; wine replaced the lemon tea, and delicate sandwiches were handed round. Outside, afternoon abandoned itself to red evening, and finally, with airy kisses and laughter and promises to renew meetings, it was time to leave.

A week later Rosaleen and Frederick were amongst the many guests at 6, Rue des Pelletiers. It was the much publicized third Impressionists' exhibition and everybody who had an interest in art, and a few who did not, attended in order to observe, comment, criticize – and even ridicule this new style of art. Renoir, Monet, Morisot, Cézanne, Degas, Pissarro . . . Eighteen artists in all, exhibiting their works in the hopes of luring the public away from stereotyped ideas – and convincing it of their genius.

And who could not be charmed by the lemon skies and speckled waters, by the flower-studded meadows and sun-ripened girls, by the evocative scenes which made one's heart yearn? Apparently there were several; and a man whom Frederick knew slightly cornered them and proceeded to air his views in an indignant tone.

'I sincerely hope that one day Monet learns the sky is neither speckled nor yellow, and that Renoir learns that women's bodies actually have structure and are not streaked with green and blue. Anyone who claims to like this rubbish is a fool.' He bristled with annoyance, drawing furiously on his pipe.

'Then I am a fool,' Frederick said, taking Rosaleen's arm and moving away.

'People are so vehement in their dislike of anything different,' Rosaleen commented.

'Well any artist is immediately public property when he exhibits his work, and lays himself open to criticism. He has to expect it if he strays from the conventional. It is the public's prerogative to be scathing.'

'But it's so disheartening.'

'Yes it must be . . . By the way – you look beautiful.' He had to say it, despite her distaste for compliments. Daily he had watched her blossoming, and this afternoon, in emerald-green silk and with her hair piled high, he thought her more exquisite than ever. There was a womanliness now about her, and her recent sadness had lent her expression new depth.

She said simply to Frederick: 'Thank you.' But he knew her – and changed his mood accordingly. He pointed people out to her; a game she loved.

'There is Antonin Proust, the writer and philosopher and friend of Manet . . . And there is Manet. Oh – and I believe that is Hector Berlioz the composer . . . And Fantin-Latour with Whistler whom you already know . . . That woman in fuchsia pink is the talented American artist Mary Cassatt, whom I have heard is in favour with Degas. She showed her portrait of Zola in the Salon in 1874, so I read . . .'

Rosaleen's eyes darted hither and thither. She was caught in the excitement of the moment, lightheaded with the intensity of her feeling – the thrilling effect of the paintings themselves, the assortment of people, the French voices, garlic and wine on breath, women's perfume . . . The place pulsated and she was enveloped by the atmosphere.

And then in a wonderful moment of dawning, the inspiration came to her: 'I shall follow their school – become an Impressionist.'

Elated she looked around the room, across bobbing heads and excited hands, and she saw him – slight, boyish, narrow of face and soulfully dark: the violinist from the other evening, Lorenzo Mellini. She recalled his name. He was with another young man of similar age, fair beside the other's darkness and of the same slender build. They leaned a little towards each other, serious faced, seemingly engrossed. She stared – and the violinist glanced in her direction; his eyes widened and for protracted seconds their gaze fixed – questioning, half smiling. Then his fell away and he turned back to his companion.

·§ Fourteen §·

THE IMPRESSIONISTS

I was lured by the lemon skies
Of a motley bunch they called the Impressionists.

There was a small dance floor in the restaurant of L'Hôtel Palais Royal and that night Rosaleen, who had drunk more than she was accustomed to, swept tipsily and gaily around it with Frederick. He clasped her firmly, his forehead perspiring, his hair falling over one eye as they twirled through dance after dance.

'Enough, enough,' he protested, laughing. 'Even the musicians are packing up now. It is bed-time, dear girl.'

They went up the central marble staircase, leaning slightly against each other, giggling at nothing in particular. They had adjacent rooms on the third floor and as Frederick was about to go into his Rosaleen announced, 'I've decided to follow the Impressionist school.'

His hand was on the door knob, half turning it, and he stopped to face her. 'I was wondering when you'd come to that conclusion.'

'You knew I would?'

'Of course.'

'May I come in? Talk to you about it?'

He hesitated. 'Yes. And I have a bottle of port which might not go amiss.'

She followed him inside – a spacious room with sepia flower-patterned wallpaper and heavy mahogany furniture. His possessions were laid out neatly. On the washstand were a silver hairbrush and comb, razor and brush, cuff-links in a container, some sort of ointment, a bottle of cologne and other bottles . . . On the table were pens, a writing slope, sheets of paper covered with his quick and untidy hand, and a pile of books stacked beside the notes. A waistcoat was draped over a chair back.

Rosaleen noted all these personal details, pieces of his life, as Frederick went to the armoire to fetch the bottle of port and glasses concealed among his clothes. He smiled with faint embarrassment.

'I had a bad experience once,' he explained, studiously filling the glasses almost to the brim with the deep-coloured liquor. 'A parlourmaid with an insatiable penchant for the stuff. Hence the present precautions.'

A thin buzz came from the wall-mounted gas lamps, and their glow dissolved the room in friendly orange light, blurring the outlines of objects. Rosaleen was replete – the alcohol, the copper light, her excitement with her day, her illuminating decision – all these filled her with sensuous, light-headed well-being. She floated with it. She could have been benevolent to her worst enemy.

She took a long sip from her glass, savouring the fruity taste. 'I love port,' she murmured, coiling up to Frederick on the chaise-longue, unaware of his body's tension as he tried not to react to her closeness.

'So you have decided to be an Impressionist,' he said, holding himself stiffly away from her.

'I must, do you see?' She slurred the words a little.

'I think you will be admirably suited to it, my dear. And of course you must take up Renoir's offer to visit his studio. And some of the others besides.'

'If they will not mind . . . Frederick, you have moved away from me and I was so comfortable and snug.' Her voice was reproachful.

This was his domain, his retreat where for the past ten days he had sat every night after parting from Rosaleen, enjoying his private tot of port and regaining his detachment, in so far as he was able. On his own he would talk to himself, reason with himself and try to ignore his ever burgeoning love for the woman whom he knew better than anyone else and who innocently and inadvertently made impossible demands of him Occasionally he became morose, deciding that after Paris he would sever her from his life . . . And then following this came such agony that he knew he would rather see her on any terms than not at all.

Was he so very weak? Or perhaps it was strength? He did not know; and here she was in his room destroying his resolve by the minute.

'Rosaleen . . .' he said thickly.

'Mmm? Will I be a famous artist do you think, Frederick?'

'Is that what you desire?' He could barely bring himself to speak.

She leaned forward and drank some more port – a couple of longer sips this time so that the glass was almost drained – and lay back again, languorous, her lips glistening. She was impervious to his predicament.

'I desire to be good. A good artist . . . How hot you are, Frederick. Have you a handkerchief? I shall wipe your forehead and you can be my little boy . . .' She gave a small giggle, and wriggling against him struggled to sit up. He pushed her gently down once more and encircled her in his arms.

'But I was going to wipe your brow.' She giggled again, trapped in his embrace.

He knew she was drunk, that later he would feel guilty, that he would regret his actions, that those actions might well destroy their friendship; but he was utterly lost. He kissed her with every particle of the love he had for her, nibbled the softness of her full lips and tasted the sweetness of port on her breath. And when she did not resist and seemed pliant in the confines of his arms, he began to partially undress first her and then himself.

'Rosaleen . . . Rosaleen . . .'

Her skirts were bunched up beneath them – her nakedness, slender and smooth-skinned; he marvelled at her flesh, the texture of her skin, its colour. He stroked and fondled her – and still she seemed submissive. What was she thinking?

'I am violating her, and I cannot help myself . . .' He paused in his caressing of her and asked hesitantly, 'Do you – mind?'

'No.' The answer came from far away, and the voice did not sound like Rosaleen's. But he had her consent. Oh the joy! The warnings in his head with their distant repercussions he could ignore. He was tender with her. He wanted to pour his being into her, to explore every tiny nook and probe beyond. He knew only one simple word for how he felt: ecstasy. Beneath him she was light and yielding, but he became aware that she made no sounds, that as he stirred himself around in her and rapturously explored her, she was only tolerating him. Selfishly he knew he had to go on, to take and take from her; and with each blissful, self-indulgent moment he was more conscious that he had ruined everything. Eventually he was overtaken and as he gushed into her, clutching her and trying not to cry out, her hand came round his neck to stroke him – before falling away again. This belated little gesture was the final thing for him – and he grabbed her face and kissed her as though he were giving and receiving life.

He lay, spent, on top of her, sprawled half on the chaise-longue and half on the floor; he felt deadened, despairing, and knew that he had lost her. Beneath his weight Rosaleen, as limp as a doll, fell asleep and began to snore gently.

Very carefully he got up, and carrying her over to the bed laid her on it, arranging the covers over her. She woke briefly, smiled, murmured, 'The room is revolving,' and returned to sleep.

He slid under the bedclothes himself, careful not to disturb her, and for the rest of the night remained awake gazing at her, listening to her, smelling her, thinking of her, and aching, aching, aching . . .

The sun filtered in a thin strip through the indoor shutters and Frederick lifted the latch to open them so that daylight flooded in. Paris was exposed: the Tuileries, manicured and frothy with pink-tipped trees like outlandish ballgowns . . . And beyond, the line of the Seine and the Left Bank. Frederick stared out broodingly.

From the bed Rosaleen watched him standing by the window in his paisley silk dressing-gown. The night's events were vague and hazy – too remote for her to relate to and hence she could easily accept them. This was Frederick – dear and familiar, and nothing which had occurred seemed unnatural. If in an unguarded moment they were carried away – what matter? She remembered warmth and gentle pleasure and a feeling of safety, and now seeing him standing there, his shoulders drooped, so obviously despondent, she was filled with tenderness for him.

He was so immersed in his moodiness that he started and whirled round when she appeared and laid her head against his back.

'I thought you were asleep.' He couldn't bring himself to look at her.

'Frederick – don't be sad.'

He turned his back on her once more and said angrily, 'I've ruined it. I'm sorry, Rosaleen. I'm truly sorry.'

'What have you ruined, dearest Frederick?' Her voice was gentle.

'Our friendship.'

'Oh no, that is not true.'

He faced her then, his forehead wrinkled in anxiety. 'You mean that?'

'Nothing could ruin our friendship.'

'You felt so beautiful,' he burst out.

She was silent then, uncertain how to respond, suddenly aware of her own responsibilities to this man. 'I care about you,' she said eventually.

'But not sufficiently to marry me,' he stated dismally. Then he gave a harsh laugh. 'Oh well – hung for a lamb, hung for a sheep and all that . . . I'll be reckless and dare ask you: will you marry me, Rosaleen?' He knew the futility of his hopes even as he thought them and voiced them, and the sweet concern in her expression and lack of reply endorsed it.

'Oh well,' he said again, with forced brightness, 'it was worth a try, dear girl.'

She caressed his arm. 'What I feel for you is a closeness I've had with no other man. But it is a different kind of closeness.'

'I know. And I am being most unfair.' With considerable effort he was managing to sound quite cheerful. 'I promise I won't mention the matter again, and – forgive me for last night?'

'There is nothing to forgive.'

'Ah how charitable you are. One final word: you know I love you, but I can suppress it. Most of the time I can control what I feel for you and be objective. It would hurt me infinitely more not to see you at all.'

'That would be unthinkable, Frederick.'

'Good, good. Now what say you to a hearty breakfast, dearest girl?'

A couple of days before they were due to return to England they visited Renoir at his studio in Rue Cortot in Montmartre. It was a charming place – part of an outbuilding belonging to an old folly, and there was even a garden – overgrown and untamed, with flowers spurting joyously upwards and weeds run wild. Renoir showed them round courteously. He was paternal towards Rosaleen and respectful to Frederick.

'I often paint outside,' he told them. 'Cafés, gardens, even boats . . . Where I find myself, there is my studio. For example – here is my very great friend Claude Monet and I have painted him also painting in his garden at Argenteuil. Argenteuil is a pretty place outside Paris. I used in this painting little motions with the brush and it does make the effect rich . . . And this one – I have called it *La Loge*. It is at the theatre and I first showed it at the exhibition of 1874. I like the man in the picture for he looks not at the play, but at the audience . . . And here I am in the middle of painting a model who comes here to the studio. She is pensive. Please notice I am using black when I paint. My colleagues, they do not use black. I am using the free style in this painting. Please also note the many colours I'm using for her skin. You like her, I hope . . .'

He showed them painting after painting, explaining his technique in each one, his experimentation with new styles, his progression, the influence other artists had had on him; and Rosaleen was ensnared – by the pictures, by Renoir's conversation, by the artist himself. At last it was clear – the reason for her previous doubts, her disgruntlement, her sense that there was more to be derived from her art than she did. Here, encapsulated in these paintings, life was as she observed it – vividly coloured and patterned, with its startling impact caught and held. She relished the prospect of the future.

But it was almost time to go and she had not dared voice what she wanted more than anything. Frederick was already thanking the artist for his kindness. She had to ask him . . .

'Monsieur Renoir – if I were to stay on in Paris, might I work alongside you for a while?' She felt Frederick's surprised glance but kept her own fixed determinedly on Renoir, her fists bunched in tension as she awaited his reply.

His face broke into a smile and he took both her hands in his own. 'Mademoiselle, it will give me much pleasure to have you with me.'

Frederick was about to depart for England. Downstairs in the hall of the hotel he gripped Rosaleen's shoulders and scanned her face with a rueful expression.

'You know what I admire about you: you will not be deflected from whatever decision you make.'

'Sometimes you think I make the wrong decisions.'

'Sometimes I believe you do, nevertheless the trait itself is praiseworthy. You have such strength. I have no doubt you will achieve your aims.'

'And you yours.'

'Whatever they might be . . .' He looked embarrassed, and his awkwardness became hers. This particular parting marked the end of several months together. He had rescued her, harboured her, briefly been a part of her – and finally set her on the path to her decision.

'Since I met you that day you called at the inn you have been instrumental in my fate, do you realize?'

'That is a weight to bear indeed,' he said seriously. Then

lightly: 'However, I have broad shoulders. I shall think of you accompanying Monsieur Renoir and his colleagues on different jaunts and I shall be able to picture you perfectly; and when I next see you you will be a newly fledged Impressionist.'

Rosaleen moved out of the expensive Hôtel Palais Royal into a small room above a café off Avenue de l'Opéra. The proprietress was a small dark woman who spoke scant English, but whose face, voice and gestures were so expressive that Rosaleen had little trouble in understanding her. A formidable woman, despite her lack of stature, she was almost obsessively clean and tidy and the little white poodle which accompanied her everywhere was washed each day just like the white lace curtains and tablecloths and bedspreads. Madame Mireille, as she was known, kept an 'honourable' place, and as she bustled about she clicked her teeth over everybody else's inadequacies and inefficiencies, keeping up a running commentary as her critical gaze swept over her empire.

Her strict glance had assessed Rosaleen with its usual accuracy and she had noted – apart from the fact that the girl was a beauty – her neat, fresh appearance, the intelligent calm expression, and the small amount of luggage with her. She had noted, too, the lightweight easel and the painting equipment. Then, with her quick decisive step, she had led Rosaleen up the narrow staircase to her room.

Outside the Café Mireille with its tilted tables balanced on wedges of wood, the cherry tree discarded its blossom on to the pavement where it lay curling and brown-rimmed. Rosaleen, holding the little coffee cup in her two hands but not drinking, smiled slightly in absent meditation. The warmth from the cup seeped into her hands and the aroma and gentle quiff of steam rose to her nostrils. She sighed contentedly and inhaled her own sense of well-being, pulling her Joseph shawl round her. There was an early-morning cool hovering still in the air, and the sky was not yet quite blue, the street only just stirring itself for the day's business – figures appearing and disappearing; a bucket or two being emptied; shutters being opened; a voice, and another; the milk cart stopping, unloading and moving off again;

278

cats around piles of rubbish, a dog eating breakfast from a bowl . . .

A figure hurried over to her table. *'Mademoiselle Rosaleen, bonjour, bonjour. Est-ce que je suis en retard?'*

She understood that he meant he was late and said, 'Monsieur Renoir, it is only half-past seven.'

'Ah that is good. My clock – it is not working.' He sat down next to her, took a cup and poured himself some black coffee. They sat without speaking while, like her, he surveyed the little street gradually shedding its inertia.

'Eh bien,' he said, banging his hands down lightly on the table. 'So today we are to visit my good friend Claude Monet at Argenteuil. I think you will like him and he you. We will take the train from the Gare St Lazare – Monet is doing a painting of the station at the moment. Argenteuil is about ten kilometres from Paris, and it will not take long to travel there. You are content to come with me, Mademoiselle Rosaleen?'

'Oh yes, Monsieur. I am greatly looking forward to it.'

'Et bien,' he said again, and sat back contemplatively.

Rosaleen had been in Renoir's company for the past week and had painted alongside him both in his studio and out of doors. He had said very little to her by way of instruction, but before they had started he said, 'You must look – quick, like that – and paint as you see the impression. You must paint as you feel.' Her heart had lifted when he had said that: it was how she had always longed to paint; to capture a moment's mood. 'A lazy man's way out,' Oliver would have said disapprovingly. But Oliver was gone and her time spent with him seemed to belong to someone else.

In the studio a pert-faced, dark-eyed young actress by the name of Madame Henriot sat for Renoir, and before making a start on her canvas Rosaleen watched the master: both his canvas and the one he had given her were already thinly primed with pale, dove-grey ground, and he proceeded to mix alizarin red with yellow ochre and paint an outline of the girl. Next he scumbled thin layers of colour into the relevant places – and at that stage Rosaleen picked up her own palette and brushes.

Intermittently, between looking at Madame Henriot and her own canvas she stopped to watch Renoir – how he tackled the dress slowly, painting wet-in-wet, how he built up skin tones . . . Over the next couple of days she saw the painting develop and take life, and would, with renewed zest, return to her own.

'*Pas mal*,' he encouraged her occasionally. 'Not bad.'

Another time they had painted outside the Café Mireille – and Madame Mireille, her poodle on her bony lap, had consented to remain still for ten minutes and allow them to paint her in the shade of the cherry tree, her best side presented to them. They had worked on the café scene for the next two days, and by the end, when they packed up their things, Renoir congratulated her: '*Bon*, Mademoiselle Rosaleen. It's coming. You comprehend well. Your painting is coming along.'

She hugged him impulsively then – basking in his compliment, assured at last of what she was doing.

'*Eh ma petite* . . .' He shook his head fondly and gently disentangled himself from her.

The countryside around Argenteuil was flat and lush with trees which edged the broad expanse of the Seine. And this morning they were mirrored in the sparkling water which had taken on the blue of the sky. Small pleasure-craft were dotted about, mostly moored to jetties and awaiting their occupants. But Argenteuil was beginning to sprawl nearer to Paris's environs – the town itself, with its attractive colour-washed houses and the dominating church spire, was more and more being drawn in by the tentacles of the metropolis.

'One day Argenteuil will be devoured –' Renoir made a suction noise in his throat. '*Comme ça* – it will be gone. I am sad when I think of it.'

When they arrived at Monet's house they found him in the garden playing with his ten-year-old son, Jean. Of medium height and stocky, he romped in the grass with the handsome fair-haired child. He looked up to see them, and his smile grew wider.

'*Mes amis* . . .' He stumbled up gladly to meet them, brushing down his trousers and putting on the round-brimmed hat which was his trade-mark and which had been dislodged during the romp. He butted a hen out of his way with his toe.

'And you are Mademoiselle Rosaleen, *n'est-ce-pas?*'

She nodded, shaking his hand, immediately liking the amiable chubby-faced man with his bushy dark beard and unruly hair.

'I was in London,' he said proudly, 'in 1870 and 1871. I greatly enjoyed it. I studied your very fine artists Turner and Constable . . . *Bon, mes amis, on y va?*' He straightened his back to indicate his readiness to go, and the three departed with their painting equipment and easels to the banks of the Seine, passing Monet's small boat which he had actually converted into a 'studio'.

Like Renoir his canvases and colours were bought ready-prepared and he used pale grounds, and Rosaleen, in between the men, found it interesting to compare their techniques: Monet used more white than Renoir and built up a thicker texture, often applying colour directly, without using the palette and sometimes dragging the wooden end of his brush through impasto layers to reveal the light ground. His brushstrokes were short, whereas Renoir's tended to be longer and silkier with a sweeping action; although when he painted water he used shorter strokes.

She thought again of Oliver – his dark colours, his rigid adherence to rules, his continual frustration – and she felt a fleeting sense of pity for him that he had missed so much.

The day unrolled, mild and smooth. It was Saturday and the boats – row-boats or sailcraft – were untied to bob about, glittering under the blue and white sky, voices drifting from them occasionally; men with straw boaters courteously lent their arms to ladies picking their way along the towpath; the willows' branches drooped into the water and through them poured the sun.

'It is too lovely,' Rosaleen said at one point, to neither of them in particular. The loveliness of it all made her throat catch.

Monet smiled kindly. 'It is good, life, no? We Impressionists are poor, Mademoiselle, in the sense of money. But we are rich. *Ah oui* – we are indeed rich.' He bent his head again in concentration and his words played in the air.

They painted on, Rosaleen consciously emulating Monet's technique, which she thought lent itself to the landscape. She began also to experiment on her own. Every so often either one of the men would look at her work as it progressed, give an encouraging word or grunt and perhaps a small pat on the back – and leave her to continue, unhindered by their interference.

At some time in the early afternoon a voice was heard calling, 'Claude!' And another, thinner, younger: 'Papa!' And Camille Monet appeared, accompanied by their son, each carrying a wicker picnic basket. Rosaleen looked up, thinking how pretty a picture it would make: the fair-skinned, dark-haired woman in her white dress and the child with his knickerbockers, his straw hat pulled over his eyes, and the long grass brushing against them.

'Papa!' The boy ran up to his father, while the mother stood behind him, her hand on his shoulder and smiling a little shyly, her eyes narrowed against the sun.

They set aside their palettes and gathered round the hampers, Claude Monet making appreciative noises as his wife unpacked the food. Jean went from easel to easel. He stopped at Rosaleen's.

'Est-ce qu'elle est vraiment douée?' he asked his father with the tactlessness of a child.

'Yes,' Monet smiled, answering in English. 'She is good.'

Rosaleen's heart swelled, and she turned away briefly to hide the sudden watering of her eyes . . .

Later they were joined by Manet and Berthe Morisot who talked quietly with Camille as the others painted, while Jean played with his ball – tossing it in the air and clapping before he caught it again. He was just in Rosaleen's line of vision, and on an impulse she included him in her picture, a merry little figure at the water's edge.

Two months elapsed, two months of painting and picnics and boating parties and guinguettes – dances held out of doors in the suburbs of Paris where a city gentleman might find an attractive country girl to be his companion for the evening. It was a time of late nights and friendships; drives in gigs borrowed from wealthy friends – to Fontainebleau or Versailles or Chantilly; café sessions and dinners at Eugène Murer's restaurant in the Boulevard Voltaire. Wine flowed freely and conversation even freer – sometimes there would be a dozen or more of them at a table, banging down glasses, bellowing with laughter, shouting a viewpoint – and a sleepy child might crawl on to its parent's lap and submerge its head in a strong protective shoulder.

Rosaleen, welcomed into this unique circle of people, thought as she sat amongst them one evening: 'I'm glad I'm independent and that I am not shackled to a man. How could I enjoy myself so wholeheartedly wondering about *his* enjoyment and feelings the whole time?'

They were superlative days and she feared their end – leaving them to pall into memories, leaving Paris and her new friends. She feared being friendless in London, having to start all over again, pioneering a movement to which she was already committed.

'I don't know what to do,' she said to Renoir one day.

'I cannot give you advice, Rosaleen,' he said. 'But as an artist you must travel – visit places, and look at art.'

'I can see art under one roof in a gallery.'

'It is not the same. You must see art in its own environment. You must see through the eyes of other artists – what they have seen.'

'But now – what must I do now? I'm afraid of being ridiculed in London.'

'Ah, *petite* Rosaleen, I cannot answer you. But you must not be afraid. *Et malheureusement* – unhappily – you will be ridiculed. That is certain.'

A letter from Robbie forwarded by Frederick provided her solution:

Dearest Rosaleen,
    Why do you never write? It is spring and all the way up the flanks of the mountains you can see the white dots which are the lambs, and their tiny cries along with the

deeper ones of the answering ewes resound throughout the valley. And they are joined by the barking of sheepdogs. The weather is unusually fine, and today (Wednesday) Laurie and I drove the pony and trap to Ambleside market. It was particularly busy on account of the mildness and I suddenly thought of you and remembered – just – the day you came back with the baby rams and mother berating you . . .

We got back laden with produce, and as the afternoon was my free one I met Vanessa – you know, the vicar's wife's niece I told you about – and we walked to Torver Back Common and then took the footpath to the western lakeshore. We're still sweethearts and I wove some hay and made it into a ring for her. She wears it on her wedding finger. In a year's time we'll get engaged. We both want that.

Mr Ruskin has been away since February in Venice – he was very downcast when he left England – and the other day I had a letter from him, which surprised me I must say, since I am only an employee, although I know he thinks well of me. Anyway the letter was most strange and rambling, and in it he claimed to have seen signs of Rose La Touche's spirit! Brantwood itself keeps me busy as Laurie is often involved with other matters and increasingly I take over his role. I am fairly capable with my hands as you know, and anything which needs repairing I can at least have a go at. I am also sorting out some manuscripts Mr Ruskin asked me to. This, as you can imagine, is most exciting. With regard to my own poems, another was accepted last week – that makes four in all now and they talk of me contributing on a regular basis! I am happy, Rosaleen – I want so little really. You were happy here once. Do you ever think about it – back to how it was, and me following you everywhere like a shadow? Five years – over five years since you left, Rosaleen, and you came to see me in my room with your bruised face.

How I hated Father for that. I'll never excuse him, but at

least now I understand him better. We both want the same things even. We're not looking far – just out of the window, that's all. I visit the inn once a week and nothing really changes. It survives. They survive. Nothing more or less. I'm writing now by candlelight in the room I share with Laurie. He's out and Brantwood sighs sleepily. It does sigh, I swear it – creaks and heaves like an old man resting his bones. You'd scarcely recognize Brantwood now, so many changes have taken place. Well that's not quite true – the main building remains essentially the same. Do you remember that jaunt in the row-boat you and I took? I huddled inside, terrified we'd capsize and then terrified we'd be caught – and now here I am in Mr Ruskin's employ!

I have not asked about you: are you feeling better, and has the horror of those months back receded a little at least? Will you write to me with your news, Rosaleen? I so long to hear from you and it's been ages. Will you not come back and at least pay a visit? I never dreamed when you bent over and kissed me that white night that it would be years before you returned. It was better I didn't know it at the time.

I think about you often.

Your loving – Robbie.

After reading the letter Rosaleen was overwhelmed by a feeling of nostalgia, a yearning to see her home; and in Renoir's studio she told him of her decision. Of all the other artists, he was the one she felt closest to. She had seen his many moods and facets – and some were not pleasant. He cultivated wealthy friends to be used to his advantage; he had anti-Semitic tendencies; he was prone to depression about his work – but paradoxically he was the humblest and kindest of all men, was close friends with Pissarro, who was half-Jewish, and his more usual buoyancy compensated for his depressions.

'I have decided to go back to England in a couple of days' time,' she told him. 'I think I must face things.'

'I will to miss you, *ma jolie petite*,' he said sadly. 'But you are brave and you have talent. You will win your battles.'

'You have been so kind . . .'

He shrugged. '*De rien.* I have enjoyed it. And you have learned much, *n'est-ce pas?* But I think it is my good friend Claude Monet whom you prefer to copy.'

She blushed, thinking that he felt slighted – and then noticed the humour in his eyes.

'I like to mix my styles,' she answered carefully.

'*Mais quelle diplomat!* Ah Rosaleen – it is a pity that you must depart. A pity . . . A pity.'

He and Monet saw her off at the station. It was early in the morning and the rain fell in a fine drizzle from a sky that was two shades of grey. She kissed each man and was hugged in turn, and for a moment she clung – and another moment, clung again. She felt like a young child leaving her parents. She did not want to see their faces fade in the distance, pale and hazy in the greyness of the sky and the steam from the wet dark platform. Like an Impressionist painting.

'I don't want to leave.' The plaintive words remained unuttered. She wanted to appear composed. But they both saw; they spoke of her after the train had carried her off – *la petite* – so pretty and brave and determined, so alone and little and uncertain. What would happen to her, they wondered?

❧ Fifteen ❧

THE DISCIPLE

I shall follow their ideals
But my battles will be my own.

It was evening, and raining in London when she arrived. A North wind blew the rain across the platform and drove it, silver streaks, into her face.

'Wonderful weather isn't it?' a man said, eyeing Rosaleen curiously. They were the first words anyone had said to her since leaving French soil, and the very Englishness of the remark almost made her wince.

A figure hurried towards her and she saw him with relief. 'Rosaleen!' Frederick kissed her. 'Have you been here long?'

'No – a moment, that's all.' She felt forlorn, imagining herself wan and waif-like, and the image made her feel worse.

He took her case, and ducking their heads against the sleet they dashed from the shelter of the covered platform into the street where a hansom cab waited.

'Was it wonderful?' he asked when they were settled and on their way to Chelsea.

'Wonderful, wonderful, wonderful,' she said with longing in her voice.

He glanced at her keenly. 'I thought you might stay. Your telegraph quite took me by surprise.'

'I had a letter from Robbie – I thought I would go home for a week or so. I shall take some of my paintings to show him and Father – one or two old ones as I don't know that Father would approve of my new style. That's if he will agree to see me at all. I thought if I could at least show him something I'd done he might be mollified.'

'Rosaleen –'

'And then when I get back I'll look for somewhere to live and a studio.'

'Rosaleen, I must tell you something. Your paintings – the ones you left at my place – have all been destroyed.'

'Destroyed?' She smiled confusedly, running a hand through her hair.

'Someone has ripped them to pieces.'

Rosaleen was silent for a moment, digesting the information: months of work – destroyed. And among them – her two unsold paintings which had been such a bone of contention between Oliver and herself.

'Ah well, I shall have a clean palette with which to start anew, if you'll forgive the pun.' She gave a tremulous laugh, then added, 'I suppose we both have a good idea who did it.'

'I suppose we do,' Frederick agreed grimly. 'I'm so sorry . . .'

'It is hardly your fault.'

'She visited, then insisted on staying when I had to go out. She made some excuse about wanting to look at one of my books.'

'She was very bitter about our Paris trip.'

'I have of course told her what I think of her in no mean words. But she – of course – played the innocent: what *was* I talking about; and how could anyone do such a thing. It must have been her, but I did not go to the room for a couple of days after her visit and then it took me a moment to link the vandalism to her . . . Oh Rosaleen, you look so upset.'

She stared out of the cab window at the night-time London scenes moving by, illuminated in bursts of light from the street lamps and the semi-moon. 'It makes me shiver to think someone should hate me so. And there again I am sad because I was hoping to go home.'

'But you still can.'

'No. I've nothing to show for the years except a few paintings in my new style which would mean nothing to my father. As I've said before – when I've achieved something, then I shall go. I want him to be proud.'

'You have such a strange outlook sometimes.'

'Maybe. But that's the way I am. So tomorrow I shall look for an apartment and a studio . . .'

She found them together in a Kensington square. The rent was low and the landlord and his wife, Mr and Mrs Bedford, were a pleasant elderly couple who warmed immediately to Rosaleen and would invite her to join them on odd evenings, or go up to her studio on the slightest pretext.

The weeks passed and slipped into late summer with its unpredictable weather. Most days found Rosaleen outdoors with her easel and paints, along different stretches of the Thames, or positioned in a pretty garden square, or at the riding stables in Hyde Park . . . She painted Frederick in his dressing-gown having breakfast in the courtyard, and another time grooming Edgar; she captured the changing of the guard in a blur of red, gold and black. And if it rained – then her streets gleamed with puddles that were blue, yellow and rose, and the carriages would shimmer and the ladies' hats drip.

She was the disciple faithfully following her masters, and her paintings were infused with light and that vibrancy which was part of her nature. Her children were real children, not the miniature models of decorum as usually portrayed; her women exuded sexuality, not as idealized by the Pre-Raphaelites, but in an earthy way; her men might be beggars or aristocrats, but they must have in their faces something which sparked her interest. Sometimes onlookers would gather round her as she painted, and sometimes a person would pass a comment, or grunt, or be silent. Perhaps he might even laugh; but Rosaleen worked on as if they were not there, a solitary figure with a lone voice.

Socially she had resumed a few contacts, but of the old circle some had moved away, or given up painting for more lucrative work, or apparently, as Rosaleen had once done, disappeared from the face of the earth. She saw Frederick regularly, and it was with him, at a fashionable Soho restaurant, that by chance they met Effie and John Millais together with Henrietta and Edward Ward.

'But you must join our table,' Millais said, and beckoned to a waiter who scurried over to adjust the seating arrangements. Another poured wine into the crystal glasses.

'So my dear – you are living now in London again, I hear,' Mrs Ward said to Rosaleen.

'Yes. I stayed in Paris for a couple of months, studying under Renoir, and now I am following the Impressionist school.'

There was a hush. And the whole table, it seemed, focused on her. John Millais was the first to speak. 'My young friend, isn't that a rather odd choice, if I might say so?' He himself concentrated mostly on portraiture nowadays.

Rosaleen looked stricken and under the white tablecloth Frederick's hand found hers and squeezed it encouragingly. Everyone continued to stare at her, expectant, waiting for some qualification. Millais's expression was puzzled, whilst the others looked as though they had found her remark mildly amusing.

She squeezed Frederick's hand back and then loosened his hold, bringing her hand up to her face, to hide the rising colour in her cheeks.

'I do not see that it is an odd choice,' she said evenly, and then when they apparently expected more of her, added – stammering a little, 'I mean I think their art very beautiful . . . It is surely lively and also evocative.'

'Evocative of what, dear?' chimed in Effie Millais rather scathingly, and Rosaleen looked at her resentfully, thinking, 'Her face has become thin and severe. She looks grasping and petty-minded . . .'

'It conjures up pleasure and enjoyment . . . sweet memories . . . wistfulness . . . longings. I feel all those things when I look upon the Impressionists' paintings.'

'But their style is a little unconventional is it not?' ventured Henrietta Ward.

'Outrageous, more like,' laughed Millais.

Rosaleen's eyes glittered. 'Once your work found as little favour,' she told him heatedly. 'Once the Pre-Raphaelites were as isolated as the Impressionists are now, and it was thanks to the likes of John Ruskin they became established.' And immediately she wished she hadn't spoken. Millais's face had set angrily, his lower lip sucked in.

'Well really,' exclaimed his wife – once Mrs John Ruskin, a fact she preferred to forget.

And Edward Ward said, 'With respect, Miss Ruddock, I do not think you can compare the Impressionists with the Brotherhood.'

'No, I cannot and do not,' she agreed trying to remain calm and catching Frederick's eye. 'But each group paints as it believes art should be. You think one is more realistic and therefore more valid than the other, but the other inspires the onlooker with sentiments he or she can relate to – those are real enough. I look at Monet or Pissarro's landscapes and am more drawn to them, feel more – as though I am there – then when I look at a Constable which I admire formally but am not part of. The Impressionists' art is like looking at a pretty pattern one never tires of – and surely must be accepted on a different level: for what it is, not what it is *not*.'

Frederick listened to her proudly. 'Wise girl!' And he gave a few short claps, laughing. This broke the strained atmosphere, and soon everyone was teasing her lightly and joining in the friendly laughter. She herself pretended to partake – but inwardly she was disappointed in them all except Frederick; they were supposedly enlightened but were as intolerant as anyone else; and the more they jested and she feigned reciprocal humour, the more separate she felt from them, resenting their assumptions and their smugness.

Afterwards, back at her apartment, Frederick said: 'I am afraid you have just had a foretaste of the opposition you will encounter, dear girl. And that was from friends.'

It was, as he said, a foretaste. In October Rosaleen amassed her collection of pictures and began to tout them. She went from gallery to gallery, person to person, place to place, even to restaurants – and at first she strode out confidently, her sense of purpose lending a springiness to her step, but then as the weeks wore on her walk became slow and reluctant – in anticipation of yet another rebuff.

Her work was greeted with scepticism or with stony-faced displeasure, with embarrassment or mystification, or derision. And at the end of her humiliation someone might say to her, 'However *you* are another matter. What would you say to a spot of dinner tonight – heh?'

She loathed those types – invariably overweight and loud-voiced and conceited – and she became increasingly embittered towards the close-knit art establishment. She thought frequently of Oliver, and although she could not liken her style to his, nevertheless she was now experiencing what he had experienced: rejection. And one could only take it personally, one could only feel withered and despondent. With the passing of the weeks winter lurked, and money became a serious problem.

'Don't fret yourself about the rent,' the kind Mr Bedford said. 'Give us a picture instead. We like your pictures.'

With relief Rosaleen let them choose. Soon after that, shortly before Christmas, she sold two – to a Frenchman called Pierre Chenier for the restaurant he ran – and it was then that Frederick conceived the idea of holding an exhibition there in the new year.

'We shall be very selective,' he said as they made plans. 'You must include only paintings you yourself are entirely happy with. And we must choose the guests with care.'

'I cannot think of anyone to invite,' she said, sitting cross-legged on the floor of her studio. 'I can't think of a single person who will feel favourably towards me. Those same people for whom I used to sit for hours at a stretch, passive and obedient to their commands, will react either with embarrassment or with viciousness, and I dread it. You saw how Millais was, and Burne-Jones would be the same. Rossetti would be worse. And Mr Ruskin – oh Frederick, what would he think?'

'To be truthful I am not sure. But do not forget he championed Turner, and surely Turner must be a forerunner of the Impressionists? Now you mustn't feel hopeless, Rosaleen – we shall invite Tissot and Whistler, both of whose art veers towards Impressionism . . . Oh I have just recalled that Whistler is in the midst of suing John Ruskin for libel!'

'Goodness, why is that?' For a moment Rosaleen forgot her anxiety.

'Do you recall at the exhibition at Sutton House, years ago, you said they were quarrelling over a particular painting?'

'Yes.'

'It is over that same one! Whistler has renamed it *Nocturne* and showed it at the opening of the Grosvenor Gallery. Ruskin reiterated his complaints – unfortunately in public this time, in *Fors*, calling Whistler a "coxcomb" and referring to his picture as "flinging a pot of paint in the public's face".'

'Oh no. Oh dear. But it is funny. Ruskin is so cranky sometimes, and I like him so well despite it.'

'I too.'

'As long as he is not as harsh about my paintings.'

'There is that possibility, Rosaleen. There is also the possibility he won't attend, for it is only polite to warn him of Whistler's invitation.'

'Such politics!'

'Talking of which we must invite Lord Taggart-Laughton.'

She looked aghast. 'That old man? But I couldn't.'

'You *must*,' he insisted firmly.

'But you know his opinion of me.'

'That's as maybe, but he has a reputation for being fair nonetheless and is certainly a well-respected judge of art. And by the by, I have heard he is most dissatisfied with his son's marriage. No heir-apparent, and the young lady becomes a little tedious with her fainting fits. He probably thinks back to you with great regret.'

'Who – Tags or his father?'

'Both, dear girl. I meant the father. But both, assuredly. Now, that is settled . . . And we *must* invite Frederic George Stephens – he is on your side . . . And a few men of business with money to spend . . .'

They set the date for February 15th, 1878, and the invitations were sent out. Frederick went to Tuscany for a fortnight, and while he was away the replies came trickling in – acceptances and regrets – and Rosaleen ticked off her list, becoming more apprehensive as the day itself drew nearer.

It was an evening occasion and Rosaleen wore a Prussian-blue velvet and satin gown she had bought in Paris; it was stunningly sophisticated with its long tight sleeves, and her bared shoulders gleamed ivory in contrast to her bright hair which was caught with a simple ribbon then left to billow in curls to her waist. Those who were not impressed by her paintings could not fail to be moved by her appearance, and as she shook hands or greeted guests everybody was riveted by her. No one would have guessed at her nervousness or noticed the tiny muscle quivering at the corner of her mouth.

She knew about half of the forty or so guests and there were many faces she recognized from the exhibition in which she and Oliver had participated a year and a half before. She thought with amazement: 'It doesn't feel like a year and a half – yet so much has happened . . . Bad things . . . Good things . . . And now?'

And now – smiling a bright smile which masked her trepidation, she mingled, listened to conversation, odd remarks; and she heard little that was favourable.

'She might be a beauty, but that does not quite excuse her this . . .'

'Why does the woman's hand apparently suffer from leprosy? . . .'

'I confess I fail to see the charm of orange and blue trees . . .'

'But the buildings are crooked – blurred. I mean to say buildings are just not like that. If she weren't so young and damnably charming I'd tell her what I thought of 'em. By Jove I would . . .'

She moved from person to person, her despondency growing all the time. Then, appearing in the doorway, a fair and delicate-looking woman drooping on his arm, was someone she knew well.

'Tags . . .' she murmured under her breath. And then after the shock she felt a surprising gladness. She approached him. 'Hello Tags.'

He was less calm than she; he flushed deeply and was almost curt in his formality, even going so far as to address her initially as 'Miss Ruddock'.

'Good evening, Miss Ruddock . . . I trust you are well . . . This is my wife.'

'I believe we once met, years ago,' Rosaleen said. And the girl smiled a pale, fragile smile and lowered her lashes as she replied, drooping a little more heavily on her husband.

'He has the bloodshot eyes of a drinker,' Rosaleen thought sadly. 'And he's become stout. I knew it would happen.'

'My father apologizes,' Tags told her with the same formality. 'He desired most strongly to attend but was taken severely ill, and insisted I took his place.'

'Then I am glad you did,' she said gravely. His eyes rested on her, a penetrating sorrowful look which elicited from her a sudden tenderness. He saw it in her face and seemed to draw back from her.

'Well, to business.' He was brisk. 'Let me see what you have been doing. Come, my dear . . . Are you feeling any better?'

She watched them – saw Tags take a couple of glasses from the waiter and motion his wife to do the same, and knew that she would not take a sip but would hand him her own two glasses when his were empty. He stopped at the first painting and lingered, a look of astonishment crossing his face. Tags knew about art, and she watched him intently to see his reaction. She saw the astonishment change to consideration, and the consideration to approval, and with that she knew a mild feeling of victory.

Tissot – accompanied by a beautiful young woman not known to Rosaleen – Whistler and Ruskin arrived simultaneously. The three were together, Ruskin on his own, and he regarded Whistler malevolently. 'I do not appreciate your ploys,' he said as he brushed past.

'Nor I your principles,' the other replied in his pleasant American voice.

Rosaleen overheard, but thought it best to pretend she hadn't. She greeted Ruskin first, appalled by the deterioration in his appearance: he seemed a haggard old man. 'It is so good to see you.' Although in her heart she dreaded his opinion of her work. More than anyone's she depended on his word.

'Little Rosaleen.' He always called her that, and with his obvious affection her anxiety fled. She kissed his whiskery cheek, thinking how frail he was.

'I'm terrified you will not like what I've done,' she confided.

'There is that chance,' he agreed. 'But that need not dissuade you, and I shall always respect your talent. If you believe in what you are doing, then even if I dislike it I shall trust its authenticity. Your convictions have never been lightly founded – unlike a certain character there.' He motioned impatiently to Whistler, diminutively elegant in the opposite corner of the room.

'How was Venice?' She changed the subject.

'Incomparable,' he answered. 'And of course I think of Turner whenever I am there.'

'Turner was an Impressionist,' she dared say.

'Yes and no. He was a draughtsman first, and within that he could explore. Now I am going to leave you to form my own conclusions.' He noted her anxious expression and added kindly, 'Rosaleen – I am growing old and increasingly stubborn. But I am not infallible – besides which you and I are friends and I certainly do not desire to snuff out your enthusiasm. By the by, your young brother is progressing well – a charming young man with a keen intellect.' He walked away with his slow and stooping gait.

She looked around the room. Frederick was playing the host, welcoming people. Fragments of his conversation drifted over to her and she smiled as she heard him acting as her publicist; Pierre Chenier was more interested in publicizing his own restaurant and hovered importantly by the splendid display of food laid out as a finger-buffet; Tags was talking animatedly to Whistler; and James Tissot – a handsome dark man with a moustache that gave him a faintly nautical air – was with his woman friend, each pausing long before the pictures, their heads inclined in concentration. Rosaleen knew little about Tissot except that he had sold his painting *Hush* for twelve hundred guineas to the dealer Agnew. She also knew that Ruskin had loftily called him a glorified photographer.

She went over to them and introduced herself, and his deep eyes shone with pleasure as he shook her hand. 'I am delighted to make your acquaintance,' he told her in his lightly accented voice. 'And this is my friend Kathleen Newton. Kathleen is from Ireland.' The woman, who was considerably younger, smiled.

'We have both been admiring your work. It is delightful.'

Rosaleen's heart lifted. '*Really?*' she asked guilelessly.

Tissot laughed. 'You are that uncertain? Well I can understand, because you are a controversial artist. But in my opinion your pictures are well balanced and presented and beautifully composed.'

'Thank you. You are most kind –'

'Not kind. Honest,' an American accent said over her shoulder.

'Mr Whistler – I am so pleased you could come.'

'I wouldn't have missed this for the world – despite him over there.' He gestured with his head to Ruskin, now speaking with Frederic George Stephens. That pair caught Whistler's eye and immediately looked away.

'Oh dear . . .' Rosaleen murmured, but inwardly felt a mischievous laugh rising to her throat and suppressed it. 'It's not all disastrous then,' she thought. 'Some of them like my work – people I respect. It will take time. I must expect that . . . I knew it . . .'

'Excuse me . . . Excuse me . . .' She had to move on, to mix with everybody, to hear what was being said.

Frederic George Stephens caught up with her at a point when her spirits were flagging. Weary from tension, and weary of so many adverse comments, she was beginning to wish the evening were over. Millais, Burne-Jones, Rossetti, Hunt – they had turned on her together as if it were their right; single-minded and arrogant, they had spoken to her as though she were a child.

And now she was scalded by their criticism and airs of superiority, by their masculine presumption that they could speak to her in such a way.

'Miss Ruddock?'

'Oh – Mr Stephens.' It was all she could manage. The smile which had been frozen on her face had gone and her lips quivered in a tired effort.

'I have found this evening most – interesting,' he said.

'You do not approve,' she said dismally, winding a long strand of hair around her finger and staring at it intently.

'But that is not the case,' he said gently, waiting for her to lift her eyes, and when she did, seeing to his dismay that they glistened.

'Here – what is wrong?' he asked.

'No – nothing – absolutely nothing,' she reassured him hurriedly. 'I have something in my eye.' She made a pretence of rubbing it, and then said in a deliberately lively tone, 'There – that is better.'

He went along with her little act. 'Are you sure it is better?'

'Yes – oh quite sure.'

'And you are happy to discuss your painting?'

'Oh yes – quite,' she said again, adding gaily, 'That is why I am here.'

He smiled gently and she thought: 'Before the killing, the stroking . . . But it is not his fault.'

'Miss Ruddock – I cannot profess to be an expert on Impressionism. It is not a style I know or appreciate, but –' he held up his hand as her face fell, '– nonetheless, that does *not* mean I cannot see its merit. I think your subject-matter is delightfully thought-out and structured, that as in your other work you have shown some skill and draughtsmanship, and that certainly your pictures are vivacious – as vivacious as you yourself.'

'I was not feeling so a moment ago.'

'No, I realize. But if this is something you believe in then you must bear with it. As I said, it is not a style which greatly moves me, but this does not mean it doesn't have virtues and I shall mention them in the *Athenaeum*. I wanted you to know that.'

'You are very kind.' She felt quite weak from her fluctuating emotions and sat down on a conveniently placed chair, and only then fully realized the significance of his remarks. If he was at all complimentary, even guardedly so, she would at least retain some dignity, and the same people who slated her would have at the back of their minds that 'Frederic George Stephens had been mildly impressed'. Then came another thought: 'They'll find an excuse – I'm a woman, I'm attractive, I'm an innkeeper's daughter . . . Whatever it is they'll say that he was chivalrous, or attracted by me, or sorry for me, and that is why he was nice . . . And maybe they are right.'

'Miss Ruddock –'

She interrupted him: 'Are you sincere in what you said? I do not mean to be rude.'

He looked so taken aback that she could not doubt the truth of his reply. 'What *do* you mean – sincere? But of course I am sincere. It is my job to be so.'

'I'm sorry, I had to know.'

He patted her arm briefly. 'You must relax, and take things as they happen.'

She thought: 'Once I never worried or thought about the day ahead, or planned or searched. I had no ambitions then . . .' Fleetingly she craved for the simplicity of those days and she closed her eyes and could almost taste the fresh air.

Towards the end of the evening Tags – red of face, his bow-tie slightly askew – found her by herself. 'I have bought one of your paintings. I gather Sir Frederick is acting on your behalf,' he announced loudly. Then his voice dropped and he said almost humbly, 'They are amazingly good. I could not believe it. I bought the one of the Changing of the Guard.'

'Aristocratic to the core,' she teased – wanting briefly to hurt him – and watched the red of his cheeks deepen. She relented then and said quietly, 'I'm glad you like it.'

'I was torn between several.' He sounded so anguished and defeated, so different from the boy she had known; but she had known how events would turn out for him. She asked gently, 'How is life treating you, Tags?'

'Oh just fine.' But the compassion in her face seemed to undermine his strength and he said in a low but impassioned voice, 'That is untrue. Nothing is fine. Nothing. Absolutely nothing is fine.' He left her abruptly.

People started to go and Ruskin came to say goodbye.

'Well?' She raised a quizzical eyebrow. 'You have been avoiding me.'

'Yes, but only so I could gather my thoughts.'

'And?'

'You are wearing your disarming smile, Rosaleen. Is that deliberate?'

'No.' She laughed huskily. 'It is my relieved smile. It has been a varied evening, but I have got through it. I have faced everybody as I am, and now I must be accepted for myself. It was my first hurdle tonight and therefore my worst, and I can tackle anything that follows.'

'You are a brave girl. Well, little Rosaleen, I have bought the one of Frederick in the courtyard.'

'You have bought it!'

'That is what I said!'

'Oh sir . . .' She kissed his bearded cheek. The beard had grown longer and greyer recently.

'No doubt you are waiting for my verdict: well, my dear, as you know I have always admired innovation, and your designs – I call them that deliberately – are well drawn and executed. You have used the paint more generously than I expected, which I liked, and there is great sensitivity in your use of colour. There is also a typical boldness in your style. I cannot like it all, but nor did I actually dislike anything. There you have it.'

Her tired face glowed at his words and he tilted her chin. 'Rosaleen, I can do very little for you: the odd article, the odd purchase, but Impressionism is not a cause I wish to tangle with. And there are others, people who were here tonight, who will be unkind. Brace yourself. They resent women in art. And a woman Impressionist – well I hardly need say more!'

'It is so unfair.'

'It is that,' he agreed.

300

As he left she heard someone remark, 'Of course he has become quite mad. He hallucinates apparently. One can no longer believe anything the man says . . .' And Rosaleen was filled with sorrow and defensive anger.

Two other paintings were sold – one to Frederick and one to James Tissot – then, during the course of the week various articles appeared in different papers and journals. Frederic George Stephens was true to his word, as was Ruskin in his article in *The Times*. However, all the others – there were five – were scathing, in particular James Dafforne of the *Art Journal* who had entitled his column 'Call This Art?' and then proceeded to destroy her, accusing her of a 'demonstration of female hysteria', and ending by suggesting she put aside her paints and concentrate on setting a better example of womanhood. Another article in *Punch* was headed, 'Well, the Food was Good', and even merited a cartoon. In this report there were phrases such as 'curious flights of fantasy', and 'deterred by the blobs of rainbow colours meant to represent trees . . .' Thomas S. James of the *London Review* had used the opportunity not only to belittle Rosaleen, whom he referred to as a 'slip of a girl', but Ruskin too, implying that his judgement could not be trusted.

'I will not be disheartened . . . I will not be disheartened . . . I will not be disheartened . . .'

But it was no easy task she had set herself, and as she tried to establish herself, tried to persuade galleries to buy her work, she felt very solitary. She had sat at tables amongst friends and danced at guinguettes and lazed in row-boats like one of Renoir's characters; but the cornucopia which had glittered before her then, now seemed distant as she suffered insults and rejection. People started to rebuff her socially. As a pretty and quiet 'curiosity' she had been amusing to have around, but now that she had learned to talk she was too controversial . . . And her lifestyle was well known – hadn't there been a murder and a suicide? That was what the Baroness von Hoffnung had said anyway, and she was on everybody's party list . . .

Then one afternoon towards the end of 1878, a year which had used so much of her fortitude, Rosaleen returned to her lodgings to find a calling card for her in the hallway. It bore a family crest she recognized and was from Lord Taggart-Laughton, its message curt: 'Please visit me at the above address tomorrow, Wednesday, four o'clock p.m.'

It took no account of the possibility that she might not be free; it was presumed she must comply; and at first – in a rush of resentment – her instinct was to send an immediate reply, declining. Then she became curious, and with her curiosity came a light-hearted recklessness: 'Why not go? I've nothing to lose . . . Lecherous old man probably wants his thigh rubbed – hah! Please pay me a visit . . . Well at least he said *please* . . .'

She sat on the chesterfield in the library where she had once sat with Tags, having tea with his father. The fire crackled in the grate, and the curtains were already pulled against the dark foreshortened day. Outside a cold wetness hung in the air and lingered treacherously on roads so that horses slipped and carriage wheels skidded. The sounds of traffic in Park Lane could still be heard, but through the closed windows and heavy drapes they were muffled as though from another world – and here cocooned in the warmth of Sutton House, in the panelled room, Rosaleen heard with growing disbelief what the old man had to say.

'. . . To tell you that I was astounded by the painting my son bought from you, would not be putting too fine a point on it. I was positively exhilarated by its vividness and impact – its immediate effect. I wanted to contact you then, but was ill for many months with severe bronchitis and went abroad for an equal length of time to convalesce. Now I am fully recovered and I wished to see you to speak about your art.'

His watery and pink-rimmed eyes regarded her shrewdly, but her face was expressionless and from her silence he could not guess her feelings – that her heart thumped and her excitement was a surging heat within her.

'Possibly you are angered by our previous meeting,' he said bravely, clearing his throat and blustering a little. 'I can assure you no harm was intended . . . tradition in our kind of families and all that, you know ... You're a likeable gal – it wasn't that ...'

'I understand your reasons. I always did,' she said quietly, sorry for his predicament and beginning to like the old man, who seemed harmless now and rather defenceless with his runny eyes and dribbling lip, and gouty leg which he rested on a stool.

'So there is no ill feeling then?' He sounded relieved that business was done with.

'None whatsoever,' she reassured him with her sweetest smile.

He looked at her regretfully, shaking his head. 'What a fool I was – still, that is in the past, and my son would have made you unhappy if I'd let him marry you ... To revert to the reason you are here: I am extremely interested in your work and should like to visit your studio to buy at least a couple of your paintings; I should also be delighted to hold an exhibition here at Sutton House for you. That is if you would be agreeable.'

She could no longer contain herself. She leaped up, clapping her hands together, her face ablaze with happiness. 'Oh!' The small exclamation was restrained – almost a sigh, but it said everything.

The following day he bought three of her paintings for the combined sum of eight hundred guineas, a price suggested by him for she had had no idea of their value, and even then he told her, 'I may be cheating you. Perhaps they are worth more. But as yet you are an unknown –'

She felt a sudden affection for him and cut him short. 'You have been most generous. And you are holding an exhibition for me. What more could I want?'

'A patron perhaps? A benefactor?' He looked meaningfully at her. Seeing the range of expressions which crossed her face he realized she was not quite certain of his proposal. He elaborated: 'I am offering to become your patron, Miss Ruddock. By that I mean to give you support, financial backing, to promote you in every possible way and commission works from you. I have the utmost faith in your ability, young lady. Will you consider it?'

Her incredulity became elation. She was weak with it and sank on to her stool, holding her head in her hands. 'I cannot believe it. I just cannot . . .'

And then she began to laugh – unable to stop, and the old man joined in: the two of them, conspirators, sitting in her untidy studio with the thudding of the rain on the glass, laughing.

Sixteen

THE VIOLINIST

I thought him such a gentle boy –
Though his fawn-like eyes looked inward.

On a morning at the beginning of March 1879, Rosaleen sat at
the rickety table by the window overlooking the square. Everywhere were signs of spring – in the trees, the bird-song, the sky,
the crocuses, the daffodils . . . In front of her were paper and ink
and she sucked the end of her pen thoughtfully, narrowing her
eyes against the piercing white light which suddenly beamed
through the pane as a cloud disintegrated. Then, dipping the nib
in ink, she began to write:

> Dear Father,
>   It is a long time since I last wrote – I think it must be
> almost three years – and as time goes on and on and we go
> on and on with it, I think: surely he'll be just a little more
> lenient now . . .

She paused, watched the sun slipping into obscurity again. What
to say? How to word it so that she didn't frighten him with
words and phrases that were second nature to her now? Assuming he let Robbie read it to him . . .

> Father – once you loved me and I bounced on the feed sacks
> in the cart beside you as you drove, and you'd let me hold
> the reins; we climbed Old Man together, and you gave me
> my first sip of beer when Mother wasn't looking. And when
> she died I cared for you like you were my child; I scrubbed

your back and spoon-fed you gruel. But I grew up, Father, and left when I knew you could all cope, and now – I wanted to write to you because something has happened which I thought might make you proud: I am now making a living as an artist, and my patron – a kind and very rich old man who likes my work – is holding an exhibition for about four hundred people at his private mansion at the end of the month. I am a little nervous as you can imagine, as it's very important for me, but this man has faith in me, so I must in myself.

I am living in respectable and clean lodgings at present with a studio above and views over a garden square – very different to the view from the Coachman's, but pleasant enough for London, and the elderly landlord and landlady are ever such a dear couple. So you see, Father, I am not living a bad or wicked life . . .

She thought back to the many events in her life which would have been beyond his comprehension.

. . . I think of you and Nana and home often – truly I do – and I only wish you didn't feel so badly about things. I'm sorry for what happened, but Father – it's a long time ago now. Maybe you'll find it in your heart to forgive me for something I had to do.

I hope you are keeping in good health. I can visualize you suddenly with your great red beard, and the string hoisting your trousers round your great belly, and hear your voice: 'Aw lass, don't you be rude 'bout my gut . . .' Father – can't I be your lass again now? Give a big hug to Nana for me.
Your loving – Rosaleen.

She received a letter from Robbie ten days later:

Dear Rosaleen,

This is a short letter as I've got to go into the town with Mr Ruskin in a few minutes, but I just wanted you to know

I read Father your letter. I said to him: 'I've heard from Rosaleen — I've a letter from her for you. Would you like me to read it?' And in return he neither turned his head nor refused, but gave that sort of grunt he has which is half affirmation. So I read it — shouted it on account of his deafness, and his eyes watered. I swear it. Then he said: 'So she's all right then.' Just that: 'So she's all right then.' And he went to pour himself a beer and spoke no more about it. But you and I know him. He cares, Rosaleen. He still cares . . .

The publicity preceding the Sutton House exhibition built up gradually — from the first short notices to lengthy pieces in the art journals. Critics who had previously esteemed Lord Taggart-Laughton now hinted at his senility or suggested he had fallen prey to the charms of a 'delectable redhead', and letters bandied back and forth. But Lord Taggart-Laughton's printed replies left no doubts that his wits were unimpaired — and the tone of the articles subtly changed, becoming less sure of their ground. By the evening of the exhibition the general mood was one of receptive curiosity.

Rosaleen waited nervously with her patron for the first guests to arrive. She glanced at him — at his stoutness exaggerated in his tight military uniform with all its regalia, and the smoke from his cigar floating in soft puffs around bewhiskered jowls — and his comical appearance made her smile a little.

'That's better, m'gal,' he said. 'Where's that Northern spirit, eh? There you are, gorgeous as a jewel in your ruby red, or perhaps like a delightful glass of claret — and I can only ogle you with the useless pangs of an old man. Pity me, my dear, will you just a bit?'

'Not in the least!' she teased.

'Ah, you tantalizing creature. Well at least trust my ability to judge paintings, will you? And now, Rosaleen, I am in earnest.'

His rheumy eyes focused on her, and she looked back at him searchingly, longing to put her trust in him; her face then was very young, very innocent. He watched her expression relax, and said, 'I think we're comrades now, what do you think, eh m'gal?'

She laughed and sat straighter. 'Yes I think we are.'

'Good,' he said briskly. 'I believe our first batch of guests has arrived. Now stick like a leech by me. I'm used to handling the lot of 'em.'

The exhibition was organized in the same way as that other one five and a half years previously, and the vast ballroom with its tinkling chandeliers soon filled with guests. Flunkies with their laden salvers wove their way amongst the crowd and offered champagne or tiny biscuit squares topped with pâté de foie gras and caviar. People spotted friends across the room and called out, women commented on each other's fashions, and there was a loud buzz of conversation interspersed by the sounds of different toned laughter.

Protected by her benefactor, Rosaleen studied everybody – faces she knew and strangers, a cross-section of people, most of whom were invited, but others who had inveigled their way in, for Lord Taggart-Laughton's patronage of this unknown woman artist was the talk of London society. He defended her energetically:

'What do you mean a "novel approach to art"?' his sonorous voice rang out. 'I should jolly well hope it *is* a novel approach. That is the *point*, don't you see?'

Or: 'You lot are so dreadfully trapped by your outmoded opinions I feel rather sorry for you. You fail to use your imagination. No doubt it was your nanny's fault. Shut your eyes tightly. Open them – quick, and what do you see – your first impression? Is it not of spots and colours and indistinct outlines? Or imagine that your eyes are screwed up against the sun – that is how that tree might be seen. And tell me is it not a tree which makes you crave to rest beneath its shade?'

Or: 'Surely the whole essence of Impressionism – of Miss Ruddock's paintings – is *ambiance*; that delicious French word . . . But perhaps *you* do not understand French. You do? Good! Then you will know exactly what I mean.'

He was enjoying himself thoroughly and said to Rosaleen, 'The main thing is not to be apologetic. If you show humility it merely boosts your adversary's arrogance. Now I have to leave you for a while. You remember what I've told you.'

On her own she circulated – greeted Frederick who apologized for his belated arrival, chatted to Tags, his sisters and his wife, to Thomas Carlyle, Ruskin, Cézanne and Pissarro, who had travelled to England especially, and others she knew. People continually came up to her, and her fervour was such that her listeners were bound to respect her views. But there were many whose opinions would not be swayed – and they included that little band who had once been her friends and now spoke to her with barely disguised condescension.

Jane Morris sounded scornful when she said, 'Perhaps you should have left painting to the experts, Rosaleen.'

Her husband looked embarrassed. 'My dear, it is all a matter of taste.'

'It is not, and it makes me angry.' His wife wouldn't be repressed. 'After all the efforts of the Pre-Raphaelites to establish pure art in this country ignorant newcomers do their utmost to destroy the good work. It is heartbreaking.'

'I do not see it like that, Jane,' Rosaleen said quietly.

'No – you do not see at all. Or else you would not paint in such a – flippant – way.'

Rosaleen shrugged. 'I cannot please everyone,' she murmured, 'it isn't possible. Excuse me . . .' Still within earshot she heard William Morris mildly berating his wife.

She flitted from person to person, caught more snatches of conversation:

'She is prolific if nothing else.'

'Her paintings are a tonic to my eyes. Her use of colour is the sun on my back.'

'One has to admit this new style is rather pleasing to the eye.'

Whistler tapped her on the arm. 'Clever girl, clever girl. And how lovely you are – but I recall you don't like flattery. Miss Ruddock, you have my full admiration for having the courage of your convictions. My good friend Edgar Degas will be delighted to hear how splendidly you are getting on. I shall of course tell him.'

'Thank you, Mr Whistler . . .'

She passed a group of young matrons, so engrossed in their malicious prattle they didn't see her: 'They say she was involved in a murder and drove a man to his death. What sort of woman must she be?'

'She has bewitched Sir Frederick Walton, so I hear. He is completely under her spell. Look how he has treated Leonora von Hoffnung. Such humiliation. I do not know how the poor Baroness holds her head up.'

'It is obvious that our host has not art in mind as far as Rosaleen Ruddock is concerned. Really, what fools old men make of themselves.'

She overheard their gossip with a sense of resignation. She thought: 'How smug they are. I shall never have a woman-friend again. Women will always suspect me. I could have been friends with Berthe Morisot or Camille Monet or Mary Cassatt, but they are in France . . .'

But then her mood swung again as several people congratulated her, among them Frederic George Stephens with three colleagues, also critics. One of them was a woman, Elizabeth Russell, and she spoke to Rosaleen with the relief of having found a kindred spirit.

'We must keep in touch,' she said when they parted. 'Here is my card.'

They drifted off, and Rosaleen, her confidence restored, recognized other guests – Gladstone, the politician Earl Granville, a well-known actress, the author Henry James, the sculptor Frederick Leighton . . . And an elderly woman with an intelligent expression and straggling grey hair.

'Who is she?' Rosaleen wondered. 'I shall go up to her. Why not? It is my evening.'

The woman saw her staring and smiled, and they moved towards each other simultaneously. 'I must congratulate you on your delightful exhibition,' she said. 'I am enchanted by your paintings; they breathe with atmosphere.'

'Thank you. I seem to have enraged more than a few people – quite as many as are pleased.'

'Oh that must not deter you. It is the penalty you must pay for originality, my dear, as I am sure you were aware before you set out on your adventure.'

Rosaleen laughed. 'That's true . . . I feel sure I know you.'

'My name is Mary Ann Evans.'

Frowning, Rosaleen repeated the name, and then her brow cleared. 'Mary Ann Evans! George Eliot!' She clasped the other's hand. 'But how wonderful to meet you. I have so enjoyed your books. And I greatly respect your principles.'

'That pleases me very much. And you will appreciate the obstacles which have hindered me throughout my career. I expect you yourself have met them.'

'I have. To be born a woman is to be born disabled. It is so *frustrating*.' She made an exasperated gesture with her hands and the older woman smiled understandingly.

'You at least have objectives and are doing your utmost, my dear, that is what is important. How fortunate you are to have Lord Taggart-Laughton as a patron. You must feel proud to have achieved the position you are in tonight.'

Rosaleen glanced quickly at her, almost in surprise – and only then did it fully register: her achievement, the fact that this huge gathering was on her account. The realization filled her with a sense of intoxication as sweet and heady as port.

'I am famous,' she thought in wonderment. 'Just for this evening anyway, I am famous. Or even infamous . . . I think I prefer that.' She gave a small giggle out loud.

In the dining-hall she stood next to Frederick and watched, with the same astonishment as that other time, how civilized people behaved when unlimited food was displayed before them.

Lord Taggart-Laughton joined them for a moment. 'Well, m'gal, how are you faring, eh?' And without waiting for an answer continued: 'By the by, we have sold eight of the fifteen so far, and it is only half way through the evening, so be encouraged. Oh, and the self-portrait of you brushing your hair in front of a mirror, you might wish to know, has sold for six hundred and fifty pounds.' He gave his most benign smile and left them.

Rosaleen shrieked, and flung her arms round Frederick. 'I am dreaming . . . I am surely dreaming. Do you realize what it means? No more worrying about the rent and not being able to afford paints and materials – and of course I shall pay back the money I owe you.'

Then seeing heads turned disapprovingly in their direction she moved away from him. 'I must behave properly,' she said demurely. 'I seem to shock rather a lot of people.'

'Those people you refer to suffer from mental constipation!'

'Frederick!' Her burst of laughter caused more glances. Then in the midst of all the faces she singled out one – a narrow dark face that she knew. The young man regarded her gravely from the other side of the room, and raised his glass in a silent toast to her: Lorenzo Mellini, the violinist from Paris.

'Frederick – I have to see someone, to speak with him . . .'

The abruptness of her departure from his side surprised him, and he watched her make her way purposefully towards a slender young man he had seen somewhere before . . .

'What are you doing here?' Rosaleen addressed him as though they knew each other.

'Here in England, or here at the exhibition?' he asked in immaculate English, his long-lashed eyes fixed on hers, and she was struck by the gentleness of his face and by its almost girlish beauty.

'Both,' she answered, then added impetuously, 'When I first saw you performing at the Conservatoire I longed to paint you.'

'Do you still wish to?' he asked with such seriousness that his vanity became endearing.

'Yes, I'd like to.'

He continued to stare at her with his fawn-like eyes and she thought perhaps he was shy and waiting for her to make conversation.

'You haven't told me why you are here.'

'You haven't give me time.'

He was so solemn, so still. He confused her.

'May I sit and eat with you? There are two chairs together here.' He gestured to them – and then immediately apologized:

'I am sorry – you must have many people with whom to sit.'

'No – I should love to sit with you.' She looked in Frederick's direction and saw that he was watching her. She smiled gaily, but his in return was less wholehearted. 'It isn't my fault he feels a certain way about me,' she thought. 'I'll not be made to feel guilty.' She turned back to Lorenzo.

'You're very beautiful,' he said, in such a manner that she didn't have her usual urge to dismiss the compliment. And as if he had never uttered it, he bent his head and began delicately to eat.

'My mother is English,' he explained in his soft voice over the meal, dabbing at his lips carefully with the napkin. 'And my father is half Italian, half French. I was born and lived in Paris until I was seven, and then they separated so I came with my mother to live in England. My interest in the violin began then. She took me to my first concert and I begged to learn to play. My uncle, her brother, is a sculptor – that is how I am here this evening, I have come with him – you see he sits with his wife over there –' he pointed over the heads to a fair man and woman. 'Well my uncle had a violinist friend who offered to teach me. So it started. And then when I was seventeen I returned to Paris to study the violin privately before going to the Conservatoire. I came to England for several reasons –' he seemed to blush. 'The main one being that there are too many violinists in France, and I believed I had a greater chance of succeeding in England; of being special, if you like. It is important to be special if one is involved in the arts. You are special in that you have selected a field of art that is new.'

'I did not select it for that reason. I selected it because it appealed to me.'

'It is the same, *n'est-ce pas?*'

'No, not at all.'

'Shall we quarrel? Perhaps no one would win.' He gave his half-smile which flickered on and off. 'Perhaps we're alike. When is your birthday, Miss Ruddock?'

'May the first.'

'That is mine also! I was born in 1854.'

'But I was too!'

'It does not surprise me. I sensed a rapport between us immediately. Possibly you did also.'

She didn't reply and thought back to the two occasions she had seen him – the one at the concert, the other at the Impressionist Exhibition, with his friend. She recalled him – a fair boy with the same build as Lorenzo.

'You were deep in conversation with your friend the second time I saw you,' she said. And this time there was no mistaking the pink in his cheeks.

'That was Auguste,' he said, lowering his lashes. 'Auguste was – is – my closest friend. He is a clarinettist.'

'And he didn't want to come to England?'

'No,' he answered with obvious reluctance to discuss the matter further.

They sat in silence for a while, then people started to leave and Rosaleen got up from her seat thinking perhaps she should be saying goodbye. She was perplexed by her companion – by his quietness, his lack of interest in the exhibition or in her paintings. She had asked him about himself and he had asked her nothing about herself in return. It was as if he were disinterested. Yet that did not seem to be the case.

'May I see you again?'

'Yes.'

'I have no money to take you anywhere smart.'

She smiled at him, feeling older than him. 'One doesn't need money to listen to music in the park or walk by the river, or simply to talk with one another.'

He took her hand and kissed it. As always she was conscious of its ugliness, but he held it against his lips as though it were the smoothest, milkiest-white hand in the world. Frederick, watching from the other side of the rapidly emptying room, felt a tightening in his forehead. He saw Rosaleen take one of her calling cards from her little bag and give it to her companion.

'Ah Rosaleen . . . Another diversion.' Sorrowfully he continued to torture himself. He would go to Tuscany for a few months, he thought. A visit was overdue, and a trip there was always balm for a troubled mind.

On May 1st Rosaleen and Lorenzo celebrated their birthdays. Like most other days they spent it together. 'You are a full-time career,' she teased him once.

'That is how it should be surely,' he retorted with a perfectly straight face.

She had never visited him; he always came to her. And he joked, as far as he ever joked, that he belonged to the 'garret set'.

She envisaged some rat-infested attic and asked him if it were like that.

'Oh no. I could not live like that.'

So how did he live? But she didn't press the point.

Gradually he moved possessions and clothes into her apartment. 'May I stay with you for the night?' he had asked at first in his hopeful-boy's voice which sounded as though it expected nothing – but he had brought things with him for the following day, and those things remained and others joined them. He kept them tidily within his allotted space. Rosaleen had never known such a tidy man.

She felt duty-bound to ask the Bedfords if they objected to the change in her circumstances. 'Do you mind,' she asked Mrs Bedford, 'that I have a man who is sometimes here with me? I shall pay you of course for the extra meals.'

The other chuckled heartily. 'I don't think I've a right to mind dearie, when Mr Bedford and I never married.' And she chuckled again at Rosaleen's surprise.

Sometimes she felt that she knew Lorenzo no better than when she'd first met him, and thought he probably didn't know her at all. Occasionally she tried deliberately to pick a quarrel, but instead of becoming riled he looked so devastated that she would be immediately contrite.

'Oh I am truly sorry. It is only that I try to provoke a reaction from you. I don't *know* you, Lorenzo. I want to know you.'

'You do know me,' he told her, apparently bewildered. 'What more do you want from me?'

315

He was so self-involved that she would have thought him totally narcissistic had he not occasionally revealed glimpses of a deeper self. And the more he withheld from her, the more infatuated she became with his enigmatic ways, his docility, his beauty.

She adored his body. In bed – there they knew each other as well as two people could. In bed there was no reticence. He rolled her over on her stomach and pinioned her as he entered her, straddled triumphantly over her; he made her sit up and sat rocking with her, inside her; he made her kneel and took her from behind – and she arched her back and her buttocks against his strength, and fought back whimpers of excruciating pleasure that no one must hear.

Afterwards she would stroke him – sleek and olive-skinned and flat-bellied with the light sprinkling of body hair damp with perspiration. She would kiss the sticky, denser hair between his legs and the small defeated curl half hidden amongst it. Soon she would feel it pulsing and swelling again, and then he would push her on to her back and hold her still as he kissed and licked her with a flickering tongue all over, before entering her again. When he was inside her his eyes never left her face, but bored into her as his body did; and afterwards he often wept.

'We shall shut ourselves off from the world and nobody will ever intrude,' he said to her, as she painted him seated with his violin in his lap. 'I want no one else. Nothing else. I am bored when we have to see your friends.'

'But that is not *real*, Lorenzo.'

'I think it is very real. When two people are happy they should need no one else.'

'Don't you enjoy going out? Seeing different things? Taking part in discussions?' She put down her brushes and palette.

He gave a very French shrug which did not enlighten her one way or the other and, exasperated, she picked up her tools again. 'Well *I* like to see people and go to places,' she told him. 'I like to walk in the fresh air and feel as though I am *alive*.' She stroked on some dark blue over wet grey for his trousers.

'I like night best,' he said. 'Darkness. And in it I can make love to you and be part of your darkness. And then *I* am alive.'

'Sex is not *everything*.' She was ready to quarrel. 'And what about your violin practice? I haven't heard you practise for ages.'

'You want to get rid of me.' His gentle face was elongated with hurt, and Rosaleen felt in her the same protective instincts she had used to have for Robbie.

'No, darling, that isn't so. But I must work. And when I have finished this portrait of you I have several commissions which are very important. You must accept that I am busy. And as for your violin practice – surely you must keep at it? The little I know about musicians is that they must practise all the time.'

'I shall practise,' he said obediently, throwing his head back a little, exposing his strong neck. 'I have been too involved with you to think of it. But you wish me to, so I shall . . .'

He moved in with her completely, and Rosaleen found herself busier than ever; besides her commissions she was working on other paintings. But Lorenzo was not having success at finding regular work and he always seemed to be about. His constant presence inevitably added strain to everything she did. He had no money of his own except from the odd performance he gave and she often wondered how he had lived before.

'In Paris my father helped me,' he told her.

'What does he do?'

'Oh this and that . . . He is actually a *pâtissière* – a baker.' He said it slightly defiantly, blushing frantically at this little offering about himself. And Rosaleen realized then that this could be the reason he asked so little about her – because he was ashamed to reveal himself.

'But Rosaleen, I shall earn money soon,' he continued. 'It isn't right you should have to pay for me. I know that I am a good violinist. Soon I shall be recognized. It takes time to become established.'

She was struck by the truth of this and believed him when he said that he was a good violinist. As long as she could hear him practising regularly she felt that at least he was making an effort.

In July Frederick returned from Tuscany and immediately came to see her – tanned and fit-looking. She thought he seemed very content.

'Your holiday has agreed with you, Frederick,' she commented, pouring tea for him. It seemed ages since she had seen him, and she longed to talk with him intimately; but Lorenzo was there and their usual easy conversation was precluded them.

She saw him out afterwards, stood alone with him by the front door in the mildness of the afternoon, smiling up into his familiar face.

'I'm thinking of buying a small vineyard in the hills outside Chianti,' he said, tweeking her chin affectionately. 'It could be amusing.'

'Oh Frederick – how will you have time! Medicine, research, lectures, travel, exploring, "non-politics" – and now a vineyard! And poor Edgar. You spend so much time abroad now. Who talks to poor Edgar?'

He held her against him for a second, and Rosaleen smelt his body.

'If I buy the vineyard then perhaps I shall take him down there. He can tread grapes.'

For a moment she believed him, then she stood back and lightly tapped his nose, laughing. 'Oh Frederick. I bel*ieved* you. I did. I bel*ieved* you.'

The sound of her own laughter caught her by surprise, and she thought, dismayed: 'I don't laugh much nowadays . . .'

'Rosaleen, are you happy with Lorenzo?'

'I think so,' she answered cautiously.

'Good. Because, dear girl, I have seen you hurt quite enough.'

'Oh Lorenzo will never hurt me,' Rosaleen said positively. 'He is the most gentle boy in the world.'

'Well that is fine then. And do you love him?'

'You are a determined protector of my well-being,' she joked, evading the question.

'That I am,' he replied.

Rosaleen looked up and saw Lorenzo at the window; his face framed with the loose brown curls seemed very sensitive, and his tiny smile flashed and was gone. She turned again to Frederick. 'I think I love him.'

'It is your downfall, dear girl, that you love too easily.'

'Perhaps it is,' she agreed, 'but you cannot worry on my behalf for ever.'

'No,' Frederick said soberly and in a way that made her glance sharply at him, 'I cannot.'

That summer Lorenzo, as a result of placing an advertisement in the *Evening Standard*, had several teaching jobs.

'It was such a sensible thing to think of – such a good idea,' Rosaleen said.

'I cannot have you paying all the bills. No self-respecting man could permit that.'

'But you didn't come to England to teach.'

'No, but I'm performing in several recitals and concerts during the next few months – and perhaps they'll lead to further bookings.' He looked at her serenely and taking up his violin said, 'I shall play for you.'

They were in the sitting-room of the apartment and the evening light threw oblique shadows across part of the room. It had rained for most of the day and now, looking out of the window, Rosaleen saw that the dramatic sky was composed of irregular lines and layers of varying reds and charcoals. She turned back, rather wearily, to her lover – it hadn't occurred to him she might not want to hear him – and prepared herself to listen.

'I shall play a sonata by Wieniawski,' he stated tersely and, adjusting his standard position so that his feet were slightly apart, he began to play.

He had said he was playing for her, but watching him she realized it was not true. It was for himself – except his vanity needed an audience. He looked not at her but past her, and perhaps he even confronted his own image as he stared beyond her with that impenetrable expression. Perhaps the self-image acknowledged the musician with approval and an adoration she could never give him. And the lovely notes he dragged from his instrument – did they lack some subtle element?

Closing her eyes against the furious sky outside, against the shadowed untidy room (he never complained about her untidiness), against the sight of Lorenzo sawing away, his face tranquil, Rosaleen willed the music to envelop her . . .

There were occasional times when she thought she knew him, and those times were always at night – when it wrapped about them and Lorenzo talked. Lying in the bed's comfortable hollows with the rumpled disarray of the bedclothes pulled over them, she loved to let him talk – about a book he had read, a piece of music he longed to play, a childhood recollection, his strong sense of Catholicism. The topic was irrelevant; what mattered was that those moments were revelations. But they didn't last. His voice would slur and fade, and with one of his heavy sighs he would fall asleep and be gone from her.

That summer she sold two paintings to two different galleries: the Grosvenor Gallery, and the German Gallery in New Bond Street, where Renoir had exhibited seven years previously. Her paintings were still frequently the subject of controversy and discussion and the last one she had done, commissioned by Lord Taggart-Laughton – a big canvas featuring a mother, child and dog on a fine day by the Serpentine – was reviewed in the *London Review* by Thomas S. James who had once been so abusive about her. The article read:

> The other day I was invited by Lord Taggart-Laughton to view his latest painting commissioned from the artist Miss Rosaleen Ruddock.

'. . . Oh what a name,' she thought for the hundredth time; 'one really *cannot* take it seriously!'

> As the reader may recall, this young woman enjoys the patronage of the above gentleman and I have to admit that initially I was shocked by his interest, unable to believe that one of our most respected authorities on art should be showing signs of the same madness which has of late gripped Paris.

However, I confess that during the last months I have been amending those early, possibly rather dogmatic opinions, and this has in part to do with my recent visit to Paris where at the Salon I saw Renoir's portrait of Madame Charpentier and her children. I could not fail to be delighted and could even see that the price it fetched – one thousand and thirty-five pounds – was justified; a sum which has no doubt rescued the likeable Monsieur Renoir from the straits of poverty and will keep him in paints for a while at least.

It was thus in good spirits and an amenable frame of mind that I returned to English shores and was invited to Sutton House to see the said Miss Ruddock's portrait entitled *A Fine Day*.

This portrait, of Lord Taggart's niece, Mrs Menzies, her child, and a dog of doubtful parentage, is done on a large scale and must certainly be the most ambitious of the artist's works to date.

The first thing I noticed was that the characters were appealingly placed to the right of centre so that to the left one is granted a view of that lovely stretch of river and trees, with a rowing-boat disappearing from sight, its occupants with their backs to us. Mrs Menzies herself, wearing a peach-toned summer frock and matching hat, is shown sitting on the bank, a book on her lap, while beside her, her young son, his clothes awry and cheeks grubby, lies on his stomach playing with his spinning top. The mongrel – I trust it will not be insulted to hear itself so described – is captured as it is poised to pounce on the toy. The entire scene is placed low enough down the canvas to allow Miss Ruddock free rein with the sky – something she obviously enjoys.

I could not fault her instinctive sympathy for composition, or her draughtsmanship skills – with the exception of the dog's head which might be a trace large; although one never knows with mongrels! Nor could I fault her eye for detail; indeed this is one of Miss Ruddock's strengths. She appears to use several techniques – painting in sweeping motions when it comes to Mrs Menzies' dress, but in shorter strokes with the background, and silky, fine strokes for the faces. She uses her paints thickly, working wet in wet, and then with further layers over the dry, so that the texture of the canvas is masked and the luminosity of effect achieved by her lavish usage of white and yellow.

Looking at this picture with my reformed outlook, I realized that here was a beautifully planned and constructed work which may not be art as we are accustomed to it, but which is certainly worthy of admiration in its own right.

In early October Rosaleen went to Paris for a couple of weeks to see her friends and report on her progress.

'Come with me, won't you?' she asked Lorenzo beforehand, but knowing his answer.

'I can't. I have three engagements during that time. You know I have,' he added, faintly accusatory. 'Why can't you go later?'

'Because I have to prepare for an exhibition at the Guildhall. *You* know *that*.'

'So you will just have to go on your own then,' he said with martyred calm.

It didn't help matters that at the last minute Frederick decided to go with her.

'He cannot go if I cannot,' Lorenzo said, aggrieved. 'That isn't right.'

'Why?' Rosaleen asked, baffled. 'Frederick is my greatest friend. My brother.'

'*I* should be your greatest friend. *I* – your lover,' he reproached her.

It was true, and Rosaleen felt sad, but then she thought: 'It is him – he doesn't give of himself.' But tears were in his eyes and she couldn't say it.

'Darling, just two weeks then I'll be back. And you are my greatest friend too.'

'I don't believe you.' He averted his face. 'And you are missing my three performances . . .' Then, with a venom in his expression she'd not seen before, Lorenzo turned to face her, and there was spite in his voice. 'I shall invite Auguste to come over.'

'Auguste?' She was puzzled.

'Yes – Auguste,' he shouted, flushed and excited. '*My* closest friend.'

And it was with this antipathy between them that Rosaleen departed to Paris for two weeks. She and Frederick stayed again at L'Hôtel Palais Royal, and their first evening together was their first alone for many months. It was a cold damp night and the strong wind had made the Channel crossing rough, but now, after a luxurious bath in the newly-installed bathroom, changed into fresh clothes, and perfumed, Rosaleen felt livelier than she had for a long time.

A waiter served their food – roast stuffed quails with an assortment of vegetables – and the sommelier filled their glasses with red Burgundy. Rosaleen leaned back and made a small sound of pleasure.

'Oh it is so good to be here again – and with you.'

'Likewise, dearest girl.'

'And this time I am paying completely for myself!' She gave a little laugh of satisfaction.

'I trust you will not become *too* materialistic,' Frederick said anxiously. 'I like you as you are.'

'You mean, dependent.'

'Now that is unfair.'

'Well you know I'll never be materialistic, Frederick. Money for me is only a means to my independence. I need only sufficient to live on.'

'And to stay at L'Hôtel Palais Royal.'

'It is lovely here,' she demurred. 'And tomorrow we are meeting with Pierre Auguste Renoir, Claude Monet – and Manet if he is well enough. Pierre Auguste wrote to me that he has mysterious bouts of illness which affect his limbs. It must be ghastly for him . . . And after tomorrow we could go to an exhibition perhaps? Or take a drive to Fontainebleau if it is fine? . . .'

He let her chatter on; he had never heard her so garrulous, and at first thought it was the wine, until he saw her glass was barely touched. He realized then it was simply her relief at being able to relax and speak freely; lately she seemed to have become withdrawn and he suspected that at the root of her problem was this latest lover of hers. He didn't like Lorenzo, although he could not say why, for the young man was polite, handsome and paid his way; but the dislike gnawed at him and troubled him. She was still talking, and Frederick took her hand across the table. Anyone watching would have assumed from their naturalness together that they were married.

The fortnight passed – a period of renewed friendships, and a whirl of social events and outings. Frederick prepared to go on to Florence and Rosaleen to England. Early that morning they stood together at the Gare du Nord, about to go in their separate directions.

'You could change your mind and come with me,' he said hopefully.

But she shook her head and smiled affectionately, noticing lines around his eyes and across his forehead she hadn't seen before.

'I have to get back for this exhibition.'

'I shan't see you for a while. After Florence I'll go to Chianti.'

'To survey the vineyard?'

'It is a temptation,' he admitted. Every time he parted from her for any length of time he felt the same – this gaping sense of sorrow.

And then the train arrived and Rosaleen was climbing up the steps in her agile way, her body a flash of red hair and bright blue coat. From the steps she kissed him. Their lips brushed, and the hair of his beard tickled her. Momentarily she looked startled and she thought: 'I wish he weren't going for so long.' She hugged him rather longer than usual, before disappearing into her compartment. Frederick watched her from the platform – untying the ribbon of her frivolous little hat and setting it on the overhead rack, unbuttoning her coat. The rain had made her hair wilder than ever so that it curled defiantly about her small face.

'Goodbye dearest girl,' he called through the window as the train gave a jerk.

'Take care,' she mouthed. 'Oh *do* take care.' And she sank back into her seat repressing a strange urge to cry.

Night had fallen by the time Rosaleen arrived in Kensington. Wearily she climbed the staircase to the apartment.

'Rosaleen!' Lorenzo leapt to his feet when she entered, a startled expression on his face. 'I hadn't expected you so early.'

In the room was another boy whom she recognized – slight and fair – half lying on the sofa. He smiled easily at her and did not get up.

'It's not early,' Rosaleen said, putting down her case.

Lorenzo came up to her and kissed her, composed once more. 'Rosaleen, this is Auguste.'

'I saw you in Paris,' she said, but could not be bothered to explain. Instinctively she mistrusted him.

He continued to smile and said in heavily accented English, 'I have heard much about you.'

'Are you staying long in London?' she asked, trying to be polite, but inwardly infuriated by the sight of him lolling on her sofa.

'Perhaps. But I do not like to make decisions. Decisions are tiring – are they not, Lorenzo?'

Lorenzo looked uncertain, and he put his arm around Rosaleen. 'I am so glad to see you. Was it a good trip?'

'Yes it was lovely. Lovely,' she repeated. It was absurd – as though she were an uninvited guest here in her own sitting-room. She moved away from him.

'Oh – I have just remembered that you have a letter. It's on the chest in the bedroom. I shall fetch it for you.'

'Do you wish to sit here?' Auguste asked finally, not getting up, but making a space for her.

She said stiffly, 'I shall use a chair.' And she sat down and opened the letter which was from Robbie.

She read:

Dear Rosaleen,

I hope that you are well and that everything is fine with you. How is the painting? Rosaleen – I'm writing to tell you that Vanessa and I have just become engaged and plan to marry in a year's time. Mr Ruskin has been very kind and has offered her a job, and then when we are married we shall live together at Brantwood. I am so happy! I never thought I could be so happy. Why don't you come back and see us? Father would be fine, I am certain, and think how pleased Nana Annie would be. But I know you're busy, so perhaps you can't . . .

Father seemed really glad about the engagement and quite perked up when I told him, and Nana Annie touched Vanessa's face all over with her grizzled hands and said she was a homely lass. Am I not fortunate? I think I could rush up to the top of Old Man and shout of my love, and hear her name echoing through the valley.

My other news is also good – I am writing a book of poems which the publishers have already agreed to buy, and I am busier than ever with Mr Ruskin's manuscripts; I feel very honoured that he trusts me sufficiently to assign such important work to me.

Well, there is nothing else to say. Nothing much happens here, as you know. That is its beauty.

Your loving – Robbie.

Rosaleen glanced up from the letter. The two men watched her, and looking at Auguste she was reminded of a waiting wolf.

'My brother has become engaged,' she said, trying to smile. She should have been happy, but instead felt a great loneliness and a yearning for the past. Which aspect of the past she could not have said.

'That is wonderful surely. We must have a celebration.' Auguste clapped his hands and stood up. 'Let us go to a restaurant.'

'No,' she said firmly. 'I am tired.'

'But it is only a little after nine o'clock,' Lorenzo said.

'Yes, but it has been a long day.'

There was a pause. 'You two can go to a restaurant. I shan't mind. I shall go to sleep.'

'But *chérie* – the celebration.' Auguste stretched out his arms towards her to pull her from the chair.

Rosaleen resisted. 'No – another time. But you go. Really.' More than anything she wanted to be on her own.

Lorenzo asked anxiously, 'Are you certain, Rosaleen?'

'Yes. Now – off.' She feigned a bright expression and he seemed reassured, stooping to kiss her fully on the lips. And then the pair of them were gone.

Much later she heard them return together, and then much later still – she thought it was probably well into the early hours of the morning – she awoke again as Lorenzo climbed into bed beside her. Drowsily she responded to his caresses, then clung to him, fully awake and whimpering softly when he was inside her, prodding her with tantalizing little thrusts, his body smooth and cool against the warmth of hers.

'*Est-ce que tu m'aimes?*' he murmured before he fell asleep. Not, I love *you*, but Do *you* love *me*? She felt him stretch, re-establish his body as his own, and then he turned on to his belly and lay with his head protected by the crook of his elbow, his breath, which smelt slightly of garlic and more strongly of coffee, reaching her in little gusts.

That December it snowed heavily and an outbreak of influenza spread through England. London, normally so cheerful at this time of year, was dismal, with its inhabitants remaining behind closed doors, muffled in woollens.

Rosaleen began to vomit each morning.

'I am going down with the 'flu,' she told Lorenzo, yellow-faced and panda-eyed. 'Don't kiss me – you'll catch it.'

But it was a strange type of 'flu; other people's symptoms were those of a severe cold accompanied by a fever. Rosaleen had no cold and no fever.

Christmas came, and in the morning, dressed in their best clothes, they went to church – Rosaleen and the Bedfords to theirs, and Lorenzo and Auguste to theirs. Afterwards Mr Bedford's deaf old sister and her unmarried daughter joined them for a traditional lunch and they all crowded round the table, which was decorated with holly and mistletoe and candles. Rosaleen was unable to join in the festive spirit, and hugging her stomach picked miserably at the slices of goose on her plate.

'Eat, *chérie*,' commanded Auguste with his white-toothed smile and hard eyes.

She disliked him increasingly as she came to know him. He was parasitic, she thought, making no attempt to find work and taking it for granted he was welcome to spend as much time at their apartment as he wished. Lorenzo frequently had to lend him money, and in return Rosaleen had to lend money to him.

Mrs Bedford said, 'Don't you like the food, dearie?'

And Lorenzo looked worried. 'You really must see a doctor, Rosaleen.' He had bought her a huge and extravagant box of chocolates and she was unable to contemplate them.

But Rosaleen didn't need to see a doctor. She knew now what was wrong with her. She was pregnant.

She told Lorenzo in the new year, 1880 – the beginning of a fresh decade. She chose bed as the place to tell him, because bed was where they were happiest together; because this bed was where she had conceived; because the night which he loved so much made it easier for her. She told him after they had made love and still lay moulded together.

'We are having a baby,' she said simply, in a low voice. And in the pause which followed she tried to imagine his expression, tried to feel what he was feeling; understand his enigma.

His arm crept closer about her. He buried his head with its silky hair in the cleft of her breasts – and then moved upwards, kissing her passionately.

'I shall be a father . . . We must marry as soon as possible . . .'

His voice quavered with suppressed emotion, and if Rosaleen had felt any doubts they were dispelled in that moment, when he wept with happiness over their future child.

❦ Seventeen ❧

MARRIAGE

There is no wealth but life.
JOHN RUSKIN

Frederick had only been back in England for a day when Rosaleen visited to break the news. She heard the sounds of the flute coming from the parlour, and whispered to Mrs MacDonald, 'I'll see myself in.'

She opened the door quietly and saw him, his back to her so that he faced the fire. She felt a rush of happiness at seeing him, quickly followed by apprehension.

'Hello Frederick.'

'My goodness – Rosaleen. Who surprised me then? But what a lovely surprise.' He bounded up to greet her – hugged her, released her, and hugged her again. 'How good it is to see you. I am coming round to visit *you* later.'

'Well I have saved you the bother,' she smiled.

'It's no bother, dear girl, although I admit it's a bonus seeing you on your own. Sit down . . .' He rang for Mrs MacDonald to bring tea.

'Have you bought the vineyard?' Rosaleen sat beside him, and removing her boots followed his example and stretched her feet towards the flames. Frederick touched her toes with his own.

'I have made an offer, but it rather depends on whether or not the manager I want to employ is able to take up the position. He has been seriously ill, poor man. The owners are in no hurry to sell either, so it could be months before a final decision is made.'

'Did you have a fine time in Tuscany?'

'Yes – the people in the area are most hospitable; I was well-entertained. And you, what about you?'

'Well –'

Mrs MacDonald knocked and brought in the tea and Rosaleen fell silent. Frederick, always astute, glanced quickly at her. Neither spoke until the housekeeper had poured the tea, captured the cockatoo who had swept down from her shoulder in the direction of the cakes, and left them once more.

'What's happened, Rosaleen? You have something on your mind.'

There was no point in deliberating. 'I'm expecting a child. It is due at the end of July.' She met his gaze defiantly; his expression registered shock then mortification, and her feeling of defiance left her.

'Please don't be angry,' she said softly. 'I didn't plan it.'

'No, I didn't think you did. So what are you going to do?'

She was dismayed by the hardness in his voice. 'We're – getting married next week . . . Will you be witness?'

'No!' He shouted the word and stumbled up from the chair. He lowered his tone. 'No I will not be witness. I will have no part in this appalling mistake you are about to make. Oh God, Rosaleen, what are you thinking of *doing*?'

'*Please* Frederick . . .'

'No – I cannot be appeased this time. I cannot be your nursemaid. I cannot and will not watch you commit yourself to repeated catastrophes and afterwards expect me to be there – nice Frederick, kind Frederick, *idiot* Frederick – to pick up your shattered pieces. I think, Rosaleen, it would be better if you left. Really. I am sorry. I do not wish to say anything more I might regret. Oh *id*iot Frederick, yes really I am an *idiot* . . .'

The wedding on February 4th took place at Lorenzo's Catholic church in Notting Hill Gate; he had insisted on this. It was a flat little affair with Auguste as witness and Mr and Mrs Bedford as the only other guests. From somewhere at the back came the sounds of a stranger weeping. Rosaleen, wearing one of her most ordinary dresses she had altered to accommodate the slight thickening of her waist, stood beside her about-to-be husband and exchanged vows.

'Do you, Rosaleen Emily Ruddock, take Lorenzo Christian Mellini to be your lawful wedded husband as long as you both shall live?'

A wave of nausea threatened to overtake her and she fought against the urge to retch. 'I do.'

'And do you, Lorenzo Christian Mellini . . .'

The short impersonal ceremony continued without her, and she heard the words almost in a trance. And then it was over and they were outside in the ugly street with the previous day's snow turned to slush, and drizzle falling from a lowering sky.

They went to a local tavern where Mr Bedford became drunk and nostalgically reminisced about earlier loves – oblivious to his commonlaw-wife's darkening face. Lorenzo, his arm about Rosaleen, shot fleeting looks at Auguste who was unusually taciturn and sombre, whilst Rosaleen glanced from time to time at her plain silver wedding ring, and thought what an odd assortment they were gathered at this table.

Later, at the apartment, Lorenzo asked her, 'Do you feel any different?'

'Not really, do you?'

'Yes.' He stroked her rounding belly. 'I feel very proud. I feel a man instead of a boy.'

'You must feel that because of yourself, not me,' she told him gently.

'I want to be a good father. I wish you did not feel so very ill all the time. Do you feel ill now?'

'No. Right now I feel only hunger. I should love – you know what I should love?'

'No, I cannot guess.' He nestled against her.

'I should love a toasted muffin!'

'Well you will have to wait until tomorrow and I shall buy a dozen muffins from the muffin man! But now *I* should love to *make* love to my wife.'

By March Rosaleen felt better, and busied herself making baby-clothes. She knew an extraordinary inner serenity during this period, yet she was unable to contemplate the prospect of the birth without fear, recalling the scene of horror at her mother's deathbed. She dreamed of it sometimes, a chillingly real dream which, when she awoke, she could not dismiss as an impossibility.

'I don't want to die.' Once she had spoken this thought to Lorenzo.

'You won't die. You are young and healthy. Why should you die? You couldn't, could you?' He had sounded alarmed and she had immediately reassured him.

'No, of course I couldn't. I have no intention of it!'

'I could not bear it if you did.'

But they quarrelled increasingly. Auguste's attitude had changed since their marriage; he had become aloof, and the rift affected Lorenzo.

'Auguste is *bête*,' he said petulantly. 'He has no right to treat me in such a way . . . To – discard me.'

Rosaleen, who was gratified by the other young man's absences, said, 'Perhaps he respects that we need a little privacy together, that's all.'

It was the wrong thing to say, and Lorenzo turned on her. 'You don't like him,' he flared. 'You are jealous of him.'

Rosaleen, who had never known jealousy, was bewildered: 'What do you mean? Why should I be jealous of him? What is there to be jealous about?'

'Nothing. You know there is nothing.'

'Then why say it?'

'Don't treat me like a child,' he said sulkily. 'You always treat me like a child.'

'That isn't true.'

'And you didn't come to my last two recitals.'

'I was *ill*, Lorenzo.' She was exasperated, ready to leave the room.

'You are not interested. Music doesn't interest you. Only art does.'

'I never pretended to know about music, but of course it interests me. Especially because you are interested in it.'

'Oh Rosaleen . . .' He laid his head against her and she rumpled his hair. 'Silly boy.' Then she thought: 'Oh dear, now he will protest that he is neither silly nor a boy.' But he only leaned more heavily against her, yielding himself to her stroking of his hair and massaging of his neck.

She was tired and longed to be soothed herself, and for someone to cosset her. She thought of Frederick and was filled with sorrow at the way their friendship had been curtailed. 'I cannot blame him –' absently she manipulated the little bone at the base of Lorenzo's neck, '– but I wish I could speak with him.'

As her body became more full-blown Rosaleen was fascinated by the changes in herself, and would stare at her reflection in the mirror, observing each minute alteration and marvelling at it. But Lorenzo could no longer bring himself to look at her naked.

'Lorenzo – I am swollen because of our *baby*. Don't you think that beautiful?' Nude, she stood in their bedroom in the evening light, the profile of her belly firmly lunar, her shoulders, hips and limbs unchanged. She thought herself graceful and gloried in this new beauty. She ran her hands sensuously up and down her body, lingering over the taut crescent, stroking her enlarged breasts.

'Please touch me.'

'I *couldn't*.' He gave an involuntary shudder.

'That distresses me.'

'I don't mean to. Put your smock on. Then I can hold you.'

'What – and forget what goes on beneath? Oh really, Lorenzo, that is just too absurd. You make me feel unclean. We haven't made love for over two months because of your revulsion. How do you think I feel?'

'I'm sorry. I cannot help it . . . I have an aversion to fat.'

'I am *not* fat. This is a baby. Our baby. *Feel* it – it just moved.'

She reached out for his hands and he snatched them back. 'No!'

The look on his face so stunned her that she became immediately self-conscious about her nakedness. She shed her beauty – it slid from her like a silk chemise. She was not graceful; she was misshapen, gross and ungainly. Her sole thought now was to cover herself as quickly as possible. Fumbling, she pulled the smock over her head. But when he came towards her she pushed him away: he had debased her femininity. And suddenly she thought of those little acts of nature she had not considered previously – using the chamber pot at night; an inadvertent attack of flatulence brought on by pressure from the child towards her back; cleaning her teeth in front of him; bending down naked to pick up something, her breasts dangling . . . How disgusting she must seem to him.

Towards the end of June Rosaleen had a letter from the Royal Academy of Art. She read it as Lorenzo was shaving in front of the mirror, and he watched her in it – the widening of her eyes and animated face. He was tired and thought he might return to bed after breakfast. Rosaleen's obvious excitement threatened to weary him further.

'What is it?' he was compelled to ask.

'The Royal Academy has just accepted *two* – not one, but *two* – of my paintings.'

'That's wonderful,' he said dully.

'*Finally* they have conceded! Oh I am so happy. It means so much to be accepted by an establishment such as the Academy . . . Why are you looking sulky?'

'I am not sulky. I'm a little fatigued, that's all.'

Her elation withered. 'Why is that?'

'Well, you take up so much of the bed nowadays I cannot sleep.'

'I apologize, Lorenzo, that our baby takes up so much room.' And when he didn't reply she tried different tactics and said gaily, 'Tonight let's go out with friends for dinner. Would that be a good idea?'

'I don't feel inclined to see friends.'

'But Lorenzo, we can't sever ourselves from everyone. That is so anti-social.'

'You made me sever myself from Auguste.'

'That's unjust! I had nothing to do with it. It was of his own volition.'

'He knew you didn't like him.'

334

'I'm afraid I cannot credit your friend with such sensitivity,' she said coolly. 'Now I must hurry – I'm meeting Elizabeth Russell at midday.'

'Who is she?'

'You know – the art critic. A friend of Frederic George Stephens. I told you I was meeting her today for lunch and that afterwards we were going to Kew.'

'I thought perhaps we could go to an afternoon concert. We can't now.'

'Lorenzo, the thought has only just occurred to you. And you are mentioning it now to make me feel guilty.'

He said nothing, but narrowed his gold-brown eyes, and Rosaleen saw a flicker of expression come into them: a look of resolve.

'Lorenzo –' Her voice held a pleading note and she held out her hand in a gesture of peace. In return he gave a brittle smile, ignoring her outstretched fingers.

'What time will you be back?' he asked later when she was about to leave. And she felt a sense of relief at the breaking of their silence.

'About four-thirty. What will you do today?'

'I shall practise the violin – of course. And possibly go to the tailor. I need a new suit.'

She smiled at him – blew a merry kiss, and was gone; glad to be away from the place, to be outside in the summer air.

'How wonderful you look,' Elizabeth greeted her. 'A woman proud of her condition. I admire you, Rosaleen. You are so superbly your*self* always.'

Rosaleen laughed. 'The admiration is mutual, Elizabeth.'

They were upstairs at Simpson's in the Strand, a discreet place popular with women who didn't want to feel conspicuous when they went out to dine.

'There really should be a woman's club,' Elizabeth remarked as they were shown to their table. 'It is about time we were given more consideration . . . When is the baby due?'

'In a month.'

'Are you excited?'

'Yes . . . Yes I am.'

'You have reservations.'

'Not about the baby. But – forgive me saying it, Elizabeth, only I have nobody in whom to confide – Lorenzo is something of a child himself. He is a good husband, he is working hard now, and I cannot fault him there . . . Oh I have no wish to be disloyal . . .'

'You are not, my dear. You are merely consulting a friend.'

'Thank you, but I must say nothing more. There is nothing, anyway, that I can actually pin-point.'

'Rosaleen, I am unable to be more than an hour. I'm sorry. I know we were going to the Royal Botanical Gardens, but I have to work on an important article.'

'It doesn't matter. We can make it another time. I shall go home early and surprise Lorenzo. Perhaps it is better, as it happens.'

'And meanwhile let us hear each other's news . . .'

Rosaleen took an omnibus back. It was crowded and she climbed to the top and sat in the open. The day was hot, and dry London dust blew up her nostrils. She scanned the passing street scenes eagerly – she'd never lost her delight in the mundane, in observing the daily theatre of life perpetually changing; she saw the street sellers, the hoardings on buildings, the never-ending construction work, markets, children piled into a horse-tram . . . They passed St James's Park where she had views of deck-chairs and parasols, strolling couples and nannies with prams; around frantic Hyde Park Corner, into Knightsbridge, and then Kensington, where she got out. She walked along the High Street, stopping on an impulse at a small goldsmith's to buy a cravat pin as a present for Lorenzo. Purchasing this gift gave her pleasure, and her mood – already cheerful from having spent an hour with her friend – brightened further. She turned down a side road – where an organ grinder was surrounded by children wanting to pat the monkeys – and then turned right into the garden square. A church clock chimed two.

She came to the house and unlocked the front door, remembered the Bedfords were out visiting Mr Bedford's sister, and went upstairs to the apartment. Lorenzo wasn't in the sitting-room and she thought perhaps he was resting, and so opened the door to the bedroom quietly, her present for him in her hand. From the bed came the sounds of groaning, and the shape under the sheets writhed around.

At first she thought he was in the throes of a nightmare; she heard a moaning and the bedclothes moved like some undulating white monster. She stood there mesmerized, caught in a state of unreality, for a few seconds that seemed endless. Then the shape split into two. Arms emerged from under the covers, and Lorenzo's curly head. And then another. A man's. Auguste.

A low buzz started in Rosaleen's ears, and escalated into a high-pitched ringing. The room span. She was spinning with it – an absurd doll from a musical-box dancing, whirling round . . .

They stared at each other horrified. The men, instead of springing apart, huddled close, united against her. Their torsoes were alike in their muscular masculinity, glistening with perspiration; their nakedness taunted her, mocked her white face, her frozen half-open mouth, her pregnant belly, her womanhood.

'Rosaleen –'

His voice broke her trance and she screamed at him, 'Get out . . . Get out, both of you. Get OUT.'

She began hurling their clothes at them – strange that she hadn't noticed the two sets of men's clothes earlier – and getting up from the bed they dressed hurriedly, shamefaced now and diminished before her anger. A vigorous feeling of energy swept through her, a fury like she had never known. Anything within reach she grabbed from its place and threw at them, watching with mad delight as they ducked and averted blows and protected their faces with their hands. Her fingers lighted upon a pair of scissors and she came towards Lorenzo and Auguste with the points directed at them, laughing as they cringed like two small boys.

And then she turned them towards herself, continuing to laugh wildly. 'You think I'd use them on you? Stab you? Harm you? A little incision here or there or perhaps a couple of snips at those oh so male organs . . . You want a boy?' She addressed Lorenzo. 'My dearest, you *have* a boy.' And she started to hack at her hair. 'A pregnant boy,' she sobbed, hacking away savagely, lengths of hair falling to the ground. '. . . A pregnant boy- . . .' When they had gone and her rage was spent and her shock become numbness, she lay exhausted on the hated bed. There were so many things to consider: her future without Lorenzo, bringing up a child without its father, the prospect of divorce . . . And other things: the shattering experience of discovering her husband in an act of homosexuality (oh, she should have realized earlier – all the signs had been there), the chaotic state of the bedroom, her lovely hair lying in coils on the ground . . . It was all too much, and she gazed up at the ceiling at a small damp patch, imagining its irregular shape as a wide-branched tree or a lady with an oversized hat, or a cloud over a mountain. She lay for some while breathing deeply and focusing her attention on this meaningless little map to the exclusion of all else, so that without being aware of it she was reaching a state of meditation and began to float – out of herself, away from her troubles.

And then the pains started.

They were so slight at first that she barely noticed them, but then they became more persistent and she could no longer dismiss them. She was in labour. Rosaleen forced herself to be calm, tried not to think of her mother – 'She was a month early' – and waited for the Bedfords to return.

It was another couple of hours before they did, by which time her waters had broken and her pains were intense and regular. She heard their voices downstairs, their feet – the relief – and called them. She thought she called them, but there was no response and she knew she had called only in her head. There was blood on the sheet; she felt its stickiness first and then, lifting the

338

bedclothes, saw it between her legs. The sight of it made her panic and she summoned her strength and called again properly, and heard Mrs Bedford running upstairs. There was a knock at the sitting-room door and the landlady came in. 'Rosaleen?'

'In here. I've –' And she was gripped in a spasm of pain so severe that her back arched with it and she almost flung herself from the bed.

The old woman called to her husband, 'Derek – a bowl of water and towels – fast. She's in labour.'

The contraction passed and Mrs Bedford wiped Rosaleen's waxen face with a towel. 'I'm bleeding,' Rosaleen said from between cracked lips. 'Could you find Frederick? He's a doctor – the man you liked with the flute. If he's away get anyone . . .'

'I don't want to leave you. I shall get Derek to go in a hansom.'

'Thank you.'

She gave herself up to the pains, to the emptiness in between, and waited for Frederick. 'Please let him be there. Please . . .' Mrs Bedford held her hand and Rosaleen gripped her as a new tide overtook her; somebody was surely ripping her insides apart, slowly and with relish, in order to torture her longer. '*Mother* . . .' she screamed, unable to stifle it and continued to scream.

'Ssh dearest girl . . .' The hand holding hers was now Frederick's, and incredibly, with his arrival the paroxysm dissipated and she stretched out her arms weakly to him.

'Thank God you are here.' Her face puckered and she averted it from him to hide her tears.

He sat on the bed and tilted her chin gently so that she had to look at him. 'Ssh, my little love. Rosaleen . . . Of course I'm here.'

'My hair –' Her shoulders juddered and her nose streamed, and he took a handkerchief and made her blow into it.

'You are beautiful. Your hair will grow. You are *beautiful*,' he repeated. His hands felt expertly all over her. 'You are ready to push. When I say, you must start.'

'I've another pain coming on.'

'Push *with* it, Rosaleen. Go *on* . . .'

339

Almost three hours passed and she was weakening. Outside, night descended. Frederick paced the room. He had removed his jacket and waistcoat and rolled up his shirtsleeves. Dark patches were under his arms and down his back, and his face was as grey as Rosaleen's. He turned back to her and said forcefully, 'Rosaleen, if you do not push the baby will die. It has to be now.'

'I *can't*.'

'Poppycock, dear girl. That is most unlike you.' He tried to smile but his mouth struggled in a different direction. Another agonizing wave was overtaking her.

'Push, *please*.' He willed her on through screams which she thought were her mother's screams. '*Push*, for God's sake.' She saw Flora's glazed open eyes and then she saw Frederick's eyes as a dark dewy line – was he crying for her? 'Push – there's the head.' His hands were groping inside her to pull the baby from her, and then it was out, with a thin cry. Frederick snipped the umbilical cord and severed the little girl from the mother.

'I am alive.' She slipped from consciousness. Frederick cleaned the mucus from the child, and after wrapping her in a towel put her in bed beside Rosaleen. He himself sat on the edge, put his head in his hands and quietly broke down.

Rosaleen named the baby Kate Amelia after her friend. 'If she could have Kate's serenity then I would be glad,' she said to Frederick who visited her each day.

Kate Amelia had Lorenzo's narrow face, golden skin and almond-shaped eyes – at present navy-blue. 'But they will turn brown,' Frederick said. 'And her hair will be yours.' He stroked the copper cockscomb as the child sucked at Rosaleen's exposed breast, its fingers kneading its fullness.

'Mine as it was.' She smiled ruefully.

'It's not that short. In fact now you have cut it properly I like it; the curls frame your face.'

'Once a gypsy woman tried to cut my hair – to sell. It was when I lived in Battersea . . .' Her voice wavered and she bent her face to rub her cheek against the baby's downy head.

'Things will improve from now on,' she murmured, and

Frederick felt a tightening in his chest. She was so fine a person, and she trusted everybody she met, crediting others with her qualities, launching herself wholeheartedly and unwittingly from one disaster to another. And as life dealt its lessons he had to watch her suffer, watch her confront disillusion, and then with typical courage confront it and start again. He had seen her in despair, he had seen her degraded and he had seen her without dignity and he had loved her throughout, in all her guises. He wished she could be sheltered from pain. He wished it might be his role.

'I have my daughter now,' Rosaleen said, settling her on her other breast. Her voice became stronger and more positive. 'She will be everything to me. I need nobody else now I have a child.' And with that declaration a burst of maternal love flowed through her, unquestioning and straightforward, and Rosaleen cuddled her baby to her, marvelling at this miniature person for whom she alone was responsible. She didn't notice Frederick's expression; it was as though his face were a door which had closed.

When Kate Amelia was a month old Frederick left London for Tuscany. He said goodbye to Rosaleen on an overcast late July day, unusually subdued.

'I shall be away a long time,' he said seriously, cupping her chin and looking penetratingly into her eyes; he thought he might find something – an ember – that would give him hope. Her light lilac gaze held his with customary sweetness. He saw tenderness, affection, friendship: all sentiments he valued. But nothing else.

'I shall miss you,' she said lightly, touching his cheek.

'You have Kate Amelia.'

'Yes . . .' She looked down. 'I think she's had enough milk. She is falling asleep – aren't you, darling?' Unselfconsciously Rosaleen adjusted her clothing and got up, carrying the baby to its cradle. She laid her in it and rocked it, humming softly. With her back to Frederick she said, 'You saved both our lives. And don't try and deny it.'

He didn't reply.

'I shall paint a picture especially for you.' She turned to him with that quicksilver change of mood he knew so well. 'Would you like me to? It will be a special present.'

'I should love you to.'

'It will be finished by the time you return from treading grapes,' she joked, then added, 'You look downcast, dearest Frederick.'

'No – no – it is only that I must be going.'

'I shall visit Edgar in your absence. Poor horse.'

'Mr MacDonald is kind to him.'

'He cannot play the flute. Edgar's musical. Frederick – play me a tune before you go, please? Just one.'

She curled up on the chair and closed her eyes, allowing the sounds to seep into her being, and Frederick watched her all the while he played, knowing an ever-deepening sorrow.

Four weeks passed. Friends came and went, more freely than they had when Lorenzo was around. Rosaleen began working on her painting for Frederick – a portrait of herself with Kate Amelia in her arms. In the background was a cane table upon which was a vase of summer flowers. She went for walks; to exhibitions, to open-air concerts – and wherever she went she took her daughter. 'You will be a cultured little girl,' she whispered to the sleeping form in the perambulator, stopping to look at her yet again, the minute and peaceful perfection.

But Rosaleen could not sleep at night. In the cradle beside her Kate Amelia's breathing was light and regular, and she awoke at about midnight and then again at four in the morning to be fed. But in between those hours her mother dozed only fitfully, listening to the precious breathing, dreading it should stop. And while she lay awake she had all that time in which to reflect, and be listless, and lonely.

'Why should I be lonely?' she wondered, lying on her back with the light of the full moon on her face. 'I have my child. Some good at least came from that ill-fated liaison . . .' She had pushed Lorenzo from her mind. But it was Frederick she could not. He was there at the fore – his kindness, his eccentricity, his reliability, his foibles, his intellect . . . His hang-dog eyes, his full mouth, his voice . . . She began to think of Frederick the man.

'I wish he would write,' she thought after another month had passed. The baby slept through midnight now and Rosaleen no longer feared she was going to die in her crib; but she herself still slept badly. 'I miss him,' she realized later on that day. 'Funny Frederick . . .' She wondered if she had ever shown him gratitude for the many things he had done for her. '. . . He knew that I was grateful. I'm not a person to gush. It wasn't gratitude he wanted . . .'

She was bathing Kate Amelia in a tin vessel in her room. The child splashed her starfish hands in the water. Rosaleen said aloud, 'He saw you come into the world. He *brought* you into it, out of me – with my knees raised and my thighs apart enough for a tram to go through, and the mess – and not a moment's shame between us . . .'

A slow flush pervaded her. 'I love him. God, after all this time – I *love* him.'

That evening she wrote to him, sitting at the table by the window which overlooked the square.

September 30th

My dear Frederick,

It is after seven-thirty in the evening, and as I write to you I look through the window at the low sun and realize that summer is over. That is always sad. How are you? I have been very busy; Kate Amelia is, at three months, quite big now and her little crest of hair has become more respectable (as has mine!). She is very strong and supports her head well by herself and smiles at me a great deal. At least, I *think* she does. Is it possible she knows me? She keeps me occupied, as you can imagine, but is an extremely placid little thing, thank heaven, and I cart her everywhere: she goes into the perambulator along with my painting equipment! How she has enhanced my life. I see friends

343

often, which I missed during that 'certain period', and in particular I have become close to Elizabeth Russell whom I like greatly, although no one will ever replace Kate in my affections. She has been gone for almost exactly four years now and I have an impression of her face burned into me. My painting is going quite well, I think, although there is always someone eager to deprecate it. But Lord Taggart-Laughton is a continuing support. He has suggested I try to exhibit at the Salon in Paris next spring. Now that *would* be a privilege. Meanwhile – I earn a crust. On the subject of painting, I have almost completed the one I am doing for you. I hope you will like it; it is a small token of my gratitude to you, which I am not always good at expressing. I am not good at expressing my feelings at all; I never have been, and I suppose it has to do with my upbringing.

Are you having a fine time, and have you bought your vineyard? More to the point – when are you coming back? I have visited Mr and Mrs MacDonald once and showed them Kate Amelia; they were most complimentary, although I had to ward off the attentions of one of the cockatoos. I saw Edgar also. He told me to say he misses you. I miss you too, Frederick. This is so hard for me to write, after all these years and all that has happened – and yet in another way it is not hard, because there is a relief in telling you my sentiments, which for the past few weeks have been altering and developing, as I myself have been. This letter is my link with you and although it is a poor medium, nevertheless with you so far away it is the only one and will have to suffice. I love you, Frederick. There, I have said it – and will again: I love you in the truest and deepest sense, you funny, dear man; and I only hope I am not presumptuous in saying it or burdening you in any way. My feelings are so powerful that even as I write I am filled with a happiness that brings tears.

I trust that you are having an enjoyable time and can imagine you sitting on the terrace of your rented farmhouse, surrounded by olive trees and vines and pines, writing your journal, or perhaps reading one of your 'tomes' which is quite beyond my comprehension!

I long for your return, and to voice in person the things I have dared write in this letter. Take care, dear Frederick.

Your loving – Rosaleen.

She addressed the letter and went out to post it immediately. The sun had disappeared and the air was cool. Rosaleen pulled her Joseph shawl closer around her shoulders, and her own gesture made her smile at the recollection of a fateful evening a traveller had dropped by at the Coachman's and tried to explain the meaning of art. And who could explain it literally, she thought? It was all-embracing. But she was enriched because of it.

On a Tuesday morning, a fortnight later, she received a letter from Italy, and as she opened the envelope her fingers trembled. The letter bore the same date as the one she had sent him – September 30th. 'How funny we should have written on the same day . . . Oh I wish this were a reply to mine . . .' She began to read:

Dearest Rosaleen –

I hope this letter finds you in the very best of spirits and in excellent health – and that you are remembering to take those iron tablets I gave you! I trust also that Kate Amelia is fighting fit, and not causing her mother too many sleepless nights . . .

'How formal he sounds – but then he doesn't know my change of heart.'

. . . Tuscany is as glorious as ever, with its untamed, tangled countryside and mountains, and of course Florence not too distant. But Rosaleen, I write this letter for a particular reason . . .

She read faster:

> . . . I got married ten days ago, to a widow in her thirties. I
> have known her for the past couple of years. Her name is
> Giuliana and she is a good and loyal woman for whom I
> have admiration and great liking . . .

'*No* . . . It can't be *true* . . .' Rosaleen leapt up from her seat, the
letter in her hand. Tears poured from her eyes and her outburst
woke the baby who started to scream. Rosaleen went over to her
and picked her up, pressing her wet cheek against her daughter's.
She rocked her, rocking her own grief, and returned to her chair
where she absently undid her bodice and let the baby suckle. Her
tears continued as she read on, slowly now and with reluctance:

> . . . I hope this is not too much of a shock, but it seemed a
> reasonable idea. I am not growing younger and should like
> a family of my own. I suppose in the end it is every man's
> wish. I hope you will be happy for me – you know that we
> will always be special friends and that should you need help,
> support or a word of comfort I shall always be delighted to
> 'lend an ear'. Nothing has changed in that respect . . .

'But it *has*.' She began to sob again, leaning back in her anguish
so that her nipple slid from the baby's mouth and a wail
superimposed itself over Rosaleen's sobs. She repositioned
herself and the wailing immediately ceased.

> . . . We shall be living partly in Tuscany – I have just signed
> the contract for my vineyard – and partly in Chelsea, and
> needless to say I hope you will be our most regular visitor.
> Indeed, you must come to see us in Tuscany, too – the
> scenery would certainly inspire you to paint.
> Well, dear girl, I close now as it is gone midnight and
> Giuliana has long been asleep. This has not been an easy
> letter, but now I have written it I shall post it in the
> morning – and try to imagine your reaction. We shall return

to England at the end of next month, November, so I look forward to seeing you – and Kate Amelia of course – then.

Ever affectionately yours,

Frederick.

But he could not imagine her reaction. Not in a hundred years could he have imagined her reaction – that she cried in a way she had never cried, that she was broken-hearted as she had never been, devastated as she had never been, that at that moment, were it not for her daughter, she would have been prepared to kill herself because she knew that she would never love any man as she loved Frederick.

Mrs Bedford had heard her crying. She knocked timidly on the door and receiving no reply came in. She found Rosaleen in the nursing chair gazing ahead with streaming eyes and blotched skin, a letter dangling in her hand and the baby asleep against her pale bared breast.

'Rosaleen? Dearie?'

At the kindly voice Rosaleen looked up with despair in her face and dissolved into fresh sobs. Mrs Bedford took the sleeping child and laid her in her crib, before returning to Rosaleen and taking her in her bulky arms. 'What is it, dearie?'

'. . . I cannot bear it.' Her voice was scarcely audible.

'What can't you bear, Rosaleen?'

'Frederick – he has married.'

The other woman was bewildered, and then understood. 'Your feelings changed for him then?' she asked gently.

'I love him. I *love* him. It hurts . . . I cannot bear it.'

'Oh my poor dearie, there, there . . . What can I say? Oh my poor dearie.'

'It hurts. *I* hurt. I *hurt* . . .' She wept quietly against the other woman who could do nothing other than hold her and murmur soothing banalities – and try to remember what it was like to feel such pain over a man.

For a moment Rosaleen stopped crying, and instead began to laugh harshly. 'My letter – he probably received it this morning. He is probably reading it now.'

347

She heard her own laughter and it jarred her. The pathos, the irony, the tragedy of it all struck her, and a fit of weeping took hold of her again.

Only three days later she received another letter. This one was from Robbie, and it was short.

> Dear Rosaleen,
>   I've some sad news. Nana Annie died this morning – Wednesday – after falling down the stairs. She died instantly, that's the only good thing. Father is pretty bad considering he never took any notice of her and hardly spoke to her for the last five years. Do you think you might come back for the funeral? It will be next week. Father mentioned you after it happened. Of course I'd have written to you anyway, but nonetheless he said: 'Better write to Rosaleen. She'll be wanting t'know.' Well this isn't a letter for other sort of news and if I go now I shall be in time for the post.
>
>   Yours ever – Robbie.

She had opened the letter unsuspectingly and read it downstairs during breakfast with the Bedfords – the early-morning desultory conversation, the sounds of eating and drinking and the clinking of china and cutlery . . .

Mrs Bedford had seen the postmark. 'News from home?'

'My grandmother has died.'

'Oh I'm sorry. It's one thing after another.'

'Poor Nana,' Rosaleen murmured. She slumped back into her seat. 'Poor Nana,' she repeated, but it was seven and a half years since she had seen her, and her tears had been used up over Frederick. Fleetingly she saw the hag-like and solitary figure tucked out of sight on the window-seat, knitting and slurping cider, her eyes unfocusing, but her ears not missing a trick.

'I'll go back tomorrow.' And as she said it there was a subtle and slight shifting of her sorrow.

Mr Bedford said, 'You spend as long as you like, we'll not let your rooms in your absence, will we, dear?' He turned to his commonlaw-wife who shook her head in confirmation, and they both looked at Rosaleen with compassion.

And so at five to eight the next morning, with Kate Amelia in a Moses basket, she boarded the train at Paddington. A porter carried her case, her painting equipment and a package containing a couple of her smaller paintings. He helped her into an empty compartment and then left her regretfully – too smitten to remind her she had forgotten to tip him. She wore a tight-waisted light-blue woollen suit, and her Joseph shawl was draped around her head and pinned at her shoulder with a cameo. From it her face peeped out, wan and lovely.

She bent to adjust Kate Amelia's quilt and lingeringly touched her cheek before sitting back with a sigh, bracing herself for the long journey ahead. The train drew out of the station and quickly gathered speed. Through the window Rosaleen watched the dismal streets and buildings and factories flash by. She was remote from it all – from the train, the events which had led to her being on it, from the ugly suburbs. A great weariness lay solidly and heavily within her, and besides her weariness was a ridge of pain lodged across her chest; constant like a chronic disease. She was already growing used to it.

As London and its sprawling environs were left behind and the train charged on north-westerly, so, like disjointed jigsaw pieces in no particular sequence, thoughts flitted into her mind. The years became an accordion contracting and squeezing out its sounds, here discordant, there harmonious; events recurred; voices came and went; faces appeared and retreated – apparitions from the past.

She saw herself, bruised and hopeful and veiled, arriving at the Burne-Joneses'; then Tags, boyish and charming, later defeated and bowed; the basement cell in Battersea and her landlord standing in the doorway chewing a raw onion. Kate eclipsed him, a guardian angel stretching out her long-fingered hands – blocked suddenly by the cowering figure of Talwyn. And Oliver, huge in physique, his head thrown back in laughter – and then lolling forward, blue and distorted. And Renoir said resignedly: '*Les critiques* – they do not like me.' Now she herself was sitting in the audience of the Conservatoire, listening to a boy called Lorenzo Mellini play the violin. The Baroness von Hoffnung rose before her as the incarnation of wickedness: 'One day you will realize you are out of your depth here . . .'

And throughout, linking it all, was Frederick, reliable and caring. The ridge of pain moved and twisted before lodging itself again. Rosaleen nursed it conscientiously, accepting it as retribution for her own foolishness.

At one-fifteen they arrived at Lancaster where she had to change trains and take the Lancaster and Carlisle railway to Carnforth. Overhead the sky was dark and the air was noticeably cooler than it had been in London. Shivering a little, she enlisted the help of another porter, this time remembering to tip him.

This part of the journey took only a half-hour or so, and at Carnforth she changed trains again, to the Furness line which would take her on the final haul to Coniston. Her daughter whimpered in the Moses basket, and Rosaleen picked her up and took her in her arms. Once more she fell to thinking and reminiscing.

'How strange – Robbie, who so feared Father, is the one who is close to him now. And he'll be married soon . . . Goodness – my young mankin! And it'll be myself the stranger back home. A guest. And Nana Annie gone. I should have liked to have seen her . . .'

'. . . I understand a lass's moods, I do . . . Oh I was the same age as you – it don't seem so long ago . . .'

Beyond the window the countryside became familiar; stopping at Silverdale, Grange-over-Sands – and onwards towards Ulverston. And the start of the mountains, pale and dark and partially concealed by mist; invoking in Rosaleen ripples of excitement.

John Ruskin appeared before her as he had looked when she first met him: 'I have only just come to this haven. It is strange to imagine someone would wish to escape it. Remember, Rosaleen

– "There is no wealth but life."' And later, in a letter: 'Never forget your roots, Rosaleen. All else is transient . . . Please convey my best wishes to Frederick. He is a good man.'

Her eyes watered and she rubbed them with her free hand. 'Did he feel for me all those years as I am feeling now? But Frederick is unselfish and I am not. He asked that I should be happy for him – but *we* could have been happy.' She pressed her fingers to both eyes in turn, but the tears trickled through. 'I should be exported to the Sahara: miracle remedy for draught – Rosaleen Ruddock offers her unique services. Hah!'

They stopped at Ulverston and the familiarity of the station made her smile despite herself, and evoked a host of memories. Her earlier twinges of excitement grew and spread. A few people got off the train. More got on.

'Oh please – not in here . . .' She held her breath, but nobody entered her compartment and she sat back again, hugging her sleeping daughter closer.

Rosaleen stared through the window. The last lap. Coniston drew nearer by the minute. 'Nothing changes here. That is its beauty,' Robbie had written, and she realized the truth and wonder in that as she saw the countryside becoming more and more recognizable, and spotted old landmarks – and the years fell away.

Gradually a slow and gentle joy rose in her, expanding and replenishing her. It was tempered with the old pain, but it was there nonetheless.

'Nothing changes' – but the sky, and now it parted to reveal the mountain peaks.

'. . . Eight years ago I set out only to see what might be beyond the periphery of my experience, and never imagined what a farrago lay ahead. And if I reflect on all that has happened and all that did not, and how my questing nature led me from one event to another, should I not feel some satisfaction? I sit in this train with my baby snug against me and my paintings at my side – my creations, both. I am intact. What is there after all, that cannot be recovered or replenished or restored? And where have I left behind that I cannot return to? I can no longer envisage anything

351

which is not immediate; I want only to exist, to feel, to be. The French verb, *être* – to be. Just, to be.

'And when we arrive at the inn Father will not be expecting me. I shall surprise him. He will not see us arrive. He will, in his deafness, perhaps hear a slight sound – the vibration of a door banging, or my footsteps, and he'll call out: "Who's there?" and I shall reply: "It's only me, Rosaleen. I've come home."'